TIM FINCH

The House of Journalists

Tim Finch has worked for more than a decade on refugee issues in the U.K., including as director of communications at the British Refugee Council. Before that he was a political journalist for the BBC. Recently he has been working with the internationally acclaimed artist and activist Ai Weiwei on *The Human Flow*, a documentary film on the refugee crisis.

T0057960

THE HOUSE OF JOURNALISTS

THE HOUSE

OF JOURNALISTS

TIM FINCH

FARRAR, STRAUS AND GIROUX | NEW YORK

Farrar, Straus and Giroux
18 West 18th Street, New York 10011

Printed in the United States of America
Published in 2013 by Farrar, Straus and Giroux
First paperback edition, 2017

The Library of Congress has cataloged the hardcover edition as follows:
Finch, Tim.
    The house of journalists / Tim Finch. — First edition.
        pages   cm
    ISBN 978-0-374-17318-0 (hardcover)
    1. Journalists—Fiction.   2. Authors, Exiled—Fiction.   3. London (England)—Fiction.
 I. Title.

  PR6106.I5344 H68 2013
  823'.92—dc23

                                                                    2013006520

Paperback ISBN: 978-0-374-71785-8

Designed by Abby Kagan

Our books may be purchased in bulk for promotional, educational, or business use. Please
contact your local bookseller or the Macmillan Corporate and Premium Sales Department at
1-800-221-7945, extension 5442, or by e-mail at MacmillanSpecialMarkets@macmillan.com.

www.fsgbooks.com
www.twitter.com/fsgbooks • www.facebook.com/fsgbooks

P1

FOR MY FATHER AND MOTHER,

Alan and Julia

CONTENTS

ARRIVAL

THE SENSE OF BANISHMENT

Exile is like some herb which gives its distinct bitter flavour to many different forms of writing. Graham Greene.

To experience exile a man doesn't necessarily have to leave his country. The sense of banishment can be felt on one's own hearthstone. Graham Greene again.

Graham Greene is one of the best-known writers in this country where you are unknown as a writer.

WELCOME TO THE HOUSE OF JOURNALISTS

We assemble for the welcome ceremony in the library and Julian, our founder and Chair, leads you in. A small party of other visitors—friends and donors—follow. The mood among the fellowship is relaxed and informal. We are laughing and chatting. Then Julian claps his hands and calls for silence. Up to that point, Mr. Stan, our Father of Chapel, has been sitting quietly, unnoticed, in his corner. Now, as he is introduced by Julian, everyone turns towards him. He insists on standing on ceremony, despite the great strain this puts on his tiny, twisted body. The minute or two it takes him to get to his feet is almost beyond endurance. Then, having hauled himself into his crutches, he grinds his confounded bones into the centre of the room. His voice is a crushed peppercorn whisper.

"Welcome to the House of Journalists. We are pleased to receive you into our House and our fellowship. The fellows are most glad to greet you as our brother in exile. This is a place of sanctuary for all those who have used the power of the word to expose tyranny throughout the world."

We know nothing of your condition or destiny but we see straightaway that you have a writer's eye. There is that glint in it. You would not be a writer if you did not see stories under every stone, never mind this roof. But what an introduction! You have no sooner arrived than you are greeted by Mr. Stan, a piece of work beyond imagination. This special place has thrown open its doors to you, as it did for us. Welcome to the House of Journalists.

| MR. STAN WAS NEVER TO UNCURL AND ASSUME A PROPER SHAPE

At first, not even Mother noticed: Little Stan was her scrunched-up bundle, squinting and bubbling; he was the apple of all the aunties; a late gift from a lamented God as she pushed hard at forty. For a few weeks the neat single-story breeze block house, with its roof of corrugated tin and its dusty, bare-earth garden, marked out with whitewashed stones, knew true heartbreaking happiness. The one photograph Mother kept on the mantelshelf through all their suffering was of Little Stan as a newborn in her arms.

As time went on, however, it became clear that her tiny miracle was never to uncurl and assume a proper shape. They tried callipers and corsets and leg irons; his baby-bird body was subjected to every form of correction and humiliation. Still he was all stunted hump and stoop and stump and spindle. And his humpty head had, it seemed, cracked open and bled a port wine map of Africa from crown to temple. At most, at best, a tuft or two of baby elephant hair sprouted in clumps on the mottled eggshell.

But Little Stan did have the most beautiful hands. When the other children threw stones at him out on his sticks in the street, Mother ran out to shield and protect those hands—so slender, articulated, and exquisitely veined. The baby sobs, the head bumps and body bruises, were taken in her stride. She waved them away. Her one concern was for his precious hands.

Mother put them to the piano at an early age—but Little Stan's soupspoon ears couldn't pick up the music. He read the scores studiously; played them by the book. But there was no feel, no touch. The sound was mechanical: like a piano roll. His true instrument turned out to be the typewriter. His first one was bought for him as a toy and he took to it instantly. The journalist in him found his voice in its clatter and ring. He was never able to write as well in longhand; and this stopped him performing to his ability in the stifling stillness, the dust-mite-dancing, the sunlight-shafting of the high-windowed grammar school exam rooms. That ruled out the university—his mother's dream; and led him instead to his home from home—the newsroom.

"Thank you, Mr. Stanislaus," Julian says, as our much-respected Father is helped back into his customised chair, wheezing and triumphant. Julian—a very popular writer and broadcaster in this country—turns to you, the new fellow. "As you may know, Mr. Stanislaus was the editor of the main newspaper in his homeland, a small island in the Indian Ocean. A hero of the independence struggle, he became a fearless critic of the repressive regime of President . . ."

You nod, apparently attentive to Julian's words. But we can see that your eyes are drawn to Mr. Stan's hands, now cushioned on their protective armrests.

You will be imagining the tiny, pink, pearl-nailed fingers that his mother cherished; and the thumb he used to suck in his sleep; and the little knuckles that he pressed into his cheeks as he sobbed in the corner.

———

There are so many ways to cause pain—and to break the spirit. They used hammers.

Mother was called in to witness her gibbering, shiver-shuddering son as the prison doctor tended to the bloody mush stumps. "Oh, Stanley, your precious hands!" These guys—the interrogators, the torturers: call them what you will—are butchers certainly, but they usually have some intelligence. On this occasion it was spot-on. "What have they done to them!" Mother was dead from the shock within a week; Mr. Stan's resistance, so spirited until then, was broken.

"The House of Journalists," Julian says, turning his attention to the friends and donors, but not neglecting you, our new fellow, "was built in the eighteenth century as a fashionable London town house, but over the centuries it has housed Russian Jews, Irish immigrant families, Jewish refugees fleeing from the Nazis, Bangladeshis, and, more recently, Somali asylum-seekers. Speculators did have plans to redevelop it as luxury flats, but we were able to block that. It is modelled on the Maison des Journalistes in Paris. Some of our leading writers and broadcasters went on a fact-finding mission; a committee was formed and funds were raised to buy the building. We got a Heritage Grant for the conversion, and we have won a number of architectural awards. As well as providing a residence for thirty exiled journalists and writers, we have a newsroom, conference facilities, and this magnificent library. One way or another, this building has been a place of refuge for new arrivals for more than two hundred years. Now this state-of-the-art centre provides a more fitting welcome for those seeking protection and—I like to think—stands out as a symbol of our commitment to uphold this country's noble tradition of providing sanctuary.

"As I say," Julian goes on. "At any one time we have some thirty journalists and writers in residence. Only a very few are long-term residents; for the others this is a halfway house. The fellows all have prima facie claims for asylum, but have not been given formal status. They are assigned to us from arrival camps and clearing centres or sometimes straight from ports of entry. If they get status—and most do—they move on. Assistance is provided to find housing in the community and jobs—in the profession, if possible. Among our funders is the government." He stops for a moment and surveys the room. "We have criticisms of government policy, of course, but that does not stop us working in fruitful partnership with ministers and officials. As well as assisting individual exiled journalists and writers, we are helping through the project to advance public understanding of the complex issue of asylum. Our fellows are encouraged to write, to broadcast, and to make films about their experiences. We hold lots of workshops, study groups, and seminars."

This is the signal for assigned fellows and volunteers to invite the friends and donors to see more of the House of Journalists. There is much good work and profitable industry to show off. We all have our tasks.

Julian turns his attention to you.

"So, let me introduce you personally to Mr. Stanislaus," Julian says, all smiles. "Mr. Stanislaus, this is our new fellow, AA."

You step forward. "Please, don't get up, Mr. Stanislaus," you say.

"You are welcome, AA," he says to you. "I trust you will fit in well here." His tone is warm.

Julian continues: "Mr. Stanislaus, as well as being our Father of Chapel, is our longest-serving fellow, a stalwart of our Committee, and a true symbol of this special place."

There is a pause. Mr. Stan is offering you his hand.

Mr. Stan cannot use a pen, or a knife or a fork or a spoon. The only thing he has learnt to hold is one of the bidi cigarettes that are bought for him at the Asian corner shop on the High Road. He cannot light it. You will do that for him out in the Central Courtyard where we all stand, and Mr. Stan alone sits, smoking in the white breath of this cold foreign city. Mr. Stan sucks deep on the hot, noxious luxury of the home island and spits wet flakes of tobacco from his lips. He is ecstatic at the lung-burning pleasure of each infernal drag.

———

If you were to try to uncurl Mr. Stan's crablike hand—go on, bend it back as far as it will go—you will see that the inside of the shell is blackened by smoke. Now let his hand go. You have caused Mr. Stan real pain, you must understand that.

Mr. Stan shows no hurt. His hand remains outstretched.

Crablike is not quite right, is it? A better description might be knotted tree root—suggesting, as it does, a certain gnarled damp fleshiness. At their zenith, when, fired by ideals betrayed, they were hammering out those blistering editorials, Mr. Stan's hands were hard long-boned configurations. Mother hated to see them being hurled at the machine. This was not what she had dreamt for them. And now look: all her dreams shattered. Yes, look! Hideously *re*configured by those hammers, those *claw* hammers, all sense of elegant extremity is lost.

Finally, you take the proffered hand. We watch to see how you will handle it. (Forgive us, but as we pick up the language we cannot resist the odd pun.) In the end, you choose to encage the repellent flesh club, studded with half-fossilised fingers and thumbs, nails, and knuckles, as lightly as possible between your two hands, in a gesture that conveys a sense of touching warmth, while allowing you to avoid any real contact. You may feel that you have failed the first test of true fellowship. We notice that you keep your eyes downcast for a moment.

But when you look up you will see that Mr. Stan is nodding his head appreciatively. You have, as it happens, shown the restraint and civility due to these formalities. Mother would have approved. You have gone some way to reassure Mr. Stan. And if Mr. Stan is reassured, then Julian is reassured. A new fellow is always a cause for joy—but also some anxiety. You have been assigned to the House of Journalists by the authorities, but you are not carrying papers. Like many fellows you have arrived armed only with your story. Julian will be interested to hear it. We all will.

| THE FIRST FEW PAGES OF A NOVEL

You will doubtless compare your arrival at the House of Journalists—as we did before you—with the first few pages of a novel. We are all writers after all, so it is only natural that we should make this comparison. There is the same sense of displacement; the same sense of being plunged into proceedings, while still standing apart. You are a stranger in a strange land. The old clichés. It will take some time for you to adapt to these unfamiliar surroundings and to get to know the people. It can be difficult to understand the peculiarities of the language and to distinguish between the different voices. It is natural to feel disorientated and anxious—but exhilarated too. You—like us—are here because of the irrepressible power of great stories, great characters—great truths. Whatever came before (there will be time enough for that), it was somehow written (more playing with words) that you should end up at the House of Journalists. What will unfold over the coming pages, none of us knows. And therein lies the strange beauty of this shared experience.

| EVERY NEW FELLOW EXCITES SOME INTEREST

The Central Courtyard is where we gather to talk—and to smoke. Smoking is banned inside the House of Journalists, as in all public places in this country. PROHIBITED BY LAW, say the signs. We respect the laws of this country of course, but for us there are no private places—and most of us smoke. We are journalists and writers after all. We have all spent time in prison. We have all had many long hours to kill.

They have put an ashtray out here for us now—a small defeat for Julian and the Committee. But, as if to say that his vision for this place will prevail in all circumstances, Julian commissioned a leading young sculptor to design an ashtray in keeping with the grey flagstone courtyard with the modernist fountain at its centre. Thus it is that we stub out our stinking butts in a stainless steel, semi-spherical bowl filled with fine grey sand, sitting atop a fluted plinth. The irony is not lost on us. We are fastidious about disposing of our fag ends in the elegant receptacle provided. But we carry on smoking all the same.

The House of Journalists puts on courses to help us to give up smoking and classes which promote "healthy living." But we are journalists and writers. We have been in prison and we have been tortured. We have spent days hiding out in cellars or warehouses or travelling in the back of containers. We have breathed foul air and eaten stinking food and been deprived of sleep for nights on end. Our health, in all sorts of ways, is precarious.

Have a look at our teeth. Mossy tombstones that move around in the soft earth of our gums. It is a bit late for "healthy living," we all think with a laugh—that is something that goes with home and family and the expectation of a long and happy life. Still, there are small pleasures to be had in any life—and one of ours is the induction of a new fellow. It is always a talking point.

You need not look so anxious, AA. Every new fellow excites interest and speculation. Come and join us. You are a smoker, that's good. There is great fellowship in that. Julian will not like it, but Julian doesn't rule the place! Oh, it might seem that way sometimes. You know what these institutions are like: they always have their petty rules and restrictions, their tin-pot tyrants and traitors—and their pipsqueak rebellions. But we have all survived a lot worse, have we not?

By the way, feel free to smoke in silence. Not everyone wants to open up the moment they arrive. Keep your peace. We all feel that the House of Journalists sometimes makes too many demands on us. Yes, we have our stories to tell. But we have our secrets to keep too. Both have their power. Do not give too much away, AA. Hold back. Deploy your story to maximum advantage. That is our advice to you.

| ROOM 15

You have been assigned to Room 15, we notice. Is there any significance in that? you might ask. None at all. It happened to be vacant, just as Room 22 is vacant now. You might have been assigned to Room 22 if it had been vacant then. But it was occupied, as it will be again very shortly. You see what we are saying? Fellows move on. New fellows arrive. You have arrived. You will move on. All new fellows are made to feel welcome at the House of Journalists, but you should be under no illusions about the place. This is not where it all comes right. Don't make that mistake. The exile has to learn that he belongs nowhere, that the journey never ends. This is both our great misfortune and our great liberation.

We should leave you now. You will want to rest. But remember, we are always here. You have already met your neighbour in Room 14, as he is one of the smokers. But what about your neighbour in Room 16?

| I AM MUSTAPHA

I am not a smoker. It is one of the things that sets me apart from the other fellows—though I would not want to suggest that this is something I set out to do. I value the fellowship of this place. But I find solace of a different kind in solitude. The House of Journalists respects that in its own way.

We all understand how precious this place is to the good people who first established it. They have built something here; they are proud of it; and in their minds it should be reverenced for the good work it does. But this mind-set makes them somewhat unyielding towards anyone who would in any way undermine or even make light of their mission.

Few seek to, it must be said. But whatever Julian and the Committee contend, the establishment of the House of Journalists was as much a political act as a humanitarian one—and a political act will never command consensus, let alone unanimity. Indeed, as Julian must know, the generous attention that such a project attracts excites its own brand of resentment; a resentment that tends to fester by dint of the inhibition people feel in voicing criticisms which tell against the general praise. Beneath the most splendid palaces run sewers more stinking than the open gutters, as the well-known saying goes. Well-known in my home country, that is.

I am reminded of a piece I wrote for a briefly fashionable periodical in my home country. "There are those who will oppose, or at least question, an action because it is a step too far," I wrote, "while others will regard it as a gesture so insultingly small that it would have been better to do nothing. Some will say action of this sort was required, but not this *particular* action, which, sadly, is so misjudged that it amounts to a step in the *wrong* direction. Others will oppose the action, and with a peculiar bitterness, not because they think it wrong, but because they would have taken it themselves had they not been pre-empted in this hasty way. (There is no enemy like an enemy who opposes you for doing what they would have liked to do themselves.) Finally, there are those who, having supported an action from the start, feel they have not received the credit due to them, or that you have received undue credit (the same thing, more or less), and whose support diminishes to such an extent that in the end they are opposing you, if not the action, with all their power."

It is writing that captures well I think the political tenor of the time. Ours was the only democracy in the region, and we were rightly proud of that fact. But our democratic institutions were in the hands of the wealthy elite, which ruled largely in its own interest, if benignly by the standards of our monarchical or one-party neighbours. Coalitions were put together, broken up, and reassembled so as to give the impression of change, but the same old men stayed in power and the same old politics went on. Venerable senators, with skin like tobacco leaves, wearing elegant suits, double-cuffed white shirts, and hugely knotted silk ties, wandered the corridors of Senate House on the Corniche, stopping to chat with deep-tanned young deputies, in suits of a slightly racier cut, sunglasses riding the waves of their swept-back glossy hair. Conversations had this sort of tone: "A good deal is on the table, and you should be using your talents to persuade your faction of its merits. Your late father would be disappointed to see you playing your hand so ineptly, I must say. But my love to your dear mama—we hope to see her at the yacht club on Saturday. Antoine will be back from Paris . . ."

Many of those who imagined themselves like me to be part of the "radical opposition" were from the same elite and we too played the game—attacking the corruption and ineptitude of ministers, and demanding change, without really expecting or wanting any great upheaval. We were liberals, not revolutionaries.

It was in this spirit that we toyed with the new prime minister, an oil engineer from the north, a hardworking outsider who had manoeuvred himself into the inner circles and clambered to the top by making himself indispensable to a succession of superiors, the last our weak, lazy, and infirm president. His was a surprising appointment; progressive in its way; indicative of a certain openness. He was an intelligent man and was a far more competent administrator than the country was used to. But he was treacherous towards colleagues, hectoring with juniors, dismissive of long-standing conventions and established civilities, intellectually unsophisticated, and culturally uncouth.

At first he exhibited a brittle tolerance for our raillery. It did him no harm with his cabal and his constituency to be carped at by the likes of us. We wrote as much. It was clear that he had no natural sympathy with the perquisites of a liberal democracy even though he had been confirmed in his post by a popular vote. We wrote as much. For him to take offence at our barbs and charges, to rant that they were an affront to the people who had elected him, to allege that we were at the core of what was so rotten in our system, to parade before the people as the one true democrat: all of this was risible and we wrote as much. Our friends and relatives in government circles were now warning us that we were threatening the country's stability with our attacks; that the prime minister was more powerful and dangerous than we imagined; that the game was up. But the game was all we knew.

Then one bright morning I went out onto our balcony and saw the tanks surrounding the president's palace. "I didn't know we had so many tanks," I remember I said to my wife. She didn't think it was funny. She feared for me. She was right to. I spent that night standing up in a packed cell in the headquarters of the security police.

Everyone in the House of Journalists has, in his own way, seen the tanks, made light of the moment, and then found himself in a police cell. For most there was a sense of destiny in it. It was a culmination.

I, by contrast, waited in that cell for the door to open and the light to flood back in. I had made a small name for myself in those circles I have talked about; and I had played a minor part in attacking the growing authoritarian tendency of the new prime minister and his faction. But I never imagined there was any real danger in it. In the months running up to "the clampdown" there had been an increasing number of instances of journalists and activists being arrested and even beaten up. But such abuses were not unknown under previous governments. Were the "human rights violations" of the new administration that we railed against really any worse than those we had been pointing out for years? We remained confident that those picked up would soon be released and patched up, as they always had been in the past. To talk of outright tyranny, as we did with some relish, was overdone, surely?

I would certainly have dismissed the notion that I was risking my life or even my freedom to uphold democracy and the rule of law. Such a claim would have seemed to me showy, vulgar: a pose. And I was not alone in thinking this way among my class of countrymen. We were all infected by the same fatal insouciance.

The executions began at dawn.

There was no resistance from our side. All the fight in us was mere words. The prime minister knew that. It could have been a bloodless coup. All the blood was for show—like the tanks. So vulgar, we thought. The prime minister's class of countrymen sensed our distaste and slaughtered more of us, spurred on by our insufferable fastidiousness. Soft, effete, spineless—they spat it out, and we just stood there. Some of us—more and more during the day—they took out and shot;

others of us, including me, just waited . . . into a second day . . . into a third. It was a humbling experience: I was not such an important person.

Stay that way, a snivel spirit whispered in my ear: *make yourself small; crawl under a stone, like a bug; crawl out only when it is safe.* In the years to come, the years in the camp, I lived this way: low to the ground. It was the only way to survive. But in those first days, I was still possessed of a stronger, self-important spirit which urged me to stand tall. *When they come for you*, it said—as surely they will, as surely they must—*you will face torture and death with pride and defiance.* Yes, pride and defiance in the face of torture and death. *You can face it.* Yes, I could. Then. But only because I still didn't quite believe it would happen; I still thought they would open the door and the light would flood back in . . .

Then the thud of a gunshot from the execution yard overhead or the unmanned pleadings of another hero being dragged by his heels along the concrete corridor would knock the knees from under me.

Believe it now?

Back, buglike, under the stone, scuttle.

Then, on the fourth morning, they released me. There was no flooding in of light; the door had slammed shut on any possibility of that. They took me for a broken man—and they were half right. It should have been a snivel-spirit victory: home, family, head-down safety, a keep-out-of-trouble future; a second chance, clouded only by the luxury of survivor guilt. Most men, in most of the world, for most of history, crave nothing more. But the new authorities had dismissed me from their sight so quickly that such a victory was not quite enough for me. My will to resist, my pride in doing so, had not quite been broken. It was a tiny miscalculation on their part; a grotesque folly on mine. My wife, my children, my mother, pleaded with me to *please, please, think of your safety, think of ours* . . . (The echo of it haunts me still.) *Please, please, think of yourself, think of us* . . .

But I would not listen.

I wrote the article: "an unchained howl of outrage and anguish"; "a devastating philippic against oppression everywhere"; "the last word on lost freedoms"—I use some of the descriptions which have been attached to it since—and yet, in truth, above all, this is how at the ultimate reckoning it will be judged: a mere bauble to flatter myself. It was published in a newspaper that was closed down within days. That article, eight hundred words closely typed on flimsy paper, would be much revered in this place. If a copy existed they would frame it behind glass and display it on the wall. But in my torn-apart country, in those tumultuous days, my article was contemptuously ignored by the people, who despised my class—a self-serving bunch that had led the country to this disaster—and who were intent only on their own safety. I was rearrested, at their leisure, by the security police. I was waiting for them and they kept me waiting. (It was a form of torture.) I really was no danger to them and could be left to swing slowly in the susurrus of indifference I had stirred up. They broke me in those few days. Thereafter I lived to the law, the one law that reads: there is no heroism; there is only survival. The snivel-spirit law.

The House of Journalists, Julian and his Committee, does not welcome such talk. I understand that and I speak only for myself. Others must tell it as it was for them.

| YES, I AM MUSTAPHA

I should introduce myself. I am Mustapha. (In the same way you are AA?) It is not my real name. I am reluctant to give my real name for fear of reprisals at home. My wife and children are still there: lost to me, safe from me. To imagine that I am protecting them is perhaps a vain and selfish comfort? It is a comfort all the same.

But I "must 'ave a name"? I looked at the immigration official, a young lad with laughing eyes, in terror. My fear shook him. I think he was new to this line of work. "Okay, don't worry about it." He didn't want to scare me. "Really. It just means I 'ave to be your mum and dad." I didn't understand what he meant, of course. "Gotta fill in the form, 'aven't I? So I'm writin' down 'ere—Mustapha. Get it? No, course you don't. No worries, mate. You." He pointed to me. "Mustapha." He pointed to the word on the form. "Mustapha. Must 'ave a name." He laughed to himself—a rather hopeless, empty, not-much-of-a-job-not-much-of-a-life sort of laugh. "And me, I'm Barry." He shook my hand. "Nice to meet yer, Mustapha."

I know that some of the staff and volunteer supporters at the House of Journalists regard this name as demeaning. They have suggested that I change it. But I try always to remember that the small men of any system, the petty officers, face their own pressures and difficulties. They take it out on us in different ways. Most choose indifference; some, mockery; a few, cruelty. (The godly and the righteous are the worst of all.) But there are also the ones with a twinkle of humanity. They are usually the jokers, the drinkers. True, they can turn nasty in a flicker; but if they can win a smile out of you, there is some kind of bond. "Smile, it may never 'appen," they say—or would do if they spoke like Barry. And you think: that is a terrible thing to say; it is their job to make it happen. But then you think: at the moment of saying it, they mean it. It is a way of showing some common humanity, no less, no more. They do their job, they don't dwell on it; they couldn't do their job if they did. "You'd have to be a sadist," as they say, though it is true too that there are sadists among them. The godly and righteous: the worst of all.

I am taking myself back in my mind to the gulags out on the ice-bound plains, the freezing interrogation huts, the wind-beaten execution lots. My own country has become the worst place on earth for me (and that is the saddest thing a man can say). But I am dreaming now, as I dreamt then, of how it was, in the past, of my wife and children, of our apartment in the city and our house along the coast, of lunches and picnics and long evenings around the fire or out under the stars, evenings full of talk and music and poetry, of father and mother, of my brothers and sisters, of riding out across my grandfather's estate to swim in the lakes or driving up to ski in the mountains, of friends at my private school and at university and at the newspaper and at the publishing firm. I am dreaming, as I dreamt then, of the people I love, of the places I hold dear, of cherished times, prosperous, peaceful, privileged, carefree, only to wake up drenched in a fright sweat as icy as the driving sleet that freezes our bones as we labour to build the new military airstrip. I am on my pallet bed, trying to clutch some warmth from a mealy blanket. I am here in the House of Journalists. I am warm, but I will never feel warm. I am safe, but I will never feel safe. I have escaped, but I can never escape.

So when I arrived in this country and a petty officer, making light, chose to extend his hand, I chose to hang on to the humanity in his small gesture. I chose not to take my new name as a joke at my expense. I am Mustapha. I am a *"play on words."*

The language classes at the House of Journalists take account of the fact that we are all writers or broadcasters, that we are all "wordsmiths." Peculiar local idioms will interest and amuse us, they think. One we learn early is "windbag." There is always a lot of laughter, perhaps because the construction immediately suggests to us flatulence, farting, guffing—there are so many words for it. "Yes, yes, there is something of that," our teacher, a young writer called Esther, agrees. "A windbag may be said to be full of 'hot air,' to be 'gassing on,' but also to have 'verbal diarrhoea' or to be—if you'll excuse me—'full of shit.' And 'windbags' are often 'old farts' as well." She has lost most of us by this stage, but she does not need to give us an example of a windbag. We can all think of one.

"All is well with you, dear fellows?" Julian says right on cue. He is constantly "popping in" on the classes, and always says a "few words" by way of encouragement. On this occasion he sees us struggling not to laugh. Esther too is trying to suppress a "fit of the giggles." Julian smiles, he tries to play along, but we can see that he feels left out. And he does not like the feeling. He likes to know what is going on. At all times. He is the Chair and protector of this special place, and so it is his privilege and duty to know about everything that goes on here.

My family might say the term "windbag" applied to me—surprising as that must sound to everybody at the House of Journalists. Here, after all I have gone through, I am quiet, watchful, and wary; I am, as you say, *"of few words."* By nature, however, I am a loquacious man. I like to talk, to argue, to debate, to speak my mind. It is the reason I am here; as it is for most of us.

There is a knock on my door.

"Ah, sorry, Mustapha. I hope we are not disturbing you?"

I am lying on my bed. It is a prison habit—hard to break. I have a desk in here, a chair, a television, an easy chair from which, it is supposed, I suppose, that I will watch the television. I am reminded too of the hotel rooms in which I spent so many nights on assignments as a young foreign correspondent in our region. I would set up to write at the desk, but otherwise, if I wanted to think, or to read, or to watch television, I would lie on the bed. I would never sit in the easy chair. And never unpack, however long the stay. Here it is the same. My belongings are in a couple of canvas bags in the bottom of the wardrobe.

"No, not disturbing at all," I say, jumping up. The group comprises Julian; the House manager, Solomon; and a woman I don't know, who betrays the only genuine embarrassment. She shapes to voice an apology (and is reassured that I see it and I understand), only to be voiced over by Julian.

"Mustapha, you must forgive us. It is a terrible imposition on your privacy. If we had realised . . . Please do not get up." I am already up. I could not possibly be in any position other than standing with visitors in the room. And I do not mind. I understand. The woman I do not know is no doubt an important donor. "Miriam here is a friend of long standing—we go back yonks. She is a fantastic supporter of the House, and a very generous one." Miriam is every inch the sort of woman who supports the House of Journalists fantastically and generously (I leave you to picture her); and she smiles in a way that a friend of Julian's of long standing, who goes back "yonks" (I trust you understand this word), would smile in such circumstances, the circumstances being: Julian being Julian as he shows this place, which is so special to him, to a person who is special to him too. I smile back. We all forgive Julian in such circumstances. Solomon is smiling too: it is a practised and professional smile, but no less genuine for that. So we are all smiles. We are all disarmed. We all feel good about ourselves. The House of Journalists has this effect on people. "Miriam was very keen to see 'behind the scenes,' as it were," Julian resumes. "I wanted to show her that the House is also a home."

Home. It is a sacred word, and the moment Julian says it—a rare misjudgement—it turns to wormwood in his mouth. Miriam Stern is an old friend of his and a strong supporter of the House of Journalists; they are proud of this place and they have the right to be proud; there is a lot about the place that placates the heart and encourages hope. But their pride in this place does not blind them to the limits of the comfort it offers. She/he sees a room—and me/he in it—that, to their eyes, and mine, is absent of all that makes for that sacred place: home. It is a room like all the others in the House of Journalists and not in any way like a room in any place that anyone would call home.

The reclaimed wood floors, the sand-blasted bare brick walls, the tasteful kilims and carefully chosen wood carvings, the classy black-and-white photographs of world writers, the foundry-forged double doors giving out onto the grey flagstones of the Central Courtyard with its modernist fountain: the whole unifying aesthetic of the building, that is so pleasing to the eye as one is escorted around it, completely lacks the scuff and clutter, the accumulations and lapses, above all the *warmth*, of a family house or a comfortable apartment. It is *not* a home. No, *never*! It is another institution that we must pass through on our journey *away* from home. It is a cold, impersonal place in which we *long* for home.

For a moment I am convulsed with anger and bitterness—and ha-tred. "It's okay. Let it out," the counsellors are apt to say here, but that is not my way. It is not *our* way—the way of my culture and my people. And it is in this thought that I find comfort and recover my poise.

"Well, perhaps 'a home from home,' as you say here," I say with good cheer. "At least, we wish it so. It is difficult, however. In my house, in my country, I had many, many books. Here, you see, very few."

"But you are writing, Mustapha?" Miriam asks pleadingly.

"Not so much."

"The most beautiful fragments: lyrical ellipses," Julian says. I know what is coming next . . .

You hear the loss when my voice falls silent . . .
In the spaces between the words.

I am not comfortable hearing these lines spoken out loud. Much too much weight is given to the exercises we do in the classes and workshops; our exilic experiments in a new language. Many of us are embarrassed by the praise, almost reverence, with which our tentative first steps into a literary world not our own are received. I was a very minor poet in my own country. (In my culture, most educated people write poetry.) I think of myself as a journalist and a publisher. I would never compare myself with the great writers in my language, most of whom are unknown here. When I achieve some mastery of my new language, your language, I will devote my time to translating these masters. The task will be the greatest of comforts for me: linking the past with the present; home with exile; my humble love of literature with its highest achievements; allowing me, if you will allow me, to bathe my torn soul in the sorrowful and comical beauties of stories familiar, but not my own.

"That is very beautiful," Miriam says. There are tears in her eyes. It is often the way with visitors. We have experienced so much. It is as if we have experienced it *for* them. How profoundly we have touched them. We are such moving characters.

"We will leave you now," Julian says. His work is done.

THE SUN NEVER SHINES, THE WATER IS BRACKISH; THE ENDLESS STEPPE IS BRAMBLED WITH WORMWOOD

Today has been, is still, a monotonous day, weather-wise. The monotone or monotint is grey—every day grey. One day merging imperceptibly into the next and so on. The grey blocks, the glass towers, and the classical stone edifices and spires of the city are understated against an undifferentiated grey sky. The sun's blazing arc across the sky (burning in the mind's eye) has been all but invisible, although occasionally a muted white disc can be made out. What warmth, if any, can it be giving out? And yet it is not a cold day: it is neither cold nor warm, though it is colder than it is warm, and it is warmer than the seasonal expectation. The season is winter, the month is February; the hour is three.

Such weather, one might almost call it anti-weather, seems to promise no hope of change. It feels like it has always been like this, and always will be. One day bleaching into the next. Perhaps to a habitué of these latitudes there is the making of other weathers in this weather; but to our fellowship of exiles, it seems to rule out different patterns of light; to rule out the unbroken blue of tranquil morning or the ominous plum purple of electric late afternoon or the watercolours of cloud chase and spring shower. It seems to rule out, with its iron meteorologic, any weather pattern other than its own flat uniformity.

No one knows quite how to dress for this weather; not now that the lighter raincoat is so rarely worn. The lighter raincoat over a shirt and jacket, a pair of long trousers (or a long skirt), and closed-in shoes would suit; but when it is like this every day (or so it seems), who can be surprised that the people of this city adopt the extremes and everything in between? In a short walk down a single street one might see a woman in a heavy fur coat and another in a light sari; a youth in a Puffa ski jacket and another in a football shirt; an old stager in the kurta pyjama and another in a heavy wool suit. The only person in the lighter raincoat over a shirt and jacket, trousers, and closed-in shoes is likely to be one of us.

It is routinely said that such weather is depressing, but to the busy people of this city (and all the citizens are busy, or so it would seem) the weather does not register, either way. It is the neutral background against which they lead their lives, more or less colourfully. The weather doesn't set the mood of this city. Still, *we* are oppressed by it; we fellows. And that is as it should be. On afternoons like this one we feel the dolour and limitlessness of our exile.

"Enjoying the view?" One of the sunny young volunteers comes out to join us. "Getting some fresh air?" We nod. "Another grey day," he says, laughing. "It must depress you sometimes," he says, still laughing. We smile. "It depresses me sometimes." This city is his home; his birthplace. He cannot escape that fact. He cannot keep the luck out of his voice. Maybe his time will come. Maybe this country will descend into dark days. (There are some who talk of it.) Maybe we secretly wish for that. No! We will not be revenged in this way or any way. We are better than that. We know where it leads.

We have taken the escape route—a robust exercise in matt-black urban ironwork—out onto a railed-in roof space. We come up here to look out on the limitless city. After a while, one among us is moved to the following observation. He is a man of great learning and distinction.

"Ovid in Book III, Volume I of his *Epistulae ex Ponto* tells of biting cold holding *all* seasons in its grip. Tomis in the Dobrudja is, in truth, 'continental-temperate' in climate and on the same latitude as Ovid's place of birth in the Abruzzi. Thus Ovid's bitter description of perpetual ice tells more of his *experience* than his place of exile.

"The observation is not mine, I should add; I paraphrase a professor of classics at the university I attended in my home country, speaking to us in a lecture theatre so perishing cold that we sat in our balaclavas and our greatcoats, with ice in our beards. There were maybe ten students in a hall that could have held five hundred. Snowflakes fluttered down from a broken skylight and settled on the huge stage. The professor wore some sort of military cap with earflaps. He had once been in the camps and knew cold beyond our imagining. And suffering. But then, my country has known a hundred years of suffering. And we, his students, were all to know our own. Yet, let me tell you, I miss the old place terribly, for all its horrors."

The volunteer, an intelligent young man, with a big heart, smiles. "*Epistulae ex Ponto.* My Latin's not up to much, but I guess you mean *The Black Sea Letters*?"

"Quite so. *The Black Sea Letters.* Ovid wrote of Tomis—now a popular holiday resort in Romania—'The sun never shines, the water is brackish; the endless steppe is brambled with wormwood.' If he was here today, how might he describe this great city, your hometown?" Our colleague turns to the volunteer. "You would not recognise his description, I would wager. He would see it through the tear-clouded lens of exile. We will not make Ovid's mistake. Here we are, and we must learn to love—or at the least, live tolerably in—this alien place. To London!"

"To London!" We all cry.

And we all feel a little better for it.

MR. STAN LOVES THE HOUSE OF JOURNALISTS

Mr. Stan has been woken from his midafternoon nap by his favourite volunteer and wheeled into the fellows' common room where tea is served. He enjoys a cup of Earl Grey and will take a tea cake or a Dundee slice. He uses a straw to drink and volunteers take turns to feed him. Otherwise, he would have to struggle with his special implements, and latterly he has not had the energy. He is read to—light verse or a country-house crime novel. On days like today there is a fire. In summer, the doors are thrown open onto the courtyard. There is usually a visitor paying an informal call to whom he is introduced with affectionate ceremony. Or a fellow may want to talk to him about some matter or other that he can take up with the Committee.

Mr. Stan does not write anymore. Indeed he has not written since he came to the House of Journalists. Of course the pitiful state of his hands frustrates the endeavour. But the technology is available if he wanted to write. He is just exhausted, that's all. All his writing power was used up in fighting to save his home island. A lost cause. He devotes himself instead to Julian and the Committee, to encouraging and supporting the younger fellows. He is tireless in the promotion of the House of Journalists—if, incidentally, himself.

For, although he does not write, he is always ready to tell his story. It is among the most harrowing of all the testimonies in the House of Journalists, and it is always painful for him to recount it. But each time he does so he is saying thank you to this special place. That is how he thinks of it. So he tells his story again and again, however many times he is asked, to whoever wants to hear it. Film crews, television documentary makers, radio producers, playwrights, and student journalists—there is hardly a day when they are not setting up their gear, or finding a quiet place to record or to take down his words.

Despite the anguish and fatigue it causes him, Mr. Stan tells his story with an old pro's sense of pace and timing, a practised feel for the play of light and dark. He takes the listener down with him into the blackest pits of cruelty and despair. He spares no detail; nor does he spare himself. But then, changing tone, he leads the listener up into the sunnier places, where the human spirit soars and fellow feeling shines through. He tells of men's most monstrous deeds, but brings his tale back to the best in men. Among them—listeners are left in no doubt—he numbers himself. But at the same time he also gives all the other fellows their due; and does not forget to include the staff and volunteers; the Committee; Julian, Julian especially; and above all the listener, the person he is talking to now; you, the people of this country. He leaves all those who hear his story feeling so much better about themselves, and by so doing does a great service to the House of Journalists.

Which he is happy to perform—as he owes the House so much. The staff and volunteers and the other fellows are like a family to him. And, yes, in his case, the House is like a home. He will always be grateful to this special place. He is not such an old man. But he has suffered much and does not think he has many years left. He is not troubled by death. Death, he is sure, is nothing. Nothing beyond this life: a benign extinction. That is the end he would wish for. Though he would be very happy, and grateful, to have a few more years at the House of Journalists. All his life he has been in pain and plagued by many illnesses. Much of his life he has lived in fear—of Mother, of other children, of other journalists, of the more hard-line figures in the opposition movement, of the security forces. Even here, in this place where he feels so safe, he suffers from flashbacks and nightmares. Alone in his bed, he fears to sleep. Volunteers are on hand to comfort him when he is seized by the night terrors. He is most grateful to them. But eventually they drop off beside him as he sits out the hours until dawn. Only in the warmth and chatter of the fellows' common room, in the light of another busy day at the House of Journalists, does he dare to doze.

One thing that we all understand about Mr. Stan is that in coming to this country, to seek protection, he was, in a sense that none of the rest of us feel, coming home. He was brought up to revere this imperial isle, and although he fought against it, the fight—just and right—was for independence from a mother country that deep in his heart he still loved. No matter that this country, in pursuit of its interests, was an accessory to tyranny; that it sold the arms that his government turned on his people; that it trained the security forces that lashed him to that chair and splayed his hands on a workbench, while an array of hammers and other tools were laid out before him on a piece of silk. (The memory of that piece of silk is essential to Mr. Stan. He dwells on it to great effect in the telling of his story.) No matter. This country had no direct part in his torture. He will hear not a word said against it.

He is a citizen now, of course; among the proudest. There is a photograph in the lobby of him bowing respectfully before the King. The monarchy here is constitutional. But not everybody is happy to see this picture hung so prominently in the House of Journalists. This is not a place of obeisance to one man's rule, however ornamental, however benign. Mr. Stan is at one with us in our republican and democratic values, but he has a soft spot for rank and tradition and, more to the point, was fulfilling his official role in welcoming our royal visitor, in deference to Julian's wishes. The visit would, Julian had told him, help the House of Journalists to attract donors and would be viewed favourably by the government. Of course he also had in mind the memory of his mother.

She was devoted to the present King's grandmother. A photograph of that stern royal matriarch stood on her mantelshelf alongside the photograph of Little Stan as a baby—and, in truth, the old Queen remained more constantly in her affections. For Her Royal Highness stayed true to the old ways: the rigid hierarchies, the entitlements and deferences. The same was not true of her Stanislaus, who allowed himself to be swayed by fashionable theories, to fall in with a bad lot of hotheads and liberals who, as Mother predicted, would destroy the peace and order of the island. When the crackdown came, with martial law and mass arrests, Mother took some little satisfaction in seeing herself so, as it were, *royally* vindicated. She had long despaired of Stanislaus, his "activities" and his "associates." "None of my business or doing," she told neighbours and fellow churchgoers. "It is my view that we were better off as a colony. Only ill can come of native rule."

She was indignant, however, on that sweltering afternoon when three "native thugs" burst into her nice and orderly little home, looking for Mr. Stan. "He is not here," she said unconvincingly to the sergeant, who could hear the clatter of crutches and built-up boots out back. Her escaping son had failed even to get through the scullery door. She was not surprised. Stanislaus was always letting her down. He was carried into her living room by the two constables, their arms hooked under his armpits, and dumped at her feet. "Not here, you say?" the sergeant said impertinently. Mother was unmoved. Her concern was not so much for her son's safety as with this "unwarranted violation of private property." Indeed she might have watched them drag him away with little more than a promise of an "official protest" if one of the officers in his manhandling—the clumsy brute!—had not knocked her precious photographs off the mantelshelf. The old Queen was left lying face down—a gross indignity! Worse, however, befell her baby boy who, smiling up at her, had the glass which had protected him for so long crushed into his face by a brute boot. In that instant, she forgot her rugs and knickknacks, she forgot the dethroned monarch and what the neighbours would think. Now this invasion of her home was bonded in her mind to her buried-deep but still burning love for Little Stan, her pretty baby boy, before he had gone all wrong.

Mr. Stan was conscious of that, even as they knocked his glasses from his nose, slapped him about a bit, and read him his fucking rights a blurred, foul-spittle-spraying inch from his pug-ugly face. Perhaps it was this language (Mother could not abide bad language). Or perhaps it was the violence (she had often beaten Little Stan, but that was discipline; discipline was necessary; the violence of the street had no place in a respectable person's home). More likely it was that in the ensuing scuffle Stanislaus and the arresting officers stamped all over poor innocent Little Stan once again. Whatever the reason: her shouting and pulling at sleeves turned to punching and kicking and biting and scratching as they dragged Mr. Stan off to a Black Maria. It took two other officers to subdue her, pacify her, and leave her, spent, lying on her living room floor—such a gross indignity!—amid the crushed glass, the broken frame, and the image of her bonny baby boy in her strong arms.

She recovered herself quickly. She was up and sweeping in minutes.

The noise would not have escaped the attention of her neighbours, a nosy lot; but they must never see the house in such a state, *her* in such a state. She bathed her ravaged face and put a comb through her hair. She spent an hour picking glass fragments from her knees with tweezers sterilised in hot salt water. She took a bowl of soup. The photograph of Little Stan, muddied and crumpled, was ironed out and, for that evening only, took Her Majesty's place in the unbroken frame. The following day he was restored in his own frame to his place on the other side of the mantelshelf. And she was out around the small hilltop capital demanding to know from startled police officials where her son was being held. "I recall, not so long ago, when this was a civilised country, with the rule of law and a proper respect for the rights of Her Majesty's subjects. Yes, before your time, young man, before we decided we were better off ruling ourselves. We see now where that has got us. Now, where is my son? I will stand here at your desk until you give me the information. It is up to you how long I wait. I am in my eighty-ninth year, but I am as strong as an ox."

Whenever Mr. Stan jolts out of his naps, it is Mother whom he expects to see. It is her voice he expects to hear. "Now, Stanley, this has *got* to stop. You need to consider your own safety—and mine. Even you must see that this lot have gone to bad. They are thoroughly rotten. You need to tell them whatever it is you know—or whatever they want to hear—and get yourself out of here. Playing the hero will achieve nothing. Please listen to me, son. For once." Her words ring in his head. And when he raises his hands to his eyes and sees those wretched stumps he cries out for her.

| MUSTAPHA? YES, COMING

I know that tea is being served in the fellows' common room and that I should be getting up off my bed and joining the other fellows.

Although afternoon tea, like all meals at the House of Journalists, is optional (there are also communal cooking facilities where we can cook for ourselves, if we prefer), all the fellows attend. My absence will be noticed if I leave it much longer. A volunteer—there is an army of them—will come to enquire of me. Most solicitously; most respect-fully; most insistently. It is easier just to put in an appearance—to take a cup of tea or to eat something; to join one of the gatherings or sit at one of the tables in the refectory—than to stay away.

I should add that the food here is excellent, though it is not quite to anyone's taste. It is the sort of food that is laid out at buffets in interna-tional conferences. Every food culture is catered for, with every im-pression of authenticity. But we all notice that we tend to enjoy one another's national dishes rather more than our own. The essential in-gredient that is missing is—please forgive the inevitability of it: *home.*

I am the only person from my country at the House of Journalists, but there are two fellows from the biggest country in the region, with whom I can converse in an almost common language. There is a certain commonality of experience as well. One of the men, Matthew, spent an extended period in a labour camp, just over the mountains from the place where I was imprisoned for so long. We laugh about it now, per-verse as that must sound. We take a certain pleasure in the fact that men of different classes, different nationalities, opponents of different regimes, opponents of *one another* in different circumstances, should have shared the same fate, divided only by a border, a disputed border at that. Such are the curiosities of the politics of oppression.

Here we are united in exile and nostalgia for the food of home. It was while standing beside each other in the refectory queue one eve-ning that Matthew spoke for me when he said:

"The slop they served us in the prison was the most disgusting shit." (I would not have used quite such coarse language myself, but there we are.) "We wolfed it down because we were so damn hungry, but it rotted our guts, made our shit green and liquid. The latrines were stink-ing lakes. When my belly was empty, a twisted empty dry sack, I used to dream about the meals I would pig down when I got out, and in the wildest of those I never dreamt it would be like this." We both con-sidered the food in front of us: the evening selection at the House of Journalists, a banquet, wondrous and bland. "What I dreamt of, of course, was my mother's cooking—it was always my mother's, not my wife's cooking, that gave me the comfort I needed. Simple things; basic foodstuffs: rice, beans, flatbread. I come from a poor family and we did not eat well. And in the city, I was poor too. My journalism did not pay well. I ate in the poorer cafés. You know the places: chipped Formica tables, dirty linoleum floors, fluorescent lighting, a tinted poster of the president in youthful middle age. Places where students and junior city clerks went to eat. There would be some stew, some rice, some flatbread, some sheep's yoghurt. And to drink: sugary, fizzy pop in a can with a straw. I rarely ate at home. Our apartment was tiny—just two rooms. The kitchen was shared with the others on our floor. My wife—she was a cousin, we married very young, she was beautiful at sixteen but that beauty faded fast; childbirth, children, my neglect, the life I subjected her to—all of them wore her out—anyway, she was not a good cook. I believe she is dead. It is better that this is so. (Matthew crossed himself. He is a Christian—a minority religion in his country, as in mine.) But do you know what is so strange now? Now, sometimes, I dream about that prison food. Yes, I want to savour that shit again. I don't know what it is about it: something in the cooking oil perhaps, rancid as it was. Here the food, so perfect and wholesome, is tasteless to me. It is capsule food, like they said we would all be eating, in those American programmes on the TV about astronauts, when we were boys."

I laughed. None of this talk of a mother's cooking or cheap cafés really aligned with my memories of immense family meals prepared by the family cook, Alana; or nights out with friends at the best restaurants in the city—Persian, French, Moroccan, Italian: our city was the culinary capital of the region. But I was with him in spirit. "There is a café, like the one you describe, on the High Road, near the over-ground station. We should go there for lunch one day. Relive prison days and mother's cooking!"

We followed up the suggestion and now we eat there once or twice a week. The food at the café is terrible, but at its best/worst it is only a pale imitation of the really terrible cooking that our home region can produce. "It is definitely the oil," Matthew says. "They cannot get the oil. It is not totally dissimilar, but it is too *good*."

Still, he enjoys the trips out; I, less so. The café is a haunt of his fellow countrymen. They are numerous in this city. They are teachers and professors, lawyers and trade union officials, working in this country as mini-cab drivers or night watchmen. The diasporic conversation is animated and sometimes there are leaping-ups: staged displays in which the small glasses of the impossibly bitter coffee of our region are swept away and the chessboard overturned. The owner, who is second-generation, runs out from behind his humming cold counters, waving a carving knife that he has just wiped on his filthy vest, to interpose his malodorous, hairy, proletarian bulk between the warring intellectuals. "Filthy immigrants," he shouts joyously. "This is how you repay our hospitality."

I do not find any of this play-acting congenial. I find myself thinking that it is true what my countrymen say, that our homeland is the "little gem" of the region and our big neighbour is slovenly and boorish. I find myself thinking that it is true that our language (so much more than a "dialect" or "variant" on the common tongue of the region) is much more nuanced and civilised; that our literature, both in style and subject matter, displays the finer bone. I find myself thinking that all this is true even though it is in our homeland that an ill-bred oil engineer from the north rules with a brutish disdain for the value of our culture. And that it was brother intellectuals from our neighbouring country who spoke up for us, the imprisoned elite, when our own countrymen in their fear deserted us, turning out in their thousands for the weekly spectacle in Revolution Square in which independent newspaper editors, dissident filmmakers, and liberal playwrights, their hands bound with polyurethane cords, their heads bagged with meal sacks, were hanged, legs kicking, from cranes. There was no opposition at home, only oppressed masses. It was pressure from the novelists and poets of our neighbour, exerted through PEN and through Amnesty, which led to my release and that of many others.

And yet, I couldn't abide their capital of concrete and dust, which sprawled across the grey steppe and crawled up the dry mountains which bowled around it. At its heart was the "Old City"—once, in history or legend, an enchantment of domes, minarets, and perfumed souks; now, in present reality, a stinking and graffiti-scrawled warren; its elegant *riads* partitioned into tenements, flagged with drying bedsheets;

its great mosques—once centres of learned discourse—now heaving with the fundamentalist masses at their nodding-dog prayers; every alleyway snarled with street stalls, taxis, rubbish and vegetable waste, mangy dogs and muscled rats, under a cat's cradle of power cables and a floribunda of satellite dishes. You stumbled out through its crumbling arches into the urban wastes of bus station and public plaza, the parched gardens and blistered fountains of the city's boulevards, marooned by multi-lane traffic. The city centre was ringed by vast residential zones of psoriatic apartment blocks set in empty, windblown, rubbish-strewn squares. Somewhere, beyond the tram lines and the bus routes, there must have been middle-class districts with lawns and pools, air-conditioned malls and country clubs, but even these, I imagined, could not compare with the crisp sea air and the elegant art nouveau sweep of our coastal capital.

There was a community of my countrymen living in one of the poorest and most densely packed parts of the city. We had our own shops and cafés, a newspaper and a writers' club. I was welcome there—lionised even—as a known, if minor, opponent of the home regime and a long-serving political prisoner. There was a sort of life there: drinking the bitter coffee of home, endlessly raking over the old failed politics, stringing out the days until the next national holiday, when we all gathered to dance to the scratchy old tunes. The émigré writer Alexander Herzen wrote of this existence in *My Past and Thoughts* (the book will be known to you, I'm sure) as *"a closed, fantastic circle consisting of inert memories and hopes that can never be realised."* That about captures it!

There is a knock at my door. This time there is no intrusion. I wait for another knock before answering.

"Mustapha."

A solicitous, respectful, insistent voice. I get to my feet, put on a smile.

"Yes, coming . . ."

THE FOREIGN PRESS BAR

You did not appear for tea in the common room, AA, we noticed. You did not appear for dinner in the refectory either. No one questioned that or sought to rouse you. You have just arrived here and you would have wanted to rest. You would have unpacked your few things. There is always heartbreak and realisation in that. It will hit you harder still in the days to come, but this evening there is at least the euphoria of arrival.

Buoyed by that, you venture out into the common areas. It is around nine when you are first spotted. There are no talks or other events going on tonight. Some fellows are watching television; two of us are playing table tennis in the games room. But the place has rather a deserted feel to you, we imagine, particularly after all the activity earlier. The night staff and volunteers will also have noticed that you are up and about; they are here to help you if you need help. They are quite insistent, you will find, in offering assistance; it is hard to escape from them after you have been here for a while. But it is recognised that a new fellow will want to explore his new surroundings, to "find his feet," on his own. Tomorrow you will have your full induction session. The rules and protocols—not over-onerous, they trust—will be explained to you then.

In the course of your wandering, you will come across one of the House of Journalists' little mysteries: the Foreign Press Bar. Have a look around, because it is most unlikely you will come in here again. There is no one drinking in the Foreign Press Bar tonight or any other night.

Intriguing, you think. We are all intrigued by the Foreign Press Bar.

Who was the last fellow to have a drink here? The honesty book, in which fellows are expected to settle their bar bill for any alcohol consumed (we all receive a small cash allowance), records one name: S'petim Klogg. A made-up name? It would be wrong to assume that. At the House of Journalists the unlikeliest of names (unlikely to the ears of others, that is) are the most likely to be real. And anyway, what is real? Is not every name a made-up name? Given or imposed: culturally, parentally; the name recorded in the state register. Most of us here at the House of Journalists were looking to make a name for ourselves with our writing or broadcasting. Then that name (birth or de plume) put us in danger. In prison, or awaiting execution, we were often reduced to a number or were counted only among the numberless nameless. In hiding, or in flight, we sought anonymity or assumed another name. Sometimes these were the names of the dead. Here some of us have reclaimed old names; others, still fearing for our safety—or looking for a fresh start—have adopted new names. (I am Mustapha. You are A A?) There are a number of quite famous names among the fellows of the House of Journalists; famous here, that is, in this country. There is perhaps some redemption in that. Perhaps that is what you seek, AA?

But S'petim Klogg? Let's not forget him. Sadly, everyone has; under that name at least. (That is the way of it. Becoming a fellow of the House of Journalists is no guarantee that you will be remembered. That is a mistake, in our innocence or otherwise, that many of us made when we arrived. Though no one just disappears. This long-lost fellow will be recorded somewhere on the books, in some locked file.)

The honesty book, if it is to be believed, records Klogg as having enjoyed? drunk? paid for, at least, a cherry brandy. How unlikely is that? Cherry brandy translates more or less in every language as cherry brandy. In more or less every culture it is a drink that given a choice no one would choose. And choice is not an issue at the Foreign Press Bar. It is, you will have noticed, well stocked with spirits from around the world: rice wines, cane rums, fruit liqueurs, brandies of all sorts, vodkas, araks, every sort of moonshine and firewater. A mystery, then: both S'petim Klogg and his cherry brandy. All we really know is that it must have happened in the very earliest days of the House of Journalists, when the place first opened, when the Foreign Press Bar seemed like a good idea, a novelty. Because since those early days, hardly a drop of the extensive range of world liquor on the shelves has been touched. The Foreign Press Bar is the one neglected corner of the House of Journalists. Of course there are some among us who are forbidden by our religion from touching alcohol. But there are plenty of drinkers. We are journalists and writers. We smoke. We drink. We smoke together fraternally. So why do we not drink together?

One of those things. A mystery.

| AGNES IS ONE OF THE BOYS

You find us at last out in the Central Courtyard. Where else? Here we are one collective—smoking. You are welcomed and take a place in our circle. It seems that you enjoy being in the company of fellow writers.

When you arrived at the House of Journalists this morning a member of staff would have welcomed you warmly, but the first thing he would have done was to cut off that plasticated white wristband you were wearing. These bands are bestowed on new arrivals by immigration officials and resemble those they put on corpses in the morgue. To prevent mix-ups. Is this what happened to you?

You do not look too sure, but this is the normal procedure, so it must have been so. If you followed our example, and we assume you did, you would have said to the official at the border point just two things: "Asylum" and "I am writer." A lot of arrivals try it these days. Word has got around. You would have been taken into a room to wait and wait and then to be "interrogated." We laugh, because what they call interrogation here does not come close to our understanding of the word. Sometimes they rough people up a bit—and that causes outrage among the human rights groups here. Again laughter: this time at the thought that these groups can get so passionately exercised by so little. Letters to the papers, petitions to Parliament, marches and demonstrations. Still, we go along with these groups in protesting about our treatment. It would be churlish to do otherwise when they do so much to help us in our claims. Even so, we've lived through a lot worse.

We notice that you have a cut on your lip. Did you give them some? Lip, that is—that's what they call it here! *Lip.* You seem keen on this idea. Did they advise you to "button it"? But how can you be expected to tell them your story if you cannot open your mouth? Did you ask them that? We'll take that as a yes. It is always a mistake. You will not make it again, we can see you agree. Better to be like Mustapha, "of few words": the quiet, sad, mysterious type. This approach always works very well.

Still, even if you nearly messed it up, "you and your big mouth," in the end your plan worked out, and an order came from somewhere that you should be dispatched here, "the cushiest fucking lock-up in the country," with your lucky wristband saying: *AA—Writer*. You protested at its removal. Are we right? The staff member laughed—but not unkindly. "We take that one, but you get this one," he said—and handed over a laminated security pass with your photograph on it which said . . . *AA—Writer*.

You must wear this pass around your neck at all times. Around your neck, at all times, for security reasons, you are to wear this identity. *AA—Writer*. Whatever you have been through and wherever you are going, it is something, is it not, to be recognised officially in this way?

Of course, questions remain about your status: your right to be here, your right to remain. There is still a struggle ahead. But there is no question, apparently, about your right—self-proclaimed, but established in this fellowship—to the status of writer. *Writer*: Novelist? Essayist? Aphorist? Poet? Memoirist? Journalist? Yes, questions remain. Exile and the writer is such a commonplace after all—in so many traditions—that the condition of exile could be seen as an obstacle to the writer looking to escape from the tyranny of influence. But that was the old world, your old self, your old life. You are free of that now. Exile offers you the chance to invent yourself anew. You are in a new world of your own making. You are here at the House of Journalists. You have been admitted to the fellowship. It is a rich seam: now, to mine it; to make it yours.

We see your high spirits and smile to ourselves. As is fitting for a new fellow, you are invited now to perform the honour of helping Mr. Stan to light his evil little bidi cigarette. It is chilly tonight and Mr. Stan is wrapped in a large dark blanket. He is using its woolly wings to protect the fluttering flame. Leathery of head and rodent-bodied: he looks like a bat in the darkness.

You straighten up. You are a tall man, straight-backed: handsome, in a drawn, disappointed way. You are the sort of man who should have been a greater success with women than you have been. Standing beside Mr. Stan, towering over him, you smoke an elegantly elongated cigarette. It is obvious that you cling to a sense of style, however threadbare it is now. Otherwise you give nothing away. That is sensible: make the most of the mystery of arrival. Any glamour attached to the writer in exile does not survive very long in this place. Sorry to prick the bubble, but there it is. You are just another sad, lonely, unknown refugee looking to start again. Welcome to the House of Journalists!

You look rather downcast now. But it was never going to be that easy—even with all that this place offers you. You realise that, surely. Anyway, time to look up, Agnes is approaching you. We laugh. We know what Agnes is after.

But one moment: Women at the House of Journalists? Yes, indeed, did we not mention that? It is true that we, the female fellows, have not featured as yet. In the House of Journalists, as elsewhere, the male voices tend to dominate. But the women of the House will certainly pop up in our story, your story, going forward. The men will not get it all their own way. This is a place of strong women: fellow fighters and survivors.

There is the male wing and the female wing—though Julian and the Committee don't like that word "wing": ominous echoes of prison. The only divide—Julian and the Committee point out—is that the female fellows have their rooms on the far side of the courtyard, in the mews building; while the male fellows are accommodated in the original house. There are no restrictions on our movements. All the other facilities are shared. We enjoy free association at all times. We are brothers and sisters together.

Agnes embodies that spirit. She is just twenty-three: our youngest resident. She is tall and rangy: hard-bodied. When she is inside (the House of Journalists is always kept warm) she wears white sleeveless T-shirts or vests that show off the hard knots of her muscled arms and shoulders, and her hard, flat chest. Her hair is worn so closely cropped that it looks almost shaven. To some of us, the men among us, this is an uncomfortable reminder of seeing women prisoners in the distance in their own barbed-wired compounds. But of course Agnes does not resemble those wrecked specimens in any other way. She is self-confident, strong-willed: she wears her hair this way because it is the way she likes it.

Outside in the courtyard, in the cold, she wears a hooded top—like the faceless youths huddled on the street corners of this sometimes threatening foreign city. But Agnes does not withdraw in on herself like they do. She is open-faced: all laughter and chatter, opinion and point. She is not looking for any trouble, but no one messes with her. Just let them try! The slouching toughs of this neighbourhood show her respect without knowing why she attracts it. She is very popular with the fellows, with staff and volunteers.

Her smoke of choice is the roll-up. She constructs each with sensuous long-fingered care, completing the act with a slow lick of the tongue and a soft-fingered rolling. It is a beautiful act to witness, but what emerges, every time, is a broken-backed, drooping, flaky specimen which she contemplates with astonished bewilderment. How did that happen again? her look seems to say. She sucks on the thing with sceptical determination. There should be pleasure in it—she surmises that from the deep satisfaction we are all drawing from our cigarettes—but as ever it is escaping her.

Agnes smokes to be one of the boys. Since she was a little girl she has always been one of the boys. She never wanted to help her grandmother and the other women in collecting water or preparing the meals: she wanted to be out stoning the street dogs or killing snakes. In the city, now an adult and a professional, she insisted on joining the all-male Press Club, and made her editor send her on the most hazardous assignments. When the new government carried out its first round-up of journalists, she was the only woman among those held downtown in the police station.

If Agnes is out of tobacco or papers—a frequent occurrence—she cadges whatever other smoke she can. So that is why she is approaching you, AA. If you don't mind she will try one of your slim, silver-banded cigarettes. We laugh to see your rather flustered gallantry, as you tap a slender filter tip from its box.

Mr. Stan looks on. He adores Agnes and is ever eager to be of service to her. But, game as she is, she draws the line at his lung-burning little bidis. She tried one once. Never again.

"Jeez U!" She cursed. "That is one rank cigarillo, Mr. Stan. You must have lungs of leather."

Mr. Stan giggled and blushed as she threw the bidi to the ground and stamped on it, as if putting out a small bush fire.

"Yes, Mr. Stan. You are the maaan," Agnes said, seeing his delight and shaping for a high five. Mr. Stan, ecstatic now, held up his stumps and Agnes bumped them joyously with the flats of her hands. Mr. Stan was happy for the rest of the day.

Of course, as much as Mr. Stan loves Agnes, he respects her too. We all do. She is one of the bravest of the fellows. Her grandfather came to the capital from a remote province, established a small photographic studio, and went on to work for a highly regarded newspaper in the city. His pictures of women dancing for joy on Independence Day won the approval of the new president and were published around the world. Agnes was her grandfather's favourite, his protégé, and she helped out in his studio after mission school. As soon as she was old enough and strong enough to hold his Pentax steady and true, he taught her how to take pictures with it—but "more important, to *see* through it." She took over from him as a chief photographer on the newspaper when she was just eighteen. By this time, however, her grandfather's studio had been ransacked more than once and the dancing women had become women sitting, women squatting on their haunches, women waiting and queuing: for rationed bags of maize and for cooking oil. The president was a distant, angry, delusional figure, locked away behind the dirty pink crenellations of his palace on a crumbling bluff overlooking the great lake. The round-ups had started; protests were broken up in the streets by police wielding batons and whips; and corpses, imaginatively mutilated, turned up on the doorsteps of their houses. "At first sight," a foreign correspondent wrote in one of this country's most distinguished papers, "they look like drunks, sleeping it off in the early morning sunshine. Then you look closer . . ."

With the chief news reporter, now her lover, Agnes went out into the opposition strongholds in the northern suburbs, out into the outlying villages and the bush, to record the superabundance of atrocity. Bodies hung from trees, or lay rotting among the rubbish heaps beside the roads, or floated bloated down the slow brown rivers where they were eaten by crocodiles. The tracks of beatings and torture ridged and criss-crossed many a back that was unsheeted for her magic eye. She came across a whole congregation preserved at prayer in charcoal inside the blackened ribcage of their church. Villages, from which the men were marched to mass graves now heaving with decomposition, were repopulated overnight through the ferocious, sweat-stinking, heavy-membered fecundity of soldier rapists. Agnes was twenty-one, twenty-two, and she was the world's most important witness to her country's descent into barbarity.

Martial law was declared. Her newspaper was closed down; its proprietors arrested. Agnes and her lover took to the interior, but her photographs continued to appear in underground publications, poorly printed but widely circulated. Some of them were smuggled out and reproduced overseas—first in relatively obscure publications, but later in prestigious international magazines. Maybe her fame protected her, because of those inside the opposition hideout which was raided by government troops only she escaped with her life. She may have had some help from contacts in the foreign press corps; there may have been diplomatic representations made on her behalf. Many of us have interventions of this sort to thank for the fact that we are here, alive and safe, at the House of Journalists.

Agnes is a *photo*journalist; the only one at the House of Journalists. She both relishes her unique status and makes light of it. "These writer boys, they are the ones that topple rulers and change the world with their words. Me? A picture doesn't express outrage or argue for justice. It just *shows* how it is. It just takes you there. It just puts you in the frame. If you feel outrage or want justice—that is your doing." The House of Journalists has of course given due weight and prominence to her photography with exhibitions and catalogues. But it tells you something about the way this place works, as well as the power of its marketing, that Agnes is almost as well known now for two short poems, written in a therapeutic workshop. They are printed here in full.

HEAD

They hacked your beautiful man head
From your beautiful man body
With a dirty, rusty, blunt machete,
And stuck it on a stake to rot in the sun.

But they did not cut off your love thoughts,
Our sex secrets.
They did not cut off your burning desire to defy them,
Your plans to destroy them.
They did not cut off your brilliance,
Your humanity,
Your hatred and heart.

It is still all up there:
All of you that I loved.
In your head.
And I cradle it in my arms in the same way I always did.
I rock you to sleep like a baby.

BODY

They called me into the morgue to pick up your body.
They thought that without your head I would find you
ridiculous.
They thought that now your body was starting to putrefy I would
be repelled by you.
But what I saw lying there on the slab was the beautiful man body
I knew so well.
The same strong chest, strong arms, strong legs.

I lay with you in the heat and the flies.
It was just as it was:
Making love.
And there is still no bed I would rather share than your grave.
I am sharing it now.

These two poems have a raw power, no one denies that. But there are those of us in the House of Journalists who, in truth, would prefer more polish and control; more of the practised poet's art. There is an element of envy in our opinions perhaps. The camaraderie of exile has its limits. This special place has the same professional jealousies and rivalries that divide newsrooms and common rooms the world over. Agnes may be a favourite among all of us, something of a pet; but her success, with pieces so slight and so crude, must necessarily rile and antagonise.

We have learnt to keep our mouths shut, however.

For Agnes's poems are the sort of writing that Julian and the Committee value above all else. The House of Journalists is *about* such writing. It exists for it and because of it. Without the naked pain, the uncensored horror, the howls of injustice and fanfares to the human spirit, this place would lose its hold on public imagination.

We understand that. We only point out—gently—that it is sometimes the mark of good writing that it inhabits small spaces wholly; that it convinces quietly; that it does not say what seems obvious and important. Good writing can be ironic, domestic, difficult—on the wrong side of the argument.

But fate has bestowed on us these great stories, these great themes. That some of us respond with agonised silences, muted utterances, tentative answers to small questions, disquisitions on our own private concerns, must frustrate. After all—they say to themselves: the writers who visit us here and mingle among us—we are free of the cramped chambers in which they must work. After all we have been through; after all we have seen and could say; after all they have done to help us, how can we be so constrained?

So Agnes—the ingénue—is the godsend, the sensation. "These two unadorned, untutored verses," Julian has been heard to say—more than once—his voice wobbling with pride and emotion—"tell you everything you need to know about the House of Journalists; all about the awesome courage, the heartbreaking hurt, and the defiant humanity of the place."

It is said by some that Julian and his Committee purloined "Head" and "Body," tearing them from early classes, with the unconsidered consent of Agnes, who was then a very new fellow. But their action has been allowed to pass. Agnes can always be prevailed upon to read the poems in public. She displays no false pride in disowning them. She is, if anything, awed by her ability—now lost forever—to capture the desperate erotic anger she felt in that first dwelling on Jean-Paul's death. "These poems," she says, always effectively, to the audiences who gather for readings, "are not political, but they are propagandist. I think of them as propaganda for love."

What of the facts? There is serious doubt as to whether Agnes was taken to see the headless body of her dead lover or that the placing of his head on a stake in a public place happened at all. They are "true" incidents only in that they are true to her poetic memory. And Jean-Paul, as well as being a journalist, was an officer with the rebel forces, perhaps one of their most senior commanders and responsible, it is alleged, for many atrocities of his own. It is not clear how much, if anything, Agnes knew of this side of Jean-Paul. Many in the fellowship know from our own experiences that there are no hands clean of blood in a civil war, so we do not feel that even complicity condemns her. But it is important for the House of Journalists that Agnes's reputation both for veracity and for innocence is protected. Julian and the Committee have some powerful friends in the media and they have made use of them. We understand the forces that are at work here and how two simple poems by a young attractive woman who has survived so much have the power to be used for good or ill. We must welcome the fact that they are being used for good.

You are talking to Agnes, sharing a word or two with her, though giving little away. Perhaps you are already a little sweet on Agnes? (We all are, if we're honest—all the men, certainly; and perhaps some of the women as well.) Agnes brings out the charm which we already suspect that you can turn on if the mood takes; she makes you feel good about yourself. Better, certainly. Don't be fooled, though. Agnes may develop a soft spot for you, as she does for many of us, but it won't go further than that. As we have said, Agnes is an attractive young woman, and she is not short of offers from the attractive young men of this city. Until recently she had a boyfriend—on the outside; an occurrence rare enough to excite real interest and some concern.

It is not against the rules or regulations. The House of Journalists is much too liberal and right-thinking to inhibit our personal freedoms in any way. It is not, after all, a boarding school or a monastery. Or a prison. We are all adults, free to come and go as we please. There is no prohibition on visitors, even those who stay the night. But, all that said, there was a sense that the relationship between Agnes and her boy-friend was in some semi-official way—out of a fiduciary concern for her welfare—frowned upon. Not that Agnes cared about that. She rather enjoyed that it should be so. She has a rebellious streak.

Alexei was—is—ganglingly tall, strong-shouldered, concave of cheek-bone and abdomen. He was—is—a jazz pianist. And when he wasn't "on the road"—which was most of the time, it seemed—he habituated the House of Journalists, day and night. He ate in the refectory and played the piano in the fellows' common room and shot pool in the games room. We got used to him, even if we didn't like him very much. But there was one thing which disturbed us. Because, with a frequency that exhausted the imagination, and not just at night but also during the day, the quiet sanctums of the House of Journalists, its cloisters and courtyards, its libraries and common rooms, were shaken by the rhythmic pounding and ecstatic cries of Alexei and Agnes's lovemaking. No one wanted to complain, but there was disquiet. It had been going on for some little time when Mr. Stan, who so adores Agnes, and who is quite deaf, was, much to his embarrassment, prevailed upon to approach her about the . . . well, about the volume.

In that cracked, peppery voice of his, Mr. Stan put it to Agnes—and to Alexei—that the House of Journalists was home to the survivors of rape, to men and women who had lost loved ones; that her behaviour (their behaviour) might be viewed as somewhat insensitive and inap-propriate; that she (they) were perfectly at liberty to enjoy the freedoms of this place, but that some thought for others would be appreciated. Agnes took it all very solemnly and respectfully, but Alexei—who was stark naked—seemed to think it was all a joke.

"I correct myself," Mr. Stan said. "He, Agnes's gentleman friend, was not stark naked—he was wearing a pork-pie hat." As if somehow the

hat, but more than that the pork-pie nature of it, were a peculiar inde-
cency in the circumstances. Mr. Stan—like so many men and women
who have suffered so terribly—can find these small embarrassments
hard to bear. And to make matters worse, Alexei—unforgivably—shaped
to "Stan the Man" Mr. Stan, to high-five him, to bump his stumps,
while still stark naked in his pork-pie hat. Agnes jumped up to stop
him, to stop Alexei, that is, and he did desist—laughing as he flopped
back onto the bed. But the damage was done. Agnes tried to cuddle
Mr. Stan's head, but he was too upset to enjoy this, his greatest comfort.
He shook Agnes off—really quite violently, such that she looked at
him with real hurt in her eyes.

That night we were out smoking in the Central Courtyard as usual
and we could hear Agnes and Alexei arguing. There were shouts and
screams, slamming doors and tears. Then there was silence. After a while
Agnes came out to join us in hastily pulled-on jeans and hooded top.
She grabbed a cigarette out of the mouth of the first person she passed.

After several deep drags, and long exhalations, she handed the cigarette back. "He's gone, okay," she said. "Yes, that's right. He's FUCKED
OFF!" She gave us a stare. "That's what you wanted, wasn't it? Well,
that's what you've got. Thank you, my brothers and sisters. We can all
sleep soundly tonight."

And then she burst into tears.

She was all right after that.

| THE END OF A LONG DAY

It is the end of a long day at the House of Journalists. We retire to bed
weary of it—as we weary of every day, if we are honest. We will take up
our story at a later date. Until then: one more observation.

Sewn onto the upside of the mattresses on our single beds at the
House of Journalists is a plastic-covered square of fabric that "guaran-
tees every SuperSlumber purchaser a good night's sleep." There is always a point early in the stay of every fellow when, standing aside to

allow the cleaner to carry the stripped-off under-sheet out of the room, he or she notices this bold assurance. The word "guarantee" translates more or less into every language as "guarantee"; as does the expression "a good night's sleep." So, we ask ourselves, how could any company make a claim so fabulous?

The mattresses, it must be said, are excellent. Most of us have never slept in more comfortable beds than those at the House of Journalists. (New arrivals often find them *too* comfortable after many nights in the back of lorries or many years in prison bunks. To break ourselves in, we sleep for a while on the floor.)

Firm, but with plenty of give, the mattress moulds to the contours of the prone figure, while providing support to the shoulders and lower back. (We find ourselves lapsing into the language of the manufacturer when we try to describe the SuperSlumber experience.) When we lie on our beds to read in the afternoon we often drift off to sleep for a few minutes. These are sleeps of immense physical lassitude; luxuriant and sensual. But they are not deep sleeps—quite the reverse. They are shallow dips below the sparkling surface, where a refracted sun still warms; not a total plunge into the dark totality of night. There is a sense, so comforting, that from these warm shallows you can drift back to the surface at any moment. It has been observed, more than once, that SuperSlumber might choose to advertise its mattresses thus. What it cannot "guarantee," however, is a good night's sleep. Not to a fellow of the House of Journalists at least. There is no good night's sleep in the House of Journalists.

Is that what you are finding in Room 15, AA?

There's no sound from you. Perhaps the SuperSlumber mattress has worked its magic this once and you are sleeping soundly?

More likely you are lying on the floor, staring up at the ceiling, and thinking about what will happen next. And what—and who—you have left behind.

Now is not the time to tell us about all that.

Maybe tomorrow?

THE VISIT

YOU COULD SMELL DECAY

Like Artur Sammler, we have seen the world collapse once, so we entertain the possibility it might collapse twice.

And we, and others who cluster around the House of Journalists, identify with Sammler's disquiet, accorded him by Saul Bellow in 1969 in *Mr. Sammler's Planet* (Viking Press), that "liberal beliefs did not seem capable of self-defense, and you could smell decay."

THIS IS AN IMPORTANT VISIT FOR THE HOUSE OF JOURNALISTS

"Good morning," Julian says to the assembled fellows. "And what a very pleasant morning it is."

We take this to mean that the weather is rather brighter today than the norm, though we would observe that it is no better than a lighter grey or—if we are generous—a *silver* grey. (It is still winter: early March. A month has passed.) Julian is of course silver-grey himself; a rather beautiful man, it must be said; and those massy silver locks are offset today by a long dark coat and a knotted scarf of rich dark softness.

"Very pleasant indeed."

He claps dark soft leather gloves together to show enthusiasm for the day and then clasps them together to celebrate the boon of fellowship.

But we have drawn him out into the Central Courtyard. A small victory. After breakfast is a smoking time: that is now established. If he wants to speak to us he must come to us out here. He does so with reluctance. It is an effort for him every time to disguise his particular loathing that so many of us smoke. Julian is a non-smoking writer; his writing has that non-smoking quality. It is clean living, and has self-discipline. He is not really what you would call a writer's writer.

"Today," Julian reminds us, "though you will need no reminding, we have a VIP visitor, the playwright and poet Edward Crumb, a Nobel laureate and of late a noted political activist and controversialist. This is an important visit for the House of Journalists for reasons that I will not repeat, so I would ask that all of you be there to welcome him. He is, I know, greatly honoured to be meeting you. He asked me to stress that—which is good of him. We will gather in the library at three. I will not detain you further. I know the morning schedule is a busy one."

We take that as a signal to disperse to the various classes and workshops, but we notice that you, AA, linger: a rare mistake. Julian will have been informed that you spend most of your time in your room, that you seem to have lost your early pleasure in our fellowship, and that no one knows any more about you than when you first arrived. Yes, he has his "spies"—though, don't be alarmed by this expression—it is used in a light-hearted way in this country.

Of course the fact that you have not shared your story is respected. Stories are precious. All we have are our stories. And we are writers and so we want to shape them and present them in the best possible way. It has been noted that, in your case, none of your writing has travelled—though you are not alone in that. Neither do you do any writing here—or, at least, none that you care to share with the other fellows. That too is respected. No one is forced to write, although attendance at writing workshops is encouraged. You do not attend—or rarely; and then only to sit and to listen. That is not a problem. There are no rules. We do not *have* to write. And we can write what we like. Maybe you are writing alone in your room? In which case, we/they will respect your privacy. But do remember that you cannot stay silent forever. In the end you will have to account for yourself.

At last, you take a final drag on your cigarette, exhale, and—belatedly conscious that Julian's eyes are on you—extinguish the butt in the elegant piece of public sculpture provided for the purpose. At some stage Julian will want to return to you, AA. But for the time being his mind has turned to a more immediate worry: Ted Crumb's visit. Julian loves to show off the House of Journalists, but sometimes it means opening this place up to influences and forces which seek to disrupt and even corrupt. With that in mind, he heads off to check that all the contingencies are in place to protect the House from Crumb's malign influence. He will not have anyone destroy his good work.

| WORKSHOP 1

So this important visit will take place this afternoon. But it is not allowed to disrupt the normal rhythms and routines of a morning at the House of Journalists. The fellows are about their various tasks and undertakings, supported by a dedicated team of staff and volunteers. A small group of fellows is gathered in a bright, state-of-the-art multimedia room for Workshop 1. None of us here today will yet be familiar. Workshop 1 is a gathering place for newer fellows, where we share stories about our experiences, but also look forward to finding a new voice in a new language in our new country. Mustapha is sometimes of our number—but he is absent this morning. He is not feeling up to it. We wish him well. But his absence presents an opportunity for others among us to introduce ourselves.

| HELLO, MY NAME IS JOSIAH

"Josiah, you are very welcome."

The welcome is given by our teacher, Esther, who has already been introduced. We are all very fond of Esther, as she is of us. Esther is the best of the House of Journalists. When a fellow is first enrolled into Workshop 1 the senior staff member completes the little ceremony which is made of it by introducing Esther, who until that point has kept out of the way, her head bowed, her back pressed against the wall. Esther is "a very talented creative writing student, of whom great things are expected," it is said. "We await publication of her first collection of short stories with enormous eagerness," it is also said. Esther, fair hair scraped back into a ponytail, pale blue eyes cast down, her bumpy, bony hands clasped together, seems to cower in the face of this expectation. The blush that blotches her pale cheek and neck is a self-scalding pink. She burns with shame that we should think she is worthy to compare herself with us—and yet she is desperate to succeed in her writing.

The agony of her ambition is hard for us, the fellows, to understand. Yes, she writes—but we all write. Yes, she writes, but more than that she teaches. She does not see it this way, of course. In her own mind she teaches because she has so far failed as a writer, young as she is, so new to everything, so far from failing to our older, wiser minds. To teach is so much less valued here, we notice. That is strange to us, because what could be a higher calling than to teach? To teach is to open up the world of civilisation. It is the path out of darkness and into light.

"Thank you, my friends: those are very powerful and heartfelt words."

Esther, released from reference to her writing, is much more at ease. And when she is not weighing it against literary ambition she does take great pleasure in teaching. That is only right, as she is a wonderful teacher of her own language; wonderful because she loves it so. Yes, much the best way, perhaps the only way, to teach a language is to love it and to communicate that love. The love can take many forms: there are those, strange to some, who love the rules and formalities; there are others, the poets, who love the cadences and metaphysics; for Esther, the most lovable aspects of her language are the foibles, the eccentricities, the comedies. "Oh, listen to me." She laughs as we all laugh, she having taught us some nonsense verse or play on words. "I'm supposed to be teaching you how to 'speak proper.'" "Speak proper," we all parrot. "No, no, no," Esther squeals. She has one of her "fits of the giggles" but regains her composure. "To speak properly. After me: 'To—speak—properly.' 'Properly,' not 'proper.' We must speak the King's English at the House of Journalists."

Yes, we are all enjoyably diverted when Esther is teaching us the little turns of phrase which give this language its peculiarity and charm, or when she is gently correcting or commanding us. Yet, central to Workshop 1, as it is to the House of Journalists as a whole, are our stories. We must always get back to those—and they remind Esther, as they remind all those who hear them, that we can draw on experience beyond the normal scope. Ours is an epic canvas. And that inverts the normal relationship between the teacher and the taught. We, her students, have this great status. There is no getting away from that. Welcome to the House of Journalists!

"Yes," Esther says. "Welcome, Josiah. Now, we like to start our sessions by learning more about one another. Perhaps you can tell us something of your life? Anything at all: perhaps something about your childhood?"

Josiah looks alarmed

My childhood? I'm sure I understood it right: she asked me about my childhood. Isn't that rather strange? Why do they want to know about my childhood? How could that information be useful or interesting?

"Josiah?" Esther is now looking alarmed as Josiah seems paralysed by fear. He sees her reaction and smiles to reassure her.

Of course, I am at the House of Journalists now. I am safe here, they assure me; those people whose job it is to assure me that I am safe here. They are nice people; well-meaning in their way. Though I do not think it is sensible to trust them entirely. Even the sympathy of the most sympathetic is constructed in such a way as to disorientate. I say something. They sympathise. I never know quite where it leaves me.

But Esther is our teacher and our friend. She only wants to help me. The other fellows tell me that she is very good at helping them to regain their confidence with words. She is light and funny, but does not mock.

"*Still, this is a struggling language for me. Like my other fellow colleagues, I making small mistakes which for the reader render myself slightly comical in complexion.*"

Oh, we know that is how our voices are sometimes conveyed when it suits the House of Journalists, and we understand the conventions that are at work here. But I have always been known for my command of my own language, so it is an indignity and embarrassment that my inadequacy in this one should be so obvious, so laughable.

(You are now hearing what I hear inside my own head when I talk to myself. This is not foreign to my ears or yours. And this is how you, dear readers, will hear me—and the other fellows—henceforward. The House of Journalists allows these little liberties, I trust.)

I will work hard to learn this language. Like most of the fellows, educated men and women all, I knew something of it, spoke something of it, before my journey into exile. But still, to have to live in it constantly is strange to me, as everything about this strange place is strange to me. I will banish this sense of strangeness, however. I must do so because this country is now my home. There is no possibility of return for me. That may not yet be accepted by the authorities here—my claim has yet to be heard—but it is the case. So, I will take on this language; I will learn to live in it; it will be the language of primary residence for me.

Still, my place of secret refuge will remain my mother tongue.

Inside my head, it is gabbling away, talking about our shared past, praying, singing, telling old tales, incanting the verse that all our countrymen know by heart. My language is not understood by anyone here. Even the simplest sentence—"I do not understand"—is met with incomprehension. I understand why. My language is composed of the most improbable clacking and gutturals. We smack our lips and stick out our tongues. We gurgle and whistle and spit. Sounds are rolled around in our mouth water. Respect, even reverence, is paid here to its outlandish music. But I am not seduced by this false sentiment. I want to be understood.

Therefore I will master this master tongue. Without such mastery, I will not be able to do justice to my own story even though my safety hangs upon it. I will be "assigned" an interpreter who will speak for me when my case is heard. I have no doubt that he will be friendly and sympathetic. He will do his best for me. People here are generally most helpful. But his grasp of my language will be excessively literal and he will have no *feel* for my words. No, I cannot entrust to him, a stranger in a strange land, my only possession of any worth: my story.

At present, however, I hear/say in a broken tongue. Or to be precise (I am "a bit of a stickler," as we say in my language and, I think, yours?): broken and blurred. My own efforts are at best stop/start; while the oncoming traffic flashes past too fast for me to make much of it. It feels like driving the wrong way up the highway in a broken-down vehicle. But I must not make light of my deficiency. We all know the importance of this language. It is the international language of communication, diplomacy, and transaction; and as such, it is also the international language of war, imprisonment, torture, trafficking, human rights, and sanctuary. It is, in so many words, our various journeys through politics and oppression and into exile. In this world, in the end, there is no choice but to learn it; to subject oneself to its demands.

"Esther, I think, on reflection, I would prefer if I could just listen today. I do not feel confident enough to tell my own tale today." It is a surprise to me that I have the confidence to relieve myself of this burden, if only temporarily. I see it as a good sign. I hope that Esther and my fellows will not take it the wrong way.

"Of course, Josiah. Of course," Esther says, reassuring me. "I hope you didn't feel under any pressure? Another time perhaps?"

ADOM CONJURES UP MOST MAGICALLY THE BEAUTY OF HIS COUNTRY

Esther looks around the gathered fellows in Workshop 1. The other relative newcomer among us is Adom. Esther is rather afraid of Adom—or perhaps more accurately, intimidated by his presence. Every fellow has experienced things almost beyond her imagining, but the immensity of Adom's experience is especially forbidding.

———

"Adom, it is good to see you in the workshop again. We have missed you for the last few days. I hope you are feeling a bit better. Perhaps you would like to come forward to tell us more of your story?"

This young woman Esther is perhaps twenty-five. It is strange to me that a young woman should show such easy familiarity towards a man who is more than twice her age; a man of considerable status and bearing, even if these qualities are diminished somewhat by my supplicant circumstances. I have adapted well to my new situation, however. I am humble, but not wretched. I am sure the other fellows would agree. I maintain a good humour and high spirits. I show due gratitude and deference, but retain self-respect.

This country is admirable in its regard for justice and its respect for the individual. It is why I chose to put my fate in its hands. Though ultimately of course I am, as we all are, in God's hands. It is in Him that I reside ultimate trust. It is to Him that I look for deliverance—both here and hereafter.

And yes, I am feeling better, thank you very much. There was some business about my status to attend to, and I was laid rather low after that. But I am not a man to give in to low spirits. And I am indeed willing to share my story. It is important that people hear it. I will not spare myself. It has its own peculiar force, but its lessons are universal.

My country, Esther, is a place of great lakes, of mist and mountain. See there: it shimmers mauve and pink and silver in the twilight of memory—and my brother and I are the small black boys, standing hand in hand, silhouetted against its grandeur. There is no prouder or sadder yearning than the yearning for homeland. But such yearning is treacherous too. It cheats recollection of strict veracity. For my country, I must tell you, is also a place of flesh-eating jungle, of roadblock and militia; of plantation, poverty, proxy, and resort. It has long been so, and yet until disaster befell me, I lived untouched by these realities, in a state of blissful innocence.

I played and roamed as a wide-eyed boy with my brother among giant plants which bent low to offer us their fruits, among vines that curled around our waists, swung us into the air, and landed us safely on the other side of rivers, pools, and waterfalls so crystalline we could drink from them as well as swim in them. Great languid, long-legged, long-necked, tall-storied creatures came down to the water holes where the women washed, while parrots chitter-chattered in the trees and hummingbirds, wings ablur, made electric raids on nectar cups. The mountain behind my home was a black-fanged dragon which spat fire into the starry night—but it was far-off and thrilled us as much as it scared us. One morning I went out into a clearing in the sunshine and a corps de ballet of white butterflies settled on my head and on my shoulders and on my hands and on the pages of the book of poetry I was reading. It matters not at all what the poetry was. I could be reading those poems now. All else is lost.

"I'm sure we all agree that Adom conjures up most magically the beauty of his country and his love for it," Esther says, enchanted. "But please, Adom, continue."

My home, Esther, was a college for boys in the northern region of my country, the most beautiful region of all. The school had been established by my father, who also served as its first headmaster. My mother died when we were small children so there were just the three of us: my father, my younger brother and I, plus a housekeeper, a cook, and a few lowlier servants. Our father maintained a God-fearing household. Discipline and learning, and all forms of cleanliness and observance, were valued very highly. Students and servants were regularly beaten. My brother and I could not expect to escape—though our punishments took account of our status. As we grew into manhood, our love of all that was wild and beautiful was tamed and circumscribed. We came to understand what was meet and right. Nature was brought within proper limits as we were taught all of civilisation's benefits.

My father was our guide, stern and loving, God bless his soul. He died when I was seventeen, and young as I was, I took over as headmaster. No other appointment was conceivable. For more than thirty years after that, I lived with my brother and his wife in a modest villa on the grounds of the school. It was a peaceful and orderly life. With God occupying His rightful place among us. Bright boys from all around the country flourished under my tutelage, amid those flowers, birds, insects, and animals of such array that they made of the well-watered lawns and flower beds places botanical, zoological, and, yes, magical. Such is His garden if we abide by His rules.

I installed my brother, who did not possess my didactic gifts, as head groundsman and gardener. I passed over to him responsibility for everything that grew in such profusion in that wet, hot, rich, dark, good earth. No gardener could have been more blessed by nature and the divine than to bring forth flower and fruit in this Elysium.

Of course, all this easy, almost indecent abundance needed good firm management. My brother employed a small army of village men, from the local tribe, armed with machetes, to cut back the wilder jungle that would have eaten our ordered paradise alive in minutes. Theirs was the backbreaking work. My brother was not born for it. He was a gentle man, a man of God and of peace. That was the man I knew. He respected me greatly. My sister-in-law, who supervised the kitchens, was of similar disposition and goodness. And that remains my view.

A man of my stature and wide interests was bound to involve himself in the greater affairs of his region and in due course his country. Politics absorbed a good portion of my time in later years, as I became a trusted advisor to and confidant of our president, a kinsman and cousin. I also embarked on my writing career, publishing essays and short stories. I became a public figure.

But my main position in life was always that of headmaster. I remained devoted to my school and my boys. I never married. I was not suited to the institution. So, my brother (limited though his company was to a man of my intellect) and his wife (a village woman, if truth be told) were my only family. I thank God for them nonetheless. There were no harsh words or strictures between us. We lived respectably. We loved nature and God. We lived always in peace, and latterly in some prosperity, in our little patch of Eden. They were simple people, my brother and his wife: good people. I will not hear another word.

They nailed this sweet couple to facing trees, the village men, from the local tribe. They cut them open with their machetes, leaving their organs to spill onto the ground. The village women, their babes at their bare breasts, their broods around their filthy skirts, came along to watch. They dipped their hands into the bellies of the martyred couple and smeared their faces with their blood and gore. They had prepared for these barbarous rites by sacrificing wild animals on crude altars. They were wearing skins; sporting fangs and antlers.

What explains this descent into barbarism? A single word. Revenge.

There had been arrests and some deaths among their people after protests about land rights and food prices in the regional capital. The police were perhaps heavy-handed, and the fatalities—though few—were certainly regrettable. But one of their preachers, a notorious rabble-rouser with links to extreme opposition forces, took to the airwaves. (I have no doubt it was all planned.) Rise up and kill them, every one, he cried. Yes, slaughter their tribe—by which he meant the minority tribe, the ruling tribe, my tribe. So they did. A radio broadcast, to such savages, is like the voice of God. Not of course the voice of our Lord, our merciful Lord, though they claim the same. That in itself is a sacrilege—and they are damned to hell for it! No, not our Lord, our vengeful Lord, who lived among us as a man, and who will raise us up—or cast us down! Theirs is a disgusting perversion, a demiurge, something drawn from the stinking well of animalism which still runs deep in my country.

I was in the national capital, on urgent instruction from the president's office, when the outrage was committed. It tears at my heart that I was not there to defend my brother and his wife or to share their fate. Yes, I would have willingly borne the indignity and agony they suffered if it had pleased God. But I could not have foreseen this outburst of savagery in my region, which even a man of power and influence—and I will not exaggerate mine—could not have prevented. Nothing could have prevented it—forces stronger than we could ever have imagined were at work. Forces diabolical; forces geopolitical. So, my absence was untimely, but not causal to the fate of my brother and sister-in-law. Of that I am convinced. Still, it racks my heart and soul.

And these villagers, turned barbarians, had previously—passively—submitted their destinies to my care; they were peaceful and pliable; they had given themselves over to the order that prevailed in our region, through my fiat. I had dictated and overseen these advances in all their sweep and particulars. I had helped to establish the regional and local government; I had solely built their school and their church. So it is beyond my comprehension that they should have turned against me, that they should have fallen so low—that they should have perpetrated such a gross betrayal!

| THESE ARE NOT JUST STORIES

Having unleashed his final thunderbolt, Adom is left standing shaken by the power of his indignation. We, the other fellows, are his thunderstruck flock.

We note that you, AA, have ghosted into the room and are sitting at the back, near the door. You think you are not noticed perhaps, but we saw you taking it all in, mesmerised by the potency of the story, almost relishing—yes, *relishing*—the horror of the aghast return, the burnt-out school, the wanton destruction of the paradisiacal gardens, the slaughter of the enchanted beasts, and the lamentable parody of our Lord in the deaths of two such simple souls. Out of order, chaos! Out of light, darkness!

"Adom, please! Please spare yourself any more torment. That is enough for now."

Esther goes up to Adom and touches his mighty forearm. It quivers and stiffens. She leads him back to his seat.

This too often happens in Workshop 1 for Esther's liking. The power of personal testimony, the cornerstone of the House of Journalists, its very

point and mission, necessarily summons up these deep dark dangerous spirits. They shake even the strongest fellows and, frankly, they
scare her. Of course there is no denying the richness of the stories.
(Many of the domestic writers drawn to this place would sell their
souls for a tincture of it.) But—Esther tells herself—if you can resist the
mesmeric pull, look away from the dancing flames of the fire, see the
tellers not as shamans and oracles, but as ordinary men and women,
racked by bitter experience and heartbreak, what you hear is . . . bitter
experience and heartbreak.

These are not just stories; these are people's *lives*.

SUCH TALK WOULD SHOCK

Thank you, Esther, yes, I will spare myself and the fellows. I have burdened you all with it, when it is my burden to carry. And I have the
broad shoulders of the powerful man to carry it, I am still proud to say.
Yes, Esther, there are other fellows who need your gentle attention.

And why should you, Esther, a young woman, almost a girl, pay
special attention to me? You have, as I say, a whole class to attend to.
You are moving among us, and as you do, you are brushing against
me only very occasionally. These brushings-against are ethereal more
than material, and no special intimacy is implied by them. Though, of
course, one never knows with the young female. The whisper of your
long swishing skirts and your clean girlish smell excite and stir me
nonetheless.

God forgive me, but I would possess you this very minute if it was
the custom of this place, which it is not. I do not forget that. I would not
force myself upon you, God forbid. I have never forced myself upon
any young girl, however brazen and deserving. But it is the case that
when I ran the school all the female staff were available to me. I liked
the shy, delicate, skinny ones, with the paler skins. I took them simply
and in an upright manner. They gave themselves up to me because I was
in a position of authority over them. I had no illusions about that. But

there was no question of violation. They yielded. They yielded willingly but without any desire. It was duty, that was all. So they at least were without sin. I comforted myself in my shame that this was so. I took the sin upon myself, which was only right.

But this is a delicate and difficult subject to discuss. Of all the cultural dislocations between this place and my homeland, this is one of the most profound. The relationship between men and women is so different here. I respect this difference, as I respect all the rules and mores of this country, but it makes satisfying my needs difficult. My heart, which has always been cold, is colder still. How could it be otherwise? I am incapable of love. And I will not pay. I have never paid! A proud boast for any man! The sexual morals of this city are palpably a lot looser than is our way. But to lie in mutual lust is quite alien to me. I do not think I would enjoy a woman's lust. There is feeling in it. For me there has never been any feeling in it. There is only the urge, the need, the shame, and the sin.

Esther wraps up Workshop 1 a little early today. It is a big day. We take up our folders, our papers, our pens. You, AA, have slipped out again.

I am met at the door by my "assigned volunteer," a young man called Adam. The near coincidence of our names—which is not a coincidence: he was surely assigned to me *because* of his name—is seen by Adam as an auspice. "We will get on well," he says. "I have a good feeling about it. Leave things to me. I will see that your case works out." I have no such feeling and I will not "leave things" to him. But I like Adam well enough, even though he is, in the way of this country's youth, friendly and familiar to a point that would be considered highly disrespectful in my country. He treats me as an equal but is, in his own words, "in awe" of my experiences and my courage. I have got used to that. He performs a lot of little services for me, for which I am grateful. Recently, he has tracked down some books of my country. Have I not heard of the Net? he says. I have indeed heard of the Net, I say. But I have not as yet had the chance to explore it with the seriousness it deserves. The whole of history is to be found there, I am told. "Any book in the world, brother," he says. He calls me brother, or sometimes, man. This familiarity is not considered disrespectful in this country—or not *as* disrespectful. We explore some of these questions of idiom and etiquette, much to his amusement, during our conversation practises. These I find useful, although it worries me that under his influence I am, despite my detestation of it, picking up some of his street argot, his free forms and base coinages. I correct for these of course; which makes for, in his words "some cool exchanges."

Adam, I perhaps should mention at this point, is black. I was told I was being assigned a mentor; I was told he was a young student in the city; I expected him to be white; and so I was surprised when he was black. Should I have been surprised? The fact is I was. Adam likes to think that our shared blackness gives us a special bond—another one. He is proud of his blackness; so I do not disabuse him of the notion of the black bond. But of course there is no black brotherhood where I come from, *brother*. Which is why, personally, these days I prefer to be among white people. I find them more civilised—even the lower classes and the petty officials. I know that the white races are capable of great cruelty and violence. This is their—and our—history. But the greater nature of the white man's violence earns its own respect. It is violence for a point and to an end. The fact is that it serves their interests successfully.

Such talk would shock Adam. It would shock many people in the House of Journalists, which is respectful of all difference—racial, religious, political, sexual. Indeed such tolerance is an official policy. I suspect that many other fellows like me are less than comfortable that this is so. We think there are rights and wrongs. We *know* there are rights and wrongs. God is above, man below, and some men are cast down to hell for their abominations or their false witness. But we keep our counsel. There is not the breadth of freedom here that its supporters suppose. And, leaving the particular issue to one side, that is as it should be. Freedom is overvalued in my view. There must be order. There is no civilisation without order—and order must be strictly enforced, with liberty's wilder shores sacrificed if necessary. This talk too would shock Adam. He is a son of this city, this country, this system—much more than he likes to think.

But enough of Adam.

I will mention only that he is studying "creative writing." I rather suspect that our "cool exchanges" are the basis for the play he is working on. Out of politeness, and a certain curiosity, I have asked to read it, but he says *"Whoa!"* This, at least, is the best approximation I can find for his vocalisation. "It needs a lot of work yet." So be it. I should not take it the wrong way, he assures me. I do not, I assure him. He would be honoured to have me read it, deeply honoured—when it is in "better shape."

Adam is ready to do me any service, in which attitude he reminds me, which is a great comfort, of the due respect shown to me by the boys at my school. My lieutenants, I called them. Most remained loyal to me to the end, though few were of my tribe. It is a source of great pride that I educated them out of all false loyalties. When the rebellion started, they took to the forest depths and awaited my return. I ask myself, would the greater loyalty have been to avenge the outrage committed against me? Perhaps that is expecting too much of mere boys. They looked to me and I was not there, though there was nothing I could have done about that. Without their leader, some did desert. The most despised just slipped away. But others threw off civilisation and smeared themselves in the bloody gore of their ancestral savagery. These practises are revolting to me, of course, but those that took this course at least distinguished themselves in their new situation. My teaching made of them the leaders: the most feared and respected and disciplined and cruel. They rebelled against me, but did not betray me utterly. Those who remained loyal spoke of these others with a kind of awe.

It was some days before I visited the school. As I have mentioned, I had been called to our capital urgently by the president, just days before the genocide took place. Once reports of the slaughter reached me I determined to return. The president pressed me to stay on in the capital as the crisis for our country was not just regional. He understood however that my absence from my school and my region could be misunderstood, that my enemies could use it against me. So although the military's advice was that a visit, however brief, would be very dangerous, I went ahead with it. I had no hope of saving my home, but I needed to see what had happened—and, let me be frank, *be seen.*

I flew into the regional capital on a military plane. Loyal government forces still had control of the city centre and key strategic assets, such as the airport and power station. But all the other areas had been surrendered. Not to the rebels, who were nowhere to be seen, but to ominous depopulation. The armoured car that picked me up sped along empty, cratered boulevards, lined with burnt-out buildings. Ours was the only vehicle on the roads. Gone were the spluttering, exhaust-pluming trucks with their Hindu temple cabs. Gone were the honking herds of tuk-tuks and the occasional old Humber holding its nose above the hoi polloi. Gone were the old upright bikes carrying the whole family—dad pedalling, mum sitting sidesaddle on the crossbar, the eldest daughter, legs swinging, on the rack at the back, and the two little ones perched on the handlebars. And gone were the straggling lines of villagers traipsing in and out of the city, driving their goats or geese ahead of them, or humping sacks of maize and vegetables on their heads, or pushing barrows piled with bananas or yams or cages of live chickens. Gone were the shacks and stalls selling everything under the sun. Gone were the traders and itinerants. Gone were the beggars and pickpockets. Gone was the detritus of all this human activity. The deserted roadsides were littered instead with what looked like uncollected rubbish sacks crawling with vermin. Some were just that, but others—had I got out of the car and kicked them—would have morphed into decomposing corpses. The last remnants of mankind in this inhuman void. Monstrous man-eating weeds were already pushing through the cracked tarmac to compete for this carrion with the vultures and rats and wild dogs.

It was, if anything, even more eerily empty of humanity on the district highway out to the school. Refugees had been tramping down this potholed dirt track in their tens of thousands only days before; but now they had crossed over the border to the relative safety of the refugee camps in the neighbouring country. Now there was not a living soul to be seen.

Yet we sensed that in the dense jungle on either side of the road, the rebels were lurking. For the time being they were sated with blood, but they would strike again. The green/black foliage seemed to glint with their red devil eyes.

The driver of our Land Cruiser—his throat half cut in his own mind—was a study in concentrated terror. I could see the cords on his neck pulsing. (They did indeed hack off his head somewhat later in the proceedings, I am told. So he was not idle in fearing this end. This was days or a week after; I was long gone; but I often think of how the cords on his neck must have pulsed blood. He must have tensed his neck for the blunt blade, and the hacking through would have been muscled butchery. It is perhaps not wise to dwell on these things, but to dwell is what one does.)

Once we reached the school grounds it was the same story as in the city. What had been cleared and civilised was swiftly being reclaimed by the darkest forces of nature. In just a few days, grotesque tentacles of greenery had started to strangle the lawns and the flower beds and to crawl slimily up the sides of the outbuildings. Many of these were savagely damaged; my villa more grossly violated and despoiled. The main hall of the school itself was a black roofless shell.

The crucified bodies of my brother and sister-in-law, decomposing on their trees, swarming with white maggots and blue-green flies, had been left for my inspection. It was painful for me to see them. It was also a humiliation and an insult to a man in my position. But it was right nonetheless that I should have borne witness to this abomination. I stood for a few moments, my face unmasked against the stench, my head uncovered and unbowed. Then I authorised the cutting down of the bodies and their Christian burial.

Throughout the short internment there was extreme nervousness among the entourage that accompanied me. They were looking around, minding their backs, and hardly concentrating at all on the sacrament which I performed myself for want of a priest. I was tolerant of their distraction. The place hummed with menace. It was difficult to maintain the proper composure and authority, particularly as there were times when it was also proper to give oneself up to the exaggerated grief that is our custom. My ululations harrowed out across the school grounds, through the rift valley beyond, and over the great lake. Tens of thousands of bodies washed up on its shores in the days to come.

Other loyal servants of my administration, in the postures of their last agony, had been left for me to see. The savages, in their ignorance,

had slaughtered many of their own tribe, I noticed. But a higher intelligence seemed to be at work in their methods of killing, which were of
an ingenuity beyond the primitive mind. Outside forces were behind
these deeds, I said to myself. And forces with backing from beyond the
continent. (It is of no comfort that I was proved right within days—for
it was these outside powers which turned the minds of the president and his cabinet against me and impelled my flight into exile.)
Many pupils were among the slain, but I could see that there had not
been a total massacre. I retained my confidence, even as the sky darkened, that the best of my boys were somewhere nearby, awaiting my
return.

As I inspected my estate, however, I was being constantly advised
that it was time to get out and to return to the regional capital. The
prospect of night descending on us in this place was too dreadful to
contemplate. I could see the wisdom of this advice. I was not without
fear myself, and I was about to give the order, disappointed as I was for
my boys, when, at the last moment, a troop of them appeared out of
the forest. The sight of them was, at first, deeply shocking. They were
almost unrecognisable: their uniforms in rags, their faces and bodies
smeared with something—blood, earth, faeces, I do not know, or care
to know—and armed like the rebels with machetes. They were terrified, they were half starved, they had turned in a matter days from
civilised boys to half-wild creatures. It is said that in my white suit,
with my air of authority and calm, in the midst of this carnage and
terror, I appeared like an angel to them. Such a notion is fanciful, of
course. But I can understand why they rushed to me, crying out in joy,
clinging to my arms, and kissing my feet.

I ordered that these young lieutenants, the bravest and the best of
my boys, be amply fed and watered. (We did not have clothes with us
so could not rectify the shame and indignity of their near-nakedness.)
They sobbed and babbled and made little sense, but we pieced together
a tale of the men of the village descending on the school in such numbers and with such ferocity that its defence was impossible. Those before us had taken the only course open to them other than martyrdom
or treachery: they had fled into the forest. They begged us to accept this
version of events, and I at least was prepared to do so, though it crossed

my mind that martyrdom would have been the more dignified course. In the forest, I was proud to hear, they had rallied into an organised band—the leaders identified themselves—to await my return and my orders. Again, was it wrong of me that I was disappointed that no fight back had been attempted? The only scalps they could show me were of women and children who had strayed into their camp and been hacked down in panic. They could not disguise from me their relief that the village men and their commanders had not launched an attack. They had been overly content perhaps to sit it out.

Among my regrets is that I kept the key to the gun room in my possession at all times. We found this strong room intact inside the burnt-out main building. Its contents were undamaged. Reviewing my decision, I found nothing to admonish myself for, but all the same, it left my boys without firearms, which they could have used for their own protection and to fight back.

By now it was too late to set off to the city. We had no choice but to make camp. My lieutenants swore to protect me and my party, and said their reconnaissance suggested there were anyway no rebels in the immediate vicinity. This was some comfort, though it was still a fearful night, full of sudden noises and long silences, both of which invited all sorts of forebodings. We were all glad to make it alive to an ominous dawn, heavy-bellied with rain. As soon as this first light appeared, my entourage made preparations for the road. I spent a final few moments beside the fresh graves of my brother and sister-in-law. Though at that stage I had no notion of this distant exile, I knew there was no coming back to my region, my home, and my school for a long time, if ever.

I promised the complete opposite to my lieutenants. I am not proud of that. I do not know what has happened to any of them. I think of them constantly and they are never out of my prayers. We left them reasonably well provisioned; they were armed now with the weapons from the gun room; and the plan was that army trucks would be dispatched to collect them in a few days. (It may have happened; I do not know. Events moved fast over the next few days and I had to concentrate on my own safety.) Rain started falling, the engine of the Land Cruiser hummed impatiently, and I was led to the vehicle. My boy lieutenants watched impassively, perhaps a little sullenly. I did not meet their eyes.

We reached the regional capital without incident, but the city was tensile with fear. There were reports of rebel forces advancing and there was dwindling confidence that the central government could hold this northern outpost—or even that it wanted to. Many of the higher regional officials and other notables were pressing to be evacuated. I found myself in the difficult position of advising the military commander against such a plan, which I thought would show defeatism. It was difficult because my own flight out could not be delayed. My presence in the capital was urgently required by the president, as the political situation there was worsening by the hour. There were desperate scenes at the airstrip. Shots had to be fired to disperse the crowds so that I and my small party could get through. Angry, desperate, weeping people chased the planes along the red dirt runway. We banked out into a biblical storm; lightning forked down into the black turbulence of the great lake and electrified the jagged-toothed mountains. This was the last view I had of my beloved home region. It was as if God were punishing it for its sins. We were in the relative safety of the capital within two hours. What happened next is another story.

Adam has heard this tale a number of times. He is of an age to relish both its heroic and humane dimensions. And he hears what he wants to hear; though in no version of my tale do I spare myself—quite the contrary. Mine was one of the first internationally distributed "insider" accounts of the darkness that descended on the heart of my country. I will admit that I crafted it with an eye to Western sensibilities and assumptions, painting the bigger picture in bold blacks and whites, but at the same time placing myself at the centre of the moral complexities, admitting my mistakes and weaknesses, in a way that some in my continent, never mind my country, found naïve, even dangerous. I always had confidence, however, that it would do me credit in the long run. I bank on it still, knowing that a most important telling is to come: before the tribunal.

I am told status is a formality; such is my reputation, my prestige; such is the politics of my exile. We shall see. I am a thorough man. I have not come this far, seen what I have seen, done what I have done, to be denied now. I will tell the truth as I see it, knowing that a man only sees so much. God alone knows the whole truth. I look forward to His reckoning too.

Adam accompanies me to my room, carrying my books. He asks me if I need anything and I dispatch him to the corner shop to buy some sweets. I am particularly fond of liquorice-all-sorts and wine gums. "And tobacco," I call after him. I was a pipe smoker as a young man, but fell out of the habit. I have taken it up again so that I can share in the fellowship of the Central Courtyard. I will always stand a little apart from my brothers and sisters here, I recognise that. There is some suspicion of me. That is the fate of a man of my stamp and with my story. But I would lessen the distance as far as I am able. Thus it is that I puff on my pipe contentedly enough and share a few words with other fellows. They are guarded, but that is always a wise course.

Now I will rest for a while before the visit.

| THEY WOULD HAVE ME LOOK IN ON YOU, MUSTAPHA

We all come to accept that it is the way of this place that they will not leave us fellows to suffer alone. If we are suffering, the House suffers with us. There must be something they can do to help. If not, we know where they are. Yes, we say, just down the corridor. Yes, they are very kind. They never give up. They pride themselves on it.

"Mustapha, it is Malcolm." "I was just visiting." "I did wonder if you wanted to be on your own." "But they would have me look in on you, Mustapha." "You know what they are like." "Just say and I will leave you."

I sit up on my bed and invite him in, this man who has already invited himself in. In most circumstances I am pleased enough to see Malcolm Dougan, a most gentle and friendly man, who is a professor of literature at one of this city's many prestigious universities. He does not look, it must be said, like an eminent academic. Although in saying that it would seem I reflect my own standards and prejudices and not those of this more relaxed and democratic country. For a start he wears a beard, which is never to my taste. By which I mean to say I do not in general favour a beard on a man (a dislike which predates, I should add, the enforced ubiquity of them in my homeland under the regime). Malcolm's—which is like the none-too-well-cared-for coat of a long-haired dog: dirty white in colour, yellowing into wet tips about the lips—may be particularly repulsive (it gives off a faint whiff of dog meat, unless I am imagining it); but those box-hedge elaborations, redolent of neat clipper, hot towel, and bay rum, are, in their way, more ridiculous.

Malcolm's unkempt beard is of a piece with his exceptional slovenliness of dress: the prisoner-of-war parka, the shapeless, hangdog sweater, the jogging bottoms with low-slung crotch, the trainers so foul and broken-down that this dog—which hangs about every aspect of Malcolm's toilet—has surely chased and chewed them, then slept with and slobbered over them in its warm, hairy, meaty beard of a dog basket.

I am perhaps more than usually struck by Malcolm's turnout this afternoon because I have myself fallen far below any acceptable standard of personal cleanliness and attire in the last few days—going down to lunch and dinner, unshaven, unwashed, and in crumpled shirt and trousers.

Today I am, I am ashamed to say, still in my pyjamas at approaching two in the afternoon. Malcolm makes no comment of course, but I see the distress in his eyes that I—normally so punctilious in matters of dress—should be reduced to this state. He may be more than happy to slob about in his study all day, in an old dressing gown, drinking tea and dunking biscuits, with Schubert lieder on the old stereo. But that is not my style at all.

He lets it pass, however. He is so much more sensitive in this regard than the professional staff, whose concern for us can so often become intrusive and oppressive. By contrast, he does not seek to dig too deep. Something of his manner was obvious in his response on first being introduced to me soon after I arrived at the House of Journalists.

"You perhaps know, Mustapha, that there is a play in our language of that name?"

In the most kindly way Malcolm must have been well aware that I could not possibly have known that; just as he knows now that much of what he says to me I do not understand. Or at least, I do not understand it at the level of the spoken word. There is a deeper understanding perhaps; an understanding between two men who do not share a language but who share a humane and liberal outlook on the world, even if we do not share a taste for elegance and style. Malcolm is wise enough to know that I can enjoy the warmth and generosity of intelligent conversation even if I can do little but nod in response.

"Yes, indeed. By one Fulke Greville, Lord Brooke: a contemporary of Shakespeare. It is said that this play, *Mustapha*, may have had some influence on *The Merchant of Venice*. So, Mustapha: there's a certain literary heritage in that name. Well chosen, I would say. And Greville sounds like an interesting character—one of those great men of the Elizabethan age—soldier, parliamentarian, courtier, wrote a biography of Sir Philip Sidney, but found time to knock out a couple of plays. You don't see his like these days, of course. More's the pity."

Malcolm is uneasy about some aspects of the House of Journalists and knows that I find some of the expectations it puts on me difficult to live up to. The fellows are constantly in demand to attend events, to speak, to read, to appear. We have all noted that there is in this country a huge "industry" (this is the word used here) around literature in all its forms—and we are stalwarts of one of its subgenres: the refugee memoir. I, of course, am a very minor figure in this, being relatively new to the House, but even so there is a certain demand.

"Mustapha—it's all part of the game. Don't be too concerned about it. People here are very interested to hear your story—that above all. The House of Journalists, very shrewdly, makes literature of that. They do it to help them provide the safety here that you need as human beings. That is not an ignoble trade-off, I think. You know the worth of what you have produced, and it may not measure up to the very highest standards, but do not make the mistake of judging it too harshly. We do need to hear what you have to tell us. There is a greater scheme in all of this. A greater good. I think we can trust in that. I hope so anyway."

This afternoon Malcolm has the good sense and good manners to make his visit brief. He hands me a book of poetry and a tin containing a homemade (by him) fruit loaf. He hopes the former will become as much of a favourite of mine as the latter already is. I thank him. Malcolm's twin passions are reading and cooking. We have discussed his cooking. Men of class and learning in my culture do not do any cooking, but it is common here and anyway he is a widower. He lives alone—though recently he has found a "girlfriend." I am ashamed to say that the look on my face when he first mentioned this news must have betrayed my mild disgust at the idea. Malcolm looked a little hurt—and he has not raised the subject again.

As he leaves, he reminds me (he was asked to expressly) that we have an important visitor at the House of Journalists this afternoon. "Edward Crumb, no less. He wouldn't remember me, of course, but many moons ago we used to move in some of the same circles. Yes, I don't think I have mentioned it, but when I was younger I moonlighted as a theatre critic for a few years. Anne's illness put paid to all that, sadly."

Malcolm leaves me now. He shuts the door gently behind him and I start the process of dressing. When I am in this condition it is always a long, long haul.

IS THAT NOT A FORM OF TORTURE IN ITSELF, MUSTAPHA?

I find myself in this condition—no more than setbacks, I like to think they are—every few days. We all receive support and counselling at the House of Journalists—and it has helped many of the fellows, I am sure of that. But my "issue," to use their terminology, is proving difficult to resolve.

For it is my view that I was *not* tortured. I am resolute in this opinion. I know what torture is. I have heard it taking place. I have moved among its victims. I know what it does to a man who waits on it day after day.

"Is that not a form of torture in itself, Mustapha?"

That is a form of words, I replied to my counsellor.

"But to have been imprisoned, abused, and half starved? To have spent ten years in a labour camp and then been forced into exile?" My counsellor thinks—he is not completely wrong—that I draw some comfort from hearing the full litany of my suffering spoken of.

But it doesn't alter the fact that I was *not* tortured—unlike so many of my fellow countrymen, my fellow detainees, and most of the fellows here. And yes, it is vile perversity, but I am tormented by my lack of this badge of belonging. Why was it my destiny to escape both death and torture? Am I the lucky one? What does it say about me as a man that I should have been spared in this way? That I am a lesser man? Lesser men, I am sure, were made to suffer more. Where is the justice in that?

"Mustapha," my counsellor said with artificial emphasis (he is one of those who do not like this name) . . . and he went on to say something from a textbook about survivor guilt. He misunderstands me. It is not guilt I feel, but rather this sense of envy. Yes, I am *jealous* of all those others because my suffering was not of the same order of magnitude. I tried to explain this to my counsellor and he looked horrified. "Mustapha," he said, "there is no hierarchy of suffering."

I dispute this. There is hierarchy in every play of human affairs. The index of this place is suffering as measured in a man's ability to tell of it in the most hideous detail. The wise fellow, I told him, pours out the torture and death he has witnessed. He piles up the dead and dying and stands atop. Better still, he parades the stigmata of his own physical torments. To suffer mere mental anguish does not play to the wider audience. There must be blood. That is the very ink of this place. Its contract is written in it.

"Mustapha," my counsellor said, "I must ask you not to speak in these terms."

It pains him deeply, professionally, that I do not respect my own suffering; that I belittle and diminish it. And he is also most uneasy about anyone voicing a bad word about the House of Journalists. The House of Journalists allows us—no other institution in the system comes close—to talk through and to explore the greater subtleties and obscurer fascinations of the condition of exile. Here they do not just patch up; they do not just make do and mend. They look to understand and to heal. We should be grateful, really grateful. I appreciate this.

I backtracked. I apologised. I did not mean . . .

The session petered out. Our hour was up. We were to meet again in two days' time. (In the event, I was marked down as a "no-show.") I took up my personal file; walked along the corridor and across the Central Courtyard. A lone smoker, concentrated on his cigarette, acknowledged my passing with a nod of the head. This young man was tortured—so he says, so he writes, and so it must be so. There is no basis for disbelief. He bares the scars through his writing. The House of Journalists asks nothing more of us; our testimony is proof enough; though at our case hearings House-approved doctors will stand as expert witnesses that the pattern of physical and even mental scarring is indicative of recorded torture methods in our countries of oppression. The tribunes are greatly swayed by such evidence, it is said. Little else moves them. My counsellor is only looking to me to give him what he needs for the case report. He is looking to me to say it: that I was tortured. But I will not say it.

I suffer, like I am suffering today, like I have been suffering for these past three days—but I have not been tortured.

It has taken me an hour to put on my underpants and one sock, but I will put in an appearance this afternoon.

| WE WELCOME A TRUE LION OF LITERATURE

"The House of Journalists was built in the eighteenth century as a fashionable London town house, but over the centuries it has housed

Russian Jews, Irish immigrant families, Jewish refugees fleeing from the Nazis, Bangladeshis, and, more recently, Somali asylum-seekers."

Yes, it is Julian's familiar speech. (You might begin to sympathise with those of us who have heard it many more times than once before?) We are gathered again in the library, this time to welcome Edward Crumb, the poet and playwright, Nobel laureate and political provocateur. The official party is a large one today: as well as friends and donors, the full trustee body is in attendance, and the minister. "Keeping tabs," as they say here.

The government here is nominally of the Left. The Leftists among us, a goodly band, laugh at that—though we have seen worse debasement of the coin. We are great students of betrayal. Don't talk to us—as so many writers in this country want to—of betrayal! We are sick of betrayal. That is why we are so loyal and so quiescent. That is why we do not speak out. It is why we show gratitude that some find craven towards this government of the Left, which is nothing of the sort. Call it the price of safety.

"Among our funders is the government," Julian says, turning in the direction of the minister. "We have criticisms of government policy of course, but that does not stop us working in fruitful partnership. Andrew, I like to think, remains a friend of the House of Journalists."

The young minister responds with a sort of smirk. In domestic circles, he is regarded—and regards himself—as a ruthless operator. Again, we laugh. It is not likely, is it, that he will intimidate any of us with his prefect menace. Of course we do not laugh out loud, but our politician guest senses our disdain—and it sends a little shiver through him.

"This building, one way or another, has been a place of sanctuary for new arrivals for more than two hundred years. Now, fully refurbished and equipped, with its dedicated staff and volunteers, it provides a fitting welcome for those seeking protection and—I like to think—stands out as a symbol of our commitment to uphold this country's noble tradition of providing sanctuary."

Julian pauses at this point. He looks with trepidation at Edward Crumb glowering beside him, though he might do better to observe the expression on the face of Miriam Stern—or to look in our direction, for that matter. Julian is of course only doing his job as founder and Chair. He is talking the talk. We understand that. But as he well knows, to speak of "noble traditions" of "providing sanctuary" is so much soft soap. In truth, the blackened brickwork of the House of Journalists, so admired by the arbiters of architectural taste, is the ingrain of a darker history that cries against this country's much-proclaimed glories. Do not get us wrong: we are all most grateful to the House of Journalists; to Julian and the Committee; and to the government and people of this country. But if scaffolding and plastic sheeting were put up, and high-powered jets of water pounded at the building's façade, the cobblestoned street would run rivers of black blood. In truth, what country could tell a different story?

Now Mr. Stan rises to make his welcoming speech (also familiar), and all the while we wait, with some expectation, on the words of our guest of honour. He has been described to us as a great writer, much feted and honoured, but a "controversial public figure." Julian and the Committee have been dreading this visit and put it off for as long as possible. Julian and the Committee fear any writer who is, in their view, antithetical to the spirit of the House of Journalists. They strongly believe in writing as a collective enterprise which should take place in a democratic, respectful space. Crumb, we gather, is a loner, a maverick, a troublemaker. His best writing, they tell us, is spare and menacing. It turns the thumbscrews with relish. Again we laugh at that. Do not worry: we are not offended by the expression. It is a "turn of phrase" that is much to our taste, in fact.

So this Edward Crumb is another who fancies himself as a bit of a hard case, does he? We shall see. Julian and the Committee certainly fear that he will use his visit to attack the government; criticise the House of Journalists; perhaps even say something less than complimentary about us, the fellows. And in the current political atmosphere there is extreme nervousness at this prospect. There is no electoral capital in showing even the slightest generosity to asylum-seekers. A Crumb diatribe, however predictable, will generate headlines—and the prime minister is swayed by these in ways that are most *un*predictable.

Among the fellowship there is some nervousness too, but also excitement. We do not speak out these days, but we recall the thrill of it.

The warmth and safety of this place is precious to us. But it is not in our natures to be so compliant with the authorities.

You, AA, are among us again. Doing your duty? Or perhaps you too are interested to see this Crumb character? You have not bothered to spruce up in any way for the occasion. Julian will have noticed that. You are still in that rumpled suit which to Julian reeks (metaphorically) of the slept-in condition of the disintegrating writer who has not made it home for many nights. It is a look that he loathes, and it is not one that the exiled writers and journalists here tend to affect. Standing next to you is Mustapha, who is, as ever, immaculately, almost painfully, well dressed.

Does Julian notice how dog-tired Mustapha is? Perhaps not; he has a lot on his mind today. But *we* can all feel the immensity of that tiredness: the feeling that the physical demands of standing will end with the body shattering like glass into billions of grains of sand.

Mr. Stan finishes his speech and cantilevers himself back towards his customised chair. He was all warm words towards Edward Crumb—conventionally generous; but in his spasmodic progress across the room he suddenly veers towards the writer, planting a crutch at a crazy angle, and swinging his stunted body round and up, in such a way as to alarm—and perhaps warn. Mr. Stan is most protective of the House of Journalists. Do not forget that.

Edward Crumb maintains his warm smile even so. It must be said that up to this point he has been on his best behaviour. He has been outwardly amiable and patient and good-humoured, and some of us are beginning to wonder what all the fuss is about. But now the warm-ups and preambles are dragging on and on, the piss is being taken quite frankly.

Well, for fuck's sake: there is a fucking *limit*—Crumb begins to rumble. We've heard from the cringing little crookback, with his hideous stumps; we've heard from that wet fanny Julian Snowman; and now we are enduring the scripted offerings of the Minuscule of State, another beardless, milk-skinned, mass-produced nodding dog. This was supposed to be a chance for one to show some old-fashioned Lefty solidarity with brave comrades of the mighty PEN. Instead, well, what? Suckered into a stitch-up, that's what. Yep, yours well and truly is exhibit A in a propagandist photo-call for the government's pet project, with the Minuscule acting as one's minder. Jesus, he looks about *twelve*: a milk monitor in the Hitler Youth. At some stage, it's going to have to be pants down in front of the assembled and out with his weeny knob. Embarrass the Nazi fucker, that's the ticket. The one good thing about the Nobel millstone is that it confers the privilege. "This war is one big fuckup," one is permitted to whisper in the ear of the prim minister as he shakes one's hand in front of the world's press, with a fixed grin on his face that doesn't even flicker. *"THIS WAR IS AN ALMIGHTY FUCKUP,"* one screams (in one's mind's ear at least). *"YOU SCUMBAG, YOU TOTAL PIECE OF SHIT. IT'S A FUCKING MORAL OUTRAGE, THAT'S WHAT IT IS."* No response from his Premiershit, of course. He just smiles through the storm of hate spittle, deaf to the thoughts that are convulsing one's mind, the *FUCKING SCUMBAG*!

Now *calm down*, Jane says, back at the country place, fixing one a massive cobble-bottomed of something lethally peaty, which one downs in one glug, sending a honey-tone, heather-scented shiver through one's very soul. HRRRR . . .

But *calm down*? *CALM DOWN*? The fuck one will.

And to one's more delicate readers, sorry if this upsets you; if you feel these thoughts, expressed in this way, deface the pristine virtues of the early (prelapsarian) poetry and plays. Yes, Ted Crumb would like to say sorry, and at the same time, FUCK OFF. Because, frankly, it bores the tits off one to hear the same old more-in-sorrow rhetoricals trotted out again and again. Oh, what happened to the Edward Crumb whose work, whose *early* (pre-*fludde*) work, was characterised by extreme rigour and an exquisite melancholy, albeit laced with a sense of menace and even the possibility of violence? What happened that this acclaimed voice, so perfectly pitched, is now drowned out by the bilious ranting of a loud foul mouth? What happened that a writer so beautifully in command of the language is now afflicted by a form of late-life Tourette's?

What happened? What HAPPENED? A fucking war fucking happened, that's what. Another fucking war, coming after all the other fucking wars, and all the other pogroms and genocides and holocausts and humanitarian interventions and ethnic cleansings and surgical strikes in which people in their millions have been burnt alive and hacked to death and industrially destroyed and chemically exterminated and tortured and gang-raped; yes, fucked to death, literally *fucked* to death . . . that's what.

Is this coming across all right? Is there enough economy, restraint, and fucking elegance? Yes? No? Offended by the tone of the question? Well, sorry, and at the same time, FUCK OFF. Because this senile old bastard, sitting in his own piss, swearing at the nurses, is in fact the *true* Ted Crumb. The authentic voice of. So don't tell one to calm down, to mind one's pees and queues, to remember one's position, one's reputation. What reputation? The poems, the plays; all the pristine praised and prized stuff: piss in the wind. At last, aged seventy-one and half— and whatever the critics might say—one is finding one's voice. Do you hear that? FINDING ONE'S FUCKING VOICE!!!!!

Our distinguished guest, convulsed by the exuberant violence of his thoughts, looks up and sees us all looking at him. We are all smiles: deliberately hard to read.

Finding one's voice, are we? Yes, that's the ticket!

Forgive us, but all you visiting writers make it so easy for us to mock. You mock yourselves. All bluster and abase. In struggle or empathy, as comrades or counsellors, you find in *us* your voice. We have heard it all so many times.

You know what we are talking about, AA? You have been here for, what, about a month now. One day, the feminist writer; the next, the campaigning journalist; the next, the sympathetic poet; the next, the young playwright—and that's not counting all the volunteers and mentors. They write, you write, but *everyone* writes. They would give voice. Should we give thanks? We have our own voices. That is the point, they say: everyone in this country has a voice. We are all part of one mighty chorus. But who, we might ask, is listening?

There are those who play the tough guy, like Mr. Crumb here; and there are those—many more, it must be said—who are humble before us. Humble before us after what we have gone through! Oh, yes, that is what they are in awe of; what they so respect and fear and, yes, *envy*. You understand all this, AA, don't you? After what we have gone through, the voice—to their ears at least—rings loud and clear and true. After what we have gone through, the writer is exulted onto the higher plane of true harrowing, true heroism. After what we have gone through, there is something, at last, to write *about*. And in that we must all *share*. We must write, they must write, you must write: to write is universal.

"It is time," Julian says, finally drawing proceedings to the point, "and it is certainly a considerable honour, to welcome to this special place a writer, much honoured and garlanded, who has used the platform offered by this recognition of his long mastery of the word to speak out with a fierce passion and, yes, a terrific anger about a whole range of injustices and inequities. At an age when in some the fires are dying down, his are raging. That in itself is to be saluted. We will agree with him, and we will disagree with him. The important thing is that he is a symbol of the freedom we all enjoy in this country to say what we like, to write what we like, to stir up, to provoke, to debunk, to demean, to unleash. This is a precious freedom—we all choose to use it differently. But the House of Journalists—within the limits of decency and mutual respect—is a forum for all forms of free expression. So it is with great expectation, if a little trepidation too, that we welcome a true lion of literature. Ladies and gentlemen, Edward Crumb."

Crumb steps forward. Conscious of the weight of expectation, he pauses. He has been set up and now he must perform. We, the fellows, are waiting.

But just one minute, you bunch of cunts. Yes, you, Snowman; you, Minuscule; and *you*, the fucking all-knowing fellowship. Give one *some* credit for subtlety of mind. It may be less trodden of late, but a primrose path still winds through the minefield of stink bombs in one's head. It has only been in the mature autumn of one's life, amid the fruitful hillocks of rotting leaves, with so much won and nothing to lose, that one has enjoyed the freedom to let a few off. If one chose one could as easily surprise the assembled with the charm and warm words of writings springtime. But then who is one kidding? That's not what they've come for. Not this flowery poesy (and where the fuck did that spring from, by the way?); not the elegant economy of one's prized years; what they've come for is the fucking cataracts and hurricanoes. So be it. Let's see what the price is for fucking with the Maison des, the holy HoJ? Electrodes to the jolly old nadgers? Pliers applied to a crusty toenail or two? A rendition of something extraordinary? The collected works of the Snowman until you beg for mercy perhaps? This last, the worst by far. Rumour has it that friend Jules is preparing a series of short stories based on the House of Journalists. And who can blame him? It was the reason he set it up in the first place, presumably? A little bestseller by way of recompense is long overdue, is it not? Leave it any longer and the inmates will have eaten the project alive from the inside out. They'll have devoured every last morsel of flesh and gristle from his Joust of Horny lists and left its bones to bleach in the merciless sun of ubiquity. They are no fools, these fellows; they know how ruthless our world can be. It is they who stood up to murderous regimes; it is they who were imprisoned and tortured; it is they who took long and dangerous journeys into exile. And then what do they face? A battalion of soft wet saps tapping away on their own teeny tiny laptops, stealing *their* stories from under them. Well, they are having none of that, thank you very much. They will have a piece of that action, thank you very much. So, before you know it, dear Jules, it is they who are sucking the life out of your creation, your brainchild, your *baby*, like giant leeches. The impertinence, the cheek! Yes, we need to wise up to Johnny Foreigner pretty damn sharpish. Fucking immigrants: taking our jobs, writing our books, sleeping with our women! (Are they? Give them an inch—and probably.) So, let's get it over with and get the fuck out of here. Because, frankly, this place gives one the fucking willies.

———————

"Thank you, Julian" (you ridiculous bag of fart gas). "The lions of course are my brothers and sisters in this room" (though they're a mangy lot, some of them) "who have raged against the tyrannies of their own states and who must find it as pitiful as I do to hear the feline diplomacies of our own writers" (yes, you, Snowman, you miserable string of cat piss). "I will be blunt—you expect nothing less of me—" (one is becoming a caricature, of course, a joke) "this 'House of Journalists' is a show home, it's a marketing exercise." (A little shiver of anticipation around the room: *this* is more like it.) "It does good work no doubt, but it doesn't fool anyone. This country betrays most people who come here looking for shelter. It always has. Our tradition of providing sanctuary to the persecuted and oppressed is a nasty, self-regarding, sentimental myth put about by successive governments—of which this current one is much the worst." (A wince from the minister.) "We all know that the immoral and illegal invasions which our war criminal of a prime minister has thrust us into have displaced millions." (Much more like it: the home journos are scribbling hard to get it all down.) "Some of the fellows here are victims of and witnesses to these outrages. But they are the lucky ones, as I am sure they would testify. Many of their comrades are not so fortunate." (Friend Jules is palpably cacking his silk knickers now.) "Not content with razor-wiring our border and Nazifying the Border Police, we have ringed this city with prison camps." (The Minuscule is now trying his you-don't-scare-me-Crumb stare. It makes him look like a constipated toddler on his potty.) "Places of oppression and persecution for the persecuted and oppressed: these camps are this country's dirty secret. And how do we react? We keep our heads down, brothers and sisters; we keep our mouths shut. But enough!" (The journos look up. Surely that's not our lot? Not even a single lonely "fuck" to thrill the spinsters?) "One's interest in coming today" (turning, with something approaching nobility, to the exiled writers, who look startled, quite frankly) "is in meeting my comrades." (Old Crumb bottled it, that's what they're all thinking. He pissed neatly in the pot marked *piss* and handed over his sample to the nurse like a good boy.) "Friends, we'd have done this better over a few pints down at the pub" (what did one tell you: a fucking caricature), "rather than with a state visit, but we must now follow the protocol." (Full cock or no cock, but not *half* cock—that's the lesson here.) "We are guests in this . . ." (adopt tone of absolutely withering sarcasm) "house." (A nod to Snowman.) "So, Julian: the honours, if you would."

The silence that follows doesn't know what to do with itself. It looks at its feet, its hands, the ceiling; it lets out the odd cough and titter. Julian holds back, fearful perhaps of a booby trap: the device timed to go off just as the emergency services arrive on the scene; the second bomb at the funeral of those killed by the first. He looks to the minister on his right, who nods his head as if to say, *That seems to be it*; then he looks to Solomon and Mr. Stan on his left, who incline their heads in concurrence.

"Well, Edward, thank you." He bows towards Crumb. "Forthright and robust. As you said, we expected nothing less of you. We all have our criticisms of the system—and we all choose to articulate them in our own way. But I am repeating myself. As you also said, Edward, this place, whatever its virtues, whatever its faults, is really all about the fellows. So I invite you now—and our other guests—to join me in seeing the work of the House of Journalists, in the course of which you will get plenty of opportunities to talk to the fellows and to hear their stories."

And with that, Crumb and party are taken off on the standard guided tour. Julian looks relieved and is in command once more. Well, it could have gone a lot worse! A man expecting a kick in the balls cannot complain if he is only thumped in the stomach, he tells himself.

| AA AND CRUMB

But then the minister and his party have to take their leave; and a couple of representatives of the trusts and foundations also depart; and Miri Stern wants a word, if that is okay; and Julian finds, to his alarm, that he is diverted at a critical moment. Solomon assumes responsibility for shepherding Edward Crumb until Julian returns—only to fall short—as so often.

Julian finds this out the moment he rejoins the party—after no more than a few minutes away. For when he does so, it is to discover that Ted Crumb has "just wandered off." Solomon turned round and "he had disappeared."

Wandered off? Disappeared?

Yes.

Where the hell to?

I don't know.

Well, find him.

And Solomon in fact does so, within a minute or two, but still is not redeemed, because Crumb is found in the Central Courtyard enjoying a cigarette. Yes, *a cigarette* (there are a lot of these tiresome repetitions when incredulous anger seizes our Chair) with the only fellow who has thought it appropriate to come out for a smoke while an important visit to the House of Journalists is still taking place. Yes, that's right, Crumb is found with you, AA. AA and Crumb. What are we to make of that?

You cannot have planned this to happen, surely? It draws attention to you in a way that—a few lapses notwithstanding—you have been working hard to avoid so far. No one wants to draw attention, let alone invite suspicion, when they are a new fellow of the House of Journalists. But here you are, putting yourself at the centre of a turn of events which may or may not turn out to be pivotal.

For the time being, you—and Crumb—are giving nothing away. You extinguish your cigarettes in the elegantly sculpted receptacle provided and move off without a word. What if anything passed between you remains your secret. You are cool customers, we must say. AA and Crumb. If you are plotting anything, you keep it close. Where will it lead? Who knows? Perhaps we are all making too much of the incident? But you are playing a dangerous game. You should know that. The House of Journalists does not react kindly to any twist of its tale. Julian will see to it that you do not profit from his creation. Be warned.

| HE SHOULDN'T WORRY *TOO* MUCH

It is some reassurance, Julian tells himself, as he paces around his office an hour or so later. The minister, Andrew, has taken the time to phone him back to say that he appreciated the call, and that he, Julian, shouldn't worry too much.

Too much?

Well, he was hardly going to say don't worry about it *at all*, was he? After all, an official guest of the House of Journalists (albeit self-invited) had made a speech attacking the government, which, let nobody forget, is the House's main funder. Hence, presumably, that rather pointed, rather nasty, rather threatening, all-too-typical, and, yes, rather cowardly now he comes to think of it, *too* much. Though perhaps he is making too much of this *too* much, and Andrew hadn't meant too much by it? But then—another thought to undermine the previous one—Andrew always chooses his words very carefully. Or rather his advisors, his word tasters, do. Yes, Andrew, experienced minister that he is, doesn't say anything unless it has been tested and cleared. For poison. So this *is* something to worry about. The *too* in *too* much had team approval. Julian can hear the huddle in his mind. "Tell him not to worry, Minister, but leave him to sweat a bit. Tell him not to worry *too* much. That will leave him worrying just enough."

"Julian?"

It is Solomon, the executive manager of the House. Julian describes this office as his office but in fact it is nominally Solomon's. When Julian is in attendance, however—which is most days, these days—Solomon gives it up, and logs in at another desk in the outer office, where Sabrina, PA (to both the Chair and the executive manager), sits and—in truth—does Solomon's job. With ruthless efficiency, it must be said. She is a local girl in her twenties, and is not at all starry-eyed about writers in general, or the least sentimental about exiled writers. That is her secret. If only he had left Crumb in Sabrina's no-nonsense hands.

But no, Julian decides, he isn't going to pursue this. He isn't going to heap all the blame on Solomon. By and large, Solomon, a refugee himself by the way, though no writer, fulfils his role—which is not in fact an executive one; it is purely ornamental—admirably. Julian realises that he should be honest about that. Today of all days.

"Yes, Solomon?"

"Julian, I think I mentioned that I was leaving a bit early today?"

"Yes, Solomon. Thank you."

Solomon knows there will be more. Julian makes him suffer for a moment—then, unexpectedly, is generosity itself.

"Crumb was Crumb being Crumb. It could have been a lot worse. No real damage done. Hopefully. Say hi to Genevieve and the children."

Solomon hovers on the brink of a comeback, but thinks better of it. He knows Julian in these situations—and Julian is acute enough to realise that and give him credit for it. Solomon shuts the door and leaves Julian to it.

Julian resumes his pacing around the office, which, although not officially his, has been decorated according to his tastes and standards. Solomon was "only too pleased" to give his blessing to this arrangement. Dear Solomon does not have an eye for décor any more than he has an ear for dialogue, which is why his attempt at a play based on his life has been consigned, on Julian's advice, to the bottom of a drawer. It is rare indeed for Julian to judge a refugee's writing to be unpublishable. He is, he knows, criticised for that in some quarters. Solomon's play is his riposte to these miserable critics. It is greatly to Solomon's credit that despite exemplary rejection he bears no grudge. "We do not lack for writers here," Julian jokes—and Solomon takes it in good part.

Julian picks up an African sculpture and enjoys the feel of the cool wood in his hands. There are some excellent pieces in here—gifts, mainly, from visiting bigwigs and dignitaries. But just as precious in their way are the cheap statuettes and shields that have been awarded in such profusion to the House of Journalists in recognition of his work. Most of these are displayed in the public rooms of course, but a few are kept here.

Crumb was always going to cause trouble, Julian. That was what Andrew, the minister, had said next—after he had said not to worry *too* much. And that is true. But that *always* is troubling too. *Always* meaning it was entirely predictable—and yet the entirely predictable was allowed to happen. But—now he comes to think of it—it isn't the entirely predictable that is *really* (his italics now) troubling him. After all, what was Crumb's speech, when all is said and done? The dreaded Ted, the fearsome Crumb—and yet all it added up to was what? Feline diplomacies, show homes and marketing exercises, nasty, sentimental myths; illegal invasions, millions displaced, prison camps, our dirty secret. That was the top and bottom of it. In truth, Crumb had held back. He did not do his worst. Out of respect for the fellows no doubt. Julian has, he realises, reason to feel grateful to Crumb about his speech. So what is *really* troubling him?

That shared cigarette with AA; that is what. Don't ask him why. Of course he hates smoking, always has done. He hates that so many of the fellows, including the best of them, indulge in the filthy habit. But it wasn't the smoking. That would be ridiculous. It was the *sharing*. Of what, he doesn't know. Perhaps nothing? Usually—and there is some reassurance in this thought—it turns out to be nothing. But someone in this place has to watch for the first signs, and that was a first sign, he is sure of it. A first sign of what precisely? Well, he doesn't know—but of something. He has only his suspicions to go on. But his suspicions go a long way. He is an aficionado of suspicion. If there is anything about you, AA, which could destabilise the House of Journalists in any way—and he is not saying there is—he will—excuse the pun (he loathes puns)—*smoke* you out.

Enough! He has the exquisite head of this African tribal princess in his hands and he has been trying, he now realises, to strangle her; to strangle her, before hurling her long lithe body to the floor! This is not good, not least because he can be seen in here by fellows out smoking in the Central Courtyard. Yes, a good group of them is out there now—including Adom, the East African headmaster and politician, the one who the Foreign Office take a special interest in, who the secret services are keeping tabs on, who is puffing complacently on a curly briar. The smoking fellows are not obviously looking in on him, but you never know. He has a close relationship with the fellowship and is confident he enjoys their respect. He works hard to put himself inside their minds, to understand their frets and fears, to see this place as they see it. He thinks he has a good idea of what they are thinking. He prides himself on that. But they aren't under twenty-four-hour surveillance, God forbid. They are free to gather together in these huddles to smoke and to talk—and in truth, none of the staff or the volunteers has any idea what they are discussing at any one time. For all he knows they are discussing him. How he is striding around his office, talking to himself, and trying to throttle the life out of this slender ebony beauty. She had been a gift from a great African novelist who had visited a couple of years ago, made a very moving and powerful speech, and lavished praise on the House of Journalists.

The memory of that day has a soothing effect. He needs to keep control of his emotions. He doesn't want the fellows to think he is prey to constant alarms and suspicions. When he thinks about all that the House of Journalists represents, the praise it has received, the awards it has won: he can take great pride, yes great pride. But it is because this place is so special that he also has to watch for signs and never drop his guard.

| SO, AA?

So, AA: you have helped to unsettle the House of Journalists. Was that your plan? Open up! Who are you and where have you come from? Enough of this AA: writer business. Let us in on your story. We are your fellows. You cannot trust everyone but you can trust us. Can't you? Your silence speaks volumes. It puts you in danger. No one here likes a fellow who is unreadable. You are a danger to yourself and to the rest of us.

Tap, tap, tap.

First from Room 14.

Tap, tap, tap.

And then from Room 16.

You must be able to hear our tapping. We can picture you listening: tensed like a code-breaker. Thrilled and unnerved at the same time.

Tap, tap, tap.

Do you imagine there is a message in it? That we are signalling to you? That we are signalling solidarity?

Why would we be doing that?

Yes, you are a "strange one," "a bit of a mystery," as they say here. But you cannot think this enigmatic quality sets you apart? Yes, you carry with you a secret of some sort. But who of us doesn't? You'll need more than that if you are to earn your place among the fellowship of the House of Journalists.

EDSON, THIS VERY SPECIAL MAN, HAD TOLD HER HIS STORY, HE HAD ENTRUSTED HER WITH IT

Do any of us notice Vanessa Boothby, a writing mentor, arriving at the House of Journalists, sometime after Edward Crumb's visit, as afternoon slips into early evening? She certainly doesn't notice any of us. She is more than usually self-absorbed and disappointed today but is nonetheless paying her regular visit to her mentee, Edson. She always fulfils her responsibilities to others, whoever they are. If she is being honest with herself, however, which is something she always tries to be—it is so important to be emotionally truthful if you are a writer, after all— she feels rather alienated from Edson, just now; rather let down, though goodness knows, it is not his fault, it is just that, well, it didn't go well this afternoon, and she had been pinning so many hopes on it, and, let's face it, people like her, writers who give so much of themselves to help other writers, do need to get *something* out of this place. They can't just be expected to give, give, give.

Her hero—the appellation, so often casually bestowed, is entirely appropriate in this context—is an exiled journalist, based on a real man, a remarkable man, her friend Edson, whom she met at the House of Journalists, an institution with which she is sure they, the commissioners, are familiar. If she hadn't been invited for his script conference, she would have been with him this afternoon, as his guest, for the visit of the Nobel Prize–winning playwright and poet Edward Crumb, whose early plays and poetry she greatly admires, though she is less keen on his recent work, she must confess—too crudely polemical for her tastes. But anyway, Edson, this very special man, had told her his story, he had entrusted her with it. "I give it to you, Vanessa," he had said to her, enfolding her hands in his, "it is all I have and it is a great burden," and she hopes with all her heart that she has proved herself worthy of it; that she has succeeded in giving voice to his suffering, his loss, his courage, his good humour, yes, good humour—he is a remarkable man— and his dreams for the future. She hopes that she has given him the opportunity to speak through her, as it were, even though he is a writer himself, of course, a journalist of distinction in his homeland, though not, by his own admission, a writer in the artistic sense. And because of this great responsibility, she took, even by her own high standards, particular, painstaking care with this play, this monologue, yes, but she prefers to call it a play, a play for a single voice, a single voice that sings of a world of suffering and pain, but also of hope and redemption. And anyway, as she was saying, she had felt, in particular, a great responsibility to get the voice right, because it is a voice of great beauty as well as enormous power. Yes, Edson himself has a wonderful turn of phrase and his spoken English is powerfully idiosyncratic, and she has tried to capture some of that. She has drawn of course on her many years as a writer and teacher of creative writing; yes, she has had radio plays performed before, many years ago admittedly; quite small-scale projects yes, but radio she feels is *her* medium, if she could be excused making such a claim, with its powerful intimacy and immediacy, its lack of visual distractions or need for "theatrical" effects, its ability to talk directly to the listener, to talk to the inner ear, if she could put it that way. Anyway, they had read the piece. She will say only—and then she will shut up—that it has a particular poignancy and relevance at this time; it is timely, yes; that it is political with a small *p*; and that listeners will tune in to that, as it were, if they will forgive the pun.

———

All of this and more, much more, she had said to the stony-faced chief commissioner and the slightly more sympathetic-looking head of drama who were sitting—or, in the chief commissioner's case, lounging—in midcentury modern armchairs, with copies of her manuscript in their laps. Rays of late afternoon sun, appearing suddenly from behind an almighty cloud, cut in through the windows at an art deco angle and threw light on the well-polished parquet. Vanessa knew that to have been invited to this meeting was significant in itself. She has seen desk-high, yellowing slush piles not just in this office, but in any office where the chance of publication or production is a possibility.

The chief commissioner listened to her pitch, legs akimbo in his low chair, in that deadpan way they do, giving nothing much away; while the head of drama, legs buttoned up, but smiling open-faced, seemed to be willing her on a bit more. Good cop, bad cop? One of them must have seen possibilities in the material or they wouldn't have asked her to come in.

But it was so hard to tell, and now, after all she had said to the two of them, she feels—acutely—that she has sold herself short; she has not made enough of her own art. True, it is Edson's story, pretty much in every detail, and using a lot of his words and turns of phrase, but it is a mistake, a profound mistake, to underestimate the skill it takes to fashion this raw material, to give it some shape and bend it into a narrative arc. Edson himself is just a journalist and not a writer in the more elevated sense—which is surprisingly rare among the fellowship, despite the name: the House of Journalists. And, yes, Edson, to his credit, doesn't pretend to know how to make of his own story a work of art. He is peculiarly self-aware in that regard; many of the fellows buy into the House of Journalists' central myth: that because of what they have gone through almost anything they write has the power of art.

But who can blame them when they are so encouraged in this belief by Julian Snowman and his Committee, which reverences everything they write and accords it published status, via the House of Journalists' publishing arm—a profitable little business that is. Julian and his Committee make much of the place as a space for writers to come together and share their experiences and learn from one another, but in truth, people like her, writing mentors, are used as unpaid and uncredited functionaries of the House of Journalists' writing machine. That is their only role and woe betide them if they stray beyond its bounds and write something of their own based on the place and its people, because then they will find themselves accused of appropriation, treachery, cultural imperialism. Oh, a torrent of accusations! Not to their face of course, that it is not the House of Journalists' way, but she has heard such words used about previous transgressors by the more loyal brethren, the guardians of the flame, Julian's young henchmen and women. So she had certainly thought long and hard before embarking on this venture, as she knows that if it succeeds she will be cold-shouldered, if not turned out, which is rich given that rumour has it that Julian himself is working on something based on the House of Journalists, which he will no doubt justify in some roundabout and high-minded way, suggesting that he has not rushed into using its unique, rich, and precious raw material, tempting though that might have been, because his mission has always been to support the fellows themselves to tell their own stories in their own voices—and that of course he would continue to do—but that now he feels the time has come to reflect on his own part in this great endeavour, to shine a sidelight if you will on an experience that has humbled him and helped him to grow, as a person and a writer. Oh, yes, the stories themselves will be short, as Julian's stories always are these days. Highly polished little pieces they will be, sitting neatly at the high end of middlebrow, where they will sell like delicate hotcakes. But all the self-justification surrounding them will be anything but short, old windbag that he is, in these days of his pomp. She had known him slightly at university, when he had been a shy boy from the north, barely saying a word. Anyway, even without having to concern herself about the anticipated reaction of Julian and his Committee, having been entrusted with one of these stories by its owner, she did feel a heavy responsibility to be true to its essence, and perhaps that had inhibited her as an artist, leading her to stick too rigidly to the tale as told in all its particulars. But it was too late to add that now.

"We are extremely interested in this subject area of course," the chief commissioner began apparently encouragingly although somehow anything but. "It is obviously very rich territory for drama. And we are well aware of the House of Journalists. Yes, well aware. And, you know, this is not the first work we have seen based on it. Every writer in the country seems to have some connection and to have been powerfully moved by the place! But, in the end it is all about quality, what we think will appeal to our audience. And we did find your play for the single voice quite effective, but as it happens, Julian Snowman, your founder and Chair, recently had lunch with our controller to discuss something on a bigger scale, recorded on site at the House of Journalists—a mix of features, drama, short stories, conversation. A day-long special. Of course it is still in the early planning stages—but we are all very excited about it. And we were wondering if you were aware of that. Presumably this has been discussed among the writing community at the House of Journalists, though perhaps not, from the look on your face. Well, you can see how this changes things, but what we were wondering is if your play could perhaps be adapted and, as it were, integrated into the wider project. Maybe you could discuss this with Julian Snowman, just as we will be talking to our controller? And in this way your play—not in its current form, but extracts; and perhaps going back to Edson himself, working more directly with him; because he sounds a fascinating character, with a very distinct voice, something more in his own voice, less mitigated, with you bringing your dramatic skills to bear in a more discreet, behind-the-scenes sort of way, you know, a sort of consultancy role—in this way, the important essence of your play, Edson's own story, would reach the radio audience, which is the main thing after all. Anyway, could we leave you with that thought, to take that away, and meanwhile discussions with Julian Snowman will continue and who knows, we could all be working together in some capacity or other on this very exciting, though still on the drawing board, House of Journalists project."

| IN THE DRIVE-TIME STUDIO IS THE SANCTUARY MINISTER, ANDREW ALEXANDER

A woman Andrew doesn't know, or at least doesn't recognise, nods to him—rather distractedly—as he and his three advisors sweep into the marble, mirror, and chrome glories of the foyer of Broadcasting House. He nods back—more warmly. She may be a constituent; she is certainly a voter. But the woman ignores his response. Fuck you, he thinks. She is carrying, he notices, three flaccid plastic folders, under one arm.

A producer, a new keen one, is there to meet them, to show them through security, and up to the studio. He can tell she is a new keen one because she makes some effort to talk to him. The experienced ones know not to bother. She is allowed to chat on—he has zoned out anyway—but then something she says triggers total shutdown. His team steps across and wraps it up. *That's it: they are crashing this conversation.*

The trigger was her saying that the last question would be about Edward Crumb's reported comments on the government's asylum record during the House of Journalists visit.

No, no, no, not having that. That wasn't what was agreed, as your editor well knows. Not discussing it. The minister will be talking about today's excellent figures. That's the story.

She really is a new keen one. She starts to take them on. He can't help smiling behind his linebackers.

She isn't listening. This is way above her pay grade. Phil Morris is a prick if he thinks he can pull this one. Edward Crumb! The programme has zero credibility as it is. The story is the figures. End of story.

She looks as if she might come back at them again but as she squares up, the lift door opens behind her—nothing at her back—and they sweep through her, crushing her beneath their wheels: the minister and Home Team.

They show themselves into the green room and wait for the editor Phil Morris. They don't deal below his level.

What sort of a stunt is this, Phil? Do you want to look like a total prick? Edward Crumb? Zero credibility. Run with this and your programme—what were the latest ratings?—is a government dead-air zone. Yes, Phil, the whole government. Lots of time for blowing the oppo, which you seem to enjoy so much already. You can empty-chair us right up till your leaving do. Your funeral.

Andrew says nothing throughout. He keeps his mouth shut. He leaves it to Home Team.

But sometimes, in more reflective moments, he does wonder: Is this what it has come to? He came into the House eight years ago now, and has been a minister for six of them. His promo to Armed Forces in the reshuffle before last had seemed like a real breakthrough. At last, he was on his way; catching up the early high fliers of his intake. It was two wars and counting by the time of the general, and so to come out of that and to be offered Sanctuary, the wet one in Borders and Security, was a shatterer. *Frankly, you can stuff it,* he had wanted to say. Just this once. *I'm worth at least Enforcement.* He didn't of course. He accepted. Meekly. (Mother—the baroness—had said it was advisable; and Jenny—the QC (and wife)—had said it was up him. No change there, then.) Word from the whips office (it chimed with the Street) was that Gerry Southall had nailed down the hard end (no more brownies to be won there); it was the soft end that needed sharpening up. The soft end was the sloppy dog shit. Spiralling suicides and self-harm in the detention centres; too much rough stuff on the raids and returns; talk of international commissions of enquiry, unease among the crushed judiciary, some stirrings even among the inert electorate. The job of the new MOS in Sanctuary (Asylum as was—which tells its own story) was to scatter a bit of fairy dust; dream up a few heart-warmers and showpieces. "Just enough for cover, mind; just enough to confuse the migrants' rights crowd, wrong foot the Lefty lawyers, and placate the last liberals in the party." So here he was, doing his duty, patrolling the soft and sloppy. Government Good Boy. Was this why he had wanted to be a minister? Of course it wasn't. He had hoped to do the business, see some action. And, yes, make a difference; change the world; do some *good* even.

"Oh, *do* shut up." (Mother, Jenny, his SPADs, his SOS, the PM, just about everybody, in fact.)

He would of course: that's what he did. The only words that ever passed his lips were those written for him by Home Team. He could be counted on not to put his foot in it: the sloppy dog shit; his mouth, you name it. They had washed it out with soap: his brain, that is; that is to say, his brain that was! Sometimes he wondered if he was capable of independent thought or word or deed these days. He thought, he *dreamt*, in sound bites, in key messages and the lines to take. (Was even this reflection his own?) And when he gave voice, the voice was His Master's. "It's why I really want you to be a minister, Andrew."

Yes, a *minister*. He should not forget that. In such situations a minister stays silent. That is as it should be. He has Home Team to speak for him.

Phil Morris is listening. He understands where they are coming from. He sees their point of view. But they know he can't agree to no-go areas.

Phil Morris is old school; one of the last. One by one they are being put out to grass. That—to take the broader view (and Andrew is broad-minded enough occasionally to see it)—is a pity in a way. The programme editors do their jobs, and the ministerial teams do theirs. The point is not to get the editors to cave completely (as—taking the broader view again—happens too often these days). The point is to make the point: to show that we won't be messed with. To show who is boss.

No-go areas, no. But sticking to the story, yes.

He hears them.

The story is the figures.

He hears them, yes. Now he must . . .

Home Team gather round their man for a final run-through of lines. Nothing to worry about. The story is the figures and the figures are good, so the story is good. Go tell it.

And what if?

What if what?

Phil sanctions a "while you're here, minister" after all.

He wouldn't dare.

We're talking Phil Morris here, one of the last ones left with any balls at all.

I don't know.

So why did they tip us?

Tip us?

Friendly prod in the lift.

I get you. A double bluff.

Well, more a triple, if you think about it.

Aren't we making a Machiavelli out of a molehill on this one?

Okay, but how about this for size: Morris gets friendly prod to tip us, we bawl him out, he plays a half fold, we buy it, he sees that, he gives go-ahead to Nick, we sit here congratulating ourselves, and Andrew takes a Crumb question from Nick, exposed, unbriefed, word-blind.

You're not saying we should walk?

"Of course we don't walk." Andrew had listened this long. He is the minister; he has a team to think aloud for him. But now he speaks. He speaks because he has never walked. His chief advisor may have called it, but this time he is not running her play. "You think I can't busk a Crumb rebuttal?" She and the other two look sceptical. Fuck you, he thinks. But he beams. "Your tunes, guys, I'll be blowing your tunes." They warm. "Vic." He turns to his chief. "I'm taking this one, okay? I'm up for it." She's taking an authority blow, but you know what: it's re-minder time. Who's the boss? *He's* the boss. He's the minister and she's just a SPAD. He beams again. "Guys, team, no worries here, okay? It's *me* talking, which means it's *you* talking. The best in the business, right?"

They all but high-five him into the studio and then line up behind the production team in the cubicle, to listen in.

"Joining me in the drive-time studio is Sanctuary Minister Andrew Alexander."

The interview is the predictable piece of piss and when the Crumb question comes, as come it does—almost apologetically, at the end—he positively smithereens it.

"Nick, the first thing to say of course is that Edward Crumb is one of our greatest writers, so many people will be disappointed that he chose the House of Journalists, home to so many courageous men and women—and generously supported by this government—to badmouth this country's proud tradition of providing sanctuary. I was there today and I think Edward Crumb, on reflection, will know he misjudged the occasion. There is a time and place to raise legitimate questions—and we, your government, will always listen. But the House of Journalists today was not that time or place. The House of Journalists is this nation at its best. It is something we can all be proud of, and at the same time we can all be reassured that providing sanctuary to a handful of distinguished exile writers does not mean open borders and uncontrolled inflows, as today's excellent figures have shown. Edward Crumb's comments are a sad diversion on a day when all the indicators are pointing in the right direction."

| MIRIAM STERN WAS ONE OF THE FIRST FRIENDS OF THE HOUSE OF JOURNALISTS

All the indicators, she hears the minister say on the radio news, are pointing in the right direction. It is the minister to whom she had been introduced a few hours previously at the House of Journalists. And here he is on the airwaves turning the world on its head.

You read . . . (she could imagine the minister saying) . . . into my words . . . (his warm dead hand in her hand) . . . a construction that is . . . (the icy warmth of his smile up close) . . . if I may say so . . . (smile over) . . . your own.

The warmth the minister gave out seemed to be carefully calibrated—as if, like a reptile, he was controlling his body temperature. (She might be a constituent; she was certainly a voter.)

"We are all very proud of the House of Journalists," he said, as of a gifted child who doesn't always do what its parents ask, "and I know your personal backing has been very generous. It is so important that high-value individuals make a commitment, alongside government, to important projects like this one."

His warm words iced to the bone. Her only value was her high value.

Don't you . . . (she would have the minister know) . . . put your government alongside my commitment . . . (a flicker of unease perhaps). My commitment . . . (she wanted to say) . . . (too late) . . . is . . . my own.

And in her opinion, if we are giving our opinions, the reverse was true. That is to say, all the indicators are pointing in the *wrong* direction. Or is it, none in the right?

Miriam was one of the first "Friends" of the House of Journalists and, although Julian made much of the "moral" support she had given, in truth it was the financial backing, through the family trust that she had set up, which was much more important. She had no illusions about that. Hard cash to support the work of the House had bought her the Martin and Angelika Stern Library of Refugee Studies. It was, she still believed, "a fitting way to honour my beloved parents' memory," and she was proud of the work of the library "in supporting serious scholarship in this important subject area." (She was quoting herself from the modest ceremony that had been staged to mark the opening of the library.) "Moreover" (still quoting) there is no doubting the passionate commitment of the staff and volunteers at the House of Journalists. (Close quotes.) And yet today's event had shaken her faith. Something wasn't right.

As was her way, she pondered on it deeply.

First of all today's event. She had attended a number of these functions and had often found them uncomfortable. But today's had been grotesque. The parade of the fellows in order of suffering; Julian Snowman all show and unction; Edward Crumb's disintegration into self-parody; the minister's cryogenic presence; the private donors and small trust-funders now outnumbered by big corporates. But her concern went deeper and wider than that. It was the big-picture politics of the place, if she could put it that way. Once, she thought, the House of Journalists had stood for something. Stood for, stood out, stood *up*! But what now?

Certainly, the House of Journalists had become its own little world—enclosed, protected, and drawbridged. Today—as so often in the past—she had heard it described again and again as a "sanctuary" or a "haven." The designation put her in mind of weekend breaks in old smuggler villages cut out of heritage coastlines; of afternoons spent reading in front of open fires as sea storms lashed harbour walls in picturesque fury. How comforting it is to imagine that your cottage, protected by feet-thick walls, is the world—so warm, so safe. How comforting and how mistaken! For the world—as her parents knew; protecting her as best they could—is rather the bitter weeping rain; it is the sea, not just in the fury of a storm, but in its iron-grey heartlessness. Whatever men do to protect themselves—and so often they will do their worst—it is as nothing. This heartlessness is where the world begins and ends. You and your warmth and safety are nothing to it.

This great bleak thought induces oppression for a moment or two and then is blown away in a gale of laughter. Cheer up, Miriam, she tells herself through the laughter tears—just as her mother used to say to her when she was a little girl. Look at you, in your luxury car, in this smart district of the city, on your way to dinner at a fashionable restaurant with an old friend. You have a career you love; a lifestyle to envy; you are in good health; you are happy; you are in your prime. You have followed your own path. Enjoy your success, your wealth; your ability, limited as it is, to help others; above all, your goodness in wanting to. And now she could hear her father too, a man of darker moods, warning against his own tendency to dwell on the ultimate pointlessness of life. "Yes, cheer up, Miri," he would say in his heavily accented, precisely enunciated English, which he had mastered in *almost* all its parochialisms and peculiarities. "Worse things happen in sea."

Her father, because of his own nature, loved that her mother "knew how to enjoy herself." The heart of her parents' enduring love was this polar attraction: the serious young law student and the wealthy party girl; one of the great lawyers of his generation, who rose to become a Law Lord, but who never forgot or forgave; and the ever-glamorous hostess, brittle and brilliant, determined after those "wretched years" to take refuge in the civilised comedy of social life. The story of how their young love had been thwarted by the rigid class divide of the time and place (Berlin in the 1930s); of how they alone among their families had survived the ghettoes, the camps, the gas chambers, the chaos of liberation; of how they had bumped into each other in London by some turn of outrageous fortune, was, thanks to *One Bright Morning on Poland Street . . . A Miracle!*, well known. Perhaps too well known.

Miriam was a private person, determined to stay private, who had written a memoir as a personal tribute to her parents' love and had never envisioned that it would become a bestseller, still less be turned into a hit movie. This unexpected success had provoked anguished debate—particularly among fellow Jews. She was among the anguished debaters, which did not of course assuage all the others. True, she had her defenders—she was among those too; but to the irritation of some of her harsher critics she was ready to admit limited flaws and failings in her book and its many spin-offs.

Had she not diminished the apocalypse of her people by making it a mere backdrop for her parents' love story? Could it not be argued that the book was a mere palliative, an extenuation, when what a complacent, complicit world deserved was an indictment, a savage reminder? How could she possibly justify giving the tale a happy ending which at least implicitly was universal? All these questions were legitimate. Miriam asked them of herself, again and again, and it was important to her that she could answer them in some way.

In the few interviews she had given she was at pains to set the book in a graver context. *Yes, the story, read one way, is the triumph of hope over despair; love over hate. My parents were, they thought, lucky in love and in life. But it ends, as everything must, in death. My parents were not gassed in those ovens, or machine-gunned into pits of lime, or frozen to their bones in the ghettoes; I was able to lay them to rest, side by side, in a place of sanctity. But there was no escape from the great ultimate. It lay in wait and claimed them, as it does for all of us. All my parents' story shows—it was the lesson they taught me—is that life offers some of us little havens of safety and warmth and we should cherish and celebrate and seek to widen them. Which, incidentally, is one of the reasons I have long supported a project called the House of Journalists, which provides a much-needed place of sanctuary for exiled writers. We need more places like this.*

Her New York agent had phoned her the other day to say she had been approached about *Miracle* becoming a musical. Miriam's first thought, a spasm of appalled intellect, told her no; no, no, no! Then she thought: the library was for her father really, a place in which his serious soul could find lasting peace. Miriam had included her mother in the library's name because her mother would have expected to be by her beloved husband's side in this important enterprise, as in all the others to which he had devoted himself throughout his long life. "Great, gloomy books" were not for her, however; "I leave all that to Martin," she would say proudly. And he would look back, adoringly. Being brought back to high life by a high-kicking young woman on the Broadway stage was much more her mother's style. All the glamour and glitz would have delighted her. So Miriam's more considered response to the request for the rights was a great yelp! Yes, she cried down the phone, surprising her New York agent. Yes, yes, yes!

Miriam parks her car and steps out into the excited movement of early evening. She is in tears, as so often these days, but they are sweet-water tears, divined from a heart full to bursting; the sort of tears that bathe rather than burn the eyes. Even her father, who raged for justice all his life, put love, especially family love, above all else. His little Miri was the most precious thing by far that he had carried out of the infernal clutches of Auschwitz/Birkenau. "You were born there, my dearest, in my head and heart, as I dreamt of your mother, in one of those stinking bunks. The thought that one day, your mother and I, by some miracle . . . well, that kept me going. Hope and hatred—that's all there is when humanity lays waste to itself. Hatred, in truth, keeps you strong; without it you would never survive. But hope is the other part, the greater part; it saves you for redemption, not revenge. If there is only hatred, well, that was all our enemies had . . ."

More tears; she is awash. "Miri!" Her friend, from across the street, greets her and runs to her. She dries her eyes on her sleeve. She composes herself, gathers herself: to face the world. Her friend embraces her. Miriam Stern is a self-possessed woman, sweet-natured, surprisingly sentimental—but made of tough stuff. You don't get where she has got in the financial world unless you are. And look at the story of her parents: their remarkable survival against the odds. She is an exceptionally loyal and giving friend; but a loner, who has never married. No children; but she is a godparent to many. She never forgets a birthday, but is careful not to overindulge. Instead she works to instil a moral seriousness in these children, now young people. She cares especially deeply about refugees; well, that is not surprising perhaps, given her own background; but it is more than that. She talks about them, and how they are being treated, with tears in her eyes: sentimental but angry tears. She has that steely determination to make a difference, and like many these days, she is increasingly concerned about the political situation and the direction of this government. Like many, she invested so much hope in the party and the leader, believing it would govern well and he would be a great prime minister. Her disillusion is great, her fear considerable. She talks about it with feeling. Well, if your family story was like her family's story, you would, too.

ALL I CAN SAY IS THERE IS *SOMETHING* ABOUT HIM

Julian Snowman and his longtime civil partner, the multimedia artist Philip Shirley-Smith, are dining together in a restaurant around the corner from their home. Philip had had to come into the House of Journalists to "kidnap" Julian, who otherwise would have been there all evening, brooding over the day's events. He is still brooding even now, but in time the champagne will relax him and deliver him from his increasingly obsessive concern with the place. Philip, so long-suffering, looks forward to that.

————

"Who are we talking about, Jules?"

"We are talking about our newest fellow, AA."

"Surely every new arrival can have an unsettling effect? Why should this one be any different from any of the rest of them? Why let him freak you out?"

"*Freak* me out, you say? I express my reservations about him and this, apparently, is me being *freaked* out."

"Look, Jules, you must appreciate that you can sometimes seem, well, *over*protective of the House of Journalists."

"Philip, you don't know these people like I do. I know those who can be trusted and those who cannot. I would have expected you to back me up."

"Jules, darling, I will always back you to the hilt. But I don't want to see you distressed by a new fellow who you cannot quite place. Chances are he will fit in over time. They mostly do. And if they don't, you move them on."

"Look, Philip, I appreciate that you are only seeking to reassure me. But I'm quite certain about this one. True, we've had more than a few fellows who have had stories that don't quite add up, who may not be where they say they're from, or who clearly aren't telling us the whole truth or anything like. But that is only because they are fearful and confused about the way the system works. I tell them again and again that sticking to the truth is the best policy. 'A true voice rings true. We as writers know that more than anyone.' But too many believe that the path to safety lies in falsity or exaggeration, or the adoption of different personas and voices. They feel they should be telling people what they want to hear or making something up. They think the system works that way."

"So what makes this AA any different?"

"Look, if I say it, I risk your ridicule—"

"Jules, please—"

"No, because in its way it *is* ridiculous. For all I can say is that there is *something* about him. Nothing more than that. A knowingness, perhaps? Though that doesn't really capture it. A certain arrogance? Though in truth he does not cut an assured or impressive figure. And you will tell me that I really cannot make so much of the fact that he was out in the Central Courtyard smoking on his own when Crumb got away from us. But somehow it felt like it was engineered. It was a perfect little set-up. Crumb and AA together, chatting and plotting . . . Look, when I try to put it into words it doesn't make any sense."

"Well, true, it doesn't sound much to me, but perhaps you should trust your instincts."

"Really? Well, in that case my instincts tell me that the presence of this one is malign, antithetical, corrosive; that he will cause real damage to the spirit of the House. But God knows how!"

Philip takes the bottle of champagne and refills Julian's flute. Languid liquid becomes excitable, foaming up to the lip, up, up, and almost over . . . and then, as quickly, evaporating back. Philip looks up and smiles.

"Okay, you win. You are probably right, Philly, you usually are. I am making too much of this miserable AA character. It is just that I am so worried about the House at the moment."

Philip refills his own glass. He settles back. The bubbles are working their magic, but he must be patient. Julian has not off-loaded all his anxiety yet. Not by any means.

Yes, as Philip knows *(he does indeed)*, foremost among his critics are those other writers, journalists, and broadcasters who set the place up with him, but have always envied him his success. Philip doesn't need telling *(no, he doesn't)*, but the fact is, his fiction, unlike theirs, *sells*. Give the public a book by Julian Snowman and they want to read it. Both those who read a lot of books—slumming it somewhat; and those who read very few—venturing slightly upmarket. And as well as the books, there is all the radio and television; there are all the committees and commissions. That is why they—all the others long gone now—wanted him on board as Chair. He had the profile and the contacts to make a success of the project. And that is why the House of Journalists, much more than anything else he has done, has ended up being his proudest achievement, his life's work—his *baby*. And because this is the case, he feels he knows best what is needed to protect and nurture it. Philip understands, doesn't he? *(Well, he tries.)* And it is just plain unfair and wrong to suggest that he is in the pocket of the government. Simon and his ministers had made mistakes, had done some stupid, even reprehensible things; their record on this issue was patchy at best. And he had said so. But this talk, growing in their circles, of galloping authoritarianism, of outright abuse of human rights, of the curtailment of essential liberties, of the neutering of opposition and dissent, was hugely overblown. Some of the charges thrown at this government, at ministers, at the prime minister himself . . . well, really! He had known Simon for many years. True, Simon was supremely confident in his powers, he didn't suffer fools, and he was utterly ascendant in today's politics . . . but a nascent despot, a quasi-dictator? It was laughable. People needed to get real, to calm down; to desist from this loose talk. Well, he was telling Philip what he already knew. (*That was true.*) Oh, it was all very well over metropolitan dinner tables or in liberal newspapers: it was just idle chatter, ignored contemptuously by Simon and his ministers, who were much more in tune with the people, if truth be told. What worried him though was that people around the House of Journalists were being infected by this talk, saying openly that the project was compromised, that his inclusive approach put him too close to the government's asylum policies, that the House of Journalists was being used as cover. Could he believe that? (*Yes.*) And as ridiculous as Ted Crumb's attack had been—a bad parody almost—and as tame as it had been—he had bottled out at the last minute—it added something to this sense that he was hand in glove with the government. Crumb and his ilk were out to wreck and destroy if they could. Now, the House of Journalists respected a diversity of views, of course it did. But people were starting to take liberties. And worse, so much worse, the fellows were starting to pick up on this despondency and insolence. Well, he wasn't having that. Not after all they had gone through. He had promised them a place of safety at the House of Journalists and that was what they were going to get. If he had to shut out this babble, this chatter, this noise, he would. He would take the necessary steps. Whatever they might prove to be. He had a duty to protect those in his care. And nothing was going to stop him. Oh, how many times had he burdened Philip with all this?

(*This was a good sign.*)

Too many times, but darling Philly understood what a burden *he* was carrying, and he did not begrudge him a bit of unburdening surely.

(*And this was another.*)

"More champagne, Jules?"

"Well, I shouldn't . . ."

Philip fills him up.

"I'm getting a bit tiddly, to be honest."

Philip makes sure that he is topped up right to the brim.

"Well, enough of that."

(Home and dry now.)

Julian would now ask him how his day had been, and he would give the briefest, brightest summary of it, and then it would be: Love you, Philly, don't know why you put up with me, what you see in me, silly old queen—it must be love. And after that it would be: Oh, if the fellows at the House of Journalists could see me like this they'd never believe it was the same old Julian, their crotchety Chair, but that is because they never see me with you, Philly, only you really listen to me, and take the trouble to understand what I am saying.

And then their main courses would arrive, and they'd decide to have another bottle, though they really shouldn't, and they would go on to discuss, with that supreme self-satisfaction that all happy couples enjoy when discussing "the secret" of their relationship, the "secret" of their relationship. Which—no secret—is that they are happy. And like all happy couples they would conclude that they don't need to "apologise" *(though no one is asking them to)*. Let their friends carp and bitch. *(None of them are.)* Let them laugh. *(Ditto.)* And by now they would be laughing at themselves. Happy couples, they would remind themselves, are good at laughing at themselves.

And then they would have dessert, which they always did though they really shouldn't, and then a nightcap *(ditto)*, and there would be more of this silly happy tiddly talk, and then the bill would arrive. And then they would sway their way home to home sweet home, arm in arm, to climb-almost-clamber the fairy stairs to Bedfordshire. And then they would crash into the wide white ocean and billowing surf of sheet and duvet to sleep sweet shit-faced in blissful oblivion, the House of Journalists obliterated.

THIS PLACE IS TORMENTED EVERY NIGHT BY THE MOST TERRIBLE DREAMS

When I, Mustapha, first wake, I listen for sounds that locate me in this world, benighted as it is for me. For waking is a sort of home: four familiar walls. Even in the camp, even when a dream had transported me away from everyday horrors into weirdly reimagined childhood haunts or strange idylls of yearning young love, there was some comfort in waking. For the greater terror was, as ever, the abysmal fall into *never* waking. This is the endgame. There is no escaping it. And yet every waking is an escape into another day. And that is something: a small triumph of life over death.

A sound—listen!—the sonorous snoring of sound asleep. I roll over and check the shared wall with 17. No. Roll the other way and check 15. Yes, it's you, AA! A gargle gurgle and wind-whistle through nose hair and lip purse. The soft suck of stones and of dream sigh settling. I laugh to hear it. It is a funny and a beautiful sound. Such sleep . . .

It stirs sweet healing memories of my beloved Yasmin, soft cursing and soft kicking, imploring me in her own disturbed half sleep to shut up. She slept so lightly herself that she served—please forgive me my romantic fancy—as a guardian angel over my deep, noisy, untroubled dreams.

It is in these dead predawn hours that I miss Yasmin the most. I lie draped over the stone-cold but still beautiful image of her in her long-ago youth and weep desolate tears. She is not dead, which is perhaps the worst of it. She is living, estranged from me. She knows of my whereabouts, but I am long lost to her: by my choice to defy the authorities and to sacrifice safety; by all the years we have spent apart (again my choice, the harder part of her thinks—others signed confessions and were released); above all by exile, far away (another choice—there were nearer places). There is—censored letters have long reached me—another man, known to me, a comfort to her. Yet I do not doubt, and she would never deny, I am certain of it, that I am her great love. Still. I was her first love, certainly.

But life moves on. The current regime is hard on the women of my country. Careers are not open to them; work of any sort is difficult to find. It is impossible for a woman of her class, her pedigree, her line. She is forced to be dependent, as she is required to be demure. (I picture the slim, long-haired, laughing, jeans-wearing girl. Then I picture a grim-faced, middle-aged woman in a head scarf and long black shapeless skirt.) I am grateful—or should be—to this man, once a friend of sorts. He looks after her and the children. He provides for them and keeps them safe. He neutralises, through his contacts with the authorities, the danger they could face through being my family.

The children: I talk of them as the children, rather than as my or our children, because what attachment to them do I enjoy? What claim? They were six and three when I left them in their mother's sole care. They are twenty-one and eighteen now. No longer children, and certainly no longer mine. Through the post office service of the Red Crescent I have received over the years clipped and censored reports from their mother of their progress. (She never talks of herself.) Sometimes, at her urging I have no doubt, and less frequently as the years have passed, they have appended instances of bewildered, distant affection. There is, despite the censor, some sense that they respect me, that I possess a certain heroic quality; but that makes them scared of me too. I am a stone figure—monumental, distant. I sense—again it is subtly coded—that their mother's new husband, my old associate, their stepfather, is to them something of a buffoon, a clown, not quite respected by them. But what would I give—*everything* of course—to be the butt of this affection? What is their respectful, awesome love for me across these frozen years, these echoing distances? What sort of father wants his child to admire and respect him? What sort of a father am I, that I should have chosen this path and ended up here? What sort of a husband? What sort of man?

Do you, snoring away on the other side of the wall, ask yourself these questions? I wonder. Do you, AA? A loud walrus snort apparently confirms it. Or perhaps not? You make me laugh, AA, do you hear that? Where is this fellow who is starting, they say, to unnerve Julian and the Committee, in the blocked drains and organ pipes of your noisome night self? In the camp it was like this: there was a grim pleasure in finding the cruellest guards slumped and snoring at their posts. It was supposed not to happen, of course. They were supposed to be alert and watchful at all times. But the boredom, particularly during the night, was immense. They were only human. And so they slumped and slumbered and slobbered: powerless lumps of common humanity.

Suddenly—listen! on the other side from me—Room 17: a shuddering awake; a strangled shout of anguish. This place is tormented every night by the most terrible dreams: screams tear at the night as torture is relived; agonised sobs reverberate as loved ones are dragged away once more.

By day we are the quiet, quiescent foot soldiers of the House of Journalists—following orders and asking no questions. But at night, we rise howling from our beds and take over the place. Night porters don't last long at the House of Journalists; young volunteers come and go. Counselling is offered. But it taxes even the strongest of souls to spend the long dark hours among us as we haunt the corridors with our memories and cerements. You should be awake to chronicle all of this, AA. You should not be sleeping, snoring, through it. Perhaps you are dreaming it?

CONNECTIONS

| LET THE DREAM FALL BACK

I saw a dream which made me afraid, and the thoughts upon my bed and the visions of my head troubled me. Book of Daniel.

Let the dream not trouble thee. Let the dream fall back on the dreaded. Book of Daniel again.

| FULL OF TWISTS AND TURNS

Another disturbed night, like the night we all endured after Crumb's visit, full of twists and turns, ends at last in the later early hours in the deep sleep of defeated exhaustion. Such sleep does little to restore and renew the energies and spirits. We surface from it wrecked and bewildered.

The morning offers up white grey light, further filtered through the thin blinds. One yank and up they snap. We do not look out. We all look *in*: on the grey stone courtyard, with its sculptures and water features. It is an exercise in impeccable restraint. Early risers, the first smokers, are pacing the yard, hands in coat pockets, sucking deep, looking up at a square of white grey sky. All thoughts are imprisoned in memory.

We do not have long to linger and dwell. Already there is a certain bustle at the House of Journalists. The comings and goings start early. Breakfast is being served in the refectory; classes, workshops, and seminars will soon be convening. There is a sense of purpose and of looking forward. Julian is on the premises again. Young volunteers and interns are pouring in from their flat shares, bed-sits, and halls of residence. Preparations will be in hand for today's visitors and guest lecturers.

We queue up at the breakfast buffet and then carry our trays across to the usual tables. Fellows are encouraged to eat together, but communality is not required or enforced—and certainly not at breakfast. They understand that not all of us spring out of bed full of chirrup and fellowship. Indeed, in truth, none of us do. Rather, we prefer to ease our way into the day, to gather our spirits in solitude before the morning's activities and demands. You, AA, take advantage of this dispensation—as is your right. You read a newspaper, we notice. Few of us do, though they are delivered free of charge. You look first for the football scores and then turn to the quick crossword.

You have nearly completed it when a volunteer comes up to your table. She is sorry. No need to be sorry, you say. Sorry to interrupt, that is. Not at all, you say. It is just that Julian would like a word. Julian? Yes, when you have finished breakfast of course. A word with Julian? Yes, in your own time.

You take your time, we notice, though you cannot disguise that the summons has caused you some agitation. Like you, we know nothing of its purpose, though we might surmise that it relates to your case. The House of Journalists assures us that most fellows can expect to be given status and that everything is done to assist us. Even so, we all live in fear of refusal. This is the fate of most who venture to this country in search of protection. The international criteria are interpreted in the narrowest way possible. They do what they have to do and no more. We are political people and we understand the politics of the situation. But we are also human beings who are concerned above all for our personal safety. When our cases come up it concerns even the most independent of us that we have not shown enough gratitude to the House of Journalists, to Julian and the Committee, for accommodating us in this haven of sanctuary. If we sometimes chafe at its rules and laugh at its foibles it is only because we feel safe here. We trust that they, the authorities, understand this.

You still linger, we notice. A few minutes pass before you finally leave your table. We can only imagine what happens next—though no episode in the House of Journalists stays hidden for long.

Julian receives you in his office with mannered bonhomie. But your response is guarded, suspicious even, and he quickly abandons any pretence.

"Have you had any contact with Edward Crumb?" Julian asks.

"Edward Crumb?"

"Yes, Edward Crumb, the world-famous writer: who was here just a few days ago. You and he shared a cigarette in the courtyard. Has he been in contact?"

The look on Julian's face—all bonhomie abandoned—gives you to understand that it would be very unwise of you to play dumb with him.

"No."

"Edward Crumb has made no attempt of any kind to contact you?"

"No."

Julian softens. He is relieved. He has worked himself into a state unnecessarily perhaps? He is suspicious of you, he admits it. And Crumb has raised his suspicions. But he has a rule never to doubt the word of a fellow. There must be trust and respect in this place—which is why he so jealously guards it against those who would undermine that ethos. But he has asked you a straight question and you have given a straight answer. He can ask no more than that.

"Not that it is any way forbidden, you understand, to have contact with an outside writer. Quite the contrary: such contacts are encouraged. It is just . . . well, it is just in the case of Edward Crumb it would be helpful to know if any such contact is attempted."

You nod your head. Julian is still wary.

You were dispatched here by the relevant authorities, from some port of entry or holding place, the normal checks having been carried out. Or so he assumed. It is the usual way of it. True, he didn't ask any questions at the time. That now seems a mistake, but there was no obvious reason to. He trusts the system. The system is there to act as a filter. To make sure that only those whose stories ring true get through. To detect those who are just making it all up in the first place. The

House plays its part at a later stage, this stage, when subtler spinners of fiction and falsehood are apt, despite—or because of?—their deviousness, to enmesh themselves in a web of inconsistencies, contradictions, and discontinuities. If you have fallen into any traps, AA, you have escaped them up to now. But take care—there are many ways in which you can become caught up in your story.

Still, the question has been asked and the answer given: there has been no contact between you and Crumb. No further contact, that is. Not since the shared cigarette. You have given your word. So that is an end to the matter. For now.

Julian thanks you for coming in. He asks you, slipping back into mannered bonhomie, how you are finding life in the House of Journalists. He asks because he/we have not seen that much of you lately. Have you had a date set for your tribunal hearing yet? Because it is in everybody's interest that cases are settled quickly. We all want to know where we stand, don't we?

You nod your head again. Julian says nothing more. You take it that you are dismissed and leave the office with relief.

Julian watches you go and then gets up from behind the desk and paces around for a moment or two, before returning to his seat and picking up his BlackBerry. It is blinking its little red eye, as if in warning. Cliché alert. Though just occasionally, Julian reflects, the red eye does spell danger.

It would have been easy to delete Ted Crumb's message as soon as it appeared in his in-box—at 2:31 a.m.—dismissing it as a pissed piece of provocation, a wind-up to get him going, but betokening no serious intent. But no, he slept on it. (Quite literally: he kept his BlackBerry, on vibrate, under his pillow. The House of Journalists was under instruction to contact him at any hour if an emergency arose. He wanted to hear about it right away.)

And then when he woke up, the first thing he did was to read the text again. And with that clarity of mind that dawn rising brings, he read in it precisely that serious intent that he might have missed four hours previously. Though of course there was always a chance that he wasn't reading it *in* it, so much as reading it *into* it? If that makes sense. Anyway, he read it again—and was not sure either way. And so he read it again—maybe twenty or thirty times. And with each reading it became lighter outside the window, but also cloudier. It was clearly going to be a cloudy day, as it were. And though in one sense this reflection meant he was none the wiser as to the precise nature of the content of the text, he was at least certain that he could not dismiss it as inconsequential.

Hence the decision to call in AA for questioning—though that is perhaps a melodramatic way of putting it. Ask him in for a chat about an issue of concern, perhaps? Better. But either way, it wasn't clear to him now why he had bothered. AA's assurances, even if sincere—and he was bound to assume they were—were never going to resolve the matter, were they? Crumb was more subtle than that. AA may well have been recruited, but he would not have been told the whole story. Need to know. That would have been the approach.

Julian gets up and paces up and down a few more times. Then he calls out.

"Sabrina! Convene the Committee. An emergency session. The Boardroom at eleven o'clock."

| AGNES JOINS A PROTEST AT ANOTHER REFUGEE CENTRE

We notice that as you return to your room, AA, you meet Agnes in the corridor. She is dressed for a trip and carrying her camera gear. As it is Agnes, you make conversation. It is strange to hear your voice, so rarely do you speak with us.

"Going somewhere?"

"Yes, AA, I've decided it's time to see what's going on beyond these four walls, to open my eyes to the wider picture."

"Good for you," you say. You are not used to making conversation. But it is something of a relief. Perhaps you have overdone the brooding, enigmatic presence?

"We are cocooned in here," Agnes says.

You say nothing. Having started this exchange, you do not want to be drawn in any deeper. The exchange with Julian is still fresh in your mind.

"I've been thinking for a while," Agnes continues, "that it may be time to move on. I don't want to be trapped in this place, however much it has done for me."

You nod, but do not say anything more. You go back to your room, where you spend so much of your time. It is safer there. You do not see, as some of us do, Agnes walking out of the House of Journalists to rendezvous with her new "outside" friends, the City Sisters, a campaign and support group, unconnected to this place, indeed highly critical of it, who are travelling to join a protest at another refugee centre. The trip, of course, is unsanctioned. If it was known about it would at the very least be frowned upon. Efforts would certainly have been made to dissuade Agnes from going, though not of course to stop her. There is no question of restraining us or of locking us in, even if it is for own good. No, we are free to come and go as we please, to associate with anyone we choose to, to join any group in any activity. And the only reason courses are offered is to alert us to the possibility, very real given our profile, of our being exploited by opportunists or extremists, with their own agendas. Agnes, being so young, has been a particular object of this assistance, and on the face of it, she has welcomed it. But in this instance she has chosen to follow her own path. So be it. The House of Journalists can only do so much. After that, it is up to us.

And let's not lose sight of the bigger picture here. (We can just imagine Julian saying such a thing.) For the bigger picture is that Agnes—and isn't this great news—is going on this trip because she now feels ready to take a step towards resuming a career, a life, in photojournalism.

Yes, Agnes is taking photographs once more—for which, yes, we, the other fellows, give thanks. It is indeed great news. When she first arrived at the House of Journalists, she found it impossible to even pick up a camera. Every time she took the weight of one in her hands she could feel the heavy blows of the truncheons on her legs and arms and head; she could feel the heavy boots thudding into her kidneys and trying to shatter her spine. She could taste the blood and vomit and panic in her mouth; she could feel the piss running down her legs and soaking her jeans. And she could hear her precious Pentax LX—the camera which her grandfather had used throughout his career, which he had given her on her eighteenth birthday—being pounded by these same heavy boots. They were jumping up and down on it, those government goons, as if trying to pulverise it into dust, such was their terror at the power of its all-seeing eye.

In the absence of photography—and with help from the staff and volunteers at the House of Journalists—Agnes, as we know, turned to poetry; poetry that has made her a new name, and has done so much to enhance the reputation of this special place. There was a novelty for her in this form of expression—and she enjoyed the attention. There was catharsis in it too. But when Julian approached her about producing a slim volume of her poems to mark a major anniversary at the House of Journalists she called a halt.

"I'm downing tools, Jules. Let's not abuse the muse, hey! To fanzas of my stanzas, I say it's been fun, but work done. Let's call time on the rhyme. Yeh, don't mess with the reluctant Poetess. To any pleas from the Snowman, it's no man."

Julian's reaction to this outburst was, as they say here, "a picture." So rare is it for him to have his ideas rejected or his authority challenged, never mind in such facetious terms, that it took an exquisite effort on his part to assemble from teeth, jawbone, and facial muscle something approaching a smile.

"Yeh, it's time I got back to snapping a few pix," Agnes continued breezily—seemingly quite indifferent to the indignity she was heaping on Julian—"it's time to pick up a camera again. You have all been cool with me. Given me space and comfort. But it's only through a lens that I can look forward; to see myself in this new world of exile. The poetry is just raw power, man. It is outpouring. You know that in your heart, Jules. It is deep therapy and nostalgia. It's grief and anger management. I give it to the House, man. It's my payback, and I've been happy to pay. But only another Pentax will empower this woman again."

No sooner had she started speaking than Julian had discounted her. To his mind, she had placed herself in that category of fellows who had "moved on," even if they were still physically present at the House of Journalists. She was no longer of use to the House, because it was no longer of use to her. There was no recrimination or bitterness. It was natural that at a certain point there should be a parting of the ways.

All of these thoughts Julian had been processing behind his stiff smile—only for that smile to burst open as he realised that he was being far too hasty. What on earth had he been thinking! If anything, Agnes's move back into photography offered even greater opportunities for collaboration. He could immediately picture coffee table books and touring exhibitions. Or perhaps her poems set alongside new photographs? The possibilities were myriad. One moment he was discounting her, now he was counting her back in. Welcome to the House of Journalists!

To help Agnes get back into photography Luciano Huck was brought in. Before his accident, Luciano had been a highly regarded news photographer. His work in war zones and conflict situations won him many prizes. But then he lost both his legs in a "friendly fire" incident. Since then he has developed a successful second career as a counsellor and mentor to people suffering post-traumatic stress disorder and similar conditions, using photography as a means to help them to recover their mental well-being.

Luciano of course knew Agnes by reputation and he had seen many of her pictures. He respected her as a professional. But in this situation she was his client; a vulnerable individual, working through complex aversion issues. Under direction from his own counsellor, Luciano devised a step-by-step programme to help Agnes conquer her fear. There was something very touching, and both were aware of it, in seeing these titans of their profession working together in this way—starting with the photography of small familiar things, of the most intimate subjects.

Agnes had been able to bring with her into exile only a tiny, tragic, funny bundle of personal possessions. She had gathered it together in a race around her mother's house before the car called for her. The bundle was made up of the practical and the nostalgic: a few things which she thought would be useful or from which she could not bear to be parted.

Among them—and perhaps most precious—was Eric, her pocket-sized beanbag bear. Much and variably patched up, his legs and arms thinned to no more than a row of beans, his little ears torn and hanging off, his once-bright bead eyes worn dull, only the shadow of his felt mouth remaining: Eric was a survivor. He had parachuted out of upstairs windows and rafted down streams and been mauled by dogs and thrown at snakes and soaked through by equatorial downpours. Of late he had suffered hurtful rejection and had been living in the back of a cupboard, but somehow it seemed right to have him along on this adventure.

Another treasured item is a watercolour sketch of the suspension bridge over the river. It was painted by a friend from the upper balcony of the family house. It is the only image she had taken with her of home. Photographs of family and friends would have been easy to carry, but they would have been too heartbreaking a burden.

Instead, a simple spoon, useful in so many ways on the journey, served as a key into childhood memories. The memory today is of eating maize porridge in her grandma's kitchen, with all the other children, including the poorest street kids, whom her grandma invited in out of pity, in defiance of her daughter's—Agnes's mother's—disapproval. "After playing with them Agnes smells of the rubbish dump and I have to pick the lice out of her hair. She is learning their foul language and their thieving ways."

Agnes has had no contact with her mother since she fled; she has no idea if she is alive or dead. Agnes does not talk of it. To be honest, she was more respectful than fond of her mother. The two of them rowed continuously and bitterly. They were such different personalities. Agnes thinks for instance of her mother's fastidiousness about personal hygiene and how horrified she would have been to find out that her daughter had packed no knickers for her flight into exile. Of course, she had left the house wearing some, but otherwise she had just one spare pair—and they were not hers at all, but his, Jean-Paul's; and not strictly knickers, but a pair of baggy undershorts. They lacked all his grace and shape and manhood; and, having somehow turned up in her mother's house, they must have been boil-washed by the housemaid many times. In fact, it was a wonder they had not been thrown out or burnt! And yet by some alchemy they retained something of his smell. In her darkest and loneliest moments, when she was trying to sleep in those cold containers and sloshing depths, with people moaning all around her, she buried her nose deep in the musky comfort of his shorts.

How was it that Luciano could be allowed to share these secrets, to discuss them with her, and to assist her in their photographing? She asked herself these questions in his absence, and she was troubled. But in his presence, there was no question. He was so professional, so focussed. She trusted him utterly.

All that she had here—Eric, the sketch of the bridge, the old spoon, all the rest of it, so little, so pitiful, so cherished—had been carried to this country in a small sports holdall, celebrating an unremarkable Cup win by one of the more famous football clubs of this city; the sort of bag that is mass-produced abroad, not for the domestic fans, but for the poorer foreign hordes; and which ends up on street markets in African or Asian cities. She had no idea how she had come to choose it from among the hundreds of others on the stall. She had no connection to or affinity with this football club. The first time she had even thought about it was when, as she was driven in the immigration van from the airport holding centre to the House of Journalists, she noticed a vast bowl of white light in the night. She remarked on it to one of the guards. It was the home stadium of a famous football team, he told her: they were playing a big European game that night. Maybe she had heard of the team? She smiled, held up the bag, and then clutched it close. The guard, so hard-faced until then, smiled back.

It turned out to be Luciano's team; one of those coincidences that create a bond. Her favourite of all the early photographs was one of her sports bag, on the floor, in her room, with a few things, precious all of them, intimate some of them, spilling out. Luciano had taken the actual photograph. She was not ready. But the composition was hers, he insisted.

In a slightly later photograph he captured her with the bag in her arms, cradling it like a child, but laughing, enjoying the absurdity of her cherishment. And then, sometime later still, and after much gentle coaxing, he got her to hold the camera and to photograph him with the bag, wearing his club scarf, smiling and flashing a V for victory.

It is hard to imagine photographs more modest or unassuming. "Cheesy"—to use a new word we have learnt here. In any other context, they would be classed as mere snaps. Yet, in the mind of Julian, they were taken for a higher purpose, and so it is only right that they should be elevated to the status of art. The photographs were the main feature in the House of Journalists gallery until recently; they can now be found on the House of Journalists website; they've just gone out on a nationwide tour; and, yes, a book is planned.

So Luciano's work is done. Agnes would always be grateful to him for nursing the camera back into her hands, but now she must go it alone. And she must look beyond her own experience of flight and exile, and beyond the bounded world of the House of Journalists.

Hence the trip out today. She is not trying to make a point against the House of Journalists by going on it. The City Sisters have told her about these other centres, places of detention and removal, and now she wants to see one for herself. If she were questioned about it she would say that she was just "going to see what there was to see and to record it honestly." Honestly.

The House of Journalists would have respected that, of course. But had Julian known about Agnes's plan he would have had to point out that in fact she will get to see only what others want her to see—a partial record. And though she may be travelling with an open mind, that is certainly not the case with the City Sisters.

Still, that is something she will perhaps learn today.

| NO ONE CAN JUST DISAPPEAR FROM THE HOUSE OF JOURNALISTS

For the time being, Agnes's absence goes unnoticed by the staff. But soon enough it will be noticed and, if notably long—which, as it turns out, it will be—officially noted. As will her return. Fellows come and go, but records are kept. Daily records on every fellow. There are those who "move on" into a new life and with whom contact is maintained. Then there are those who are moved out and who are never talked of again. But they haven't just disappeared. No one can just disappear from the House of Journalists.

| ONE AMONG OUR NUMBER IS HAVING HIS HEARING AT THE TRIBUNAL

Today—now well under way—will be a day of waiting. The House of Journalists has its workshops and classes and seminars and visits. It is a place of great industry and endeavour, but also—and perhaps above all—of waiting.

One among our number is having his hearing at the tribunal today. We have wished our fellow well, perhaps given him some advice, or assured him that with the support of the House of Journalists he has nothing to worry about. But as he leaves us we all think of the times, mercifully infrequent but not unknown, when, having waited all day, we are informed that this particular fellow is not coming back.

The staff and volunteers are very practised in these circumstances. The departed fellow is now beyond their remit and their concern. It is us, the remaining fellows, they must be worried about. Such departures are always a blow to our morale, however. So if it can be arranged, another departure, of a fellow with confirmed status, out into the community, a flat, a job, a fresh start—a so-called "move-on"—is brought forward. But even these departures are unsettling for us, which they surely realise. Perhaps they think it is sensible to remind us that the House of Journalists is a place of transit for most of us? Only the select few are awarded lifetime fellowships. For the rest the journey must continue. Forward in the main; but in some cases back.

Still, the House of Journalists does its very best for all of us when we go—as we all must—before the tribunal. Every fellow is represented by an accredited advocate. The grounds for a claim will have been gone over, time and again, and the case will have been properly prepared. We are given every chance.

In the end, of course, our fate hangs on our story. But are we not master storytellers? And more than that: truth tellers. If our stories *are* true, then they will *ring* true. It is in this way—and only this way—that we will speak to the hearts and good sense of the members of the tribunal and gain our status. All we need to do is keep things simple and straightforward—remember what we have learnt at the House of Journalists about the power of the story simply told—and we will have little or nothing to worry about.

And that is true for most us.

We all notice, however, that it is not true for others—compatriots some of them, brothers and sisters of the same struggles, people we may have been imprisoned beside or escaped with, and who, to our ears, tell much the same stories. If we speak true, then why do they speak false? How is it that we touch, but they harden, hearts? What is this fellowship which protects us but rejects them? Why, when the time comes, do we say nothing in support of these others?

We stand apart from them, and they from us, on these tribunal days. That is just how it is. A fellow, maybe two, from the House of Journalists on one side, chatting with our advocate; a crowd of these others on the other side. They are bussed in from their detention centres, accompanied by private security guards. They are wearing their own clothes, they are not manacled or even herded, but they are obviously detainees. They flock and follow orders.

Some are clutching crumpled paperwork, but most are undocumented and all are confused, unprepared, and unrepresented. Duty interpreters will be assigned, if they really need one, and one proficient in their language is available, which is only sometimes the case—but then do they really need one?

When it comes to their turn before the tribunal, the procedure is described to them in two minutes flat by a bored official in the language of the court. We are warned by our representatives that the whole business will pass very quickly, but we should not be fooled: this is our one and only chance. It is not a preliminary hearing: this is it. These others have not been told this. They do not know what is going on, but assume that, at some stage, they will get a chance to state their cases in full. Their stories are long and complicated. This cannot be it. They have barely begun. Yet the hearing appears to be over already. They are not sure what happens next. They report back to their security guards. They get onto their buses. They do not protest.

––––––––

A tribunal is a three-person body, composed of lay members, men and women, alumni all of the "Exemplary Citizen" programme. They go through a three-day induction process and receive quarterly refresher training. They are paid a small stipend. Tribuneship is heavily promoted through official channels. It attracts a certain type from among the public-spirited. It is easy to mock them, to belittle or dismiss. But those who assume the honorific of tribune rise above the sneering. They have a difficult job. They get on with it. Their independence, if not obvious to their critics, is important to them. No one tells them what to do.

| HOW MANY TIMES HAVE WE HEARD THE SAME STORY?

How many times have we, the tribunes, heard the same story? Thousands and thousands of times; certain phrases appear and reappear: word for word—or as near as. We have heard this before, we say to ourselves. It makes us suspicious—and we don't want to be suspicious. We are by nature sympathetic. We arrive each morning as ready to believe and reprieve as to dismiss and deport. We are fair and judicious. We are swayed only by the weight of the evidence and the strength of the testimony. But we will not be had. If we feel we are being had, we come down hard. Very hard. We will not be taken for fools. And only a fool would hear the same story as often as we do and think that it was invariably true.

And yet there are all these lawyers, these advocates, these counsellors, these professionals, a whole industry of them, advising applicants on their stories. Well, let them. It is a free country. We do not allow them before our tribunal, of course. The applicants can speak for themselves.

Speak up, we tell them, we are waiting to hear what they have to say for themselves. They have nothing to fear if they are honest and truthful. We are ordinary citizens, concerned citizens, who have offered our services to the tribunal. We have open minds; we are without prejudice or agenda; we are of no party or faction. We file official reports, but we answer only to our own consciences.

The official country report in the case before us argues that beatings by the security police, although widespread and frequent, are low-level and do not amount to torture. And anyway, the wounds in this case look to us as if they have been self-inflicted, whatever MedAid says in its submission. We do not lightly disagree with the submissions of MedAid, which is an NGO made up of medical experts. Or, as they would say, an "independent NGO" made up of "independent medical experts." We do not doubt their expertise. And we do not question their independence—though we might ask, independent from *what* exactly? The government, certainly; this tribunal, unquestionably: but from the migrants' rights lobby, definitely not. We refer you to the home page of their website, which nails their colours with admirably clarity. So we give due weight to what they say—and in this case, we do not think it weighs heavily enough in the favour of their client.

We turn back to the official medical report. We are conscious that it too can be seen as partial. It is sad, but true, that so contested is this issue that the official view is regarded with outright suspicion by some. We do not take this stance, we hasten to add, but we treat the official view with some caution nonetheless. We weigh it against other views. It is an outright lie to suggest, as some do, that we are in the "pockets" of the government. And anyway, the official medical report before us in this case describes its investigation into the provenance of the injuries as "inconclusive." So it is up to us to decide: which is as it should be.

And as it happens, in this case, the case of X, we neither accept nor dismiss, but rather we recommend full review, until which time we grant X DLR (that is to say, exceptional discretionary leave to remain), revocable in the event of breach, with no recourse to public funds and the usual limits on study and work.

A full explanation can be found in the leaflet being handed to you by the clerk to the tribunal.

You are free to go.

X stands frozen before us.

Please escort Mr. X from the tribunal, he is free to go.

In the large, crowded anteroom of the tribunal, X is to be found looking for the security guards to conduct him to the bus. He is to be found searching for the others who came with him from the detention centre. He is to be found in some distress, having found no one he knows. Eventually, an employee of the building, a cleaner or a janitor or something, comes over to quieten him and to try to explain to him that he is free to go. It is all explained in the leaflet in his hand. The number here is the emergency accommodation hotline. He is free to call it if he has nowhere else to go.

In the large, emptying entrance hall of the tribunal, X is to be found looking for the pay phone.

| EVERY LUCKLESS AND RECKLESS BASTARD THAT EVER GAVE UP ON HIS OR HER COUNTRY

They come unto us, these hordes and masses, from every sovereign state, every breakaway region, every place of conflict and strife, every news story and sob story. They travel by air and sea, in sealed container and undercarriage, assisted, smuggled, trafficked, and on every sort of visa and travel document, faked, forged, and facsimile. They come from the north and the south, the east and the west. They are of all nations, ethnicities, persuasions, classes, and personality types.

They come from Goma on the banks of Lake Kivu and from the burning plains of northern Somalia that rise up into the mountains of Ogo. They are teachers, accountants, engineers, civil servants, hairdressers, and domestic servants from Avondale, Borrowdale, Mabelreign, Highfield, and Cotswold Hills. They come from the great tented camps of Southern Sudan and their tribes are the Dinka, Nuer, Bari, Lotuko, Zande, Mundari, Kakwa, Pojulu, Moru, Acholi, Madi, Lulubo, Lokoya, Toposa, Lango, Didinga, Murle, Anuak, Makaraka, Mundu, Jur Modo, Kaliko, and others.

They are former dwellers of the once-great cities of Mesopotamia, the land between the Tigris and the Euphrates. They are Marsh Arabs, Turkmen, and Kurds; they are Chaldeans and Assyrians. Mandaeans, Shabaks, and Yezidis also exist. They are of the heterogeneous diaspora of Iran. They are the hangers-on of the long-deposed imperial family, and the fallers-off from the long-discredited revolution. They are the short-lived liberals; the long-settled Christians, Jews, and Zoroastrians; they are the sassy young bloggers and insufficiently zealous old clerics; they are everyone and anyone who ever opposed or thought they opposed the current and former regimes. They are the lot of them.

From this ancient civilisation, and from others troubled by difference in orientation, come also transgender people who may identify as heterosexual, homosexual, bisexual, pansexual, polysexual, or asexual. We welcome all sorts, it seems.

Songwriters, performance poets, filmmakers, mime artists, cartoonists, hip-hop stars: opponents of dictatorships, magic and realist, Pinochet, Stroessner, Trujillo "The Goat," and the three-headed junta from the infamous School of the Americas: we have welcomed them too down the years; along with their trade unionists, human rights activists, civil liberties lawyers, opposition party leaders, and student presidents.

Once we let in the most celebrated dissidents of the Soviets; now it is the kleptocrats and the oligarchs of modern Russia but also the misfits and cast-offs of Armenia, Azerbaijan, Belarus, Estonia, Georgia, Kazakhstan, Kyrgyzstan, Latvia, Lithuania, Moldova, Tajikistan, Turkmenistan, Ukraine, and Uzbekistan. They journey to here from Saint Petersburg via Moscow, Vladimir, Nizhny Novgorod, Kirov, Perm, Yekaterinburg (or Sverdlovsk), Tyumen, Omsk on the Irtysh River, Novosibirsk on the Ob River, Krasnoyarsk, Tayshet, and Irkutsk. We get Mongols from Ulan-Ude, Jews from Birobidzhan, Manchurians and Koreans from Ussuriysk, and god knows who from Vladivostok. They are journeying too along the Silk Road, transiting from Schiphol and Frankfurt, and tunneling through from Sangatte.

We, the public, call you up, you shock jocks and phone-in hosts, to complain that while we are happy to welcome genuine refugees, we do not see why we should take in Somalis fleeing the social security system in Holland; or Togolese, Burkinabés, and Guinea-Bissauns, who prefer our bleak shores to the sun-kissed beaches of the Canaries or

Lampedusa; or every con man, abuser, chancer, and no-hoper; every luckless and reckless bastard that ever gave up on his or her country. Honestly, you could not make it up.

THE COMMITTEE IS SOVEREIGN OVER THE HOUSE OF JOURNALISTS

In the Boardroom the special meeting of the Committee is in session. Here is proof, for those of a cynical bent, that the much-mentioned Committee does exist. It does meet. It is not a fiction. It is not an invention of Julian's. It is not Julian. It has members other than him.

Though it is noted by all those who note these things that the number of members in attendance this morning is fewer even than the norm in recent months, during which attendance at the Committee has generally been thin. A number of members have of course left the Committee for various reasons and they have yet to be replaced. The question of replacements is a long-standing agenda item for the Committee. Pressing business means it has not yet been reached. And it will not be today.

The minutes of the meeting will record the attendees as:

Julian Snowman, Chair
Solomon Mongwe, House Manager (*ex officio*)
Stanley Stanislaus, Father of Chapel (*ex officio*)
Monsignor Humphrey Comfort

The minutes will also record that the meeting was deemed quorate by the Chair under extraordinary powers.

It will be a short meeting with just one item on the agenda: this communication from Crumb.

This communication from Crumb?

Yes, the Chair wanted to let the members of the Committee know that he had received the following message sent from an iPhone by Coombs, Jane (Janeconfidential.07@whizzmail.com), which reads in full:

```
Julian
    Felt one should express belated thanks for you
arranging visit other day. Trust did not land you in
too much shit. Thank AA for the ciggy. Has set me
thinking . . .
    Ted
```

And this Coombs, Jane is?

The Chair, with some impatience, explains that she is Jane Crumb née Coombs, third and much younger wife of Ted Crumb, and that her mobile was doubtless used because her husband refuses to have one, such devices being fundamentally the work of the devil, though on occasion, such as this, useful in their way for the dispatch of a message, particularly now that they've privatised the Royal Mail, closed all the post offices, and a stamp costs nine pounds fifty or whatever it is. Humphrey Comfort enjoys the Chair's mimicry of Ted Crumb, with whom—on this question at least—he is much in sympathy, as he must confess—though he does so with infuriating pride, the Chair notes to himself—that "these user names and tweeter handles are all Greek to me, Julian."

In fact Greek is actually not Greek at all to Humphrey, who is a noted classicist. The occupant of some minor honorific post in the local Catholic diocese, he is on the Committee because it was seen as politic by the founding board for the churches to have a representative. He has been that representative since the House of Journalists was set up and, though he is well over eighty now, has never apparently considered retiring. Or dying. That is unfair. True, he contributes almost nothing to Committee proceedings, but since when was that a disqualification for membership? (Julian is not above laughing at himself in these matters.) Of course Humphrey did once try to suggest that meetings should start with prayers. Julian had to invent a standing order to kill the idea, which, incredibly, attracted majority support, Humphrey—even more incredibly—having canvassed his fellow members assiduously. The standing order read: "In recognition of all faiths, and respect for their followers, the proceedings of the Committee of the House of Journalists will at all times be conducted in a strictly

secular manner." It has kept off—though this was not the intention—
representatives of other faith groups, which may or may not have been
a blessing. Humphrey took defeat in good part. He is a soft old stick
these days. One of those veteran campaigners for Leftist causes, he was a
hard-line Red in younger days, but is now tickled pink to be OBE or CBE
or whatever the BE he is in recognition of his work for charitable causes,
not least this one.

But we have strayed from the point.

The point is: the Chair felt it was important to bring this communication to the attention of the Committee at the earliest opportunity
so that a strategy for responding to it could be discussed. Who among
them cares to discuss it?

The Committee members are silent.

The Chair gives them a moment.

Thank AA for the ciggy?

The Chair explains, with even greater impatience, that AA is the
name of a fellow, ciggy is a diminutive for a cigarette, and that Crumb
and AA briefly smoked together out in the courtyard during Crumb's
visit.

The silence resumes. The Committee is not sure what it is to make
of this information.

If the members will allow, the Chair will give his own opinion on
the matter.

The members do allow it.

The Chair believes that this communication, though apparently
flippant in tone, is to be taken most seriously. He is sometimes accused
of being overprotective of the House of Journalists. The members present protest. No, the Chair knows it is so, and he makes no apology. He
would protect, by whatever means, this special place, even if that means
overprotecting. And in that spirit he sees no good coming from further
contact between Edward Crumb, a known provocateur and extremist,
and the House of Journalists, particularly if the fellow known as AA is
in any way concerned. To what end such contact would be put is a matter of conjecture, of course, but it is the opinion of the Chair that it
could furnish the writing of a book.

That is often the way of writers, Humphrey Comfort observes—he is chuckling again.

Quite so, the Chair responds drily: a novel, a novella, or even a short story about the House of Journalists, something that Crumb could dash off and rush out. A publicity coup, a piece of sensationalism: a hatchet job.

The members by their silence can be taken to agree.

The Chair should also report that he spoke this morning to AA and had from him an assurance that there had been no further contact with Crumb. Now the Chair has a rule, as members will know, that he takes every fellow at his word and so, for the time being, there is no reason to suppose that Crumb has advanced his plan through this stratagem.

This stratagem?

Using AA to pass on damaging secrets.

Damaging secrets?

Information about the House of Journalists which Crumb might choose to construe in a way that is damaging to it. That is perhaps a better way of putting it.

The Chair is a bit red in the face.

Of course, the Chair goes on, the fellows are not tagged and nor are they monitored twenty-four hours a day: they have their freedom and their privacy; they can come and go as they like, meet who they like, do what they like. Long before this episode, however, AA was arousing some suspicion. As members of the Committee know, identity is a difficult issue at the House of Journalists. Of necessity, fellows sometimes have to assume names and travel on false documents. A lot has to be taken on trust. But the question of who AA is, and where he comes from, and what are his intentions, has been a cause of some concern—to the Chair at least. It is important that the Committee should protect the integrity of the House of Journalists as a place of sanctuary for those who bear testimony out of suffering; who write and record what is most painful; who volunteer their stories. So if anyone is passing themselves off as someone they are not, well, that is a danger they have to guard against.

But the issue is Crumb, is it not?

The issue is Crumb, Humphrey, certainly it is. He has to be stopped.
No, not stopped. That is impossible. He can of course write what he likes.
It is a free country. In a free country, people can write what they like.
About anything—and that includes the House of Journalists. There are
Committee members, though none around this table, who have written
about the House of Journalists—and of course the fellows are encouraged to do so. But Crumb, as he had shown on his visit, does not respect
the spirit of the place; he does not accord it the respect and reverence
that everyone else accords it. A work about the House of Journalists—
like all his work these days—is certain to be nihilistic and destructive.
He would try to tear down this precious place of sanctuary, given half
a chance. So while he cannot be stopped, he has to be, well . . .

Dissuaded perhaps?

Yes, dissuaded perhaps is perhaps what he is trying to say, Humphrey. Because of course Crumb is perfectly free to write a story about
the House of Journalists. Any sort of story he likes. Though Crumb
should be warned that if he and his ally (and that's not to say AA is his
ally; that is certainly not proven) are intent on destroying the reputation of the House of Journalists they will find that the House of Journalists is ready to protect itself. For although the House of Journalists
is strong, any institution, however strong, needs to be protected against
those who would destroy it and all its good work, even if it and all its
good work can *not* be destroyed. The arguments are indeed complex.
The long and short of it, however, is that Ted Crumb needs to be
stopped—or if not stopped . . . dissuaded.

There is silence for a few moments.

Then—to the surprise of the Committee—he speaks rarely—and
never, as far as they can remember, to express a view contrary to that of
the Chair—it is surprising perhaps, given his background—his story of
speaking out—but then he is known to be worn out by struggle—to be
happy here—to want to give back to this place which has given him
sanctuary at the end of his life—Mr. Stanislaus speaks.

Is it in the power of the Committee to do that? Is it even in the interest of the House of Journalists to try?

Now, with the greatest of respect to the Father of Chapel, this is
disappointing, the Chair maintains. He can of course see the point

Mr. Stanislaus is making, but are they to be intimidated so easily? The Chair hazards that they are not. And by they, he means the Committee and the House of Journalists, which are anyway indivisible. So can he take it that they are agreed that action needs to be taken against Ted Crumb, and that no more discussion of this matter by them is needed?

Mr. Stanislaus?

Mr. Stanislaus nods sadly, reluctantly.

So it is decided. Now, how exactly Crumb is to be stopped will be determined at a later stage by the Chair. Pressure will be exerted, and feelers put out, and the frighteners put on. No, that is going too far. That is wrongly expressed. The Chair apologises to the Committee. He is under some strain this morning. One last time—anyone is free to write what they *like*! They are free to do so, just as we—the Committee of the House of Journalists—are free to use what power we have to stop, or at least dissuade them. And the Chair has of course contacts and he has of course influence. He would do what he could do. He would do what needed to be done. The matter could be left to the Chair. He trusts he has the confidence of the Committee in this matter? They know he always acts in their best interests. And he does not need to remind its members that the Committee is sovereign over the House of Journalists.

There is silence. It is taken as consent.

| EDSON. VANESSA. HOW ARE YOU THIS MORNING?

In one corner of the fellows' common room it is observed by a number of volunteers that the writing mentor, Vanessa Boothby, is deep in apparently anguished conversation with her mentee, Edson. And it is further observed that Edson appears to be comforting *her*; to be offering *her* support and encouragement. This is not how it is meant to be.

Edson himself is a very positive, optimistic, upbeat sort of character. He is charmingly dismissive only of his own talents. "I am, as you say, an 'ack. Do not make of me more than I am."

Well, that is very modest, and admirable in its way, but the House of Journalists begs to differ. Is there not poetry in reportage when it describes what Edson saw in that stadium? To bear witness to such suffering is of itself the act of a true artist. The true artist sees and tells the truth: there is no need for embellishment or artifice. To describe simply is enough; more than enough, if the experience is great.

So we—the staff and volunteers and other friends of the House of Journalists—wonder, that's all, if Edson, after all he has gone through, is able to judge the true purport of this writing? When we, on the other hand, can step back and see it in its proper frame.

Be that as it may, we—the staff and volunteers on duty today—observe that it can hardly be of help to Edson that he should be comforting Vanessa Boothby, his supposed mentor and support.

Advice on the matter is taken from a senior staff member and the advice is: be gentle, but break it up. A young female volunteer takes the lead.

She speaks for all of us.

"Edson. Vanessa. How are you this morning? We hope we are not interrupting you, but we just thought that Vanessa might like to hear about the guitar, Edson. We couldn't help observing that you do not have it with you, when over the last few days, since its delivery, you and your guitar have been almost inseparable. You may not know, Vanessa, that Edson expressed a desire to have a guitar again. The House of Journalists was more than happy to oblige. These are the little things that can make such a difference. They lift fellows out of themselves and give them renewed hope and spirit. And how nice to have some music about the place! There is nothing like it. We have had musicians here before, of course, and, as it turns out, we have among our number now a multi-percussionist and several accomplished singers. All of this we have discovered since Edson told us about the guitar. Perhaps he has not told you, but his guitar was a great comfort to him during the more difficult times in his country? Oh, he has: you two are so close! So you will know that he even formed a small band while in prison. But he was separated from his guitar in the later years and did not have it with him when he went into exile. Now he is forming a little group here, to play the folk tunes and protest songs of his continent, as well as songs from other parts of the world. He has been refamiliarising himself with his instrument, relearning the chords. It is all coming back to him, isn't it, Edson? Many of the songs are sad songs, we are told. But you wouldn't know it. There is a light shining in Edson's eyes as he plays and sings. Would you mind fetching your guitar and playing us something, Edson?"

This young girl just wanders over, interrupts a private conversation, and spouts this patronising, infantilising waffle, and Edson—as ever—is all smiling tolerance. And now he has gone off, as instructed, to get his guitar, leaving her, Vanessa, with the girl, who, when Edson returns, may pay for her impertinence by having the guitar smashed over her head, leaving her fretfully necklaced with splintered wood and twanged strings and broken fret board and dangling headstock, and looking out through a now-enlarged rosette, as Edson looks on dumbfounded, song mute, protest silenced.

Vanessa is shocked back into the moment by this girl touching her arm.

"Vanessa? Are you all right? It is just that we—the other volunteers—observed that you appeared to be in some distress. They—the fellows, that is—do off-load on us. We are the shoulder. We are the rock."

The girl—like so many of the volunteers here—can be no more than twenty-five, and possibly eighteen. She has such confidence, such certainty. But she has time on her side. For now she can serve and sacrifice. Her time will come. She will publish. They all publish. It is their destiny.

"You must off-load too, Vanessa. The House of Journalists is all about sharing. The relationship between mentor and fellow is necessarily close, but should not tip over into intimacy and secrecy. Mentors and fellows do not own each other. Stories that fellows tell only one another or their mentors corrode the open and honest spirit of the place. Better that we all hear them and make a collective judgement about how they should be handled. What we hear here is precious and can also be dangerous."

Vanessa just about contains her temper. This girl gets all this stuff from the handbook for volunteers and mentors. It is for her, as it is all the young postulants who take orders here, holy writ. They all swear by it, and live by it. And yet, Julian would have them believe they can go out into their own lives and think for themselves and write for themselves. Do they not see? Do they not understand?

But she is too tired to resist or stand up. She sits in her seat, in a quiet corner, not hidden—nowhere in the House of Journalists is hidden—but quiet, waiting for Edson to return with his guitar, which she will not smash over the head of this young girl, because she doesn't have the energy—or the guts. And anyway there is another part—the better part—of her which of course is cheered to hear that Edson has rediscovered his love for his guitar.

And now he has returned and has started to twang away agreeably enough, and a small group soon gathers around them: Edson; the young volunteer clapping her hands and whooping, yes, whooping! (did she mention that the volunteer is an American?); and her, Vanessa Boothby, foolishly, miserably, abjectly clapping along too, not quite in time. And there are fellows among the small group that encircles them who sing and dance and play things—one pounds out the rhythm on an upturned empty plastic water cooler drum; another crashes a tin tray against his knee, thigh, palm, and forehead with dizzying enthusiasm.

Spontaneous music making; fun and laughter; but also songs of protest; singing out for justice; all at twelve-thirty in the afternoon: Where else? Where else but the House of Journalists! Are we not privileged to be a small part of this joyous reaffirmation of the human spirit? A number of other volunteers and members of staff have joined us now. Does it not demand that we re-evaluate our own petty concerns? Must we not be reborn into something much bigger than ourselves? Julian has joined us. He has come out of the Boardroom to join the party. He dances, he sings, he jams, he scats: he takes centre stage. Only when he is exhausted is it all allowed to stop.

"Lunch!" he cries. And lunch it is.

| MR. STAN IS NOT HIMSELF

Mr. Stan is seen to pass by, to observe the scene. Normally he would take a special delight in it. He smiles when he is spotted, but we all note that Mr. Stan is not himself. The tortoise head is sunken into its shell. He is slump humped in his chair. He looks downcast, careworn; a little out of love with the place.

He is thinking about events at the Committee. He used so to love the Committee, its privileges and proceedings, which he reported back, with due reverence, to the Chapel, which in turn listened and approved. Now some fellows openly criticise; some make mock; some affect disdain. Aggravated by these attitudes, Mr. Stan points out with untypical force that he is *elected* from the fellowship to his pre-eminence in the Chapel and thus his membership of the Committee. The fact that for the last few terms he has been unopposed should not diminish his authority or his mandate. But there are some fellows, not ready to challenge his leadership through democratic processes, who nonetheless grumble about it. It is ever thus, in any system, under any leadership, Julian has reminded Mr. Stan. Mr. Stan has often reflected on the justice of this remark, but has drawn less comfort from it in recent days.

The Committee is frankly not what it was. As well as the fact that fewer and fewer members attend and a number have left altogether and not been replaced, those who do attend all disperse quickly after the formal business. There is no opportunity—or at least, no appetite—as there used to be, to discuss matters on the fringes, in small groups, out of the Chair's hearing. Today he would have welcomed such a discussion: just to see if the others—few as they were—share his anxieties. He suspects some do.

It is obvious that the dominance of the Chair over the Committee has increased to a worrying extent. The Chair—that is to say, Julian: let's be straightforward about this; let's not be afraid to make it personal—is at times an overweening, overbearing, even intimidating,

presence. The constitution, the conventions, the powers, the preroga-
tives, the privileges, and the courtesies of the Committee have not
changed. Julian likes to remind members of that. Members are invited
to ask questions, to raise points, to make objections, to voice disquiet,
to vote as they see fit, if a vote is called for and is constitutional. But the
point is—and Julian doesn't seem to appreciate this point—that they
are invited to do so by *him*. For members to avail themselves of all their
entitlements as members they must go through *him*. *He* dominates the
Committee and drives all its processes at all times.

Of course the members, few as they are, could stand up to him.
They have that right, that option, perhaps that duty. But the fact is they
don't stand up to him. Until recently he, Mr. Stan, was among that passive number. He was happy, after discussion, to bow to Julian's experience and judgement. He was happy to fall in line behind the decision of
the Committee even though that decision was invariably congruent in
all its particulars with the prior will and sentiment of the Chair.

Take the decision to try to obstruct or frustrate or in some way de-
lay publication of a book by Edward Crumb denigrating the work of
the House of Journalists. He, Mr. Stan, *agrees* with that decision. The
Committee's agreement to sanction Julian to make every endeavour to
bring about this outcome is not just defensible, it is laudable. Has not
the whole House been introduced to this Crumb character? Is it likely
that Mr. Crumb is looking to use the cherished freedoms of this country to do good by the House of Journalists, to advance even his own
purported cause, to promote anything other than his own wretched
notoriety? And yet—and here is the nub of his, Mr. Stan's, concern—
there is the decision and then there is *the process* by which a decision is
decided upon.

The distinction is a most important one. If that is not understood—
and if we will allow him, the point is born of the bitterest of experience—
then from democracy to tyranny, from freedom to oppression, is but a
small step.

All the while the impromptu music has been continuing, and Mr. Stan
has been tapping his feet on the metal footrests of his chair in an ar-

rhythmic, innately unmusical, unmistakably journalistic, QWERTY clatter. Now the music ends. Whether there are eyes on him or not, he makes a point of joining in the applause. Or rather, he makes a dumb show of the *action* of applause. His stumps come together but they make no sound. In this way—there were others—his enemies silenced him.

He was, he recalls (we are now recollecting with him), a vigorous applauder at the political meetings and musical evenings which made up so much of his life on his home island. There was a great sense of liberation in it. Mother had taught him as a boy to applaud in a refined, delicate way: so anxious was she to spare his precious hands. And anyway, it was vulgar to "thunder clap," as she put it. It went without saying that she disapproved of any catcalling and hollering; any "jungle" noises. Even a cut-glass "bravo" was, she felt, an "Italianate flourish," and she had little time for the Latin nations.

Mr. Stan has travelled back in his mind (we are there with him) to the Saturday afternoon classical series in the Kingsbridge Assembly Rooms. Mother always booked for the season, making numerous little sacrifices so that she could afford the tickets, which were expensive for a native widow.

(Mr. Stan's father, a man of delicate health throughout his life, died when Little Stan was still a baby. Mother did not speak of him, and so Stanley growing up knew nothing of him. He had been a minor civil servant and had made no mark on the world. Mr. Stan very vaguely recalls a thin face, thick glasses, the smell of cigarette smoke and some sort of rot on the breath. He, Little Stan, is lying in his crib; the man bending over him is cooing self-consciously and waggling a little finger. Mother's voice calls out that the infant should not be disturbed. Father and son exchange a look. Then the dying man walks out of his life.)

Mother always wore a hat and gloves for the afternoon classical series. The gloves, though of thin material (it was sweltering in the hall), helped to mute her occasional lapses into enthusiasm. (It is with both sadness and a smile that Mr. Stan recalls his mother's genuine love of light classical music and the tight rein which she imposed on displaying this love, as indeed on all displays of love.)

Walking hand in hand with his mother on a Saturday afternoon, wearing his school uniform, on his way to the assembly rooms to listen to classical music, he attracted much ridicule and scorn from his "raga-muffin" classmates. "Ignore it, Stanley; rise above it." It was always a relief to reach the hall, where apart from one little girl, who was terrified of him, there were no children. Adults were much more understanding. More especially, white adults. They were drawn, not repelled; they pitied and petted. What a perfect object he was for the charitable instinct they liked to show towards the native population when they were given the chance. He was expected to be grateful for these acts of kindness. "Stanley, do thank these very kind people." And he did (just as he did now, here, in another place which was alien and at times oppressive, but which offered refuge from the cruelty of his own world).

Then one season a sensation took place when a native boy, younger than Little Stan, a child from his neighbourhood, made his debut at the assembly rooms playing Chopin. The boy had been discovered by the head of music at the Hindu Grammar School (though he was not yet of an age to attend) and been taken up by her friend, the governor's wife. Mother admired both women greatly but was very uncomfortable with the exceptional preferment they showed to the boy. She regarded all her fellow islanders—aunties, cousins, preferred neighbours among them, "good people, God-fearing people"—as essentially and irredeemably uncultured. Her superior sense of herself was built upon an exquisite feeling for the inferiority of all others of her race. She was a notch above, but she knew her place. She showed due respect to her rulers and betters, but she didn't care to see her own people mocked. Nobody was elevated in her mind by the spectacle of a "performing monkey"—her descriptor for a boy she had known scratching around in a dirt yard in raggedy shorts and with scabby knees.

Her lack of enthusiasm for the boy's debut was not shared, however. Most notably, *The Gleaner*—Mr. Stan's paper in later years—hailed the concert as "the birth of a prodigy." A public subscription was raised to send "the little brown Mozart" to music college in the mother country. He was waved off from the dockside by a large crowd. Newsreel footage captured the moment.

He returned quietly around a decade later, years after quitting the college of music. There were no crowds at the airstrip to greet him. No cameras. But there was a brief mention in *The Gleaner*, hinting at the

disappointment of hopes, but with the immediate reason for his return—a sexual scandal—stripped out on the orders of the censor. Despite official fastidiousness (which she welcomed of course), Mother
fastened on this snippet and intuited scandal of some sort. She did
not care to know the details, but was pleased to be vindicated. "No good
would come of it, did I not tell you so?" she said. It was a mercy perhaps that the head of music at the Hindu Grammar School and the governor's wife had died in the meantime—though both in truth (Mother
did not care to know this either) had been more broad-minded than
their public personas suggested and would probably have found the
slim, elegant, and handsome young man who returned home—much
changed, somewhat shaken by events, but with plenty gained from his
time away—most attractive. Most women did.

True, his assumed classical abilities had been exposed in the stone-
cold rehearsal rooms of the college. His was a freakish talent, no doubt
about it, but the college was a place of serious musicianship. It was clear
to him and his tutors that he would never make it as a concert soloist or
chamber musician. But the city—this city—had many other outlets for
pianistic gifts, and it was in its dark, smoky, underground spaces, at a
time when black and white mingling still had the thrill of the clandes-
tine and decadent, that he discovered a true talent for jazz. He also developed an appetite for drink and for women, which in combination
led to an injudicious liaison with the daughter of a baronet, a sexual
assault charge (possibly trumped up), a brief spell in prison, and subse-
quent deportation.

Thus the boy prodigy's return to the island, though largely unnoticed by the public, was a source of some fascination for the handful of
people who knew the full details. Mr. Stan was one. It was he who wrote
the news item which the censor bowdlerised and Mother nonetheless
spotted. Subsequently he kept an eye out and an ear open for any news
of the intriguing returnee. When, after a few weeks, a tiny backstreet
club gig was arranged, Mr. Stan was in the audience, and a few hours
later, he scuttled back to the office, soaked in sweat and hyperventilat-
ing with excitement, to dash off a wildly enthusiastic notice which the
editor, after much persuasion and at some risk, printed.

So it was that Mr. Stan could lay a little claim to helping the musician to start up again. But of course he had never expected him to become the legendary "Piano Man," the island's only superstar, who penned the hot, smoky, snake-hipped soundtrack of its independence. (And it is astonishing to him that this music is now fashionable among the young here, in this country. He found that out when a House of Journalists volunteer who had heard of Mr. Stan's connection brought in a CD for Mr. Stan to play on his machine. He hadn't heard the music for years, but just a few chords evoked those heady days on the island with such power that Mr. Stan struggled to contain his emotions. He is now often to be seen in his special chair, with his headphones on, tapping out the rhythms with his stumps, mangling those rhythms in the process, and smiling through a mist of tears at the memories.)

"Mr. Stan knew 'Piano Man'!" Agnes cried out when she first heard the story. "He was there through it all: bumping and grinding to freedom's soundtrack. Deep respect, Mr. Stan."

Mr. Stan was of course delighted by Agnes's reaction, but he was at pains not to claim great personal acquaintance with Piano Man. He had heard him play many times—but many thousands had; he was a regular guest up at the house in the hills—but the parties were famously large. The two had been most intimate—the most hideous intimacy—in gaol together, where Piano Man, already weakened by liver disease, succumbed to the dysentery which swept through those foul dungeons. He was a most pathetic figure in those last days. He reached out to other inmates but Mr. Stan alone grasped the pianist's hands as he decomposed on his shit-soaked pallet. It was almost the last act he (Mr. Stan) performed with his old hands, his good hands, before they were smashed with hammers.

The symbolism was obvious to him at the time. Hands put to the piano clumsily and in vain held hands which had danced across the keys with such insouciant elegance. Hands thrown at the typewriter through years of struggle held hands which, it was alleged (no doubt absurdly), had accepted money from foreign powers in exchange for information on government ministers. Hands still strong (though soon to be ignominiously stumped) held hands that were clammy, clawing, clinging, for dear, sweet life; dear and sweet even as it drained away, stinking, miserable, wretched—such can be the fear of death in a man not ready.

But all this talk of death is not the way to remember the Piano Man! He was a man who loved life. And the young volunteers and interns want to hear stories of the clubs and the parties.

"He was a great one for the ladies, who all loved him. In the white spots of the Trocadero or the Lux Ballroom, in an immaculate white tux, he cut an impossible sophisticate. We were supposed Marxists, revolutionaries, throwing off the colonial yolk. But we loved to dance and in truth we danced to their tunes. Your tunes, that is! For, though he weaved in island beats, the music was essentially of the mother country, your country, a country he loved in many ways—as I do—despite its treatment of him. He often said his happiest days of all were here in this very city, when he discovered its version of jazz and developed his own style. He would have been so thrilled to find that his music is now so popular here among the young.

"He was never a spy. That was tosh. Another trumped-up charge from the regime which feared everyone who didn't conform absolutely. He was dying anyway, but they killed him because they could. Tyrants are the most contemptible cowards and bullies. They are fools too. His death in their hellish prison did them a lot of damage among the ordinary people. They loved the Piano Man because he was a popular symbol of what they came to remember as the good old days.

"Such great days. Dancing until dawn!" Yes, Mr. Stan a dance band man! Who would have thought it? Mother was horrified when she first found out. But he was an adult. He did his own thing, however much she might protest. "I will be back late, Mother. There is absolutely no need to wait up, or to worry." The dance hall always came at the end of a long day at the paper and many meetings.

Of course, his crippled state meant any actual dancing at the Troc or Lux was out of the question. But at the end of the jazziest numbers, he whooped and hollered louder than anyone; he stamped his feet harder (built-up shoes helped with that); and he applauded wildly above his head with those still-elegant hands of his. In those days, he affected a black-tie, slicked-back nattiness and smoked long elegant cigarettes. They all did, of course: it was the style, as unlikely as it now seems, of the young liberationists. The island was always a decade or more behind the fashions and trends of the mother country.

In his dinner jacket, albeit in a mismatch with rough grey trousers and the clunky built-up shoes, he cut, he thought, a figure, if not a dash. And he used to brilliantine his hair—what there was of it. And for a time, he wore dark glasses, day and night, until he was once too often helped across the road after being taken for a blind man. (Was it some confusion about the sticks, perhaps? He could laugh about it even then.)

It was in those smoky dives that a young Mr. Stan joined those plotting independence. Between the sets they sat in back booths, debating and discussing, setting the course. These were exhilarating times. Mr. Stan was admired for his intellect, his writing, and his commitment to the cause of freedom. In these circles, no one cared about, no one commented on or mocked his infirmities. Free of cruelty, free of charity. Great days indeed!

He came home to Mother less and less. When the last of the late nights closed, he was to be seen pivoting his way through the shut-eye streets, in the grey-pink foetal dawn, past mangy piles of whimpering dogs, past curled-up street kids rendered angelic by sleep, past doorway derelicts slumped in their slobber. He slept in his chair at the paper. The discomfort mattered little to him; sleep was a crippling business at the best of times. His comrades marvelled at his stamina. He seemed to survive on coffee, cigarettes, and cheap whisky.

Oh, he romanticises, no doubt. These were his ascendant years, in the twilight of colonialism and the honeymoon of independence. Stanley Stanislaus became in turn the chief reporter, a columnist and leader writer, and finally editor of *The Gleaner*. He moved in elite circles, but retained the common touch. He was high-minded in his opinions, but was popular with everyday readers. He earned a reputation (somewhat exaggerated) for fearlessness and independence of view during the last days of the colony. He carried that into the early years of self-rule when he was (with a few misgivings) a strong supporter of the government. Sometimes he spoke out, of course, but he had, as it were, a licence to do so. He was regarded (rightly) as a loyalist.

He carried that reputation into the darker days too. He was allowed to report and even condemn the ever-growing instances of oppression. Officers of the state were, he lamented, guilty of overzealousness at the very least. He was sure that they were operating without ministerial sanction, but even so their actions besmirched the good name of the government and undermined the good work it was doing. Or had planned. The silence from the ministers disturbed him, he admitted that freely, and that was why he would not let these questions rest. But he spoke out because he *supported* the government, not because he opposed it.

That was his line. And the regime let him run with it. Other journalists, with less of a pedigree and fewer connections, were silenced for criticisms far more coded. He tried to save these colleagues—but only by advising them to stay silent. Once they had spoken, there was nothing he could do to save them. Indeed he had at that point to think of his own position. So he argued that these journalists, whatever their motivation, played into the hands of foreign enemies and subversive elements, and therefore could be seen as traitors to the greater cause. He regretted the rigour, even relish, with which the full severity of the state was wielded in these instances. But he understood why action was necessary.

He was always open with his readers that some terrible things were being done in the *name* of this government. Senior ministers needed to do more to ensure that human rights were respected and the rule of law upheld. The extrajudicial killings had to stop. The trust that most people still reposed in the leadership of the country was being sorely tried. He was distressed that these men and women, whom he had known for a long time and still respected, were not more disposed to listen to advice that he assured them was helpfully meant. It pained him genuinely to find himself in the position of critic of this government when he had been among those who had fought so hard for it to come to power. However, the situation was now becoming intolerable. He told this to old comrades on the Committee for Democratic Reform bluntly. If things continued in this way, they would be betraying all that the party and the movement had stood for—and against. And he spoke up in this way because the failings of the regime were indeed terrible but the alternative was worse: anarchy, overthrow, foreign intervention.

He *begged* the government, which contained many old friends, to see the folly of their ways and to pull back from the brink.

And so it went on until finally they had had enough of his pathetic bleating. They were not alone. *He* had had enough too. The official charge was involvement in subversive activities. What a joke! And yet what a relief too. He was no threat to them of course—their grip on power was stronger than ever, the opposition movement was weak and divided and on the run, the public were cowed and docile—but his constant carping was irritating, and they could put a stop to it, so they might as well. He played his part. He refused to give up the information he didn't possess or betray the conspirators he didn't know. He submitted himself passively to the sleep deprivation, the beatings, and the electric shocks. It was a scourging for his naïvety and blind loyalty. And in the end, what need did he have for his precious hands? A torrent of words had been hammered out of that damned typewriter to no end.

Mr. Stan emerges from this bitter reverie, with a jolt, to find a young volunteer, forking food into his mouth. He chews and swallows. He has not lost his appetite, even though he has not been feeling one hundred per cent in recent days. The doctor examined him the day before and found nothing wrong—nothing at least beyond all the ills, aches, and afflictions, ancient and chronic. His medication is before him, laid out on the plastic tray that they attach to his chair. Round white tablets of chalky appearance; others, white also, but pep-pill-sized and of smooth gloss coating. There is one shaped like payload: heavy ordnance to be dropped only on a full stomach. Another is cough-medicine-pink; the bitter pink of unloving spoonful. The last is a translucent red capsule, bursting with little glittering red and white atoms. One might imagine it fizzing open in the gut and dispensing magical relief. In reality, there is no relief from the condition of being Mr. Stan. He has learnt to live with pain and humiliation. He opens wide, he chews and he swallows, and he doesn't feel any better or worse. He doesn't complain. He has been sickened by all that loyalty and idealism have inflicted on him over the years. Here at the House of Journalists, he had at first recovered some of his enthusiasm for comradeship and belonging. And then, as he settled in, he rediscovered his disposition towards loyalty and idealism too. But now, again, there is the same sickening. The doctor has not picked it up. Mr. Stan has disguised it from him, perhaps. The doctor is a House of Journalists man who reveres Mr. Stan for his remarkable fortitude and optimism. Mr. Stan is indestructible. He is the true embodiment of the spirit of this place.

Suddenly, there is a slight commotion in the refectory. Mr. Stan looks up; and his volunteer feeder looks round. They see what is happening and their eyes brighten. The waiting is over: Matthew, the fellow who left for his hearing at the tribunal this morning, has returned. Mr. Stan says a little prayer, as he always does at these times. The House of Journalists has protected its own. Whatever else concerns him, that is to be welcomed, greatly welcomed.

| STILL SOME LIFE IN OLD CRUMB

Standing outside The Cock, waiting for the landlord Bob to open up, even though it is not long after eleven; Jane's words—"a bit early even for you"—ringing in one's head when the last thing one needs is any more ringing in that thin tin bell tower, which tolls one-too-many, two-too-many, three-too-many—and which can only be dampened by more of the same, fighting firewater with firewater, a prescription the wisdom of which Jane, who always knows her limit—she counts the units for fuck's sake!—will never appreciate. Good to have her back home though. Have missed her these last couple of nights. Sometimes one finds oneself rattling around something horrible in the old stately. And never more, and never worse, than the other night.

Point of one's visit to the House of Journalists was of course to emerge with plenty of shit to stir. One imagined one would be railing and spewing forth in letters to the press, in various polemics, tracts, ventilations, and *bruto fulmina*, and, yes, in one's great late fuck-the-lot-of-you deflowering of poetry and prose. One expected one would be turning the air sulphurous with satanic industry; the poison pen would be belching out toxic fumes. But guess what? Well, you are reading it here first—the visit to the House of Journalists has thrown one off one's stride and spirit. It has disturbed and perturbed old Crumb.

When one got back to the old stately the other night, one hit the single-malt hard. (Hard as last night.) Could taste the peat and barrel in its fire-and-water tones as one stood warming oneself in the inglenook in the dark maple and red leather of the study of one's black-beamed, cripple-backed, weathered old redbrick Jacobean pile (cosy ghost story and some suggestion that a royal once slept here) as the cosy rain, the cosy outside-the-leaded-window-licked-by-the-toasty-fire rain, transformed from glistening droplets into dancing snowflakes before one's eyes—ah, a little miracle of nature!—to fall softly on the early daffodils in one's high-walled five acres, and to settle on one's long drive, and to second-fleece the sheep that one keeps to keep down the grass of one's high-walled five acres. And this same soft snowfall was, in one's cosy imagining, settling on the green-grey headstones aslant in the hummocky churchyard of the flint-stone and squat-tower church, beyond which are the cosy lights of the black-beamed, cripple-backed, whitewashed, and thatched village pub, The Cock aforementioned.

Ah, yes, The Cock, unlocked, is the heart and soul of the village, though there is still no sign of Bob opening up. And as a result, one is standing here on his hearthstone, and starting to attract greetings and even attempts at conversation from neighbours and friends. Or, to be precise: from Jane's neighbours and friends. One doesn't keep this company. One isn't part of the "community." One doesn't do village. The Cock is the limit of village, as far as one is concerned. One does The Cock because it's a walk and it's a pub, and a pub is a place to drink, and after a few one does admittedly mellow, and one can enjoy a chat with the locals or a game of darts or dominoes or even, at a push, a game of shove. But then again, if one wants to be left alone, one is left alone. With one's pint, or one's single malt.

It hit the spot, that first nice single the other night. One melted right into it, and bathing in its golden depths one pondered, as one tends to, the possibility of a fat Cuban. The problem was that a fat Cuban meant one going out onto the South Terrace. Prohibited indoors by law it is, a fat Cuban is; and now by the house rules too. That is the deal with Jane. "Kill yourself by all means, but I'm not joining a suicide pact." Darling Jane, the third and final; the posh totty to end all posh totty. "Passive smoking is balls, and you know it," one tells her. But one doesn't have them—the balls, that is—to defy her. Even in her absence. Up in town for a couple of nights, she was. Really should have thought about that when one decided to come home after the visit to the House of Journalists, because one knew it was going to knock the stuffing out of one, whatever one's hardcase persona. The thinking was that the old home fires would warm one nicely after the chill of the day. But one hadn't expected one thing.

One was braced for all the horror stories, all the human exhibits. That was what one expected, and that was what one got. They held one's hand and led one along a veritable Via Dolorosa of human suffering and misery. And in that spirit one did one's bit to go along with the whole shebang—full of praise one was for the brave brothers and sisters. One can hardly blame them after all for the shameless charade they are party to. They know which side their claims are buttered. They are not going to trash this one little beauty spot when the rest of the system is a giant shit hole. They sing the praises of the place and ring out their great tales and testimonies. But Jesus, it's a bleak and lonely business, this exile. One hears a lot of idle talk that these guys have tasted epic experience; that any writer would envy them that. Well, Crumb, for all his fighting talk, wouldn't swap places for a minute. They have got one wrong if they think that. Maybe one needed a humbling at the HoJ to bring it home, but home it came with a fucking great thwack. And the aching echoing bottomless misery of it tore most acutely at one's soul when, with Snowman diverted, one gave his sidekick the slip and stumbled on this one fellow who was out in the courtyard, smoking. VIP visit, minister in attendance, Julian all aflutter with it: it is a very cool customer who takes a fag break while this lot is in full sail. Struck Crumb most considerably, one must say.

Could one cadge a ciggy, one said first to this fellow in the courtyard. Gasping for one, but didn't bring any along because didn't think there'd be the opportunity, one told him. Health fascists have damn near made it punishable by death anyway.

Said fellow—and sad fellow too, now one thinks of it—assessed one with a cool eye—how much he understood, fuck knows—then wordlessly tapped out one of those long thin gold-banded lady jobs. Slightly threw one, that. Slightly off-centre, one thought. But then the first puff on the poof stick had one reeling back. Plenty of cancer in it; plenty of tar and nico; none of your unleaded nonsense: this really ripped the paint off the lungs.

Crumb, one said, introducing oneself—and transferred the lethal smoke to the left hand so that one could offer up the right. The fellow eyed one again, but then reciprocated. Quite a firm hand it was—and a palpable relief after some of the wet ones one had handled earlier. Some tragically sad broken fuckers among the fellowship, sadly: one was wringing the tears from one's fist after more than one introduction. Not this one, however. *Not crushed*, one thought, *not crushed at all*. Indeed one was of a mind for a moment that here was a hard case, a tough nut. So—tightened one's grip. Put the squeeze on. One rather relishes turning the thumbscrews when the situation demands. (You may have heard that?) Well, he hung in there. The cool eye was a little watery, the chin a little wobbly—but he hung in there. One final twist and then: release.

Sorry, I missed your name?

AA, the fellow says, rather reluctant to give it up, one felt.

AA?

Yes, AA.

Another thing one doesn't care for. AA? What's all that about? Dread shades of Firedoor Dost, Franz K, and Vlad Nab. Their irritating P-s and Q-s. One can't abide this pseudonymous shit; this nom de plumage; this almost nameless air of mystery. One was born Ted Crumb, one writes as Ted Crumb, and one will die as Ted Crumb. They could strap one down and do their worst and one would hold firm to Ted Crumb. One wouldn't, if you will, *Crumble*.

And yet none of this macho posturing, none of this alpha male wordplay, none of this ponderous punning, was easing the great loneliness and emptiness one felt in the company of this AA character—or in contemplating it thereafter. Every writer is in exile in some way, they say—a stranger in his own land. The writer always stands outside and looks in; he can never belong or be part. One felt the trite tyranny of this tripe trope, standing smoking with AA.

Writing was never going to fill that void; writing is only ever a papering over. One has learnt that lesson over a lifetime in which one has spent a lifetime doing the one thing one can: writing. And yet, standing smoking with this AA character, one felt moved to *help*. Yes, the utter fucking treachery of the thought, you are thinking. Not another writer attaching himself to the House of Journalists to leech off the place. Not another bloodsucker.

(You know a good trick, by the way? Burn the bastards off with a cigarette. They hate that—most of them.)

Look, it was a little shudder deep in the soul, if you will. There was this sad and lonely character adrift, and one was moved to a moment of solidarity. Give one a break! The last thing old Crumb is interested in is other writers. Everyone knows it. One doesn't do acolytes or disciples. There's no taking under one's wing or encouraging in any way at Crumb corner. A lonely business, writing; that's as it should be. Nothing communal about it. Courses, workshops, and weekends? Hate all that. Curses, wankshops, and dead ends. And yet, that notwithstanding, one is besieged by young writers. Big part of the reason one moved out here to the cunt tree, to the old stately. To escape the hordes.

But this AA was not a young writer. Tired and worn out, he looked. Fucking knackered. Spent. Word-dry. Blocked. Seen many a writer like that over here, over the years. But then if there is one bit of magic the House of Journalists can perhaps work, it is to give a fellow a fresh start, a blank sheet, a new leaf—all the old clichés. Maybe there is something to envy in that. Though as one was thinking all this, this AA character was looking anything but restored and rejuvenated by the power of the legendary fellowship. He'd come looking for it perhaps, but it was nothing doing at that moment.

It was at this point that Julian and his henchmen caught up with us.

There you are! (All smiles.) Thought we'd lost you. (All smiles again.) Out here all the time. (All smiles again and again.) Having a cigarette with one of the fellows. (Smiles that could cheerfully strangle the lot of us.) Muggins. AA. Chief sidekick. This last one—Solomon something or other—looked fucking brown-trousered with fear. Terrifying to see.

Then Jules softened it a bit—for one's benefit, one supposed. The ashtray one was to note was by the sculptor Hepzibah Fantoni. One was to note that one was stubbing one's lady fag out on a work of art by Hepzibah fucking Fantoni. One couldn't make it up, could one? And meanwhile AA had slipped away.

But, to get back to the main point (Bob, by the way, *dying of fucking thirst out here*, if you wouldn't mind): the one thing one wasn't expecting, if truth be told, was for it to hit *home*, to shiver the stately timbers, to extend its icy grip over his little island of roaring fires and leaded windows, of hummocky churchyards full of daffs, of the cosy promise of country pubs, and even—extending to old stamping grounds—the squares and town houses of Bloomsbury and Primrose Hill, Soho clubs and pubs, caffs and boozers out East, the old terrace with the brick shithouse out back (a fucking caricature, one did warn you). Yes, one rails against the dark forces, one storms and hates, one cries down destruction and revolution, but even during the darkest hours, the world wars, the Cold War, the postmillennial spasm, the War on Terror, one felt, essentially, deep down, *safe*. A thousand years of safe. But the visit to the House of Journalists had shuddered all that—and so on that first night one found one was shivering in one's cosy stately. Shivering for England.

Yes, the situation didn't just call for, it *demanded* a fat Cuban. And one was not going outside. For pity's sake, it was Stygian out there on that first night back; it was swirling with ghouls and spectres. "Sorry, Jane, darling," one shaped the excuse to suit. "But the fact is one was fucking *scared*."

And that was the low point, and Old Crumb is somewhat restored now, but would be all the more if Bob would have a heart and open his FUCKING PUB, because more villagers are coming over and trying to make conversation, to the point where one has to take refuge, as one still does from time to time, in a slim volume.

Reading poetry outside the boozer: it takes one back to skinny-arsed youth, to the scholarship and the Exhibition, and to getting the crap beaten out of one, and fair enough, for being such a preposterous little twat, Dad's reading never having extended beyond *Titbits* and the

Racing Post, and it didn't do him any harm, did it? God batter his Irish soul. Mum had dragged the old man along when the first play was put on. He sat in the stalls with his cap on, and he hadn't had a clue, and didn't give a shit. Said as much afterwards: which amounted to much the most perceptive criticism of the evening.

"You wrote that, Eddie boy? Really? *Why?*"

He liked the money though. Lovely lolly. It had come rolling in from the start. None of this taking twenty years of struggle to become an overnight success—none of that nonsense: not overnight, but *on* the night.

Now one is a sensitive soul and realises it is this success which makes other writers so scared of one. They see one as a breed apart. As if success somehow makes a difference to a writer's sense of self-worth. They don't seem to realise, or appreciate, or admit, that inside our heads we all experience the same failure. (Tricky, this, because it's inside their heads—or so one gathers—that they're having their only success.) One should have learnt earlier to respect one's success, and not just to glory in it. Problem is that right from the start they'd praised the blank sheets; that's what they'd enjoyed—not one's dodgy hieroglyphs. The writing, the words on the page, my friends, had nothing to do with it. A braver man would have said, *Hey! Don't you see what's actually there? Fuck-all, more or less.* A braver man one wasn't, so one had followed the formula, and made the silences, the white spaces, longer and wider. And there was some sort of art in it; one came to see it in the end. It was all rather brilliant after all. A brilliant white. One became one's own most generous critic. One tutored oneself to love this stuff one was turning out with such technical felicity. But was it really authentic? one asked. Was this honestly one's voice? The real—for once—*me*! Inside one's own head one didn't speak like this, that: all those lovely white pristine silences.

And then, well, we've all been there already, it happened. This lot, the present lot, on whom we had all, ridiculously, pinned our Lefty hopes after so long out of power, came to power. And it's been betrayal all the way, because it's been one fucking war after another, and cuts cuts cuts, and the rich getting richer, while the poor take it up the arse, and our bleeding liberties are trashed, and yes, one found one's VOICE.

Found one's FUCKING voice. The one that had been jabbering away inside one's head all along started speaking OUT.

Tragedy is, of course, no one wants to hear it. It pains them, the lot of them, one's public that is, one's publishers as well, to have to listen to this yobgobbery when, left to them, failing a return to the old days, long gone, much mourned, one would have slipped elegantly and appropriately into ultimate silence. They even bunged one the gong. Some sort of gob stopper. But no! Jabber, jabber, jabber. A ceaseless torrent. A relentless tide. And then the Nobel was bestowed—but still one wouldn't stop. Though fuck-all to show for it. That's the trouble with this country, AA. Well, you know it. No one wants to hear it, do they? No one is interested in what we have to say.

But thundering buggery, if that is not the sound of dead locks rising from their graves and door bolts being drawn from the stocks, signalling imminent defortification of The Cock.

Just one moment, though. What's this! Stopped at the junction a minibus, an old camper van, crammed with hot political totty, on their way—like so many before them—to protest at the local landmark, the parish's main employer, that blot, that scar, that standing indictment: the IDC, the Immigration Detention Centre. The country is fucking pockmarked with the bastards these days. They force the plans through on emergency measures; construct the warehouses from flat-pack, ready-build Swedish kits; then dole out the contracts to private security outfits. The deputy governor, Colin something, a regular at The Cock, was telling one the other day that it has a pool, a gym, a cyber-café, and a mosque; one should come and see the place, as his guest, he suggested; it would perhaps change one's view, soften one's hostility. "Oh, right, banged up in a high-security prison for the crime of fleeing for one's life, dreading return to electrodes on the bollocks, gang rape by the state militia, a bullet in the back of the head, and all the rest of that Amnesty International bleeding heart bleating, but relax, unwind, destress, have a swim, a workout, log on, chill out, trust in the all-merciful Allah, God help you." Colin laughed, no offence taken, took it all in good part. This is the trouble with these apparatchiks of oppression. They rise above the outrage and condemnation. They have their equality and diversity strategies, their Respect campaigns and their tolerance days. They are respectful of all views. So that is all right then, Colin. Get you another, mate?

So anyway, it is one's duty to give the girls a smile; a thumbs-up. Go fuck the fascists! Go penetrate their perimeter. Okay, one deviates somewhat from the gender-equality hymn sheet, but this is solidarity here, my friends, sorority.

Yet nothing from the van. Fuck-all. Thinking, no doubt: Who on earth is this fascist country land owner, this Tory squire? Much too young to know that the tweed jacket and knitted tie (with, in those days, a pipe clenched between the teeth) was once the uniform of the Left— proudly worn on anti-nuclear demos and on picket lines (though in those days one was, it is true, more often found at film premieres and bunny clubs in narrow lapels and skinny tie). Anyway, excuse one for not shedding the old threads. Hard-faced bitches all of them; sourpusses. Not a glimmer out of any of them. Until, suddenly, what does one clock?

What one clocks, cramped uncomfortably on the backseat, slung with camera gear, hood up, under escort from her shrew sisters, is none other than that magnificent black pantheress from the House of Journalists. No doubt about it.

Even though it was you, AA, who absorbed so much of one's attention on the day, there was still room for this long lean one to leave an impression. Hardly one's usual type, not greatly into shaven-headed, titless, whip-cord femininity, but in one's younger days at least one might have had a stab. One can imagine the claw marks and love bites such a hard hot feline might have given one during the spearing.

And at just that moment she spots yours truly. Sad old fucker that one is, she doesn't pass judgement, no, she flashes a full-on. Positively lights up her face, it does, and one's with it. Jeez U, the fucking simple joy of it! There is, cross the old ticker, a bit of a boy/girl thing going on. One gives her one and she gives it right back. Like an arrow from my old blood shots into the black twinkle-ink at the centre of her rich creamy smilings. Nice and uncomplicated. Sexed-up young piece; dirty old bastard: No sexual politics in that. No oppressed or oppressor. Just a bit of old-fashioned eye action. Nothing wrong with that at all.

Indeed one intuits a deeper bond, some sense that in keeping it so dirt-simple one has bridged the gulf and made an engagement: writer to writer in true fellowship. One's old eminence; her new young thing. Is this not how it has worked—so why knock it—since the dawn of letters? None of this obsequious shit; this fetishistic reverence; none of this: what-those-eyes-must-have-seen and we-are-not-worthy. We despise all that, don't we, AA? Yes, we do.

"Oi! Ted!"

"Eh?"

"Miles away. Off with the birds."

"On a higher plane, Bob. Now is this fucking pub open or what?"

THE NINE SISTERS AND AGNES MADE UP THE ENTIRE PROTEST

The journey in the cramped camper van had been uncomfortable. The heating was on too high and made the air stale. For much of the first hour, they had been trapped in stop/start traffic on one of the major (clogged) arterials. When she looked out at the drivers on the computerised bridges of the vast transcontinental container lorries; or the disco pods, with their decks and microphones, of the behemoth coaches; or the dinky ergonomic capsules of the private cars, she saw human beings automatonised as they engaged with a singular fixity on minute gradations of forward motion.

On reaching the motorway slip, however, they plunged into and were carried forwards on a flash flood of traffic. Moving at speed was suddenly exhilarating. Then they slowed and stopped again. Started, slowed, and stopped again. Screens, slung from gantries across the multiple carriageways, flashed out advisory speeds of mythic improbability.

Eventually they turned off onto back roads, and picked up relative speed again. But these back roads were narrow and twisty—and Agnes started to feel sick. The nausea was physical, but she also felt a sickness of the soul—or at least a great loneliness. The mood in the van had become more buoyant: the other women (all nationals of this country) were chatting and laughing, bouncing about on the passenger seats. Agnes wanted to go home, to have a glass of water, and to lie on her bed. She would listen to the sounds of the house and the street out-side—of her brothers and sisters playing, of her mother directing the women in their work, of hawkers and beggars calling out, of dogs whining and yelping, of chickens squawking and piglets squealing, of lorries, taxis, and tuk-tuks honking their horns. This cramped camper van, careering down the lanes of this small, inward-facing island, was carrying her ever deeper into its country and farther from her own country. Her heart belonged to the vast interior she had left behind. To its warmth and colour. To its unmeasured depths and distances. To its unspeakable terrors and tragedies.

She opened a half window and sucked in air. It had a cold metallic quality, nothing like the hot sweetness of home. But she felt a little bet-ter for it. The views opened out on a straighter road. But there was an absence about the tiny tracts of countryside and the neat settlements which unnerved her. It was not that anything lurked in the clipped hedgerows and squares of woodland, it was that *nothing* did. All the fields stood empty—of crops, of livestock, of farmhands. No agricul-ture was evident. Food was produced undercover, it seemed. The towns and villages were minimally peopled. A few early morning trains wiped out the daylight population. Now all was dormancy.

They had driven into a small village which was a quaint period pic-ture of this country as she had pictured it before she had arrived in it. This was how it was promoted internationally: through syndicated de-tective dramas, property programmes, and bake-off competitions. But she had not envisioned the melancholy of its muted tones. She had never imagined how grey-green and muddy brown the people were uniformed. And always the absence of street life: of noise, of bustle, of business, of banter and barter between people.

Outside a black and white pub there was an old man, alone. Who was this man? What was his story? As they drove off, she wished she had been in a position to photograph him. A photograph would have told her more about him. Although, thinking about it, what more did she want to know? There he was standing outside the pub, reading his tiny book, looking up and giving her a big smile. That was enough. It was a little thing that had lifted her spirits for a moment. That was all.

———

They pulled into a bleakly landscaped car park. Spindly saplings teth-ered to posts; beds of raked gravel. It was a relief to get out of the van and breathe some more clean cold air. They retrieved the placards from under the seats, unfurled their banner. One of the sisters tested the loud hailer. They walked over in a gaggle to the modern lodge at the main gates, where a couple of uniformed staff sat at a bank of screens, and others stood around, chatting, waiting to admit visitors through the airport-style security. It was at this point that Martha, the leader of the Sisters, told Agnes they were not going inside the centre.

They were not playing that game. They were not going to submit to the "two at a time" rule—and only then by prior appointment—to visit a named "resident." They were not going to submit themselves to the humiliation of a body search or to put every personal item into clear plastic bags for collection on the way out. There was no point. You only saw what they wanted you to see. You were conducted to a visitors' day room, which seemed pleasant enough with its soft seating, its tea and coffeemaking facilities, its piped music and potted plants, but which in fact was constantly under surveillance from CCTV cameras, and crawl-ing with plainclothes warders and informants. All requests to go into the centre itself, what they laughably described as the "residents' quar-ters," were refused, unless you were a VIV (a very important visitor)—for which read government stooge—an "independent" inspector, or—as was the case today—the minister himself.

"What sort of a joke is that?" Martha asked. "Andrew Alexander giving a clean bill of health to his own repressive regime. Well, ladies, we will give him a warm welcome, won't we? We will cheer him on his way!"

The Sisters let out a ragged cry of support. Agnes, feeling rather let down, added her voice halfheartedly.

"Ah, here they come," Martha called out. "Here they come—the forces of law and order. See that, Agnes; photograph that. What were we telling you about this place being a police state?"

A single police car pulled up some way short of them. The two female uniformed officers remained in the vehicle. At a previous (bigger) protest march, Agnes had marvelled to see the militancy of the Sisters mingle easily with the gentle sanctimony of the many church groups and the excitable enthusiasm of the students. The police presence was sullen, but she could detect no menace in it. Everything was under control. It was hard work to get arrested, though some succeeded.

Agnes went inside the lodge so that she could pick up a photographer's perimeter pass. The others remained outside. She rejoined them after a few minutes. It had started to drizzle. They were standing behind a crash barrier, watched over by a lone security guard from the IDC and the two female police officers in their car, one of whom was reading a newspaper. In the van there had been talk of joining up with the local "Smash the Camp" group, of others travelling down from the Midlands and the north, of trade union and faith group support. As it was, the nine Sisters and Agnes made up the entire protest.

| THE MINISTER

On the way in, the minister looked straight ahead. He ignored them with a practised disdain for the politics of protest. Lazy, destructive, devoid of solutions: contemptible in every way. He thought with a shudder of his student days. The car drove through them so quickly that Agnes, out of practise, did not react quick enough to get a shot.

On the way out, he looked at them with an expression almost of fascination, as if he had never seen anything quite like it in his life. More than that, he looked straight at Agnes. Quite distinctly. She was hurrying to take up her camera, anxious not to miss out this time.

And he held the look just long enough for her to capture a hesitant, uneasy, but somehow complicit smile.

The Sisters seemed to notice no difference and screamed the same denunciations.

| ANDREW, YOU WILL SERVE LOYALLY OUT OF OFFICE, I KNOW THAT

He puts his hand in his pocket. Still there: the small, folded piece of paper, still warm and unthreatening. Here is his treachery, his downfall. Here is his hold on humanity. Here is his weakness, his unfitness. Here is his uncovered heart. Enfolded within: a woman's story.

High up in the ministry, Andrew Alexander is sitting in the crepuscular gloom of fading office.

"Minister, would you like the lights turned on?"

"No, thank you, Magdalena."

Half an hour earlier a text encrypted to his private iPhone had come from the PM's chief of staff. He was to take a call within the hour. No aides present. Not a word to anyone.

As if? He had seen enough of these situations to know that not a word is needed. Not the faintest hint or faintest signal. Certainly sitting alone in an unlit and ever-darkening office was sheer self-dramatising theatre. A snuff is in the air and the slightest sniff of a snuff goes viral among the SPADs. Not just in the department, but across government. And not just among the SPADs, but among the ordinary civs and servs. And not just among them, but among resources and maintenance. Oh, it'll be the talk of the evening cleaning team—whispering sheepishly in Quechua or Kyrgyz.

Home Team know what is expected of them now. "Abandon Minister." Cut the cords. Don't get sucked down with him. Find a new master and attach suckers to him. Or her. Quick! This one's a dead man. No political life left in this one.

Oh, yes, his little spadpoles were already swimming away from him for dear political life. Even though one of them—which? perhaps all of them—was the cause of his demise. No other explanation. How else could Number Ten have heard about the incident at the detention centre? Heard that it happened and that it had not been reported. Heard about the meeting with all senior staff that he had called. Heard that it was to reflect on what he had seen at the detention centre and to consider its wider implications.

He is not being given face time. He is being spared the live-streamed street walk. He is being denied the final dignity of taking it like a man—full frontal. He will be back-passaged out of the ministry—like a paedo under a prison blanket—before the release of an exchange of letters written by a junior PM staffer. The ultimate humiliation of being spared humiliation.

He unfolds the small piece of paper which encloses the woman detainee's story.

There is no telling if it is true, of course. As often as not: it is not. How often had his aides given him that piece of advice? He had always listened to it; he had always stuck to the official line. "The difficulty is that there is no telling the truth. The bogus ones tell the same story as the genuine ones. A false claim takes the same form of words as a strong claim. In almost every case, all we have is the story. And the story is invariably heartbreaking and harrowing. But what of it? A story can be made up. We must not be drawn in. Fooled. Held spellbound. We must maintain a critical distance.

It had been just another ministerial engagement. He had half sleep-walked through it as usual until the incident. *At most a half memory of a straggle of protestors at the gates.* He had given his stock speech. *Not a word of that had stayed with him.* He had greeted the people set up for the purpose—a line-up of grip-and-grins. *All blurred into one.* He had taken the tour and taken more trouble to concentrate some attention on that. It was a point of honour with him that he never forgot that everyone in these centres was behind lock and key. Even so, the atmosphere had been relaxed, friendly, cheerful even—as it generally was when he visited any government facility. They laid it on for him, of course. They laid it on thick and heartwarming. He never forgot that either.

He had completed his schedule. It had not been onerous. It had gone without a hitch. He was about to leave. Then somehow one of them, a detainee, quite unscheduled, un-set-up, stepped out in front of him, quite unthreatening in her approach, and took his hand in hers— hers was soft and warm but thrusting, his was tense but unexpectedly yielding—and left behind a small folded piece of paper.

She had got to him. How had that happened? They never allowed any of them to get close and to make contact. He could not do his job if he had to do it at this level of intimacy. One human being making contact with another; reaching across the divide; her hand in his, for a brief moment: everything they guarded against.

He stepped back, into line, quite unalarmed, but with enough of a jerk to alert Home Team. In a second, they were on to the situation; they were locking it down. Room cleared. Minister quarantined. Security assessed. All of this carried out with deadly seriousness, but with no fuss or recrimination. Minimum force. This shouldn't have happened. In fact, this didn't happen, right? But they had it under control. And now they played it down. What, after all, had it amounted to: a step out of line, an approach by an unidentified female, unscheduled but unthreatening: Minister Unharmed.

Even so, within minutes he was sitting in the back of his ministerial car and they were out of there; they were speeding away.

He saw her this time. He looked straight at her. He recognised her. Yes, the girl with the camera, standing with the protestors, but somewhat apart from them, was the young woman photographer from the House of Journalists. They had been introduced during his most recent visit to the House and she had smiled at him. A sassy sort of smile, without any forced respect or deference, still less fear. *You don't fool me, brother*, it seemed to say. Though it was conveyed with warmth, even humour. He had been so taken aback that he had blanked her completely. Certainly not a constituent, not yet even a voter, and who knows what dangerous waters. Ministerial textbook. If in doubt, move quickly on. But he regretted it now with an extraordinary intensity. He would have liked to have talked to her, to have found out more about her story. He had lost that opportunity and he almost grieved for it. He sat in the back of the speeding ministerial car shaken by his state.

———

As he was getting out of the car at the ministry, he transferred the folded piece of paper from hand to pocket. He completed the operation with a certain pleasurable stealth. His aides hadn't seen it, and they were supposed to see everything. But this little victory was short-lived. Now they had reached the security point. Everyone had to turn out their pockets and put the contents in a plastic tray. Ministers were not exempted, on the orders of the prime minister. "We cannot be seen to impose on others measures which we do not impose on ourselves." An exception was made only in his own case. There were security reasons why this should be so. No one questioned them. Or rather, there were no mechanisms or forums in which the questions anyone had about this exemption could be raised. Not that there was any question of questioning on his part. He wasn't a questioner. Never had been. "This is one of the reasons why I want you in such a sensitive position, Andrew."

So, without question, he put the contents of his pockets into the plastic tray. Home keys, wallet, a variety of mobile devices—the small folded piece of paper. The paper seemed to give off light, to draw attention to itself, to demand inspection. His aides were emptying their own pockets and putting the contents therein into other black plastic trays. He noticed every item they deposited. Home keys, wallets, loose change, a variety of mobile devices, handkerchiefs, combs, notebooks, mints, glasses, sunglasses—a few folded pieces of paper. The pieces of paper he noted with alarm. They seemed to him obviously suspicious. By which he meant that they were not in the least *obviously* suspicious, but that their *lack* of obvious suspiciousness was of itself cause for suspicion. It was worth taking a look at these apparently innocent pieces of paper, surely? Unfolding them, reading what was written on them, asking for an explanation, finding that explanation unsatisfactory, calling in the high-security team, alerting the perm sec, who would in turn contact the SOS, or even the PM's office? Apparently not. The security staff did not appear to notice anything suspicious in these suspiciously unsuspicious items. For a moment he was furiously angry about it. If he could see what was going on here, why couldn't they? It was woefully lax, it really was. He had a mind to raise the matter with the head of high security; to take it up with the perm sec, and perhaps even the SOS or PM.

Then, suddenly alert to the preposterousness of these thoughts, he burst out laughing.

They noticed *that*, he noticed. They didn't notice a flagrant security breach, but were on red alert for a minister having a little chuckle. Anyway, he had passed through security now. Mission nearly accomplished. He tried not to snatch at the home keys, wallet, and mobile devices. He was positively careless in retrieving the small folded piece of paper. He scrunched it rather. A bit of paper, that's all. A note to self: that sort of thing. Don't forget wedding anniversary or something like that. Pick up dry cleaning on the way home or some such aide-mémoire. He walked ahead of his team into the secure reception area. Of course, his wedding anniversary was kept on record by his diary secretary. He was alerted whenever it was imminent, which—now he came to think of it—it was. He would approve the choice of flowers and sign the card. As for dry cleaning, he had not picked any up—or dropped any off, for that matter—since becoming a minister. Did he have a dry-cleaning secretary? He had so many staff it was not perhaps an entirely fanciful notion.

Sitting in his darkened office, waiting for the call from the PM, he reflects on the fact that he has taken very little notice of or interest in his junior non-politicals; young or old, diary or dry-cleaning; people who ordered flowers for his wife and collected his shirts and suits. That oversight seems unutterably sad now that it is too late to do anything about it.

He gets up from his desk and walks around, in a self-conscious, filmic attempt to calm himself down, to order his thoughts, to relieve the pressure of waiting.

Yes, over the last few months there had been little things he had started to question. Yes, a few doubts have been creeping in. Yes, he has been feeling uneasy about certain aspects of his job, of policy, of the effect of both on him, the man, not the minister. But nothing like this! This empathy, this concern, these human connections and contacts: what was he to make of them? That he was not himself; that was for sure. Or rather that his ministerial self, his political self, had deserted him.

The small folded piece of paper? What had he done with it?

Sudden panic. Blind panic.

Panic over. He calms himself. Deep breaths. It is on his desk. He still hasn't unfolded it. He still hasn't read what the detainee woman had written. It will be a plea: to him the man, not the minister. It will be what he is constantly warned about. What he has steeled himself to resist. So successfully. Until now. It has done its work. Unread. It has undone him. It has stripped him of office. For when a minister starts to question, to doubt . . . it's time to go. "I'm sure you understand, Andrew." He certainly did. He wouldn't question his removal when the PM's call came through.

The hysterical emotion of the day has exhausted him. Utterly. He has suffered some sort of breakdown, he realises; some sort of short-circuiting of his psychic connection to the machinery of government. And without that connection, how would he function? Was it not essential, umbilical?

He tries to imagine his empty house, evenings at home, waiting for Jen to come in. He tries to imagine "getting his life back." His life, her life, their life together, was built around his almost complete absence from home, his almost complete presence here, in office, his all-absorbing responsibilities and ambitions. He was a minister or he was nothing. His focus on that has always been his great strength. When he started to question, when doubts crept in, when he felt unease—as had sometimes happened in the past, though not like this, *nothing* like this— what? He fell back on office. Office was everything. There are things you can do, and things you cannot do, but it is only through the power of office that you can do anything, either way. "It is why I cannot imagine you not being part of my ministerial team, Andrew."

The call is coming through. He picks up his phone. An operator patches him through to the prime minister's private apartments.

"Andrew, you will know that I am profoundly grateful to you. I have always known that you, more than any of my ministers, recognise that service comes in many forms. You will serve loyally out of office, I know that. The text of your resignation letter is being released as we speak. I am sure that it does you credit. It will be forwarded to you so you have sight of it. But I am not expecting you to put yourself through any media appearances. You can step out of the spotlight now, Andrew. Job done. My best wishes to Jen.”

And so now: the silence. They are pulling the plug on all his connections as we speak. His desk is being cleared—remotely, virtually, absolutely. He is being logged out from the life he has loved. Deleted. Who or what now tells him what to do, where to go, what the form is? He is sitting in the dark here. No one is coming running. Of course not. That is as it should be. He is no one now. He’ll have to walk out of here alone. And with nothing. He’ll have to leave behind his ministerial briefcase and boxes, and all his papers. He knows that—and it tears at his heart.

And he has no personal effects to gather up. Never went in for that. A picture of Jen? She’d have laughed in his face if he’d suggested it. They’ll presumably send on those dry-cleaned suits? So he has nothing to carry. All he has are those few things in his pockets. The small piece of paper is among them. It did for him. It is his downfall. But he is still strangely, dangerously attached to it. Indeed it has taken on an added preciousness. He checks one last time that it is safe.

| GOD BLESS, STRONG MAN

Andrew Alexander sits in the back of his ministerial car for the last time. It had sped up to the kerbside the moment he had stepped out of the back entrance of the ministry. The driver (strictly speaking no longer his driver, as this is no longer his car) honked at him to get in.

The car is now racing through the city, carrying him away from office, and towards his house in an inner suburb. It is about seven-thirty in the evening. He hasn’t been home before ten on a weekday since he became a minister. Jen will still be at work; the house will be empty; there will be nothing in the fridge. There will be no calls; there will be no papers to go through. He hasn’t watched any non-news television programmes or read a book or sat and listened to music for about a decade—probably longer.

The car is speeding along. The driver is clearly set on getting Andrew home and then getting back to the ministry as soon as possible to link up with his new minister. He has his future to think about.

Sunk in despondency, a thought suddenly cheers Andrew.

Might there be a television crew outside his house to doorstep him?

They pull up outside his house.

There isn't.

The driver has got there ahead of the media pack.

Andrew knows that once he is inside the house he won't be able to come out even if crews and correspondents do descend. That would look too desperate and needy.

He walks up the steps to his front door with a laboured tread, turns to wave goodbye to . . . But the driver has sped off.

A doorstep would have allowed him to maintain a statesmanlike silence, give a steely "no comment," or perhaps say a few words in support of the government and the prime minister. But he is on his doorstep and a doorstep is not going to happen now.

He goes into the cold, dark house. He walks into the kitchen, which is as clean as an operating theatre. The cleaners—who he has never seen—spend more time in this house, his house, at home, than he and Jen. He could imagine them sitting at the pristine table, the operating table, with a cup of tea and a plate of biscuits. When was the last time he had done such a thing? Had he ever? There is no trace of the tea break now, of course. The cleaners had cleaned up after themselves. The kitchen is so clean it hurts.

He runs himself a glass of water, walks into the living room, and sits down on the sofa. Or rather, he flops down. Like a middle manager arriving home after a routine day in the office. *Home, love.* Shepherd's pie for supper and then some telly with the wife. This is the life his constituents lead; it is the life that he as a minister had pledged to preserve for the decent, hardworking men and women of this country—but it repels him personally. He has been running to escape from all that since he was at school. It was okay to preach it, but to *live* it. *Never.*

And it gets worse. Tomorrow—he could see it happening—he would be lying on this sofa, in his pyjamas, watching daytime TV. Tomorrow and for days after. Jen would leave before he got up and would come back to find him still lying here, surrounded by dirty plates and mugs, with the television on. She would despise him even more than she did already. Even more than he despised himself. "If you had resigned it would have been a different matter, Andrew. But you didn't have the spine for that. Despite all that was going on; despite all your obvious misgivings. You got sacked, whatever the official version, and now all you can do is wallow in self-pity and fantasise that by some miracle he'll take you back."

Take him back? He sits up on the sofa suddenly. A miracle indeed, but if he goes straight into the Commons first thing tomorrow and starts rebuilding, reconnecting, re-icing his soul against doubts and misgivings, then . . . what? *He would take him back?* The PM? Give him a second chance? The PM who had just sacked him because, obviously, he, Andrew, had misgivings? Well, he did, didn't he? That was the truth of the matter.

"Prime Minister, it is just that I wonder if our asylum processes have been tightened so much that they leave no scope for any show of humanity."

He had never said it—or anything approaching it. He had never even thought it in so many words. Until now. But it had been what he had been thinking in some shape or form for some time. Inchoately, vaguely, unmistakably. Even Jen, who hardly knew him and cared even less, had been able to smell it on him, so it must have been an unbearable stench in the nostrils of the PM, who knew all his ministers down to the minutest detail. Misgivings and doubts. No way back from that.

"Doubt has its place in politics, Andrew, but not in power."

He flops back onto the sofa. There are tears in his eyes. He reaches into his pocket for a handkerchief and doesn't find one, but does find the small folded piece of paper. He reads it for the first time.

> *Minister,*
> *I be no writer, but a plain, God fearing oman. I am fled, my hubby and babies dead. Much danger brings me here in hope. Everything lost, but this country my hope. Juge tell me, I must*

return. I tell to him, that is my death. He look down, they take me away. Here I an. I rite you a tender word requesting not mercy but hearing.

   God Bless, strong man
   Angel

| NO AGNES?

Again the day has drained us. Such episodes; such stories! There is a bank of TVs in the main lobby of the House of Journalists—newsroom-style; along with a row of clocks set for the major time zones. All the domestic services are running the story as a ticker-tape graphic along the bottom of the screen. *Mini-reshuffle at Home Office. Minister resigns. Personal reasons. Rising star takes place.* The TVs are all on mute, so the row of correspondents outside Parliament who are doing the two-ways on the story look like goldfish in flat-screen bowls. We look up and clock the story: 19:42 GMT.

Julian appears in the lobby, he looks up, just to confirm the news, and races on, head down. *Most unwelcome news*, his expression seems to say. Andrew for all his faults was a known quantity. Now there would be a new man to cultivate. Or rather, woman. He has had an advance warning. Julian knows her, of course. Not very well, but they are on nodding terms—and he has her number. He will call her first thing. Get an early visit to the House of Journalists into her diary: a nice safe one with a few pet writer friends and reliable private donors. No mishaps this time. It couldn't be anything to do with? . . . No, that would be ridiculously paranoid.

Agnes is still not back. It is 19:48 GMT, and she has been out since just after breakfast. As the day has progressed, more and more of us have been alerted to her absence. Until the evening, no one was greatly concerned, even those who knew the nature of her trip and disapproved of it. Of all the fellows, Agnes is the most given to venturing out. But now it is dark, and getting late, and it is not like Agnes to be out for hours on end. The volunteer on reception is wondering when or if she should officially report Agnes's absence. It has clearly been a busy day for Julian and he will not want to be troubled with a concern that may turn out to be misplaced. The volunteer can imagine him saying, irritably, that all that has happened after all is that Agnes went out some time ago and she hasn't yet come back. And she, the volunteer, didn't need reminding that the fellows are at liberty to come and go as they please. There is a prior notification rule, and a signing in and signing out procedure—neither of which Agnes has observed—but these are really only in place to aid the smooth running of the House and to ensure full compliance with Health and Safety law. And the fact is that Agnes is not even close to breaching the eleven o'clock curfew—which is there for night-time security reasons and out of respect for the out-of-hours staff and the fellows. Yet what if she doesn't return tonight at all? It is a concern which, though premature perhaps, is growing in the mind of the volunteer, and indeed in the minds of all of us. Then Julian will be annoyed that he had not been previously warned that Agnes had been absent all day, pointing out for good measure that the nature of her excursion should—we can all imagine him using this exact phrase—"*have set alarm bells ringing.*" All staff and volunteers are constantly told that the House of Journalists has a clear fiduciary responsibility for the personal safety of fellows who, for all their remarkable qualities, are classed as "vulnerable adults" under the terms of the Act. A careful balance needs to be struck therefore between freedom and welfare, respect for the individual and the responsibility to protect. So this continuing absence of Agnes presents the volunteer with something of a dilemma.

She decides to leave it for another half an hour.

"Presumably there have been people who have just walked out of the place one day and never come back?" one of the newer fellows asks us out in the Central Courtyard.

We all look at him askance. No one just ups and leaves the House of

Journalists! It is a great honour and indeed advantage to be admitted into the fellowship. Through our writing in defence of human freedom we have earned a place on its books, with all that that entails in terms of gaining a new life and career in this country, so why would we erase ourselves, just like that? In the end we all have to move out or move on, as they call it—with a few exceptions, like Mr. Stan, who has been awarded a lifetime fellowship. Ultimately, one of two fates awaits us: status or return. But if we submit to the protection and guidance of the House, we greatly increase the likelihood of achieving the first and avoiding the second. So why take a chance on our own out there? It would be a foolhardy and reckless act, but also an ungrateful and self-ish one. This second thought encourages in us the expectation that Agnes will return. Sometimes she kicks against this place, its silly rules and self-satisfied ethos, but surely she would not walk out on the House of Journalists after all it has done for her?

"It's a case of knowing 'our bread is buttered,' I suppose?" one of our number suggests. We all laugh. We will have to check this one with Esther.

Mr. Stan glides through the assembled company in his electric chair. He looks deeply troubled. He has been summoned to another Committee meeting, this time to discuss the new minister.

He sees us and enquires, "No Agnes?"

We are just about to tell him and to reassure him with our thoughts on the subject when Agnes appears. She walks through the main doors of the House of Journalists at exactly this moment with her customary sashay and lope. She is all lithe defiance.

The expression on her face is, *So what? So I've been a while. You didn't think . . . ?* Guys, *you didn't think . . . ?* But there is just enough twitch around the eyes and lips to betray the anxiety and relief behind her braggadocio. She learnt for herself today that some of her swagger comes from the fact that she is living in this safe place.

Mr. Stan is for a moment left out of the excitement at Agnes's re-turn. His electric chair is parked with its back to the main doors, so he doesn't see her entrance. But he sees the joy in our eyes and this allows him to anticipate Agnes coming up behind him, leaning over him, and giving him a hug. She then dances around from the back of the chair and squats down on her haunches in front of Mr. Stan. They do the hands-and-stumps thing.

Agnes looks up at the TV monitors, which until then she hadn't noticed.

"So the minister has jumped ship, then."

"Or been thrown overboard. The official explanation for these things is not always the true one. Julian has called another meeting to discuss its implications for the House."

"Julian and his meetings!"

"Indeed."

"I saw the minister fleetingly today. In the back of his official car, flanked by advisors. He was visiting the detention centre where we were protesting outside."

"I heard about that—the protesting, I mean."

"Look, Mr. Stan, don't give me grief about that. It's important to see what's going on out there. Not just to see everything from the perspective of the House of Journalists."

"Of course, of course, I didn't mean to . . ."

Mr. Stan can see that Agnes is exhausted. While it may have been a relief to escape from the somewhat suffocating embrace of the House of Journalists for a few hours, it is obviously a relief to be back. And that, he must say, is a relief to him. She still needs this place; and is not yet ready to venture out for good.

"You were saying something about the minister," Mr. Stan prompts Agnes.

"Yes, it's a kind of weird thing, and perhaps I'm making too much of it, but when I got a glimpse of him on the way in he was the same familiar guy, hard-faced, determined not to see anything beyond the narrow remit of his office. But on the way out, he looked transformed somehow. I don't exactly know how to describe it. He was lost in deep thought, miles away in one sense. Yet, at the same time, his eyes were open. He saw me, I'm sure. Smiled in my direction. I've got the shot in here." She taps on her camera. "One for the papers, perhaps—after what's happened. Though that's not the point. The thing is, the visit had obviously affected him much more deeply than he expected. Though, as I say, perhaps I am making a lot of a fleeting look."

"Oh, I don't know. It seems that Andrew Alexander wasn't quite as tough as he thought he was. Perhaps some of what his job is all about finally penetrated to the human being inside the hard ministerial case. Perhaps this time he could not remain unmoved by visiting such a place."

"Maybe." Agnes ponders. "Anyway, it turned out I wasn't allowed inside."

"You weren't seriously expecting to get in, were you? They only allow you to see what they want you to see."

"Now you're sounding like the Sisters."

"They are right about it. These are not pleasant places. How can they be? People held against their will; people being readied to return. People who have suffered much and hoped against hope: all that lost."

"And that's another thing, Mr. Stan. I knew all that before I went there, I saw nothing of it while I was there, and yet the thought of it oppresses me much more strongly now."

"That is only natural. You don't need to get beyond the perimeter fence of a prison camp to know what places of suffering and hopelessness they are. Though it is doubtless unfair to compare these centres with the hellholes we have all known. And I do not know what the authorities are supposed to do in such circumstances, with such cases. They can't just let everybody stay. It is a great moral dilemma."

"The Sisters take a much stronger line against the centres and the government."

"Indeed they do. And I would not wish to criticise them. They may be right. I am ever less sure of the rights and wrongs, my dear. Maybe I am too tired and old. And I am grateful, too grateful perhaps, for this place. Maybe I am afraid to look beyond its four walls. I would have the House undisturbed. I want only peace and quiet. But it doesn't work like that, does it? The world doesn't work like that. We of all people know that."

Mr. Stan glides off to the meeting, and we cluster around Agnes. Someone suggests a smoke, but she shakes her head. She decides against dinner as well. She is suddenly feeling woozy and jelly-legged—not right at all. She needs her bed. Its sly promise of sweet oblivion is a half-truth at best, she knows that. The night will not be long advanced when SuperSlumber comfort gives way to hideous nightmares. They will chase her through the night, leaving her exhausted but wide awake, to watch out the early hours hollow-eyed. Every night: the same story. But for now she is too weak to resist sleep's treacherous clutches. It takes her by the arm and leads her away.

We know where she is going.

But she is back with us: that is the main thing.

DEVELOPMENTS

| FOR LACK OF OPPORTUNITY MANY MEN DIE BEFORE THE EXPERIENCE I SPEAK OF

The following passage is from *Thoughts* by the poet Leopardi.

> No man becomes a man before he has had considerable experience of himself which, revealing himself to himself, and determining his own opinion of himself, in some ways determines his fortune and his state of life. For this great experience, before which no one in the world is much more than a child, life in ancient times provided infinite available material, but today private life is so poor in incident, and of such a nature for everyone, that, for lack of opportunity many men die before the experience I speak of, and so are like babies, little more than if they had not been born.

| THE PROFESSION OF JOURNALISM IN THE PRESERVATION OF FREEDOM AND HUMAN DIGNITY: A LECTURE BY OUR FATHER OF CHAPEL, MR. STANLEY STANISLAUS

It was Julian's idea—and a good one it is—to invite Mr. Stan to give a lecture on the journalistic profession. Julian has observed, as we all have, that Mr. Stan has been out of sorts in the last couple of weeks. He does not seem to take the great comfort he once did in the House. He appears to be troubled by the turn of recent events. And he is not—it must be said—quite the loyal lieutenant of old. Julian does not want to make too much of it. The place is not run just to please Mr. Stan, loved and revered though he is by all. But even so, it is no bad thing to have him happy and on our side.

The event has been marketed to Friends of the House of Journalists, and a number have turned up. We also recognise among those gathered the Committee member Monsignor Humphrey Comfort, less frequently seen here than of late; and over there is Malcolm Dougan, considerably spruced up for the occasion. Which is to say, he looks rather like a tramp who has spent a night in hospital. Think matrons and carbolic soap; think beard trimmed and toenails clipped. Next to him is, if we are not mistaken, a not-unconnected lady friend. Mid-fifties; shapeless cardigan and long hippyish skirt. These three and other Friends—mostly retired people who always enjoy a talk with coffee and biscuits laid on—are not the main body of the audience, however: that is us, the fellowship. The invitation was open; attendance is voluntary but attendance is expected. So here we are. Almost to a woman and man.

But you, AA, have not joined us, we notice. Though we notice too that Julian seems relaxed about your absence. Mr. Stan's agitation aside, things have settled down at the House of Journalists. The new minister has promised that her first official visit in her new post will be to the House of Journalists, which she has already praised generously in a newspaper interview. That interview is now displayed prominently on the press-cuttings board. Nothing has come of Crumb's threat/warning/hint—call it what you will—which Julian, on reflection, thinks he may have exaggerated. Julian has asked around, put out a few feelers, and no one has heard that Crumb has any plans. He has taken the precaution of talking to the House's lawyers, of having legal steps ready if anything does come to pass, but the fact is Crumb has gone quiet of late. The diarrhoeic torrent of letters and articles has ceased. There is a blessed quiet from that quarter! What could Crumb publish anyway that would really shake the House of Journalists? Its foundations are deep and its protecting walls are high. Witness this coming-together to celebrate the extraordinary courage of one of its founding fellows; a man who, whatever his doubts and dilemmas, never loses his sense of perspective or his instinct for loyalty. He is a man who has shown that he is always ready to stand up and fight when the time is right. There is a time and there is place. His weapons are the most sturdy and most trustworthy in any man's armoury: integrity and eloquence. He deploys them now to promote and protect the House of Journalists. He has always understood how politics works, how democracy is defended. He is a survivor. He is a hero of the profession of journalism, though a modest and reluctant one. He is this place's greatest servant and ambassador. Ladies and gentlemen, Mr. Stanley Stanislaus . . .

Mr. Stan has brilliantined his hair this morning. He—or rather Agnes—has taken those baby elephant tufts and plastered them to his humpty head. He is sporting too a bow tie, and a red handkerchief in his top pocket. He hopes that Mother would have been proud to see him today. She is certainly looking down on him, he is sure of that. By which he means to say, she is watching over him. Though, now he thinks of it, even when watching over she is also, in that other sense, looking down! Yes, Mother is as ever both benevolence and rectitude: so he holds himself as straight as he can to earn her love and pride as he mounts the specially constructed lectern, lays out his notes before him, and inspects his audience through his thick glasses.

Mr. Stan has of course lectured at the House of Journalists before. Indeed in his early days he was a frequent speaker at events internal and external. But there are few if any of us left from those days at the House of Journalists. Those who sat in our places have now moved on. Mr. Stan sometimes forgets that. He forgets that we don't remember him in the first pomp of his exile. He has slowed down since then and lost some of his fight and authority. Most of us only know the earlier incarnation by reputation. Sometimes we must admit that we paint him as a tragicomic figure—more apt to command affection than respect. It does not help that he is so cherished—still—by Julian and the Committee. Mr. Stan knows that he is seen this way. It has long been so. He always was a paper man, a party man; a co-optee to every committee, sub-committee, working party, and caucus. He was ever the patriot and loyalist. He was stuck too with the popular image of Little Stan, the hunchback hero: out in the streets on his Tiny Tim sticks as the protests grow, or tapping away on his typewriter as the shooting starts. Through-out his life he has had to put up with treacherous belittlement.

But many are those who have misjudged him; who have not had the heft of imagination to see that although he can be caricatured as a tiny misshapen manikin, inside is a mighty lionheart. They were laughing at him even as they set out those hammers, those claw hammers, for his exquisite anticipation. They were ridiculing him still as they pliered off the first fingernail. Oh, yes, they broke him in the end. He blubbered and he *squealed*. For Mummy! They used their power to shape him even more monstrously to their own ends. All that he hoped for and worked for on the island ended in these hideous stumps. He uses them against his enemies now—they are all he has. But he does not take pride in them. No, that would be perverse, disgusting. They are their victory, not his. Yet who in the end betrayed who? Who in the end stands the taller?

Mr. Stan must notice that the audience in the library, though sizeable, is not perhaps as big as he had hoped or Julian expected. A few loyal friends have turned out, but some of the old stalwarts are not seen at the place these days, and the younger volunteers are somewhat thin on the ground. No journalists of this country have turned out to hear him. That is a matter of regret.

Mr. Stan started in the profession in the last musical comedy days of colonial rule; the days of cat-and-mouse with pink-kneed lieutenants in long white socks and long white shorts; wet bobs and rugger buggers from places like Penge and Tonbridge, who occasionally called in the mod and rocker privates, from places like Accrington and Bow, to break up the presses and march the native boys off to the nice, neat, cuppa tea police cells. It didn't scare anyone.

It was am-dram freedom fighting. But it was all Mr. Stan had known and it must be said he loved it. It had just the right amount of excite-ment and daring for a shy, gentle young idealist finding his feet in the politics of the island.

At first, young Stan the junior reporter was sent off by *The Gleaner*—then the island's official newspaper—to cover actual am-dram. Humdrum: he did not complain; he told himself it was the perfect cover. He went straight from filing his fawning copy on productions of *Salad Days* and *The Mouse Trap* at the Kingsbridge Assembly Rooms to meetings of the Revolutionary Committee and editorial conferences of its underground newspaper. In no time he was writing most of it. The editor of *The Gleaner* knew it—and let young Stan know that he knew it. He could get up to whatever he wanted to in his own time, but he must not bring these "extracurricular activities" into the newsroom in any way. *The Gleaner* was in fact broadly pro-independence—in line with official policy. It diverged from the radicals only over the issues of the speed of the process and the details of the independence settlement. These points were not unimportant, Mr. Stan's editor acknowledged that, and he trusted that *The Gleaner* gave due weight to them. But he had to question—and *The Gleaner* in its editorials reflected this position—how such relatively minor disagreements could possibly justify talk of abandoning negotiations and resorting to violent overthrow.

Mr. Stan respected this position to a greater extent than he would ever have admitted to other members of the Revolutionary Committee. In truth, he was not a revolutionary by temperament or outlook. But he was young, he was romantic, he was eager for change—and change of a more bracing sort than that promised by the cosy process of negotiation that had been strolling along for some years, supposedly in secrecy.

In fact everybody knew the governor was talking with the independence leader over tea in his bungalow (the independence leader's, that is) in the grounds of the city prison. Sir Robin and VK were on the best of terms. They discussed the cricket and asked after each other's wives. Everyone knew the knitting needles in the telegraph room at Government House clicked constantly with messages from the Colonial Office kindly enquiring as to whether Sir Robin could advise them on a date for the handover of power, if he would be so kind. The island was one of the last colonies on the books. A minor member of the royal family was on standby to fly out and salute old Jack as it was hauled down for the last time. Everyone knew that the one thing holding up proceedings was the governor's vast wife, who loved the bougainvillea privilege of the residence, with its respectful servants and its swishing fans and great white rooms and gorgeous gardens. She was middle-middle at best, it was said, grew up in a suburban villa in Uxbridge—and could only look forward to something not much more than a step up from that when she and Robbsie left here. (Though it was also darkly hinted in revolutionary circles that VK was spinning it out too: that he was comfortable in his bungalow and loath to leave it.) Still, it was only a matter of time.

It had not always been this way. Before the war—before the fight had gone out of the colonial masters—there had been arrests, beatings, shootings in the street, torture in the cells. Some of the Revolutionary Committee members, contemporaries of VK who were no longer close to him, relished these times past and recalled them with thuggish nostalgia. *Those were the days when we rated the white bastards.*

Now the whites were weak and they wanted out.

So drive them into the sea! Why not? Humiliate them, like they humiliated us. Why should we talk terms? Why this jaw-jaw?

Old RC members had gone along with the negotiation process, but now there seemed no end to it. Let it carry on, if it must, but let it be VK's carry-on; they preferred not to put all their trust in it, thank you very much. For even as you talked you had to be ready to fight. That was the lesson of revolutionary history and they at least would not forget it. That was why the secret training camps still operated—in contravention of VK's express orders. That was why they kept to military discipline—even though the units were supposed to have been stood down under the terms of the Protocols for Negotiation. The Process, VK argued, offered them all they had fought for and more: freedom and democracy, office and power, vindication and reward. But it was all coming too slowly and—as important—too easily. It was all coming through negotiation and handover. It was breeding a generation of soft men, mummy's boys—little runts with their snouts already in the future government trough.

These old revolutionaries need not have worried themselves. No fat sinecures and easeful retirement for them, as it happened: rather violent death claimed them all within a few years. The lesson here: colonial rule may sometimes mellow in its declining years, but it always spawns a bastard child. As Mr. Stan sat in RC meetings pondering his editor's arguments against violent overthrow, he saw that child grow: a hard young cadre, harder even than the old revolutionaries—hunched and moody, mainly silent, but prone to violent displays. This group delighted in pulling the wings off any higher hopes for independence that Mr. Stan and other young idealists entertained.

It was they who planted the bomb in the phone box that killed the military policeman. The plan was to trigger a spiral of retaliation. But the response from the colonial authority was typically puny: a couple of arrests, a scheduled trial, no ill treatment, let alone torture, and every expectation of an Independence Day pardon. VK in his discussions with Sir Robin was embarrassed more than anything by this incident—though he made a point of not issuing a condemnation. In truth, he didn't know exactly who was responsible. It alarmed him that it wasn't his old revolutionary comrades, whom he was confident he ultimately controlled; they approved of the bomb—at last some action!—but it was not their work. That meant it was an element within the party he didn't control, or, worse, a new force outside the party. He needed to get out of the bungalow in the grounds of the prison, he realised finally. So perhaps the bombing did hasten the day? Mr. Stan—braver than he knew—argued otherwise. But anyway the day came not so long afterwards.

Mr. Stan was one of the reporters from *The Gleaner* covering the Independence Day celebrations. The editorial line was celebration and gratitude; fond farewells and a bright future. That, they were all told, was the mood of the country. It wasn't Mother's, thank you very much; or the Revolutionary Committee's—still less the young hard cadre; but it was Mr. Stan's. He moved among the ordinary people, as well as the nabobs and dignitaries, that day and night and new dawn, and he was delighted by the spirit of victory, magnanimity, and hope, the promise of elections and the dream of good governance. There were fireworks out at the port; there was dancing in the streets. It was a joyous day.

In the ballroom of the Hotel Imperial, he watched the small, trim President VK Vish, in white tie and tails, lead out the governor's wife for the first dance and was greatly moved by the sight—preposterous as it was. The tug and liner, the porpoise and the whale: the dapper VK nosing the colossal white bosom of Her Ladyship around the glittering sea of the dance floor. It was an image—photographed and beamed around the world—which others in the interim government and outside it would never forgive.

Every weekday in the months and few years that followed, the little puffball president, Sir VK Vishnamaswarikrishna, was driven the short distance from the Presidential Palace (the old governor's residence) to the Office of the President (formerly Government House) in his official car with the flag of the nation on it. It would have suited the story if that particular day he had been wearing morning dress, a sash, medals, and a top hat, as was his wont on any day—and there were many—deemed ceremonial. As it was, he was wearing a self-designed, wide-lapelled, double-breasted suit, in a vulgar Prince of Wales check. It was this suit, along with his legendary silk underclothes and his handmade calf-leather shoes, which were vaporised in the massive car bomb explosion. All that remained in the backseat of the steaming, ink-dripping wreckage of the Daimler when the firemen's hoses had done their work was a naked limbless torso that resembled a blackened tree stump. The presidential extremities were hurled high and wide— the head into the low branches of a jacaranda tree; an arm onto a pile of rubbish in a back alley. As for the rest of His High Excellency, the street cleaners found bits of him for days afterwards scattered among the flower beds and grassy embankments of the Mall.

Mr. Stan, now chief reporter at *The Independent Gleaner*, was dispatched to the scene within minutes of the explosion rocking the capital. There was something comedic about the scene even then—something Hieronymous at least. Offstage extras staggered about with blackened faces, their clothes in shreds, in preposterous bewilderment. There was a lot of overacting going on. Those closer to the action, the grotesquely injured, looked down at their legs and found they weren't there or tried to push brain matter back into half-blown-away heads. One woman, sitting with her guts in her lap, was trying to slop the lot back into her gaping belly. The air was thick with what sounded like laughter at its most maniacal.

But Stan was a pro. He surveyed the scene; he interviewed witnesses; he got statements off the police and emergency services. He filed the lead item and helped pen the editorial deploring in the strongest terms this barbarous outrage against nascent democracy. It ran in a first edition, and then was decisively spiked. The new editor had taken a phone call in person from the leader of the new Committee for Democratic Renewal. The new lead item and editorial paid scant tribute to the dead president; it reported that a commission had been established to investigate his assassination, but also the numerous and substantive allegations of financial corruption and abuse of office against him; it expressed confidence that the new Committee for Democratic Renewal, or CDR, would bring stability and order to the country.

Stan backed the new editorial line with some foreboding, though he was happy enough to jettison the old one. VK had become a joke, a bad joke: that was for sure. His venal gerontocracy had tested old loyalties to the limit. Without reform—the need for which he seemed incapable of appreciating—the president was inviting his own overthrow. Stan, more bravely than others, had argued that very point—in so doing testing, and sometimes overstepping, the controls on the press which VK had imposed. He had received some sharp warnings as a result.

So now the old man had been blown up. Stan was not inclined to mourn his passing, even if the act itself had shocked him. The CDR was not just the beneficiary of that act, of course, but its perpetrator. Stan knew that perfectly well. He had known most of the members of the CDR for years, though he had never really been close to them. He had never really been hard-cadre, after all. But they made overtures to him and to the paper. They flattered him and included him in their plans. He got the editorship because of the connection. He knew that perfectly well too. And so he went along, and he hoped for the best. Perhaps the circumstances of their elevation to power would not set the tone for their rule.

Some hope!

———

But Mr. Stan's subject today is "The Profession of Journalism in the Preservation of Freedom and Human Dignity" and so he includes none of the above. His talk would have been much better if he had. Episodes from his own story never fail to captivate an audience. Still, we listen respectfully enough. If there is a yawn or two as he expands on his subject, we hope we manage to stifle them quickly. If some among our number nod into sleep for a moment, we hope he doesn't notice. We still have great admiration and affection for the old fellow.

| THE TRUST HAS ALWAYS SUPPORTED THE HOUSE KNOWING ITS LIMITATIONS

"I'm ahead of you," Robert says, snapping his umbrella open in front of them and stepping out from the art gallery entrance into the hard hammering rain.

"Go on, then," Miriam says, laughing and stepping out after him to share the shelter of the umbrella.

"Well, I'd say your view is that what we have just seen is entirely appropriate to the discussion we are just about to have."

Miriam laughs again. She links arms with Robert and they walk up the fluvial street in step.

"Any preference?" Robert asks. The rain is so heavy that the umbrella and their raincoats are only going to protect them from inundation for a matter of minutes.

"This'll do," Miriam says emphatically, racing them into the first coffee shop in the square. Robert collapses his umbrella just inside the entranceway and shivers off the raindrops. There is a stash of similar half-collapsed black umbrellas under the dripping, shivering coat stand. It resembles a colony of saturated bats.

As they queue up it occurs to Miriam (because of her family history these thoughts do) that the "trainee barista," a dark-haired Polish girl whose name badge identifies her as Katrina, might have been working in the petrol station near the coach park for Birkenau if she weren't making lattes and frappuccinos in London. Somebody has to serve petrol to local motorists who drive along that road by the perimeter of the camp—right past the redbrick rail tower, the railhead for the gas chambers—without as much as a sideways thought as to the enormity of the site. If they are to have any sort of normal life, the people of Oświęcim must go about their business free of the monstrous weight of the town's history. Girls like Katrina, whether she comes from Oświęcim or not, do not live and dance and smile in the shadow of Auschwitz. It would be absurd and pietistic to think that the world would be a better place if they did. Not everyone (and her father and mother come to mind in different ways) can afford to spend their time thinking "big thoughts," and anyway, sometimes "nice thoughts" are what the world needs more. Now, snap out of it, she tells herself, as she and Robert collect their coffees.

The soft areas are all occupied; mainly it seems by single young people with laptops and fat novels. The women among them have marked out their personal space with colourful umbrellas in glistening full flower. She and Robert find two high stools facing the steamed-up front window.

"So," Robert says. Robert is Robert Lucasta, an old friend, a futures trader turned not-for-profit business consultant, and a trustee of the Stern Family Foundation. "I am right about the exhibition, aren't I?"

Miriam cradles the warm soup bowl of a coffee cup and sips through the hot foam to the bland milky mixture underneath. Like a novelty cocktail, the kick is all in the tail—with in this case a double espresso shot performing the function of a measure of spirit.

"You are as always spot-on, Robert. I think it is obvious from that show that Mark is satisfied now to play safe, to enjoy his elevation to the New Establishment. It is installation art for people who don't like the boundaries pushed too far. Look at the crowd in there, for a start."

"A lot of wealthy liberals who fancy that they are a bit radical, you mean?"

"Exactly, there's no fun in it if I am just one in the crowd."

"That's what happens though, doesn't it? That's how life goes if you're lucky? You spot them when they are raw, fresh, and edgy—and broke. You give them a Stern Young Artists bursary—"

"And they betray me."

"I was going to say they become successful. It is supposed to work like that, isn't it?"

"You are right, you are right." Miriam laughs—that now-familiar Miri Stern laugh. "I am a most ungrateful philanthropist."

Miriam and Robert have one of *those* relationships. She is allowed to hold his arm (as she is doing now); to pat him and pet him and punch him; to let her head fall against his chest, to lie with her head in his lap (in the right circumstances); to call him darling or to tell him to fuck off. She is allowed to behave as if she were about fourteen and he is an older brother for whom she nurtures a slightly inappropriate crush. It is not as if she behaves like this with any of her other male friends, of which she has many. To behave like this with anyone other than Robert would be mortifying. But with Robert, somehow, it feels natural. Never mind that Robert is now close to sixty, and she not far behind. Never mind that Robert has been married off and on for more than thirty years, most recently to a young Spanish architect, Ines, who is less than comfortable with the way Miriam behaves towards her newish husband. Miriam laughs this off: a beautiful Spanish girl of thirty-five need hardly harbour any jealousy towards a tiny, grey-haired Jewess. Though that is not the point of course. Ines does not for a minute imagine that Robert is attracted to Miriam; that Miriam is any sort of sexual threat. The thought, striking as it does occasionally, pains Miriam, even though the secret to her sex life (hardly a great secret) is that she has never been interested in sex or sexual love, with Robert or any other man—or woman. She can do without all that because she has the love of her friends. Not that this disinterest saves a woman, even a tiny, grey-haired Jewess, from vanity. She would like to be beautiful, and she was never that. The point, however, and this thought cheers Miriam—unworthy though it might be—is that she and Robert share a friendship, a sort of love, *her* sort of love, that reaches back well beyond Ines's time, just as it reaches into regions of intimacy different to those which Robert's first wife, the painter Julianne Carbody, enjoyed with him. Indeed, *her* Robert is someone they will never know.

Now, why are you in this silly, unattractive mood? What drives you to indulge in these displays? They are not very grown-up, are they? She hears the voices of her mother and father in these reproaches: the much-loved, much-missed couple.

"So, you are concerned about Julian Snowman's leadership of the House of Journalists?" Robert says, getting them to the point. He has propped her back on her stool and made it clear that now they need to talk seriously.

"Well, it is not just about Julian, it's—" Miriam stops suddenly. "No, Julian is central to this. Of course he is. Though I don't want to make this personal. The truth is, Robert, I was not happy with what I saw at the House of Journalists the other week. Or to be more precise: it was not what I saw, but the *feeling* it left me with. I felt really disheartened, even slightly sickened. Maybe that sounds a bit hysterical? I'm feeling rather out of control today. And it is not easy to articulate."

"I think I understand," Robert says. In truth, he is not sure he does, but he can see that Miriam is very worked up and he wants to help her. "There is a certain moral complacency about the place these days, is that it?"

"Yes, that is a way of putting it," Miriam agrees. "The fact is they—Julian and the Committee—have made a decision that their mission is to protect the small space. They have done it so skilfully that the House of Journalists is now almost untouchable. No minister would dare challenge the work it does. But—to me at least—this works both ways. For those it serves it still serves very well, but it has entirely stopped looking beyond its four walls."

"The trust has always supported the House knowing its limitations, Miriam."

"Perhaps, but did we not hope that it would be an influence for good; that it would be a voice in the debate and campaign for change?"

"Doesn't the writing of the fellows do that? The power and poignancy of their stories work more effectively than slogans and placards."

Miriam feels that so banal an observation cannot be said to rise to the level of her disquiet. And to bring the writing of the fellows, the holiest of holies, into all this . . . well, let's just leave it.

"I do not propose hasty action. Just to seek an opportunity to raise my concerns with Julian Snowman. He may be able to put my mind at rest."

Miriam does not need the approval of Robert or any of the other trustees to take this step. To change the terms of the funding arrangement is another matter, but she is not close to proposing such an action—never mind pulling the funding altogether. The House of Journalists is the home of the Martin and Angelika Stern Library of Refugee Studies. Above all else she wants to protect the memory of her beloved mother and father. They are much in her thoughts today as always.

She looks out on a world smeared with tears and she wonders if all this isn't all about her anyway. She is having one of her personal crises of faith. *Look at me, I'm suffering. Why don't you all suffer like me?* She is taking it out on Julian and the House of Journalists. She has got it in for an organisation which is doing a very good job in its own small way. The House is not changing this wretched world in any great way, but then how could it? Why should it? She will report back her concerns—if she still has any—to the board, and they will wonder what on earth she is going on about—as Robert quite clearly does. They will stop her from taking any hasty step. That is their job; it is why she appointed them—and why she listens to them.

For now, she takes one last sip of foul cool coffee froth and makes her excuses. Robert cannot stop her from walking out on him into the now-squally rain, without an umbrella. Perhaps it is easing off a bit, he thinks, as he watches her crossing the square.

Not Miriam Stern at her best, but there you are.

THE HOUSE WILL SURVIVE AND THRIVE WITHOUT YOUR CONCERN

Yes, it was a good idea, Julian thinks, even if the lecture itself was a prolonged piece of dull pomposity. From his seat beside the lectern, he had looked out on an audience who had fought through drooping eyelids and half yawns to connect the lofty and honourable profession of which Mr. Stan spoke with their own experiences of journalism. Like him, they know only a rough old trade—which is how it has to be in rough old times. And when are they otherwise? In the old days,

Mr. Stan was not above raw, painful, even funny confessions from the front line. Now he had retreated into windy waffle.

Still: a good idea. It had given Mr. Stan's ego a shot in the arm; a pat on the bottom. It had reassured the old fellow that he was still the heart and soul of the House of Journalists. It was worth sitting through an hour of turgid reflection and philosophising to achieve that end.

Julian is in good spirits as he walks through the lobby and into his office. He thinks to himself that he might even get down to some writing today. It has been a few weeks since he really did any of that, what with all this business at the House of Journalists, and all his other commitments. He has a lunch in his diary (he must ask Sabrina who with) and a television interview to do (ditto) but, yes, this afternoon he will devote to writing. People tend to think that because he doesn't agonise over it and pontificate about it, because it comes relatively easy for him and the fruits are so bountiful, that he does not take writing seriously. But what he doesn't do is take writing *too* seriously. He does not obsess over the process. In his mind—and he has written about it more than once—there is inward-looking writing and outward-facing writing—and it is the latter that interests him and entertains others.

The phone on the desk bleeps.

"Julian." It is Sabrina. "An outside caller for you."

"Who?"

"Miriam Stern."

Julian's expression darkens a tint. Miri Stern has been making her presence felt of late. Of course she is a friend of long standing, a fantastic supporter of the House, and a very generous one. They go back yonks and all that. But as he always stresses to the Committee, and to the friends and donors, the House of Journalists will not allow itself to be "funder-led," any more than it is government-influenced or in hock to pressure groups or lobby interests. "We pride ourselves on our independence. That is one of his proudest boasts."

"Miri!"

"Julian. Have I caught you at a good moment?"

"Good as any, Miri, good as any. What can I do for you?" *He might as well get straight to the point: they are both busy people.*

"I was hoping I might persuade you to join me for lunch in the next week or so."

"For lunch?" *Lunch? What the hell is her game? Lunch? He doesn't like the sound of that at all.*

"Well, yes, for lunch, but with the object of talking about our future relationship with the House of Journalists."

"Our future relationship?" *This echo chamber effect can get pretty tedious, he realises that, but Miri is bringing it on.*

"Yes." The irritation in her voice is obvious. "The relationship between the trust and the House, that is."

You mean whether you deign to continue funding the place. "Well, your support is certainly very valued, Miri."

"I know, Julian. And I would like to see it strengthened."

On your terms, you mean: as long as we run it in exactly the way you want it run. "Well, that is good to hear, because my only mission is to strengthen the House of Journalists, to strengthen its independence."

"I don't doubt that, Julian . . ."

But? There's obviously a but! What is it that she does *doubt? His competence? His leadership? His judgement? The direction that he and the Committee are taking to ensure that this special place has a secure future?* "But . . ." *Here it comes.*

"I've been taking a close interest in the House of late . . ."

No kidding, lady.

". . . And I've also been taking some soundings."

"Soundings?" *SOUNDINGS! Who the hell does she think she is?*

"Well, talking to a few people, inside and outside the House."

"May I ask who?"

"Julian, I don't think that really matters."

"It does to me, Miri."

"Well, some you know and some you don't." *She is sounding pretty flustered now. He has flushed her out.*

"Please tell me the ones I do know."

"Oh, I don't know, Julian, I'd rather have a longer conversation over lunch, if you don't mind."

"Perhaps, but I'd like to know who you have been talking to *inside* the House of Journalists." *Yes, names and details, if she wouldn't mind. When, how, with who?*

"Well, for example . . ."

"Don't tell me! AA!"

"AA?"

"Yes, the fellow known as AA. You know, AA. Like the breakdown service." *She doesn't know who he is talking about. That is clear straightaway. And why should she? He needs to get a grip on himself. He is supposed to have stopped obsessing over AA. (You are nothing like as important as you think you are, AA. That is clear from this conversation, if it wasn't clear already. Miri Stern doesn't even know you exist.)* "So not him?"

"No, not him. I don't even think I've been introduced. But I have, for example, had a short private chat with Mr. Stan."

For a moment, the name doesn't register with Julian, not least because he is still clearing AA from his mind. Then it hits him. *Mr. Stan!*

"So you have been having a 'short private chat,' as you call it, with my Father of Chapel. Well, I think that is an impertinence, if you don't mind me saying."

"Well, I do, rather, but let that be. It's just . . ."

"I don't think we can let it *be* at all. This is a breach of trust which I don't take kindly to. I am most surprised at Mr. Stan and at you, Miri."

"For goodness' sake, Julian, we were not swapping state secrets or plotting a coup. It is this sort of overreaction that rather goes to the heart of my concern—"

"Miri, I'm afraid your concern is seriously misplaced. I rather fear that the relationship between the trust and the House will not survive this episode—"

"Goodness, Julian, this is insane!"

"I will ignore that slur. As I say, the relationship will have to be reviewed. But that is not my decision alone. No, it is the Committee, not me, that decides these things—and I will be putting the matter to them urgently."

"Well, you do that, Julian. You put it to your mythical Committee. Or better still, just cool down a bit. Take a deep breath. The offer of lunch still stands. All I want to do is discuss—"

"—Your concerns. Yes, I know. But I politely suggest that you do not concern yourself, Miri, darling, for a moment longer. It is for the Committee, a very real body I assure you, to decide. But I strongly suspect that the House of Journalists will manage to survive and to thrive without your concern."

"Julian—"

He slams the phone down on her. He regrets it straightaway. It is an abominably rude act which he was prone to in the past when a certain type of lover provoked in him such rage that he could not control himself for a moment longer . . . And afterwards, even in those days, he bitterly regretted his lack of self-control and want of manners. But today he just couldn't *stand* to hear another word. It is shocking to say it of someone who he counted as a friend, a dear friend. But he was so shocked by what she said. He is sorry if this sounds hysterical, but really he is *heartbroken*. And it is not just that he has been let down by a dear friend, but also—he hates to say it, but say it he must—by Mr. Stan.

"Sabrina!"

"Julian . . ."

She has been listening in—he has no doubt of it. Or perhaps not, he rethinks immediately. She doesn't care about this place. She doesn't cherish it and worry for its future. It is a place to work. She just gets on with it. She takes orders and doesn't question. They could do with a few more like her, quite frankly.

"Julian?"

"Summon the Committee!"

| SUMMON THE COMMITTEE!

Somehow—it is one of the mysteries of the House of Journalists—we all know within minutes about Julian's conversation with Miriam Stern.

And yet—a greater mystery—we knew nothing of her secret meeting with Mr. Stan. How did she manage that? Mr. Stan doesn't get out alone, so he and Miriam must have met here—right under Julian's nose and our noses. How was that possible? There are fellows, staff, volunteers, spies, eyes, snitches everywhere.

Or had he help from the inside? A fellow conspirator!

Do you know anything about this, AA? And why—answer us this—do we straightaway think of you? It is true that we haven't seen you around much recently. But why is that a cause for suspicion? We can only answer that everything you do, and you don't do, is. In which case, you cannot win either way, you will answer.

Which is fair enough. This business of Miriam Stern and Mr. Stan has nothing to do with you at all. You can get on with whatever it is you are doing. The question we should be asking ourselves—you rightly suggest—is why a meeting between Mr. Stan and Miriam Stern should excite such fervour anyway.

And the answer is obvious: we are in grip of Julian's growing paranoia. It is Julian, not you, who is central to this unfolding drama. It is Julian whose actions are destroying the House of Journalists!

Now we find ourselves trying to explain all this to Shadrach, who has returned from a tribunal hearing having been granted his status. That is great news, we tell him, but we think he will be eager to know what has been happening here in his absence. As indeed he is.

Matthew, by the way, has "moved on" already. He has been given a small flat and set up with a traineeship on a free newspaper. He has already made friends among his compatriots on the "outside." He is joining the party in exile—they allow that sort of thing here, which some of us find strange. Matthew had the right attitude towards the House of Journalists. He had due but not exaggerated respect for it. He was grateful but not beholden to it. He was just "moving through" and now he has "moved on."

We all miss our fellow Matthew—Mustapha in particular. But is not Mustapha's case coming up soon? "*'E must 'ave an 'earing sooner or later, mussn' 'e?*" Esther joked at a recent class. Mustapha smiled at that, a brave smile, as he has been suffering a great depression of late.

He cannot shake off the despondency of exile. He is missing his wife and children. He is missing his homeland. He is missing—dare we say it—the long struggle he had to get here.

Because here he is. He has made it. This is it. His destination.

For if not here, where? Back again? Not that, after all he has gone through! Not that, for pity's sake! So here he stays. Here he makes his life. He starts again. The long struggle was for this.

For *this*? Safety, security, accommodation, an acceptance of lot. There is such oppressiveness here. Such restriction. We must feel it? It bears down on me so that I cannot breathe. How can we talk and laugh and smoke? There is no air, no space. I have to escape. Not one step back, or two, but three, four, five. To the time before. When past, present, and future sat nested together, with possibilities branching out, and the stem was not torn from its root.

Mustapha has apologised to all of us for his outburst. "You have nothing to apologise for at all, Mustapha," Esther reassured him. Indeed not—although we might add that we all suffer, we all miss our families, our homelands. We all fear the future and yearn for the past and find the present bleak and cheerless. There is no hierarchy of heartsickness.

Had Julian's summoning of the Committee resulted in a sitting of the Committee, the business could have been got through in minutes and that would have been the end of the matter. It would have been a one-item agenda. The Chair would have presented an oral report to the Committee, to wit that Miriam Stern, in a phone call to the Chair this morning, had indicated that she wanted to meet to discuss the future relationship between the Stern Family Trust and the House of Journalists. The Chair would have made clear his view that this suggestion carried an implied threat: that unless the direction of the House of Journalists was changed—and changed to suit her—she would withdraw her financial backing. Given that threat, the Chair would have suggested to the Committee that it should officially record its gratitude for the support that the Stern Family Trust had provided over the years, but it should remind Miriam Stern that the House of Journalists valued its independence above all. Therefore it would be most inappropriate for the Chair to meet with Miriam Stern, and arrangements would shortly be put in place to turn down all future funding from her, her trusts, and her businesses, and to terminate the relationship with the Stern family forthwith. There would have been just one item of A.O.B. The Chair would have noted with surprise and disappointment that one of the Committee members had taken it on himself to have private discussions with Miriam Stern on the subject of the future direction of the House of Journalists. He would have pointed out that such a discussion was beyond the remit of said member, that it was not in the interests of the House, and moreover that it was, the Chair was sorry to say, something of a personal betrayal. Yes, he was sorry to have to speak in such harsh terms, but there it was.

The Committee is not sitting, however. To the intense frustration of Julian. It is not sitting because Mr. Stan is absent from the House of Journalists.

Absent? Yes. So where is he? We are all asking these questions and others. In the excitement of the moment, all sorts of wild theories abound. One of our number puts us right. Of course, having given his lecture he has gone off to the hospital to have some checks. Nothing serious, we have been assured. And we are glad to hear it, though we perhaps care less about Mr. Stan's every twinge and murmur than the House would have us.

But his hospital appointment means that for the time being, everything is on hold. For there is surely no question of the Committee meeting in Mr. Stan's absence if his own conduct is to be discussed. Solomon is rightly, though uncharacteristically, insistent on this matter. Julian is heard slamming his fist down on the desk. It shudders right through the heart of the House of Journalists, so goodness knows how it shakes

Solomon's gentle soul. But he stands firm—and Julian calms down. Okay, they will have to wait for Mr. Stan. Julian accepts that. He apologises to Solomon.

The House remains in suspended animation.

| IN THE MEANTIME (1)

In the meantime, there is routine business to be got through, and Julian has received a letter from the former minister Andrew Alexander.

"Saying what?" Julian asks.

Asking for a meeting, says Sabrina. He is hoping he might be useful to the House in a non-executive capacity.

"He is joking?"

Was not Andrew a good friend in his way when he was a minister? Solomon ventures.

"When he *was* a minister, Solomon: that is the point. We need friends *in* government, not out. And it is not really friendship we want, even from the new minister. We need her to respect us, to appreciate our usefulness, to understand where we fit in to her plans and ambitions. That's how we protect what we are doing here. The word is that Andrew wobbled. This letter gives credence to that. Sabrina, we should shred it—for his sake as well as ours. Andrew, I'm afraid, is history."

| IN THE MEANTIME (2)

"Has Crumb made any more attempts to communicate with anyone, anyone at all? Staff, volunteers, fellows?" Julian asks.

"Ted Crumb?" asks Solomon.

"Yes, of course Ted Crumb. Do we know other Crumbs? Are there any other Crumbs that are not worthy to gather under our table?"

Solomon looks confused.

"Oh, it doesn't matter."

No communication has been recorded between Mr. Crumb and anyone, according to Sabrina.

"So for all we know they've all been singing like canaries to him!" Julian says, laughing at his own joke.

He is starting to frighten Solomon. And Sabrina thinks he is just plain weird. She has always felt so, but today!

"Don't listen to me," Julian adds. "My nerves are a little frayed today. We don't need to worry about Crumb, do we? We were all looking in that direction and meanwhile . . ."

| MEANWHILE (1)

Shadrach is showing us the letter issued to him by the tribunal. He has been granted "indefinite leave to remain." Esther has taught us well, so we find much to enjoy in this formulation. Who would have thought that the language of bureaucratic process would allow for such wordplay? With what stony-faced economy and irony the terms are played off against their opposites. Here is our fate sealed in a riddle. It offers us boundless uncertainty, sufferance not settlement, permission not welcome. There is precious little sense of security, and none of home, in "indefinite leave to remain." It is exile in a little phrase.

| MEANWHILE (2)

It has been quite an eventful day so far, and we, the smokers out in the Central Courtyard, have been discussing events, out in the open, out in the sunshine.

"Summer" will soon be upon us, the long-serving fellows joke. There is a handful among us who have lived through this strange, short, elusive season in these latitudes. It is characterised by long hours of inconclusive light and crazy fluctuations in temperature and humidity. Before "summer" there is "spring." We are enjoying that now, apparently. Thin stems have budded into half bloom. They hedge their bets against the possibility of night frost. The days grow longer but gain hardly any strength. And then there is this wan and sorry sunshine—which is now retreating behind a curtain of cloud—like a wallflower unused to even the mildest of compliments.

The House of Journalists' Spring Picnic is planned for later in the month. We will be journeying by coach to one of this city's many parks, where we will play baseball and sit in our coats on blankets, and drink fruit juice and eat sandwiches and other snacks. We will enjoy the fresh air, and perhaps some more of this milk-and-water sunshine. Agnes and Esther are on the picnic committee. It is not *that* sort of committee. They laugh as they see the expression on our faces—and Julian laughs along, rather too loudly. Some of the alumni will be joining us: some of those who have moved on and made a success of their new lives. They will be an inspiration and a comfort to us. The form has gone up on the notice board and we are invited to sign up if we want to join the Spring Picnic. It is entirely voluntary, but not to be missed.

And the Spring Picnic is just one event we look forward to. There is the Chess Tournament and the Summer Reception and the day-long radio special. And all the regular activities. There is the book club. There are movies and card schools. The younger ones among us have been known to kick a football around. Mr. Stan, with certain adaptations, can shoot a little pool. If time allows, a greater impression of these lighter moments will be sketched. There is, for example, a birthday tea scheduled this very afternoon for our fellow Marie-Antoinette, a poetess, filmmaker, and environmental activist. This jolly occasion, with Marie-Antoinette blowing out the candles in a gale of laughter, will be one to dispel any sense that the House of Journalists takes itself too seriously and does not know how to have fun. Oh, we can have fun, if we want to. Don't trouble yourself about that!

| A STORY THAT SHOULD BE TOLD

And yet the House of Journalists draws its peculiar power, we can surely all agree, from the darker wells of human experience. How much laughter, how much goodness and happiness flutter out when we open the pages of the great novels? Is it not the tragedies and sorrows of life that are contained therein?

So it is that we listen in now at Workshop 3, where a tale is being told that is not often heard here at the House of Journalists. It is a painful and difficult story.

That is fine. Please, go ahead.

It is one story among many of a journey to these shores. It shows that it is not just in our native countries that we have suffered at the hands of brutal authority. We die in our hundreds, even thousands—so many untold stories—because *you*, the people of this country—sorry to personalise this, but that is how it is—go to great lengths to stop us getting here—or send us back when we do. Please forgive us for being so blunt.

Not at all. Please tell the story. The House of Journalists does not pretend that because it offers sanctuary and protection that is the whole story.

Here it is, then.

I had to get out of my country. I was a journalist and poet of some distinction; I was a known opponent of the government. I had been in prison; and I had been tortured: my life was in danger. I went to your country's embassy. Armed guards at the gate would not let me through. I was directed to your country's website. It said that your country honoured the UN Convention on Refugees and provided shelter to all those who needed protection. No refugee visas were available, however. No direct routes to safety were offered or even suggested. Work permits and holiday visas were severely restricted and the waiting list was closed. Do not misunderstand me: I would have closed my country to the likes of me if I were you. A journalist and poet of some distinction, I ask you! Do we not have enough of those already? And what use are they anyway? But I was what I was—making an exception for myself, as we all must.

So, with no permission to travel, I bought an airline ticket for $800 and a false passport for $1,000. When I reached your country I would tell my story and it would suffice because it was essentially true. It was a simple story. I was a journalist and poet of some distinction. (I remained faithful to my profession, my calling.) I was travelling to an international conference. (I had read about one on the Web; in different circumstances I might have been a delegate to such a conference, I told myself.) I was not intending to stay more than a week. (The one blatant untruth.) I arrived at the airport in my country's capital but did not even get to the gate. Border officials of your country, working alongside my country's security police, stopped me at passport control. There is an ugly word for this—I learnt it that day and have heard it mentioned many times since—juxtaposition.

I was imprisoned again, tortured again. On my release, with new forged documents (which this time cost me $2,000, as I had no passport of my own to exchange), I crossed the border on foot. The border is, as you say, a "line in the sand." You drew it, your cartographers, when my country was your colony. I say sand: it is desert, but the land is hard and rugged, not soft and yielding. It has been much disputed, this line, which does not exist except on maps. Wars have been fought over it. The blood of three of my father's brothers was spilt in a conflict which pushed the line a mile or two inside one country and then a mile or two into the other, before a cease-fire agreement re-established the Empire line. Crossing it was easy enough, however, though the guards had to be bribed and my "agent" required a fee. (I will not add up all the dollar costs from now on, but I ask you to bear in mind that these sums represent parcels of family land, life-giving legacies, my mother's only chance of a respectable burial place.)

So now I was safe, perhaps? What need to journey on? I ask the questions I asked of myself. I know you ask them too. But in all truth,

I was not safe in our neighbouring country. Our security police operate there. If someone from my country, in my situation, stays there for any length of time they will be picked up and taken back. We can try again—as many times as we like. But we have to pay each time. This is how our border guards and other officials make a living. I should add that there is a daily charge for any stay in prison. I imagine they have discussed a supplement for the beatings and torture!

A contact in the capital of our neighbouring country directed me to a people smuggler. For $5,000, he would get me out of the country and into your continent. If I was to have any sort of future I had to get to your continent. I had convinced myself of that. There was nothing for me in my continent. Journalists and poets cannot survive there if they have any self-respect. There is no journalism or poetry to speak of where I come from. Only hackwork and hymns of praise to the regime.

I was taken out of the city in a taxi, as if travelling to the airport again. But this time I was dropped by the side of the road where a group of ten people were waiting, squatting by rocks. Led by a local guide, we trekked over a high dry mountain range for many days, with little food or water. Two of our number were lost along the way. I say lost. They were there with us, and then we were some way ahead. We did not turn back. We left them. We followed the lead of our local guide. That was just how it was. One was a woman; the other was a young man, maybe a boy. I do not know their names. We did not exchange such details. We focussed only on ourselves, on the journey, and on the future. I was hardened to a new way of thinking. I have not lost that. Perhaps you never do?

We descended from the mountains and crossed a salt plain, walking towards a pink and violet sunset of staggering beauty. I remember that evening. We sat down on the crust of the earth and tore at our bread. Then we walked through a night so starry it was as if we were crossing the very heavens. It was too cold to stop and sleep. When the sun rose it thrilled our frozen blood. Within an hour the sun had bleached all the colour out of the earth and sky. We walked inside the white-hot sun. We thirsted like the rocks. Our lips and eyelids and cheeks were as dry and cracked as the barren terrain. Towards evening we met up with another agent and travelled in a packed truck across stony desert and scrub for two more days.

We arrived on the outskirts of a city on the northern coast of our continent. I say the outskirts, as if they were residential suburbs or industrial districts. More precisely, we were dumped where the city dumped its rubbish. A settlement had grown up there: a stinking municipality living and making a living in the hope of admission to the next circle of hell—the sprawling slums. Downtown was miles distant. Worlds away. Following in the new-turned tracks of giant earthmovers, men, women, and children scavenged for cardboard, glass, plastic, metal— and in squawking, flapping, barking, biting competition with vultures, gulls, rats, and dogs for rotting food. This is the way of things in my continent. It disgusts me to think of it. My ambitions, sharpened by our march, extended way beyond—to the order and prosperity of Europe.

But while we were sleeping on the roadside that night our agent slipped away. We didn't know what to do next. There was cursing, shouting, accusations. One among us pulled a knife. He was pushed away. Another agent would be sure to turn up. The handover process had broken down for some reason. A day passed. The group started to break up. I was among those who waited there for another day. The others who waited were the weaker and more desperate. They sobbed with broken hope. On the third day I abandoned them. I walked away without looking back. I walked towards the city.

This city is in most respects typical of our continent. The hallucinatory come-hither of the high-rises in the city centre; a few well-watered residential and diplomatic districts which bare their clean teeth at any stray who wanders up to their gates; the concrete visions of municipal socialism in the outer districts now cracked and scabrous and partitioned among petty traders and hawkers of tat; and otherwise a vast sprawl of slum, shack, and shanty. In one respect, however, this city is unique. This is why it was a place of pilgrimage for me and for tens of thousands of others like me. For within its precincts is a tiny outpost of your continent: a colonial enclave of the country across the straits. Straits so narrow we could at night see the bright lights of your continent.

I say bright. They were lights. They were probably no brighter than the lights we slept under. They promised so much more, however. They promised a new life. In time we would take to the sea in boats in our desperation to reach them. But these straits are the most patrolled seaway in the world; they are strafed by the searchlights of naval gunboats and coast guard stations. A direct crossing is impossible. Our eventual sea route took us away from the bright lights into darker waters. Away from the straits, away from the enclave. How could this be the way to that new life that had seemed so close? No wonder we were drawn to the enclave on our shores.

Every day people crossed into it. They were few, moving slowly, in spaced intervals, through the one heavily fortified entry point. After that, to reach the border post proper, each person had to walk across an area of brutally flattened ground on which the gunsights of the guards in the watchtowers were trained. At the border post, laminated papers, biometrics, bona fides, explanations, and excuses were examined and re-examined. If they were in order, entrants were processed through a final clearance point into the enclave itself. These people, these lucky few, were people of my continent. They were the day workers. So every night they crossed out of the enclave again. Egress was expedited much more quickly.

Often as they were coming out, people from your continent were going in. The checks on them didn't take long. They were generally waved through. As they passed us, squatting in our thousands by the roadside, their faces behind the tinted windows of their Land Cruisers betrayed fear and disgust, as well as weary sympathy. What were we doing here? We surely didn't think we were going to get into their continent this way? The very fact that there were thousands of us showed how impossible that was. There had to be procedures, processes, restrictions, limits. If we wanted to come to their continent we had to do things the proper way. That meant returning to our countries and obtaining the requisite visas and permits. We couldn't just turn up at their borders and be allowed in. These thoughts crossed their minds for a moment or two, and then they were waved through, and then they didn't give us another thought, as I wouldn't in their place. Indeed in their place I would have laughed mercilessly at us sitting there beside the road in our thousands, an unmoving mass, waiting in line for a miracle that would never happen. We surely didn't think that they would ever fling open the gates to us? They would be overrun!

There was a high wall around the small enclave: a wall metres high, smooth as polished marble, topped with brilliant concertina wire, and studded with classy glass watchtowers. After a few days of squatting by the road in that queue of fools, people moved into an encampment that had grown up under these walls, as if following established protocol. It was a pathetic besiegement. I am told that international agencies had a presence there: distributing basic supplies, providing emergency medical care, and even processing people for resettlement. But I saw no evidence of these agencies and their activities. They were in a different "zone" perhaps. Yes, officially, the encampment was divided into zones, though I saw no evidence of these either.

How did we live? We ate the food waste of the enclave and shat it out again where we sat. We sat and ate and shat. We slept where we sat and ate and shat. We were often woken by water cannon. The water cannon was their sport and our renewal. It cleansed us with its torrential freezing fire. It washed everything away. Then we made foul camp afresh.

The guards in the watchtowers looked out on us from behind their mirrored aviators. They must have thought we were scum, as I would have done in their place. And it was in their place that I put myself. Each one of us does, perhaps? For in my mind I shared nothing in common with these filthy, stinking bags of bones among whom I sat and ate and shat. I really did not want to hear the stories they told around the fires of rubbish. I did not want any illumination to be thrown on their souls. I tried to block my ears to their tales of courage and endurance. And God spare me their humanity and their dreams—and even their determination and cruelty. It was hell to hear my story repeated again and again, for each time another wretch was made exceptional and worthy of redemption. I was not so special or deserving. As each storyteller took their turn, theirs was the face in the firelight we were all drawn to. There was democracy in it, a sense of shared destiny. We were a collective of storytellers. I refused to be seduced. I refused to sympathise or to share. I turned my back and waited for the water cannon to drown out this appalling cacophony.

Still, these stories worked their way into my head. I tried to shut them out, but they would be heard. They have stayed with me even though I never knew their owners, and their owners are now lost. I say lost. Perhaps I mean dead. So many died—there, but also along the rest of the route. I am one of the survivors—the victors—still haunted by these stories, which ended in defeat. You will not hear them from me. I cannot allow these other stories to drown out my story. Their owners are dead and so the stories are dead. Find them in another life if you are so interested. God, I am told, keeps them all safe in his great library. So look for them there when the time comes.

It goes without saying that I made no friends. It was no place to make friends. You had to look out for yourself. There was only one loyalty: to your own survival and future. There were robberies and beatings and rapes and murders. There were petty incidents and betrayals. The collective of the storytellers didn't last long after the evening fires burnt out. We were all on our own during the freezing nights. We made pillows of our possessions to protect them from the thieves we slept among.

After a few days, I moved on—again in line with the established protocol of the place. I walked along the coastal highway, alone, with hundreds of others. The sea it seemed did not have the energy to beach itself, so choked was it with black seaweed. I say seaweed. In fact, this wrack was a vast shoal of black plastic bags. Dry form, torn and ragged, they hung, like funeral ribbons, in the thornbushes. And, set free, they danced and swirled like black dervishes in the hot, gritty wind.

When night fell we moved in to the dunes and waited. We paid fees to "shipping agents" who moved among us. We were told that the boat owners would signal from offshore to those waiting for a pickup. We were to wade out to them. We waved fistfuls of notes—"tips"— which they grabbed and counted. We threw dirty bundles of belongings into the slosh. We scrambled over the sides as they hauled us in by our belt loops. We left others scrambling, choking, and drowning. I was the last in.

We puttered out into calmer deeper waters, trailing oil. The lights of your continent were still just visible but they were receding. The routes took us away from the patrol-infested straits, out into the open sea, where interdiction was less likely, but death much more. The boat was some sort of fishing craft. It stank of fish guts, diesel oil, salt water, and rotting wood. It was leaking and we were bailing in shifts from the start. It was a boat for five, ten at the most. There were twenty of us perched on its rims and benches. There were twenty litres of bottled water on board. There were ten packets of soaked biscuits. We were through these supplies in two days; we were out there for five.

The sun was a white-hot disc. The sky was dry vapour. The sea was a second salt plain. There was one storm. I say a storm. It was really no more than a summer squall, but we capsized within minutes. We struggled to right ourselves. The swell turned us over again. We spent several hours clinging to the upturned boat. We lost two that night. There should have been no drowning in this slight summer swell, so they must have been weak specimens, though I knew nothing about them. They disappeared without us noticing. The rest of us clung on easily enough.

Then it was back to the devil's own millpond. Our captain had no real knowledge of wind and sail. And I say captain. He was a mere coast boy—a boy who should have been making a stinking living out of fishing but who had bigger dreams. He was armed with a kitchen knife and drank from a bottle of lethal spirit. His crew was an even younger boy, crueller and more reckless. He smoked reefers, swigged from his own flask of hooch, and masturbated with monstrous deliberation. His penis, in which he took great pride, was a thick, plum-black organ, even though he was a relatively light-skinned boy. It had been blackened by the sun, presumably. We tried not to look at it. If he saw us looking we were pulled over to suck him off. I gagged and choked as he grabbed fistfuls of my shorn hair to keep me to the task. Such an act is an abomination in my culture. As I spat and retched over the side, he punched me in the face. "Next time you swallow."

One evening, having finished his own, he made a grab for his skipper's bottle of spirit and in so doing knocked it out of his hand and over the side. In a second, the older boy pulled out his knife and stabbed the younger boy in the heart. The boy tottered backwards in surprise—grinning, it seemed, at the thought that he was to die for an act of such senseless and petty stupidity. He stumbled against the side of the boat; tried to steady himself; looked up, saw the older boy, reached out to him—now imploring, now fearing death: only to have his feet kicked from under him and his legs levered over the side. He sank with a single cartoon glug. The older boy grimaced. The death was necessary. Honour demanded it. But it made landing us and getting back home much more difficult and dangerous for him.

Another one died on the last, most dreadful day. His tongue lolled black in his burning head. The sun was a perpetual damnation. The day blazed and blistered. I was spectral with thirst. The skin on my face was like strips of parchment. My hands were bleeding. Why were my hands bleeding? I do not know what that was about. We all suffered the most terrible cramps. We pissed fire and our shit was an evil slime.

By some miracle, we came upon a holiday resort coastline. It was towards dawn; too late to get us ashore under the cover of night. Having located a drop-off point, our captain—a more respected figure after the summary execution of his mate—took us out to sea again. In our hysteria for land we pleaded with him and cursed him bitterly, but in this instance he knew what he was doing.

Naval speedboats patrol these waters to stop people like us making it ashore. If they had located us they would have thrown us water bottles and emergency supplies, attached a towline, and dragged us miles out into open sea, away from their recognised waters of responsibility. This is what they do these days. They do not rescue people. They know that many die. They know that they are not fulfilling international treaty obligations. But they do not care. Who can blame them? Many thousands are making this same journey every day. Many hundreds make it as far as we did. If they rescued us all, or allowed us to land, they would be overwhelmed. We know the deal. The deal is that only a few get through. And it is only because only a few get through that there is any hope for any of us.

Darkness fell. Our captain took us in again. We spilled into the warm holiday swell carrying with us our salt-sea-soiled bags and a final corpse. We sat on the beach all night waiting for the dawn police patrols. They sweep the coast before the holiday makers come down to play. These cops were quite cheerful and good-humoured. They kicked us around a bit; slapped us, but with open hands. There was some spitting, but it was not too bad. We couldn't understand what they were saying, but it seemed they were impressed that we had made it. *Some trip, heh?* I imagine them saying. They knew of course what hell we had been through to get there. I have read since that the last summer season saw record numbers of us trying to make the crossing. We were clinging to tuna nets, and bobbing across on inner tubes and rubber rings; they were picking us up on pedaloes and surfboards. "Almost laughable, if it wasn't so pathetic, so dangerous, so tragic." These are the words of one Juan Martin Grimaud, Euro-tanned, wearing a crisp, white, epauletted shirt and expensive sunglasses, a captain in the Frontex Marine, who I have seen quoted on the Web.

We were detained in an abandoned military base, on a dry grey treeless plateau in the middle of the island, far from the deep blue and green coves and inlets of the coastline, far from the silky sands of the tourist beaches. The facilities were stark and unsanitary, the regime harsh, even brutal, but given our recent experiences we were thankful for this place of recuperation. For the first few days, at least. There was, as I have noticed many times since, a marked contrast between the attitudes shown towards us by officials and by people in nongovernmental agencies. The latter, on this island, were laypeople of the church. They were careful to offer us no false hope: "It is likely, dear friend, that they will return you. You must prepare yourself." They made it sound like death, which in a way it was. These women, for they were all women, were kindly to a fault. I say to a fault, because I and others, as the days went by, found fault with this kindness, which seemed to us to be useless. It had no fight in it. They were, we felt, meekly reconciled to our fate, these kind lay ladies of the church. When I started to shout and scream at one woman one day, a guard laid about me with his baton, as I would have done in his place. The old woman deplored the violence. She tried to interpose herself between the guard and me, and was greatly surprised when I pushed her away. She shouldn't have been. I had no more time for her. She could not help me. I did not need her comfort.

I think she may have hurt herself. I say, may. She did. She broke her wrist, protecting herself as she fell. She was an old woman. I did not know her name, although she certainly told me her name and she knew mine very well. She was constantly prefixing her weak and useless phrases of comfort with my name. I had never introduced myself to her. She had my name from the authorities, who had it from the sea-soaked passport they found, foxed and blotched, taped to my person. You may recall that this document was forged, but along with my profession, my calling—"poet and journalist"—I had kept my first name, the name my mother gave me. I did not take kindly to this old woman using this name with such familiarity. I had dealings with her only because I knew she could bring me books. But then, stupid as she was, she brought children's books in her language. These were of no use to me, I told her, as I had no intention of staying in her country. (Our shared language was this one, the language of the House of Journalists—in which I was more versed than she was.) I made clear my needs and next time she brought me a volume of poems in this language—poems of mediocre worth, it must be said—which I nonetheless valued highly, as this was the only act of hers that was of any use to me. Looking back, I wish I had made my gratitude more evident at the time.

This part of my story ends bitterly, as my kind old friend knew it would. I was taken in a security van to a naval area and put on a small marine vessel, along with around a hundred others, and returned to the small enclave of your continent in my continent. The sea journey took only a few hours. We spent perhaps ten minutes waiting on the quayside inside the small enclave under armed guard. Then a coach pulled up and we were driven out through that frontier post, past the thousands sitting squatting by the roadside, to a very well organised camp several tens of miles into the desert. In this camp—newly constructed—we were divided by sex. "For your own protection," the female guard told me and the rest of the women.

Our narrator pauses and lets this latest twist sink in. It is indeed a shocking turn of events for us, the fellows, as well as for you, our visitors, and the volunteers and mentors, who always sit in on these classes, rapt and reverential. ("One phrase you might hear to describe it is 'back to square one,'" Esther later teaches us. "A derivation from chess,

I suppose, though I am no chess player." This surprises us. Most of us are chess players. Writers and journalists in our countries are almost always chess players.)

Of course, we have all experienced setbacks; the routes of our journeys to safety have at best a tortuous logic, and always involve diversions, holdups, and lateral moves. Arrest, detention, summary deportations across borders—these are common. But today's narrator has been masterly in shocking us with the heartbreak of *her* return. We did not see that coming.

What will happen next? What other surprises does she have in store? It is a real "page-turner"—no explanation necessary. And such a description does not make light of our hardships, Julian insists. "There is adventure, and sometimes derring-do, in these testimonies. We are thrilled by some of the events. We find ourselves gripped, carried along. These tales have the taut plotting that is characteristic of life at its most intense. It is natural and right to identify with the heroes of these tales, to cheer them along. And then—perhaps when the storyteller pauses for a sip of water—we see before us the lone human being. And we get some sense of their suffering as well as their heroism, of their vulnerability as well as their courage, of their ordinariness as well as extraordinariness. This is the unique service that the House of Journalists offers to those seeking to understand one of the great issues of our day: forced migration. The House exists first and foremost of course to provide a place of refuge for exiled journalists, broadcasters, and writers. But it also has a mission to dramatise and humanise the refugee experience in ways that reach wider audiences."

Our narrator is indeed taking a drink from a glass of water. The little extras at the House of Journalists are always immaculate, as if for an important international conference. "Right from the start it was my vision that this place would avoid the dispiriting atmosphere or aesthetic of a homeless hostel or community centre," Julian tells donors. So every conference and seminar room is provided with bottles of still and sparkling mineral waters, branded pens and quality notepads, glossy literature about the House of Journalists, including its latest publications. There are plug-in points for tablets and laptops, and facilities for simultaneous translation—though this is discouraged. All efforts in the language of this country, however halting, are encouraged, even lauded. "There is ineffable beauty in a tale simply, falteringly, even amusingly told by a visitor to our language"—another phrase of Julian's. But now our narrator has finished sipping from her glass of water. Our narrator is called Sonny, by the way.

She is ready to resume, but is given pause by the hand of our moderator—one of the leading writer mentors called Rose Enderby—which has been placed gently on top of Sonny's hand. In this gesture Rose Enderby conveys—or intends to—solidarity, sisterly tenderness, the strong bond between writers, and an immense (and unabashed) sense of moral self-satisfaction, because here she is—Rose Enderby, a well-established and critically acclaimed novelist—giving of her self in the most generous way a writer can, by *listening*, and listening intently in that special writer's way, which is almost physically painful for her. By this gesture—her hand on top of Sonny's hand—she also conveys that she, Rose Enderby, would like to say a few words, not that anything she could say can add much, but that said, she just wants to express, however imperfectly, how profoundly moved she has been, and how humbled, and honoured, and proud, to have been able to hear this story, this incredibly powerful testimony, for to be a writer or, rather, a storyteller, seems to her now, more than ever, a calling of unique importance.

But she will shut up now, Rose Enderby says with a laugh—we are slow to follow. Because we haven't come to listen to her. She laughs again—we are slower still. Rose Enderby is somewhat discomposed by our response, or lack of response. She has flushed a blousy pink. Sonny, who has remained standing, her hand trapped under Rose Enderby's hand, looks at Rose Enderby. She is to go on? Rose Enderby releases her hand very suddenly.

Food, sanitation, and medical services in the camp met international standards for a camp of its sort. The officials said they wanted to help us. But they only wanted to help us to return to our countries of origin. There was a three-step process: identity verification; redocumentation; repatriation. I pointed out that I was a journalist and poet of some distinction in my country; that I had spoken out against the authorities;

that I had been imprisoned and tortured; and that my life would be in danger if I was returned. I was a political refugee. The UNRA official told me that there were no places available on the refugee resettlement scheme; the quota had been filled. I asked to join the waiting list. The waiting list was closed. I had neither been identity-verified nor redocumented, but I was slated for repatriation anyway. Or, more accurately, return to region.

After a few weeks, I was included in a returnee consignment which was trucked to the airstrip and flown by transport plane to a regional hub. The three-step process resumed at a new camp in the neighbouring country to my country. This camp was not well organised. It was filthy and disorderly. I escaped on the third day. I say escaped. I walked out of the camp at night through an unguarded perimeter gate.

I walked for a day along the road. On the second day I was picked up by a truck which was going to the capital city. I was raped by its driver each night of the three-day journey. Call it the price of the ticket, he told me, as he raped me. The following day we sat side by side in the cab of the truck. He was a corpulent, malodorous man, in a stained vest, with a dirty towel wrapped around his head. He hawked and he spat. He whistled. He laughed. I wanted to kill him. I might have done it; it would have been easy enough. There was a bag of tools behind my seat in the cab; I could have reached behind the seat, pulled out a hammer or a wrench and brained the stinking bastard with it. I smiled throughout the journey thinking about it. The driver thought I was smiling at his disgusting jokes. I didn't brain him. I wanted to, but I needed to get to the capital and I do not drive.

This was my first time. Being raped, I mean. And that is a rare thing for a female migrant to say. You might even call it a proud boast. I liked to think it was no accident. I am boyish of feature and figure, and I dressed to increase the doubt in men's minds. But I had softened in the holding centres and camps. My hair had grown. My clothes were not obviously female but I was cleaner. I gave off some femininity. I had dropped my guard. I am not saying I deserved to be raped. That is a disgusting thing to say. I just offer some explanation. Though I might just as well have been picked up by a truck driver who liked young boys, I suppose. Still, when my driver, my rapist, dropped me on the outskirts of the capital—he waved goodbye—the first thing I did was to crop my head and to roughen up. I was the tough boy on the fishing boat again. I would fight them off, or kill them, if any man tried it on again.

I found work after some days in a newsroom. It was beneath me, but I told myself—it was true of course—that I was *not* a journalist and poet of distinction in *this* capital. I was unknown and I wanted it to stay that way. My work helped me to realise my plan, although it took many months. I cannot say much more. On the whole, I'm sure you will agree, I have told my story in great detail and with a mind to veracity, though you must take my word for that. But we who reach your shores must of necessity keep back how we achieved our goal. The agents and smugglers and traffickers who help us along the way do not take kindly to clients who blab. The routes to safety are ever more tortuous and dangerous—and costly. To keep them open we must keep our mouths shut. We must protect these routes in the interests of those who make their livelihood from them, but also in the interests of those who would follow us. That is what we are told and we do not answer back.

So now my long journey ends at this city's airport? And there, you may assume, my story ends too?

Asylum. I am a writer. Welcome to the House of Journalists! Another journalist and poet of distinction becomes a fellow.

I disappoint you perhaps to tell you that at this point in my tale I am still thousands of miles, and more than a year, away from this afternoon in Workshop 3. My flight took me to a southern country of your continent, far from here. I was put into the fast track process for asylum determination. I was detained for six months. The facility—built with a European Union grant—was brand-new. It stood on the edge of a poor suburb. It was so new the white of it was dazzling to the eyes. It smelt of bleach and officialdom. In such pristine functionality the mind is maddened. I was fed and watered; I was safe; but I was never so depressed. I rocked and cried on my bunk. I went about my duties with a dead heart. But on the first day of the seventh month they released me. I was given no information as to the status of my case. I was just turned out on the streets.

I am not complaining. My depression lifted immediately. For the first couple of days I roamed in a state of wonderment. What struck me was how beautifully lit the public buildings in the city were at night. What struck me also was that the parks and gardens and verges were well kept and watered. The weather was warm and it was no hardship to sleep on benches. I kept to benches out of respect for the perfect grass. It disgusted me to see local drunks and derelicts fouling the grass with their stinking coats and matted hair and beards. The homeless have always disgusted me. A person should always be able to find a home. That I have lived so rough for so many months is a cause of great shame to me.

I did not go hungry. The food that the people of the city threw away outside the fast-food outlets was better than the food in the detention centre. I say better. It was junk. But it tasted of freedom. It tasted corporate, industrialised, first world, throwaway. One day I would throw away food like this, I promised myself. I took my finds into dark alleys, as I do not like to see people eating in the streets, even though street food is common in my country. I did not understand why people chose to take-away when these fast-food outlets had seats and tables. Perhaps it was the bright light. Only poor people ate in at these establishments, I noticed.

What next? I did not know the language of that country. I had no contacts or friends. I had no idea how to work or live there. I scavenged but I would not beg. I found a hostel for refugees like me. *Sin papeles*, they called us. I accepted help because I needed it at that moment. But I made no attempt to make friends or become part of the community. I spent some time in the public library looking at maps and then I set off. I crossed one country, and another, and a third, and—I am wearying of my adventures now—finally reached this country. Journey's end. This was always the destination I had in mind.

You will ask me, why this country? Was I not safe in the first country—and the second and third? I am told that I will have to explain to the authorities, to the tribunes, why I did not seek protection in these other countries in the safe area. All of the Union is a safe area, I am told. I do not doubt it. I will tell them—it is for them to judge—that this country is much more than a destination, or a sanctuary, or even a home. It is my *destiny*. This is a place where a journalist and poet can breathe free air, make a living, earn respect, live decently. In my short time at the House of Journalists I have had my work published and broadcast and I have spoken to large audiences. It has convinced me—though I never doubted it—of my worth as an artist. I will thrive here if I am given a chance. I will not let anyone, however powerful, stand in the way of my destiny. I trust my story makes that clear.

| WHAT COULD ANYONE POSSIBLY ADD BY WAY OF COMMENTARY AND DISCUSSION?

"Thank you, Sonny." Julian says. "Powerful testimony indeed."

He had slipped into the workshop almost unnoticed at the midway point, taking an aisle seat in the back row. Thereafter, he moved forward with mannered stealth, taking advantage of every juncture in the story to take a seat closer to the front. By the end, he was in the front row, ready to jump up and lead the thanks and congratulations to this remarkable young fellow.

Rose Enderby is left in inelegant redundancy. Rose Enderby will want a word with Julian afterwards. Julian knows that. Julian knows Rose Enderby of old. Rose Enderby can go hang, frankly.

Julian had been informed that there was a packed audience for this talk, with a lot of young volunteers and writing mentors in attendance, and so he thought it politic to put in an appearance. Rose Enderby can hardly object to his presence, or if she does, well, she can, as he says, go hang. Sonny has spoken. Let her story speak for itself. A long disquisition about its implications—moral, ethical, political, geopolitical, gender-political—can wait. And so can any discussion of the rights and wrongs of this country's asylum system. Sonny may choose to return to these broader themes at another time, when she is more settled at the House of Journalists. Some fellows choose to discuss such matters, others do not, but for now she has conveyed—in the most powerful way possible—a message which, hard as it is to hear, must be heard. What could anyone possibly add by way of commentary and discussion?

It is not a question of stopping discussion. It is a question of questioning the value of discussion when we have heard what we have heard. If anyone wants to question his attitude to discussion, he would point out that there are also those who say that as Chair of the House of Journalists he shows great courage in providing a platform for such raw and bitter testimony. Such testimony has the enormity to shake the soul and trouble the conscience of even the most powerful and important in this land. There are those who would rather these stories were not heard. But he would have them heard here. This is the place for such testimony. That is why he protects this place so fiercely. Because if these stories were not heard here, where would they be heard? He asks his critics this: If not here, *where*?

And before anyone can question him, he has left the room. The talk is over and he is out of there. He has seen something out of the window at the front entrance which demands his immediate attention.

| IT IS NOT MR. STAN

But it is not Mr. Stan returning after his check-up.

Julian, almost skidding to a halt, realises that straightaway. It was not, as he supposed, a health service courtesy vehicle that he saw pulling up; it is just an ordinary white van, which is dropping off some new books for the Martin and Angelika Stern Library of Refugee Studies. The librarian, an unassuming woman whose name escapes Julian for a moment, if indeed he ever knew it, is most surprised to see him appear at the reception desk as she signs for the books.

Mr. Snowman always expresses his immense pride in the library when showing important visitors around the House of Journalists, but otherwise he takes little interest in it. Today, however, he carefully if distractedly inspects the new volumes, and enquires of . . . Mary? . . . yes, of course, Mary . . . how things are in the library? It is a wonder, is it not, that it doesn't contain every book on refugees already? Oh, he doesn't doubt for a moment that they are publishing more and more all the time, but you have to ask yourself who reads this stuff. There are more and more scholars of the subject, Mr. Snowman. Yes, that is his point: scholarship begetting scholarship, books and pamphlets proliferating, until you get to the point where you ask yourself—just as you do with all novels and poetry and plays, for that matter—is this actually adding anything much to what has been written already?

Mary doesn't know what to say to that. She has a bachelor's degree and master's degree in refugee studies and she is completing—slowly— her Ph.D. Julian cannot be expected to take this much interest in the academic careers of any of his staff, and let's face it, the Martin and Angelika Stern Library of Refugee Studies is an outpost of the House of Journalists. Mary is grateful that it should be so, and so are the academics and students who use the library. They are happy to be undisturbed to get on with the serious business of scholarship.

Julian does not doubt it. And as he walks away, it occurs to him that herein stands the case which he will put to Committee for cutting off links with the Stern Family Trust. The House of Journalists can take immense pride in nurturing the library, he will say, but it has grown to a size where it would surely be better accommodated by a university or research institute, which has the space and specialist interest to take it to the next stage of its development. For let's not forget that this House was established not as a place of scholarship but as a place of sanctuary; a home not for books, but for writers; men and women, not objects of study or units of research; people who can speak for themselves and tell their own stories, who share their humanity and their heroism, who seek to connect and empathise, and who in doing so throw a far greater light on the phenomenon of forced migration and the condition of exile than any thesis or treatise, any tome or tract.

"Julian."

"Solomon."

"Julian, we have managed to get hold of the volunteer who is with Mr. Stan at the hospital. They are running a few tests and check-ups."

"That I think we knew, Solomon."

"But it has taken longer than they thought."

"Evidently."

"And it is not clear when they will be back."

"So, we now know that we know nothing more than we knew before."

Julian, confident that this exchange has reached the limits of its redundancy, turns away and so does not notice that Solomon is steeling himself to add something.

"Julian." It comes out in what can only be described as a breathy squeak.

"Solomon." Julian at least acknowledges him verbally—although he carries on walking, without looking round.

"Julian . . . I think you should go."

Julian spins on his heel. "Go?"

"Not detain yourself here at the House of Journalists any longer. I understood that you had some appointments, some other work you wanted to do. And although these have been cancelled I think, I do not think it makes much sense for you to hang around here waiting for Mr. Stan to return so that we can have a Committee meeting. Maybe Mr. Stan will not return until very late or he will be kept in for observation. And anyway, even if he returns now he will be tired after his tests and check-ups and I think, if you don't mind me saying, so tired that it would not be right to expect him to join an extraordinary session of the Committee, however urgent the business, even if it is a short one-item meeting. No, that would not be entirely fair, in my opinion. I really think that this matter must now wait until tomorrow, when other members may then be able to attend—though that is not the most important thing to my mind. Rather it is Mr. Stan."

Julian cannot recall an occasion when Solomon has spoken to him at such length and with such conviction on any matter; nor can he recall Solomon ever having put a contrary opinion to his own. Such are the thoughts on which Julian dwells for a moment or two. But Solomon does not need to look so alarmed. He is clearly right. There really is nothing more to say. Solomon can be reassured that he has raised a good point, made a legitimate argument, and convinced the Chair of the House of Journalists.

Julian continues on to the office, but only to tidy away a few things. Then he will leave for the day and do all those other things he needs to do.

| PALPITATIONS OF THE HEART

Mr. Stan is waiting in a hospital corridor for the final tests. He is extremely tired, but that alone does not account for his mien of dejection. The fillip which this morning's lecture had delivered to his spirits has completely evaporated. Indeed it had only just carried him to the hospital, for on arrival he received a text message from Miriam Stern. *JS agitated about our meeting—can you speak to him? He has blown things out of proportion. Best, Miriam.*

He is troubled first that Miriam had told Julian about their meeting. He had only agreed to it on the basis that it would remain strictly confidential. There was nothing in the least sinister about the meeting— Miriam had voiced some mild concerns about Julian's leadership, that was all; and he, Mr. Stan, had nodded in a noncommittal way—but he knew Julian would overreact if he heard about it, so he didn't mention it to him. And guess what? Now Julian had heard about it—thanks to Miriam blabbing (a strong word, but there it was)—and he *is* overreacting. He, Mr. Stan, was not fooled by the invitation to deliver a lecture. It was an attempt to flatter him, to divert his attention. He had fallen in with it for a morning, allowed himself a little treat, but he trusts the fellowship understands that in indulging himself in this way he has not abandoned their side.

He remains deeply concerned by Julian's increasingly manic behaviour, as demonstrated by the calling of all these the emergency sessions of the Committee to discuss these supposed threats to the very existence of the House of Journalists. First Edward Crumb, and then this fellow AA: Really, did these two pose any danger at all? The former was all empty bluster, as far as Mr. Stan could see; while the latter seemed to have absented himself from proceedings entirely. He hadn't seen the man for days. Now Miriam Stern—and indeed himself—were objects of suspicion. It is absurd. Quite absurd.

He used so to love the Committee, its privileges and proceedings, which he reported back, with due reverence, to the Chapel, which in turn listened and approved, and on occasion petitioned him as their Father to take up a matter of concern. However, at the last meeting of the Chapel strong words had been spoken. There was no point denying it. (From some quarters? Julian asked. From many, Mr. Stan reported.)

Where was the sharing of information, the respect for discussion, the spirit of democracy, the writers' collective? the fellows had asked. We are not told what is going on and our views are not being listened to, they argued. He, Mr. Stan, as the Father of Chapel, was the fellows' representative, was he not? the fellows demanded. Why then was he giving every impression that he was the Committee's creature, its stooge? (A very strong word, but there it was.) Why was he not speaking up, as mandated, for the concerns of the Chapel as expressed in various motions and composites? (There have always been a few troublemakers, Julian said. These voices speak for the majority of the fellowship, Mr. Stan replied.) Lashed by the criticism—some of it unjust, but not all; some of it intemperate, but not all—he had suggested to the Chapel members that perhaps they should consider electing another Father. But the members had reserved judgement on such a step. And the Committee in the person of the Chair had ruled it ultra vires anyway. The Committee respected the views of the fellows, but there were due processes through which concern or grievance could be channelled, and these personal attacks on their own Father, so stinging, so wounding, were not worthy of the Chapel. Mr. Stan, with a heavy heart, accepted this line. He had planned to convene the Chapel so as to tender his resignation, but given the changed circumstances, no meeting was called—and none has been called since, in which elapse of time the Committee has met several times more, and been asked to approve many decisions of the Chair. Indeed—let's tell it as it is—the Committee *is* the Chair! Why maintain the fiction any longer? The Committee is the Chair who is Julian who is all-powerful!

He has spoken out, and that is a relief.

Investing all authority in one man is not right. Mr. Stan, more than anyone, knows where it leads. He has seen this sort of process play out, in many different ways, in his own country. And it always ends badly.

The young volunteer who has accompanied Mr. Stan to the hospital appears beside him at this point and without a word starts to wheel him up the corridor for his tests.

"I am not completely useless," Mr. Stan snaps, whizzing away from the volunteer in his electric chair. There are so many of these ministering creatures these days: patrolling the corridors of the House of Journalists, keeping an eye out, making sure that the fellows have everything they need, that they are not left alone to fend for themselves for even a minute.

"Of course, I'm sorry," this particular volunteer calls after him.

The volunteer melts away, but he will be somewhere close at hand, closer than you think, ready to minister, to be of service—always at the service of the House of Journalists.

Mr. Stan regrets his outburst, but has no chance to apologise. He curses himself for taking his perturbation out on one of the volunteers, one of the remarkable young people of this country. In what other country, he asks himself, do young people show such respect and reverence for their elders? The public here do not seem to appreciate their young people. But the fellows all do. Even if they sometimes find the concern and admiration of these acolytes oppressive. And yes, that is the word that comes to mind inescapably: *oppressive.*

Meanwhile, fellows he knows, likes, and respects are meeting without him. They are discussing things behind his back. Or at least, outside the formal structures of the Chapel. Are they plotting and scheming, in the way Julian seems to find suspicious? Mr. Stan doubts it amounts to much, but he has seen how easily a spiral of suspicion can self-fulfil. He needs to exert a calming influence on Julian, who is the fount of this folly, but he has lost some of his power to do so, now that he does not, by his own admission, command the full support of the fellowship or exert his authority of old over it.

The nurse needs him to get up onto the examination trolley, but he is so downcast and weary that it is an effort to even contemplate extrication from his chair, which hums still in neutral. Yet if he doesn't stir himself, the nurse, a Xhosa woman with an impressive Table Mountain bottom, will haul him out from among his consoles and joysticks by his leathery armpits and plop him in place. He is keen to avoid that humiliation, so, taking up his crutches, he embarks on the intricacies of planting, levering, and swivelling, by which process he slowly succeeds in propelling himself from chair to trolley.

But dignity spared in one instance is immediately sacrificed in what follows, as the effort of reaching the trolley has so tired him, and so tried the patience of the nurse, that once ensconced he can offer no resistance to her hasty divestment of his bow tie, jacket, shirt, and vest. He is left to sit shivering like a child, in concave-chested nakedness—more to put him in his place than for the convenience of the doctor, he is certain.

Mr. Stan knows his own strengths. He is a good man, a brave man, who has stood up, if hunched, for all that is right. But there is a weakness within him. He recognises it and yet he has never quite overcome it. The weakness is for leadership and authority. He looked to it even in his journalism, in which he sought more than anything to write in praise. Those fierce laments and agonised denunciations of the colonial rulers and later of the usurpers of independence were hauled out of a heavy heart. He did not rejoice in the struggle, even though it was against obvious tyranny and injustice; he did not glory in the deployment of scorn, even though its objects deserved their opprobrium richly. He was not given to outrage and overthrow. Indeed it was a torment to haul himself up to his high seat and pound out a denunciation from the lumbering ironwork of the typewriter. His fingers grew leathery, black-nailed, and horn-capped through the futile labour of it. During those years Mother shuddered to see the precious little hands of her longed-for baby so hardened through this toil—even if it had been turned against a now-common enemy. And when she was brought to the security police headquarters that evening it was those baby hands, not the hardened man's hands they had become, that she saw bludgeoned to bloody, pulpy stumps. That was why the pain was so unbearable for her. That was why the sight finished her off. They had completed *his* work.

Of course there was no escape into psycho/poetical flights of fancy for him on that day. Do you hear *that*, Mother dearest! No deep readings, no theoretical meanderings. Hardened or not, horn-capped or not, there was no protection from the pain. It pulsed up from nerve endings straight into the receptors of the brain. The mind was pure-water pain. No distracting thought or diverting stratagem could live in its merciless purity. He certainly wasn't thinking of what his hands represented or symbolised, what was lost or what could have been. They were cursed purveyors of pain, nothing higher or more beautiful. He would have ripped them off with his teeth and spat them out at Mother's feet if that would have bought him a moment's relief!

And Mother, if she cares to hear this now, might ponder on the fact that the mangling of his hands has infantilised him utterly. Without them he can do next to nothing for himself. He cannot write or exercise any freedoms. He is dependent on and grateful for the ministrations of others. They must spoon-feed food into his mouth and wipe his bottom clean of shit. Yes, they must do your jobs, Mother! He slaps his stumps down on the thin plastic mattress of the trolley so hard that the nurse, scrubbing up at her sink, turns round in alarm. He smiles to reassure her.

He had invested all he had left in Julian and the House of Journalists. It was to be the end of the disillusioning journey of his life; it was to be his retirement home and resting place. Now Julian had denied him even this puny recompense. Julian's machinations, his growing dictatorial tendencies, were pretty petty stuff by comparison with all that had gone before, you might think; mere scribbling, hardly worth the paper, against those epic struggles. But therein lay its irksomeness.

Mr. Stan had often heard people say that what went on at the House of Journalists was important because of what it stood for, what it represented and symbolised. He had heard *himself* saying it more times than he cared to remember. Others could speak for themselves, but, for his own part, this sentiment now stood exposed as cant and hypocrisy! All he had ever wanted from the House was an escape from all that. He did not want to read into it wider meanings or universal values, embodiments, portents. He just wanted to live and die safely in a comfortable place.

————

"Ah, Mr. Stanislaus, let's take a look at you, then. Any trouble passing water? Any blood in the stool? Any grumblings of the tummy? Any palpitations of the heart? Good, good . . ."

| THERE HAS ONLY BEEN ONE SUICIDE

After the session with my counsellor this morning I was not of a mind or spirit for fellowship. I have spent the time since locked away. No, not locked away; there are no locked doors in the House of Journalists. *Shut* away; that is the word for it; shut away in my room, writing.

Ah, now. This is good, you will all think.

Certainly the duty volunteer who patrols my corridor was most encouraged to find me at my desk, chewing on the end of a pen, so obviously absorbed in the act of writing. He was not about to disturb me, but I anyway threw a protective arm round the pad of paper to guard the privacy of the act. Perhaps he supposed I was embarrassed by the meagreness of my efforts, but I was not shielding virgin whiteness. My once-strong sweeping hand is now reduced to a wobbly, trembling scrawl, but it had made determined inroads into the demanding lines, even as it veered off and fell away. I make no grand claims—as none of the true fellows of this place would ever do—for the artistic quality of my poetry. (Yes, I am writing poetry.) But the act of writing—this will cheer the House authorities—allows me to rediscover a stronger sense of self than the humble self-abasement I have assumed by becoming Mustapha.

I am no longer a refugee or exile; I am not an admired survivor or heroic symbol; I do not stand for or against anything. I am the man I was in my home country. I am an ordinary man, though from the upper classes, richer and better educated than the majority of my fellow countrymen. I am not of exceptional ability or distinction of character. My good fortune in life is a matter largely of luck. Luck rather than fate or God's grace, I should add: I am a rational man. I am grateful for my lot of course, though I do not make great play of my appreciation. I am no more than ordinarily charitable to those less fortunate than myself. I would like to see reform to the established order but not at significant sacrifice to myself. I am a liberal and I express liberal opinions. But the concern I have and express for democracy, justice, and human rights is only that of any educated, civilised, and self-conscious man. In truth, I care as much, if not more, for good books, good clothes, good food and wine, good company; for family and friends, for beauty and love—all of which I enjoy beyond what is fair and just in the scheme of things.

All of this, though, is but the happy and well-ordered foundation for my poetry. I mention it only because Julian, his Committee, and the House in general should know that there is nothing in it which will help to promote their noble cause or support this bloodless, sexless fellowship of theirs. Indeed what they would find if they were ever able to look and to read what I am writing—which will never happen—are passionate poems to my wife, my lover, my whole life, not as she is or even was or ever could be, but as I would have her now. The essence of her: a beautiful young girl, but ageless and unchanging. I have never stopped falling in love with that girl; a joyous endless tumbling; there is nothing in memory or expectation to break my fall; this love is utterly without end. I will fall and fall and fall, through the false floor of this life and the never-ending ones of the next, forever loving her. My love will be my eternity. The sensual sweep of her walk, the hip swing of it; but also the intelligent blue steadiness of her eyes, the elegant arch of her brows, the pout and slight overbite of her mouth: her skin glow, her peachy smell; the yielding wet sex of her: all of it brought me, senses singing, to the point of poetry. Yes, the poetry that I was guarding, which I will never share, was erotic poetry: a turn-on. Turn away! Keep your hands off it.

It is now locked away in my desk. Yes, *locked*. The drawers on the desk are not fitted with locks of course. But I went one day to a shop in the High Road and bought a small cashbox. I carried it back into the House of Journalists under my coat.

There are no searches here. What an idea! We come and go as we please, and we can bring in what we like, though most of us have little money to buy things on the outside.

I had to save up from my small cash allowance to buy my small cashbox. Nursing it under my arm, inside my coat, as I walked through the lobby and down the corridor, it felt precious and dangerous. I would be keeping secrets in it. In this place of fellowship and sharing, secrets are so precious—and treated with suspicion.

So be it. As I've already made clear: hands off. This room has been for a while a private sanctuary, and dwelling in it has had a restorative effect. But my time is up. I am shortly to be summoned with great enthusiasm to come and join Marie-Antoinette's birthday tea. It has been put to us, though I'm sure we were all planning to come anyway, that Marie-Antoinette would be most disappointed if we didn't put in at least an appearance. So an appearance it will be.

Or is that rather churlish? I am in better spirits now. I will, as they say here, "make an effort."

"After all it is not just any old birthday," Esther says to me, finding me standing some way adrift from the festivities. "It is," as she puts it, "the big Five-O."

I smile. Easy enough, this one: an idiom I can understand. "I am myself big Five-O later in this year," I tell her without thinking. I wanted to show that I appreciated her kindness. I did not think beyond that.

"Oh, we must have a big party for you too, Mustapha," she says with immediate excitement, stopping as soon as she sees the panic in my eyes. "Or perhaps something more low-key. Well, we will see. You will perhaps want a quiet day."

I smile.

"You are wearing well, Mustapha," she adds, laughing too loudly—and looking embarrassed.

She has no reason to be embarrassed, I think, and yet I start blushing, and that makes her blush more deeply still. We both end up laughing to cover our blushes. Now we stand together awkwardly.

Still, I am touched by her generous observation, though she cannot really have meant it. Just look at me. I am a broken man. I shuffle rather, and am a bit stooped in the shoulder. My hair has thinned and my teeth are not good.

If you were to see me now, my darling, you would hardly recognise me, I fear; nor I, you, perhaps? It has been hard for you too, I know.

It is one of the failings of this place—though I do not blame them for it—that they cannot imagine us as we were. We have acquired this particular status in their eyes. Esther—*you would like Esther, my darling*—Esther is the very best and sweetest of them, but even she doesn't care to see me expensively suited, walking along the beachside esplanade on the way home to our apartment, or open-shirted on horseback, or skiing in the mountains. If I were to introduce her to Raffiq she would not recognise him. And if I were to introduce her to Raffiq's lovely young wife, Yasmin, she would not make the connection. Why should she? I set myself along this path. I am Mustapha now.

Adom wanders across to join us, carrying a large slice of Marie-Antoinette's birthday cake. Adom is an immense man, but he carries his bulk most regally. His is the belly of banquets in his honour. There is no self-loathing in it. His head has a polished glossiness, as if expensive oils have been massaged into its dome and folds. Or perhaps the gloss comes from the sweat that he rubs into his head, having mopped his brow and neck with a large handkerchief. For a man who sweats such a lot, he smells good—the handkerchief is suffused with eau de cologne and he must slap his cheeks with a powerful aftershave. The odours, appropriately, are rich woods and resins, strong alcohols and bitter herbs. His blackness is immense too: a blue blackness that goes beyond skin tone to suggest some great depth. It is a surprise, therefore, and somehow obscene, to glimpse the inside of his mouth, which is the pink of frilly knickers. He guards this dainty boudoir with strong white-yellow teeth. These reassure. Perhaps the pinkness of his mouth resembles more the yawning jaw of a hippopotamus. Much better. I laugh. Much more appropriate!

As Adom tells his story, he strode around his school in a white suit and with a knobkerrie in hand. Here he favours a darker Kaunda suit with cravat. He wears glasses with large black frames. It is a look that suggests—surely deliberately—the presidential; a father to his people. The regal, as I mentioned earlier, but for republican times.

Outwardly he accommodates himself to the egalitarian spirit of this place with some joviality, but it must bear down on him. He is

clearly, though it is never said, a "special case"—parked here while decisions are made in the highest circles about the precise arrangements of
his exile. It is whispered that he is, to use another local phrase, a "diplomatic incident." "Waiting to happen," Esther jokes—a joke we don't
quite get.

Although Adom is most gentlemanly in her presence, we have all
noticed that Esther feels uncomfortable around him. He is a pedagogi-
cal as well as a presidential figure, which makes their teacher/student
relationship difficult perhaps? Or is it simply that he has an eye for the
young girls? We have noticed that too. He is a figure of outward moral
rectitude of course, but this has little or no bearing on such matters, in
my experience—quite the reverse, in fact.

On this occasion he has walked over to us in order to offer Esther a
huge slice of birthday cake, a chocolate crème concoction, showing a
rather old-world gallantry in so doing. Perhaps it is the size of the portion, or more likely a more general revulsion, but she refuses the cake
and then rushes away, flustered.

Adom's prodigious dignity is shaken, that is obvious. But my presence requires that he recover himself immediately. He looks at the
chocolate cake—it really is a preposterously large slice. He sees that,
he laughs, he shakes his head; and then he takes a fork to it himself. He
plunges in. As I have already observed, he is a man who eats well. His
magnificent yellow-white teeth are soon smeared with brown. Between
giant forkfuls he addresses me. I am drinking an orange fizzy drink
from a plastic cup.

"Mustapha," he says. "We are, I hear, to share our day of destiny."

I understand what he means straightaway. (There is a lot of this sort
of talk at the House of Journalists.) He means that a date has been set
for our cases to be heard before the tribunal. Sometimes it happens that
two fellows appear on the same day. I must say I am greatly disturbed
by the news. I do not feel that I have prepared myself as I would wish.

"Is that so?" I ask.

It occurs to me also that his appearance can only have been scheduled by some bureaucratic oversight. For reasons we do not fully understand, Adom is included in the same processes as the rest of us, but

if we are right about his special status, then the higher circles of this bureaucracy, answering to real political masters, will not want them to proceed to the point where he appears before a normal tribunal.

"You have not been informed?" Adom replies, looking up from the plate of chocolate cake.

"No."

"I must say that the office here can be slow in these matters; matters of such great purport to us. I have been checking in every morning and afternoon—and the schedule was posted through this afternoon. Still, I do wonder at the administrator's laxness. You should have been informed right away. I will perhaps mention it to one of the Committee members, or rather to Julian directly. Straight to the top man is usually best."

He laughs.

"Do not do so on my account, I beg of you," I say.

He seems surprised.

"I imagine the office will tell me tomorrow morning," I add. "They know I am expecting a communication from my family via the Red Crescent."

"A family communication," Adom says. I realise straightaway what I have done. "Sadly, I have no family living," he says.

I know Adom's story of course. The monumental sweep of it; the barbarism and elemental force; Adom's brutally honest association with its darker episodes: it has been a sensation here at the House of Journalists. If they will let him have his day, his magnificent tale will resonate with the tribunes, I am sure of that. He will stand tall before them. He will dare them to judge him: for all his faults.

At this point there is laughter from close by. Shadrach has appeared and is being congratulated on attaining his status. Shadrach is a gentle soul. His demeanour at the hearing would have been most shy and diffident. The tribunes, I imagine, would have asked him to speak up. I have heard him reading from his volume *Ballads and Reflections* and recall how he left the audience straining to make out the music of these lovely, unassuming pieces. It is a most effective technique in its way. "Silent Songs," as the fellow next to me put it. "You are familiar with the work by Valentin Silvestrov?" I had to confess I wasn't. This fellow is a most learned man; an intense, long-bearded Slav.

I should add—it will interest you, I am sure—that Shadrach was, most surprisingly, a sports journalist in his homeland. He covered horse racing, wrestling, and football. I once enquired of the mix, which seems curious to me—and to others.

"These are the sports of my country," he replied. Although his physique is not impressive, and his complexion is poor, Shadrach has something about him even now, when you look for it, which would explain his amateur success in all of these sports before he took up journalism. You might note the steel cords in his forearms or his neck, for example.

But to get back to Adom.

"With God's grace and with the assistance of the House of Journalists, we will be heard and judged as we deserve to be," he says to me.

This statement sounds profound, as much that is meaningless does on first hearing, and I nod my head as if to signal acquiescence. Adom clasps my hands in his and adds: "And, if you are willing, let my destiny be your destiny."

He is suggesting, I suppose, that I should allow myself to be carried through the tribunal in the slip tide of his eloquence. Here is another version of the deal the House of Journalists offers. Follow their line, do it their way, and they will protect us. It is a deal that should be impossible to refuse. It is in my own interests, and it offends what exactly? Some sense of independence, some notion that I am not being entirely true to myself? Such miserable stirrings should hardly inspire—but they do—a wildly self-destructive urge to throw the deal back in their faces. In Adom's face, in this case.

"I will decide my own destiny, thank you very much," I say to him, freeing my hands. My tone is rude and dismissive and aggressive—excessively so. Adom looks shocked and put out, as well he might.

"As you will," he says, moving away with some dignity. I realise too late that he and I share more than I supposed. An appearance before the tribunal is almost certainly going to be denied to him, once the higher authorities hear of it. His status will be resolved according to what is politically expedient. He will not be judged on a full consideration of the circumstances that faced him, still less the full contents of his soul. He saw in me a man of a political cast (and social caste) with whom he is instinctively comfortable. His was a small gesture of fellowship, well meant.

Adom gone, I remain standing on the fringes of this very jolly birthday tea. I stand a little apart, but I am enjoying it in my own way. I have put on a paper hat and accepted a sparkler. We are all doing our best to make it a happy day for Marie-Antoinette, who is enjoying it all hugely.

Huge enjoyment is what she does to shoo away the evil memories, to beat back the darkest of dark spirits that would otherwise surround and submerge her. It is routinely said, it is rightly said, that Marie-Antoinette is a remarkable woman. She has scars up her legs where they doused her with paraffin and set her on fire. She wears a black patch over an eye socket that was burnt out with acid. The opposite hand—the eye's would-be protector—is webbed and cracked where the skin melted and bubbled. The men who did this to her work indirectly for a multi-national oil company. The minister, Mr. Alexander, now sacked, who shook the burnt-offering hand of Marie-Antoinette, has shaken the hands of the men on the board of this company, which through backhand deals with her corrupt government despoils and pollutes the delta lands where Marie-Antoinette's people live in corrupted impoverishment. For now Marie-Antoinette contains and channels her anger and energy. But she has not forgotten or forgiven. And in time she will expose and embarrass these men. She will condemn and convict them. But now is not the time. And the House of Journalists is not the place. She is using it just as it is using her. That is the deal. It is not only the directors of multi-national companies and government ministers who strike deals.

But today is her birthday! And a birthday is a time for laughter. "Let them eat cake," she cries. (You will have been waiting for this inevitable joke.) "There is plenty more."

Like Adom, though with feminine roundness, Marie-Antoinette is, so we are told in this country of "healthy living," "morbidly obese." "But such a jolly soul," people say to comfort themselves. "Morbidly obese" captures something important, however. She eats in order to bury herself deep. "Mustapha, let me show you something," she said one day soon after she and I were introduced. She produced a photograph from her handbag of a striking young woman with a fine figure. Her daughter or even granddaughter? I did not assume so. Indeed I was ahead of her. "You were quite a beauty in your youth, Marie-Antoinette!" I was thinking of myself—of Raffiq—that handsome young man. *(And I was thinking of you, my darling Yasmin.)* "I was a great beauty, yes . . ." "Raffiq," I prompted her. "Yes, Raffiq . . ." (If she noted the name, which I have no doubt she did, she has respected my wishes since, and always calls me Mustapha.) "My former beauty is a great comfort. Why should that be, I wonder," she said. We both laughed together. It would be quite wrong to assume, as so many good people here seem to do, that we exiles, we persecuted souls, we strugglers for rights and freedoms, are above trivialities and vanities, that only the epic concerns us. We are all sorts in the House of Journalists. Shadrach used to report on the wrestling for the national newspaper in his country and Marie-Antoinette as a young journalist wrote beauty tips for a leading magazine in hers.

As the party continues I find myself, with my tissue crown and my burnt-out sceptre, standing next to Sonny. Sonny says hello. I say hello. I do not know Sonny. I was not among those who heard her story this afternoon. *(I was locked away with you, my love.)* But I will come to hear it. It is another sensation, is it not?

Sonny is quite a slight figure, with chopped-up, don't-mess-with-me hair. She reminds me, inevitably, of Agnes: the same tomboyish quality, perhaps? The same defiance. But enough of these comparisons: Sonny is her own woman.

She is wearing no paper hat, carrying no sparkler. She takes a second look at me—Lear or the Fool? (Do they teach children here that they are one and same? I won't pretend that mine was not an elite schooling.) Then she moves on. I might add—the House of Journalists gives us this licence—that I am never to exchange any words with Sonny beyond that first hello. Somehow our paths in the few days left to me here will not cross. I am among the many with whom Sonny has trekked or travelled, or slept or died alongside, or shared a meal or a fire or a word or two with, who is forever lost to her.

Sonny? Do you ever think of me?

You know the answer.

Sonny has moved on. Sonny thinks of number one. Sonny is a survivor.

The birthday tea party has now ended. I am standing here with my hat and stick as the cleaners start clearing up around us. I was determined to have a good time and I did. I didn't really want the party to end. The evening stretches ahead.

I must eat, I suppose. And the refectory is open. So it is to the refectory I go.

I eat sparingly, as is my usual way. I am very thin these days. This excessive thinness of physique and spirit does not suit me. It is not the same thing as slim or sleek. It is withered; it is diminished. It strips me of vitality and glow. They lay on this great spread of foodstuffs, and I just pick at it.

I decide to turn in early. It is around eight o'clock.

Yes, I will turn in early tonight, I tell myself, as if I have seriously weighed up other options and ever did anything else. Other fellows find some way to fill the later part of the evenings, it is true. They show films most nights and there are various talks and "events." But there is an undertow of desolation in these activities. Nothing can save us from the dread night ahead which we must face alone. I am told that at one time (not now of course) a volunteer manned the Foreign Press Bar. The volunteer was soon replaced with an honesty book. The book records one name, obviously made up. You have heard this story?

As I make my way back to my room, to my cashbox, and my little stash of secrets and longings, I think of you, AA. Why on earth is that? No one has seen you all day. Your non-appearance, so thoroughly disciplined as it was—no cigarette breaks or meal runs; just a complete absence from the scene—was remarked upon. You will be pleased to hear that, I imagine? I don't know why I say that except that we all do. We are asking questions about you. Are you sick? Are you writing? Are you dead? Do you control everything that happens here? Are you just one of us? Or are you one of them? How have you got us talking about "them" and "us"? Why is the House of Journalists such a place of splits and intrigues suddenly? Do you know what is going to happen later tonight?

Stop.

Passing your room, I think about knocking; knocking and then pushing the door ajar, and then looking in. The moment after I have had the thought it appals me. The duty volunteer is patrolling the corridor. She will have been checking up. They are always checking up. Just to see if we are all right. It would not do for one of us to harm ourselves in any way.

There has only been one suicide in the House of Journalists. And Julian has determined that there will never be another.

It was not even clean. It was not even contained. The blood—black-red and viscous from wretchedly hacked wrists—flowed under the door and pooled in the corridor. The duty volunteer was relieved of his duties. No one really knew the dead woman, and her story died with her.

You might wish to know more of this tragedy but this is all that any of us can tell. It has been "hushed up," as they say here.

| NOT JUST ANOTHER DAY ENDS

And here another day should end. It has followed the now-familiar pattern for a day at the House of Journalists. Stories are told; incidents take place; diversions amuse us; then we go to bed to face the horrors of night. Tonight however there is more to come before we face those horrors.

———

First, Mr. Stan returns. We had assumed that he was being kept in for the night: for observation or because a whole afternoon of tests had tired him out. But no, at close to eleven o'clock, a people carrier pulls up outside the front entrance, the volunteer gets out of the front passenger seat and opens a sliding side door, and Mr. Stan in his wheelchair is lowered slowly to ground level on an electric platform. No vehicles come to the House of Journalists this late at night—Julian does not allow after-hours admissions or transfers—so as soon as we heard an engine we knew it could only be Mr. Stan returning from hospital.

The night porter opens the front door and Mr. Stan glides silently into the lobby. He is slumped to the side of his hump, sacked up in a crumpled suit, his humpty head slumbering against the heave of half sleep. His bow tie is the drooping flower of its former self and yet a little miracle. How has it survived at all a day of humiliating half-stripped explorations and inspections? The volunteer—who is hours over shift— bounds into the lobby on the long legs of his youth. He wants to get ahead of his treasured charge. Getting Mr. Stan to bed is on any night a great labour and to show any fatigue will defeat the effort.

We have now come out into the corridors. The mythology of the House of Journalists would have it written that this is the fellowship at its best: no one could settle until our beloved Father was back among us safe and sound. In truth, it is simple curiosity—and perhaps also an inkling of the real drama that is to follow. For, just as Mr. Stan is about to head down the corridor to his room, there is a commotion at the entrance. First, the blast of a car horn, then an exchange of insults, then a hammering at the front doors, and finally, the entrance—of Julian.

He is—we subsequently learn and add it to our collection of idioms— "weeping pissed." Julian in this state is a Julian we have not seen before—but he is unmistakably himself. It is a late-night version, as it were. Emotion is high in him, we can tell. But we sense too that in other circumstances with careful handling he could have been talked down and all would have ended quietly.

But the circumstances are as they are: the scene must be played out.

The night porter is obliged by theatrical convention to take Julian by his forearm as he chicanes into the lobby, only for his support to be thrown back at him with some irritation. Profuse apology for brusqueness follows.

"Do exchuse me, I do not wish to sheem ungrateful. Your assistance is well meant, I have no doubt, but I think you will find that I am not incapable of walking without it, thank you very much." With which Julian crashes shin-splinteringly against the bevelled edge of a low glass table. He yelps in pain and yanks up an elegant trouser leg to reveal a bloody gash. He looks up at us. *This*—his look seems to say—*is what happens when what happened before is allowed to happen, whatever it was.* Then he thinks better of it: a gentleman bears these things. The trouser leg is dropped and the blood and pain are no more to be spoken of.

By now the other member of the night staff and the duty volunteers have appeared on the scene. Through some collective instinct they fan out in an arc, as if determined to stop Julian getting farther into the House of Journalists. "We were worried he was going to hurt himself even more seriously," they explain later, even then not breaking ranks. But whatever prompted this enclosing motion, the consequence is to provoke exactly the action it is intended to prevent.

"I have shome business in my offish if you would not mind," Julian says mildly. He appears riled, but amused. The arc of staff and volunteers doesn't quite join hands, but they do spread themselves appreciably. Julian feints to break their lines and falls back in laughter. The half ring stiffens. Then it relaxes.

Then suddenly, alarmingly, Julian runs hard and headlong at one of the volunteers, an identified weak link, who at his onrushing flings herself to the side, landing in the lap of Mr. Stan.

Julian, skidding to a halt, and pirouetting like an ice dancer, laughs madly.

"Forgive me, my friends. No wish to shcare or alarm. But a man entrapped must break through to freedom."

He appeals smilingly to us, the fellowship, now full gathered to witness the scene.

"To bed with you, ladies and gentlemen. Your dear Chair, cheer-

fully if shomewhat shamefully piddled, does not deserve thish atten-
shun, I assure you."

Mr. Stan meanwhile has off-loaded the distressed volunteer, cen-
tred himself in his chair, and driven straight into the heart of events.

"Julian, you should be heading home. Whatever it is can surely wait
until the morning when you have recovered yourself." His tone is pe-
remptory, masterly, fatherly: in every aspect surprising. He wouldn't
have dreamt of talking to Julian in such a way with others present in
any other circumstances than the present ones—the most pertinent to
him, his utter need of sleep, overriding all other considerations, politic
and personal.

"That is where you are wrong, Shtan, old man," Julian says—the
term of address so shockingly disrespectful. "We have waited all day
for your return—and we are glad to see it." He pauses to let us nod our
agreement—but we nod only in shock. Never have we expected to witness such an exchange. "But your prolonged absence has held up deshis-
suns." He now points a finger. There is a devilish theatricality of tone
about Julian's pronunciations which he seems to relish. He is having
fun, it seems. "The most pressing of which is the issue of your own—I
shall be frank—*treachery.*"

The accusation is greeted with an almost pantomimic gasp.

"Yes, old man, you have been consorting, behind all our backs, with
the enemy. Do not deny it." Julian is now prodding Mr. Stan in the
chest. "I might have shuspected many others . . ."

He looks up and surveys the fellowship. And yes, on cue, you, AA,
have appeared among us. You are right at the back, but he spots you and
makes sure you know that he has seen you. This conspiratorial business between Mr. Stan and Miriam Stern is the immediate provocation
for this crisis, but it was your arrival at the House that somehow set in
train the events which led up to it.

"But *no*, it is my most faithful and trusted lieutenant who has chosen to betray my trust."

Julian's words wound deeply—and are meant to. They belittle and
humiliate the old man.

There is a shattering hurt in Mr. Stan's eyes as he puts his chair into gear and shoots into reverse, parting startled fellows and volunteers alike. Once free of us, the chair performs a 180-degree turn at a breakneck and hurtles down the corridor, pinning an alarmed Agnes to one wall. She is the last to arrive at the scene—but the first in pursuit.

She can imagine what the old man is thinking. He needs to get to his room. He will head in there, wedge his chair against the door, and shut out the shouting world. Once inside, he would commune with Mother—the one commanding constant in his life. She will tell him what to do.

But there is a catch. The wheelchair wedges in the doorway. Mr. Stan throws it into reverse, only for it to baulk and jam again. Suddenly frantic, he shunts the chair first into one doorjamb, then the other. Mother's voice is shouting in his head. *Stanislaus! Enough!* But he is out of control. His brain careering around inside his head flipping all the switches madly. Electric signals pulse out through his bloodstream, causing his body to buck and jerk and throw itself into all manner of shapes and contortions. Mr. Stan's eyes spin. He froths at the mouth and jabbers. He bubbles and twitches. *Stanislaus, now stop that! Stop it this minute! Stop this display and show!* One final jerk; one final shape thrown.

Stop there!

Agnes is first at the scene; the detailed volunteer thereafter. Then, within moments, we have all arrived. We are confronted with Mr. Stan in the apotheosis of massive seizure. He is frozen on the cables of it: his convulsions petrified. Within seconds Julian breaks into the freeze-frame and reaches out in supplication to the thrown figure. Forgive me, Father! He seems to see some signal of life coming from the man trapped beneath the ice. It is telling him to come closer. He leans in, imagining perhaps a whispered confidence. Instead a stump in final spasm swings up and catches him square under the jaw. *Biff.* An electrified leg jerks up and knees him, deftly, in the groin. *Bosh.*

Now, however tragic the circumstances, this is funny. Julian wounded, winded, his dignity and authority tottering, is within an ace of going down in a heap. There is, God forgive us, some tittering—out of the left side of our mouths, as it were. On the right side we stick firm to grim expression.

We are paying, we soon realise, our last, twisted respects. For as we titter, the left side of Mr. Stan—one eye, one side of the mouth, left stump, left leg—trembles and drools with aftershock, while the right side is quite rigid in all its imperfections, old and new. The massive stroke has split him in two like a tree cleaved by lightning. And—worse—the tongue is stumped: trapped on the wrong side of the event.

Yes, Mr. Stan has been robbed of all speech function.

The professional side of the House of Journalists kicks in at this point. Julian is cleared away to the sidelines and tended with more dispatch and less respect than he normally would have expected and received. Meanwhile the staff medic, with the help of volunteer muscle, extricates Mr. Stan from his still-jabbering chair; carries him—half potato sack, half frozen calf carcass—to his bed; and does what he can for the stricken old character. The ambulance arrives within minutes. We all wait up to see the wheeling-away. It does not escape any of us that we are witnessing a pivotal, maybe climactic moment in the story of the House of Journalists.

And so another day, but not just another day, ends.

DEPARTURES

THE CITY

Don't hope for things elsewhere:
There's no ship for you, there's no road.
Now that you've wasted your life here, in this small corner,
You've destroyed it everywhere in the world.

These are the final lines of C. P. Cavafy's poem "The City," which was written in 1894 and was listed under the heading "Prisons." At the time he was working as a special clerk in the Irrigation Service (Third Circle) of the Ministry of Public Works in Alexandria. (*C. P. Cavafy, trans. Edmund Keeley and Philip Sherrard, ed. George Savidis (London: Chatto & Windus, 1978).*)

IMPORTANT TO HEAR

Josiah comes to the end of his story and the green light in the recording cubicle turns to red. On the other side of the glass, the small makeshift studio is packed. The studio manager, the output producer, the programme editor, and the strand editor are sitting behind the console, and a couple of senior radio executives, along with various staff and volunteers from the House of Journalists, are standing behind them.

Julian is front and centre of the standing group, and by gestures of the hand, tilts of the head, and grimaces, has given every appearance that he was both living through and directing Josiah's narration of events. Ever eager to please, Josiah is now looking through the studio window for some sign that he has delivered what was wanted. What he sees is everybody in the studio looking down; some—like Julian—with eyes closed and heads bowed.

Josiah suffers a moment of anxiety. But he is released from it in the next instant. For, as if on cue, all as one look up, smiling through tears, and with thumbs-up and little punches of the air indicate that, yes, he has delivered *exactly* what they wanted.

"Thank you, Josiah, that was great," the studio manager says through talk-back.

"Yes, *thank you*," Julian whispers to himself. Standing front and centre, he clasps his hands together in front of his chest and rings out a little prayer bell of thanks.

"Painful to listen to—" the most senior radio executive says, leaning across to Julian.

"But important to hear," Julian says, robbing the executive of the balance of sentiments. A little of the togetherness is lost for a moment.

"Painful above all to experience, I should think," the studio manager chips in. The observation is jocular in tone but not inappropriate to the mood. It is received well and restores harmony.

Many long discussions had taken place between the House of Journalists and the broadcasting people over the structure and content of this day-long radio special. But it was quickly decided that after the normal news-based breakfast show, which was co-presented from the House of Journalists and featured a number of "packages" and interviews on the themes of exile and asylum, the nine a.m. slot should be given over to a fellow of the House of Journalists telling his or her story.

There was then the question of which fellow should have this honour. There are some fellows, though few in number, who can recall when this question might have been decided in consultation with the fellowship, or at least with the Committee. Not these days. Julian made the decision on his own. He was clear what sort of story would work best.

During the course of the day a full range of views would be aired. There should have been no argument about that, not least because the radio people are bound by their duty of impartiality. So it was frankly ridiculous to suggest, as critics from both Left and Right had done, that the House of Journalists was hosting this radio day in order to "spread propaganda," whether its own, the government's, MI6's, or the tooth fairy's. The specious nature of that claim has been laid bare by the fact that many of these same critics have been interviewed for programmes or are going to be guests on the various panel discussions. All shades of opinion will be heard. Everyone can have their say: politicians, campaigners, and, not least, members of the public. The object is not to come down on one side or another, or to resolve the moral, social, and political dilemmas. Rather it is to open up debate, and explore the subject in all its richness. The issue is complex, the arguments are complex, and it is not realistic, or perhaps even desirable, that those complexities should be cleared up.

Julian recognises all that. But in deciding on who should fill the nine a.m. slot he was determined to at least set off on a straight path. Hence the choice of Josiah's story of a small-time reporter at a provincial newspaper, standing up to tyranny—and being crushed by it. No listener to this tale could possibly question the regime's evil, Josiah's urgent need to flee, or this country's decision to grant him entry. The listener is not asked to grapple with any difficult questions of moral ambiguity or political complicity. While the House of Journalists can make greater claims for its importance, there are times when its role is best seen through the celebration of small victories and small comforts. That is something that we the fellowship have long appreciated and Julian has come to realise of late. Josiah's story is the story of a good man taking on evil forces that are much more powerful than he, and—as must happen—losing that battle. But the small victory of escape and the small comfort of sanctuary are not to be dismissed. Indeed there is no small glory in it.

A volunteer notices that Josiah, headphones still clamped to his ears, is gripping the edge of the little table, trying to lever himself into a standing position. The spinal injuries he suffered as a result of the beatings means that after sitting for any length of time he finds it difficult to get up without assistance. But the urge to stand is now strong. While the broadcast was going on, he focussed all his attention on getting through his story. But after nearly twenty minutes inside this claustrophobic cubicle he is drenched in cold sweat, his heart is pumping, and he can feel a panic attack rising in him. The volunteer notices all this and moves quickly to unclamp him from the headphones and assist him out to the Central Courtyard where he can breathe more easily.

Julian is quick to check up on him and is pleased to report to the others that Josiah is feeling fine now. He has put himself through an ordeal—indeed two ordeals in one: the reliving of his experiences and the telling of them in such a public way. Then there was this third ordeal: his fear of confined spaces. But he wanted to do it. This place has been generous to him; its people kind. His story is all he has, and he is always glad to share it, if that is of help to the greater cause. It is agreed that Josiah epitomises the best spirit of the fellowship. It's hoped he can now relax, perhaps have a rest in his room, and rejoin events later when he is fully restored.

| WE PLAYED ALONG

The studio party has moved into the lobby, where it breaks up into groups. Yesterday morning at this time the technicians were doing the rig: running cables out to the truck for the live OB. Those of us who have worked in broadcast journalism might have been expected to be interested in these goings-on. And we were, to an extent. Anyway, we played along.

They recorded the afternoon play yesterday, as well as the book panel programme and some other features. Today we have all the live programmes: the news sequences, the morning service, the phone-ins, question times, and political debates. More of our stories read live will be among the highlights. Editors, producers, presenters, and famous guests have been coming and going. The refectory is operating as a continuous cafeteria, serving coffee and snacks. All the activity is a welcome diversion from the normal routine of the place. There is a drinks reception in the library this evening. We will put on jackets and ties; the female fellows will dress up too. National dress is being encouraged. The day will culminate in a visit and speech by the prime minister. The House of Journalists will receive his official endorsement.

His visit represents an apotheosis for the House—Julian's ultimate triumph. But it has also provoked controversy of course, though Julian can hardly be bothered to answer the criticisms these days. His only concern is to reassure the fellowship and the friends and donors. And they are sensible enough to see that this visit, while not compromising the independence of the House, does provide it with some security at a time of political turbulence. It stands apart, but not alone. "And anyway he's the leader of the country." This is Julian talking to his partner, Philip, the other day. "What were we supposed to say when he suggested a visit: no thanks, you're not welcome? What planet are these people living on!"

Mr. Stan has been wheeled out to share in the day's events. Busy APs rush past him in the lobby, nodding their acknowledgements; the technical guys, with due reverence, cable around him. The famous presenters and guests are brought to him especially so that they can pay their respects, just as the PM and other luminaries will do later in the day.

He experiences the world these days as though he is half under water. Or more precisely: constantly being pulled half under by some great weight. The main frustration of his half-sunk condition is that our signals and messages take their time to reach him, and before he can turn them round and send back a response we have often moved on. It is a half life, at best; but a half life, he muses, is half more than death—and he teetered on its brink sure enough. Perhaps he had even wanted to die for a moment. It was unbearable to think, as he had thought at that abysmal point, that his beloved House of Journalists was going the way of all the other people and institutions in which he had invested so much faith and loyalty. He would never be able to forgive or trust Julian fully. And the House itself is not the same and never can be. He may be a holy fool, an incurable romantic, but he is not a complete idiot. He sees things more clearly now.

Still, Mr. Stan is proud to say that he has always been a "pint half full" man, as they say here and indeed on his home island (the thought makes him smile)—and so he remains grateful for this life. Anyway, there is simply no fight left in him. And nowhere left to run to. This is where his life of pain and struggle and bitter disappointment and un-shaken belief in the decency of mankind, the beauty and wonder of life, and the inevitability of human progress, ends. As end it will, sooner rather than later—though on his own terms. One afternoon they will find him in his special chair, by the fire, with a blanket over his knees, sunk deep in final sleep. Fate owes him this ending. He feels it with a profound sense of entitlement.

Until then he will remain utterly dependent on the kindness of this place—yes, there is still plenty of kindness here. So many depen-dencies and indignities, and yet still they accord him the greatest re-spect. He is still useful to them: that is the top and bottom of it. (He has no illusions about that.) Indeed, he is *more* useful now. Now he serves as a tragic mute symbol of the place. They talk for him and through him; he conveys a message which they control completely. Did they ever re-ally think he would or could betray them? Probably not. And of course when he says "they" he means "he." What others had seen for so long had become clear to him only late in the day: For good and ill, the House of Journalists *is* Julian. It suffers from his failings just as it gains from his strengths. So it was always likely that it would be an action of Julian's which would shake the place to its foundations.

Of course, Mr. Stan had seen it all before. Theories, ideologies, sys-tems, institutions become embodied in leaders who fail, as we all fail, to live up to expectations. The best hope is that this failure can be con-tained. That is why doubters, questioners, opponents, rivals are so im-portant. A good leader who surrounds himself only with adherents, followers, and loyalists is on the path to ruin. As an instinctive loyalist who has seen that loyalty betrayed, Mr. Stan knows that more than anyone. And yet he fell for Julian, as he fell for the rest of them. It is a matter of bitter regret that he could have been so credulous after all he has gone through. Though he wouldn't want to suggest that what hap-pened here at the House of Journalists is of moral equivalence with what happened on his home island. That would be ridiculous and re-pugnant. Julian had behaved more foolishly than wickedly. Mr. Stan will go on believing that to the end.

It occurs to him—for the first time after all this time—that Mother would have had her doubts about Julian. She might have appreciated his charm and manners, but she would have "seen through him." She always did. She would have had no sympathy for him that following morning as he clung like a wretch to the spotless white rim of his toilet bowl spitting a bitty acidy trail into the mulligatawny water below.

Oh yes, how far he had fallen the previous evening, Julian reflected as he hugged that vile bowl, reeking of weakness and defeat. Years of restraint and dignity had been undone in one outburst. He was a drinker, he had always been a drinker; and he had never had any respect for those of his contemporaries and peers who were only able to control themselves through teetotalism, either total or periodic. Abstinence was another form of excess—and he had always despised excess. He prided himself on his ability to drink in a way and to an extent appropriate to any occasion, including occasions where it was appropriate to drink a great deal. He could even drink to get drunk, if the circumstances demanded it. But civilised drunk, loquacious drunk, tearful drunk—never drunk drunk. Or not since those dark nights of self-destructive self-discovery after he came down from university to the city.

During that time in his life he had woken one morning-after in a squalid bedsit; in a sheet-twisted pull-out divan bed, in which an oafish heap of pick-up slept on beside him. And in that instant he decided that this life of low-grade pleasure was sordid and shameful. He had to purge himself, to cleanse his soul, to discipline his spirit, to dedicate himself to a new life of work, wealth, fame, service, and good. So he had—how few can say it!—*changed*. Starting that very morning.

He washed as well as he was able under a piss-miserable rubber shower hose in that dirty pink bathroom spotted with black damp; dressed as respectably as he could in the rank slung shirt and stained jeans he retrieved from the floor; and marched down filthily carpeted stairs, out through a communal hallway smelling of uric acid and mouse droppings, and out into the stunning sunshine of a new life, with no turnings back, no veerings off, no setbacks or humiliations—not one.

Until last night.

Oh God! Last night, last night, Julian moaned to himself as he spat away the last wet ribbon of acid slime. The gash on his leg was nasty enough, and Mr. Stan's knee to the bollock-sac had been a sickener (literally: it had lined his mouth with liquid vomit). But it was the crack the old fellow had dealt to his jaw that had felt like a bone-breaker. It had hurt him. Really hurt him. In different circumstances, he would have taken some pride in coping with the pain. It was not something that came easily to him. The pain wailed in his head like a child—*It hurts, it really hurts!*—but he evinced at most a manly wince. Having shamed himself so wretchedly, he did not want to attract attention or sympathy. Mr. Stan's epic stroke had to take centre stage. It was not appropriate for him to try to share the spotlight, even by taking charge of Mr. Stan's dispatch in the ambulance. Instead he allowed himself to be escorted to the office and deposited on the couch. He wanted to phone the University Hospital—the CEO was a friend—to ensure that the IC unit was alert to the preciousness of their charge. But he was in no fit state. He sobered up a bit and then he phoned Philip, wanting to be brave, self-possessed, and dignified, but instead giving way, on hearing that most dependable of voices, to tears and lamentations, dressing it up as panic about Mr. Stan's condition and the future of the House of Journalists, when it was really naked self-pity, stripped of all dignity. Philip wasn't fooled for a second. He told him in the most certain terms to get a grip on himself. The whole House would be able to hear him—which was true and which only made things much worse.

So as he stood up in the pristine whiteness of the bathroom the following morning, cradling his jaw in the palm of his left hand, Julian could not escape the fact that he had heaped humiliation on himself last night in the place where he had most reason to be proud. He had defiled his reputation in a sacred spot. And what was even more shameful was that he was still thinking only of himself, his hammering head, his painful jaw, when Mr. Stan was in the hospital, after a stroke, which for all he knew (and apparently cared)—the thought struck him suddenly like a thunderbolt—had *killed* him.

"Philip!" he shouted, rushing into their bedroom, where his partner was sound asleep in the great soft white sea of their bed. "Philip. The phone, the phone!"

Philip surfaced from deep sleep to find this wailing madman wheeling around the bedroom.

"Philip, I must phone the hospital. What was I thinking! I don't even know if the old boy is alive or dead!"

Mr. Stan blows a little chuckle bubble as he imagines Julian in his frantic state that following morning. He was not dead of course. He was not even playing dead, though fellow friends who visited him in hospital said they had entertained the thought. Something about the half smile on his face, apparently. It was, the hospital director told Julian, an illusory trick of the deep coma which they had induced in order to ease the stress on the patient's brain. Though it could have been a facial-muscular manifestation of inner calm. For in the deep rest of deep coma, umbilically linked to all essential sustenance, computer-rigged for steady-state heart and brain function, Mr. Stan was safer and warmer and more protected from all harm than he had ever been in this life. He was enwombed, not entombed. He might have stayed there indefinitely, enjoying the peace and quiet, if it wasn't for Mother's remorseless promptings. She had brought him into this world and he had not yet repaid his debt to her. It was not the right time to come across and rejoin her. She would enjoy no peace—and he certainly wouldn't—if he defied her.

So he had lived, respecting Mother's wishes, and returned to the House of Journalists, where this afternoon he would be shaking hands with the prime minister of the mother country. What more could she ask of him?

Julian appears, beaming amid the bustle, and looks across at Mr. Stan. The sight brings him up short.

After making that phone call, and getting the reassuring news, he had been able to compose himself and collect his thoughts. True, when he first came off the phone he was in such an excitable state that he felt another wave of nausea rise up. But he determined at once not to indulge it. He summoned up all his will, sucked in great draughts of fresh air, and his stomach settled. He let Philip go back to sleep, showered bracingly, dressed, made himself a pot of coffee—bitter, strong, restorative— and went into his study. He intended to make a few business calls.

Already he was able to think beyond his shame at his behaviour the previous night and his embarrassment at the prospect of facing the staff, volunteers, and above all the fellowship. He must focus his thoughts—he told himself resolutely—on the future of the House of Journalists. His own feelings were a petty sideshow.

He allowed himself one more wince of pain, even a tear or two as he made another self-assessment of that jawline—not broken, but severely bruised—and then he turned his thoughts back to Mr. Stan. There was Mr. Stan the human being: brave, loved, loyal, and remarkable, whatever his foibles and weaknesses. But there was also Mr. Stan the icon: the perfect embodiment of the spirit of the House of Journalists. The latter was the more important to him, Julian realised without sentiment, because it was more important to the project, which was more important than any one individual. He never forgot this central truth; that was his great strength. Even so, he was struck suddenly by how fragile the personal connection between him and his most loyal lieutenant was and always had been. Was there any real bond at all? He had in part invented the Mr. Stan of popular legend, but he hadn't troubled to get to know the man behind it. He and Mr. Stan were proud partners in this enterprise, but it was idle to pretend that they were friends or brothers. Should he have strived for a greater intimacy? He thought not. There were supporters of the House of Journalists who vainly imagined that the fellowship itself was open to them. They strove to identify themselves with the experiences and the insights of the exiled writers. It was pitiful; worse, it was contemptible. Did they not appreciate the unbridgeable gulf? They could never get close, surely they realised that? To write out of another's experience was to bear false witness. It was his duty to repel those who even dared to trespass on this space. This thought restored him. He was proud above all in his role as the great protector of the fellowship.

Now there was work to do; not least to preserve the story which was at the heart of the House of Journalists and which gained so much from having Mr. Stan himself around to tell it. Of course Mr. Stan had been recorded and filmed many times, but there was no official, authorised version of his story for the archive of the House itself. That was a grave oversight and he was about to call Solomon and get him to set a process in hand when he remembered that although Mr. Stan had survived the night there was no certainty that he would be able to return to the House, or even to regain the power of speech. The thought shook him deeply. What had he done! In his desperation to protect the House of Journalists he had silenced its most compelling voice.

And yet look at the scene today: Julian surveys it with great satisfaction, he must admit. The place is buzzing: with radio producers and technicians, with volunteers and interns, with guests and friends and VIPs. Mr. Stan is at the centre, back where he belongs, silent but *not* silenced. His story still speaks. It will survive him. Julian has no doubts on that score. For great stories do not rely on one storyteller, but gain strength through retelling. Indeed the greatest exist in many different versions—and while the details change, often significantly, along with settings and characters, the essence of the story, its central truth, still speaks to us. The original words, the original language, the original storyteller or tellers—all may be lost to history. Think of the *Odyssey*, for instance.

At which Julian lets out a scoff of laughter. He is sometimes washed onto these shores by the wind and water of excess sentiment. Think of the *Odyssey* indeed! Today, Mr. Stan is on hand to pull him back to everyday reality: Mr. Stan, everybody's hero, but just a man all the same. A great survivor, brave and loyal, but still feeble flesh and thin blood— like the rest of us.

Julian shakes off the last of his laughter, advances towards the little man, and—in a gesture we have not seen before—holds his hands as if in prayer and nods his head: an Eastern-style greeting. There is an obvious ironic flourish to it, but Mr. Stan smiles nonetheless. We all share to some extent in Julian's high spirits on this day of honour and purport for the House of Journalists. Anyway, we play along.

| SOMEONE MENTIONS SMOKE SIGNALS

The Central Courtyard has been cordoned off for the duration and made another "No Smoking Zone." The decision has had the unforeseen and

undesired consequence of periodically depopulating the main areas of
the House of Journalists of fellows. Such is the situation now. Some of
our number are to be found sharing cigarettes with the engineers and
technicians outside their OB vans; a larger group has come up the fire
escape, onto the roof, to smoke in the upper air.

We are quite densely packed in this small space, but we would no
more blow smoke into the face of another smoker than we would into
the bonnet of a pram. We inhale therefore with heads tipped backwards, eyes closed, and exhale, eyes open, skywards. Someone men-
tions smoke signals. But if we are sending any signals, they signify very
little and expire peacefully in the clean air.

Some of the volunteers and mentors complain about the growing
dirt and noise of this city and hint at increasing social unrest and
political disquiet. We taste nothing on the air here. Maybe it is that
nothing gets through the filters. Maybe it is that we have all lived
through so much worse.

But we do hear, from four stories down, the call to assembly. Hur-
riedly, we take a last gasp; then set off down the fire escape stairs, stubbing our cigarettes out on the iron handrail. No ashtrays have been
provided up here, so the butts have to be kicked sideways into the unused courtyard of the smaller building next door. We do this guiltily,
but with the pleasure that comes from such guilt.

We clatter down the final steps of the fire escape, race through the
small yard at the back of the kitchens, and gather in the lobby. At the
assembly point we get our instructions for the day from the lead volunteer and we are stood down. Sometimes this place can feel a bit like
school. But we do not mind. It is a big day. We play along.

For most of us, though, there is not much to be done between now
and the reception this evening. The normal routine of classes and
workshops has been suspended for the day.

We do not like to mill and loiter: it is not in the spirit of the place.
But for those of us who are not specifically occupied in the radio productions, milling and loitering is rather the order of the day. Indeed
the proceedings start to take on a stale flavour. Julian, if he was not
otherwise diverted, would smell it on the air and take steps to disperse
it. Some activity or industry would be ordered. But he can hardly be

blamed for having other things on his mind. It is his big day. He has plenty to occupy him.

YES, *HER* STORY

All the output is being broadcast from speakers around the House of Journalists. Vanessa Boothby, the writing mentor of Edson, the South American journalist, who has just listened to a transmission in the library, thinks this rig-up has totalitarian echoes. Can fellows even escape by going to their rooms? she wonders. Or must they submit to the day's programming wherever they are in the House?

Vanessa is one of a number of "hangers-on" who are hanging around today's proceedings. This special day has fallen on one of her "regular days." Edson, it can be assumed, did not expect to see her here. He, as Vanessa well knows, has a big part to play today. But even so, when he spotted her during a break he ran over and greeted her with every appearance of pleasure. No, that is unfair. His pleasure was entirely sincere. He is busy today but he always has time for Vanessa.

It is however a commonplace now to observe that Vanessa needs Edson's support rather more than he needs hers. The "power relationship has shifted," as they say here. Still, today Vanessa is having one of her better days and is not here to off-load on Edson. It is *his* day. That said, she also wants to see what they are making of "her concept." Do we remember her little play? Probably not. Why should we? Though she cannot help but notice—perhaps we have too—that various single-voice testimonies feature in the day's schedule. Edson's prominently, but not exclusively.

He had asked her advice about how he should approach the recording, but she sensed that he had done so out of courtesy, even duty, as the format clearly did not lend itself to any input from her. The producer had very strong ideas about allowing the "authentic voice" of the exiled writer to come through without any outside shaping or restructuring; a purist approach which was somewhat contaminated, Vanessa couldn't help observing, by the fact that this smart, self-confident young woman would be *editing* the recording rather substantially.

The producer had asked her if she would agree to be one of the interviewees in the accompanying feature on Edson. Vanessa assumed that she was being patronised—she was getting used to that—but agreed anyway. After the interview, the girl had asked her how she wanted to be identified in the presenter's link and she had suggested: "the writer Vanessa Boothby." For a moment the professional hardness of the producer dissolved. She blushed and apologised for not being clear. But then quickly recovered her steel. "We were thinking more of: volunteer mentor." It was obvious from her tone that it was "volunteer mentor" or nothing, and it was left to Vanessa to spare herself further indignity by saying, "Oh, of course, in the context of the feature, that is quite right."

But of course it is *far* from right. Vanessa feels she has been cheated in some way. Yes, *cheated.* There, she has said it.

It has been very hard to hear "her story" given another treatment. Yes, "*her* story." She has said it again. It is no doubt irrational, presumptuous, and disrespectful to Edson, but she does feel that Edson's story, first told to her, is her story as well as his, and she certainly has greater ownership of it than these others, among whom she also counts, by the way, the staff and volunteers of the House of Journalists, who are bustling about with the same self-importance as the broadcast team.

She was also dismayed that as well as Edson telling his story—with great charm and warmth, but in a slightly confused and clumsy way, if she is allowed to be just a little critical—the producer had included a couple of his songs in the sequence. The songs, both in English, had lyrics which were banal and hackneyed to her ears. As ever, however, great respect was accorded to them—"the powerful authenticity of protest, the heartfelt sincerity of true experience," some expert of some sort called them. And while Edson makes no claims to be a writer, he takes his songwriting very seriously indeed. At least, now he does; now that the House of Journalists has elevated his songs to the level of art. There was already talk of a CD—a blend of his new songs of grateful exile and his old songs of angry protest. And people would buy it, she had no doubt. They bought everything the House of Journalists put out.

| DEAR ESTHER

But let us leave Vanessa Boothby, shall we? She is a bit of an old "booby," is she not? We will leave her to "stew in her own juice." These were some of the last expressions we learnt from Esther, who left the House of Journalists some weeks ago, we are sad to report.

We were given no explanation for her decision to leave. Esther herself was very unforthcoming and seemed even more mortified than was her wont during the unofficial farewell thrown for her by a group of fellows. She spoke only of other "commitments." Perhaps there was some progress on that collection of short stories? we speculated. But she did not mention it, so we didn't press her on the matter. She said she would miss the place and especially the fellows. "You are people," she said of us, almost in a whisper, "who I am proud to have met. And I am prouder still that I can call you friends. Yes, I will miss you all very much, just as I miss those who have moved on. You have literally changed my life; and put so many things in perspective." She was about to cry and only saved herself by making a joke which got us all laughing. It was right that it should end with laughter. That is what we will always associate with Esther: laughter.

There was talk of a disagreement with the House authorities. Certainly Esther, despite her professional focus and her sense of fun, had seemed increasingly disillusioned with the direction of the House's activities. She had been in to see Julian and he had not been able to reassure her. He had other—bigger—things to worry about at the time. That was understandable perhaps, but we think he would have done well to take greater care to keep Esther.

But let us spare Esther this attention. She would be blushing to think that we are speaking of her in this way. *Nobody is very interested in me*, she would be saying if she was here. *It's the stories of the fellows which everybody wants to hear.*

| WE SHOULD LEAVE THIS PLACE AND MAKE OUR OWN WAY

The fate of Agnes will be uppermost in some minds. So what has become of her? Another departure to report. She has moved out and is living in the city somewhere. We do not know much more than that at present. Should we know? Should we concern ourselves with Agnes's new life beyond these walls? Is it not the natural order of things, the desired outcome for all of us, that we should leave this place and make our own way? Our writing or broadcasting, or in Agnes's case our photography, has led us into exile. We must live in strange places where we are not known. It will be a struggle to settle and put down new roots. But there is some freedom in this fate. Agnes has chosen to embrace it.

"I am a stranger here and always will be," she tells audiences. "I might wish to belong or to identify, but I never really will. Still, being the outsider suits me fine in one respect: as a photographer. I did not seek exile. I was forced to flee. I am a home-lover, from a big family—and I love my country. It was out of a desperate sense of attachment that I tried to capture my country as it was being wrenched from me. There is something precious about such fervent witness. My photographs are hateful images of course, soaked in blood. But they are also, if you look into their heart, soaked in love. That is all in the past. Now, here, I see how detachment from a place helps you to see that place. "With a steely eye," as you say here. Now I have a steely eye which I will turn on *this* country—for which I have no love. It has taken me in and I am grateful for that. But I will repay it in the only way I can: by watching its every move with my steely eye."

Agnes's parting from the House of Journalists lacked ceremony and sentiment, but there was no acrimony either. It was simply time: that was all.

Of course she had been distressed more than any of us by Mr. Stan's stroke. It will be recalled perhaps that he was struck down soon after the day of her late return. Thus the two events are linked in her mind.

It had been a long rattling journey in that battered old van. Even so, she could not understand why she felt so shattered—and at the same time so agitated and panicky and fearful and clingy. They made much here at the House of Journalists of her "extraordinary resilience." She had no objection to their use of the phrase; quite the reverse, in fact. It made her feel special, strong. She fed off the power it gave her. And yet here she was, after a rather long, disappointing, and depressing journey— she put it no stronger than that—with her spirit in a state of near-collapse. What could explain that?

True, it was her first visit to one of the detention centres which we all know about, talk about, and so fear. But she of all of us most mocked that fear. "Hey, are we not the chosen people? They cannot touch us in here. We are the special ones!" One of her motivations for going on the protest was to demonstrate that her favoured status did not mean that she had turned her back on those less fortunate. She wanted to show solidarity and also to bear witness. But she had been stopped at the gates. She had not made it inside. There had, in truth, never been any prospect of getting into the centre. She had tested herself up to a strict limit and no further than that. It had proved too severe a test even so. Even peripheral contact with this country's pale approximation of evil was too much for her.

So she had returned to the House of Journalists with a huge sense of relief. And as she climbed into bed she was overwhelmed by a feeling that this place was her one haven of solace and safety. It was both a comforting and a fearful thought. She felt like a child snuggling up under the blankets as a sleet storm whips the windows. This evocation of childhood showed how the day had disturbed her, because it was entirely foreign to her own childhood, to the sweltering electricity of nights on rush beds, under mosquito nets, amid the constant crackle of cicada static. It was this thought, replacing the alien one, which warmed and calmed her and allowed her to drift off into sleep, only to be woken by the commotion in the lobby.

No, let's be precise about this. Let's set the record straight. It was terrible nightmares that had woken her that night, as on so many nights. It was a few days later that Mr. Stan returned from the hospital. It is only in Agnes's mind that the events merge into a single evening. But they were certainly connected, she feels that very strongly. And we will grant her that connection.

On the first days after Mr. Stan's return from the hospital she had taken him up as a little girl might a loved but broken doll. Again it showed her agitation, because she had never been one for dolls. Her ministrations were unstinting, intimate, oppressive. She dressed him, fed him, wheeled him around, petted him, and put him to bed. She would have slept beside him if the bed had been big enough. (We all sleep in singles here.) We could all see the deep distress in Mr. Stan's eyes. This was too much. He was an old man; he was her Father of Chapel. She was a young woman; a distinguished fellow. There was a want of decorum in her devotion to his needs. Julian intervened, showing tact and sensitivity. Agnes was quick to see that he was right: she was behaving inappropriately even if it was with the best of intentions. Yes, she could see that now.

We saw less of her. She withdrew from fellowship. She still came out to smoke, but not to share. She smoked her own cigarettes, on her own. She took to going out for much of the day. Not far, not late. She always returned well before dark (though this is not required by the House rules). But when she returned she went straight to her room.

People on the outside were offering her a way out. The City Sisters, although they feared her untamed independence, her lack of ideological discipline, her sheer irrepressible feminine cheek, were still drawn to this young woman who seemed to exemplify so many of their radical ideals. Agnes was scornful of their approaches. She was blood and dirt and sex. She was fun and laughter and what the hell. She did her own thing and she thought her own thoughts. She followed no text or tract, no sect or creed. She had no sisters.

More difficult to resist was Alexei, who started texting her again. These texts were devilishly designed to work away at her down there and dissolve her will. She was determined to resist, but Alexei did not give up. His texts weakened her in her weakest spot, but also hardened her where she was hardest. He was not to be trusted, of that she was sure. No man ever is. There was at least one other girl—probably others—on the outside. He seemed to think that because she, Agnes, was in here, she didn't know. But she had made it her business to know. She "had her spies" on the outside, as they say in here—and they had informed her that Alexei was fucking her over with at least one little white girl. And maybe another black girl. Maybe a rainbow fuckfest! He was lucky he was living in this country. In her country, with her connections, she could have had things done to Alexei for what he did to her. She had powerful friends there. Once.

It was her mother—a hard woman, a good mother—who had instructed her not to trust men, however good they might seem. They will always let you down, she told her eldest daughter. As her mother surely intended, the warning brought to mind her father—a weak man, a bad father. She thought with a shudder of his other women, his debts and dishonour, his connivance with corrupt ministers: his syphilitic death in a government prison. Her mother had not allowed the girls to visit their father in his last days. The boys were taken and shaken to the depths of their little souls. A lesson to them. She and her sisters were spared. To see her mother's tears at her father's graveside was to see rain falling softly on the hardest stone. Agnes had never seen such love before or since. It was heartbroken hatred.

Her mother had never trusted Jean-Paul, Agnes's comrade and lover. And daughter followed mother in this distrust. Oh, she loved him with a passion. And she admired him too. And followed him into very dark places. But she knew what she was doing. She had her eyes open. In a civil war on her continent you take sides. There is no protection in neutrality. There is no respect for international convention or protocol. The photojournalist is an active combatant. To pick up a camera is to take up arms. She chose her side; she chose the rebels. But most of all, she chose Jean-Paul. (Sorry, Sisters!) He was the embodiment of the cause. The bravest of them, the one who fought back the hardest, the one who hated the enemy the most. She loved that brave, hard hatred.

Do we think for a minute that she didn't know about the atrocities of Jean-Paul and his men? Do we think she followed him and the rebel group wearing her white communion dress and waving her prayer book? Do we think that for a moment she even thought about photographing *both* sides? In the interests of balance! There was *one* side and she was on it. His cause and her cause. It was made up of flesh-and-blood soldiers who killed and were killed, who felt pain and inflicted pain, who fucked and fucked with. She was one of them. She was proud of the blood on her hands.

Such a boast could never be made in the House of Journalists. She understood that. To preserve its mission it was necessary to sanctify and purify the struggle and suffering of the fellows. For a while, for her own ends, she went along with it. In the end, though, she could not live the lie. Her struggle was bloody and dirty. But it was also just. It was also glorious.

The one person who she felt might have understood was, strange to say, Julian. Of course, she did not discuss it with him. That would have been impossible. But she saw how he operated to protect the House of Journalists. And she saw parallels. Or thought she did.

There were no men like Julian where she came from. That is not to say there weren't many gay men, of course. There were. But they denied themselves indignantly, furiously, violently. To catch another man's eye was to risk a sharpened bicycle spoke in the spinal cord even if no one else had the slightest inkling. Of *what*? Yes, of what? Nothing. *Nothing!* To even hint at the notion was to self-identify. The sentence for that was death or worse. They self-policed murderously, hideously. Sometimes they cut off the cock and balls and stuffed them in the mouth—and still some men survived to serve as warnings. The community demanded they maintain this code of honour so that the community was not polluted. The country could be proud that its AIDs epidemic—one of the worst on the continent—was spread by unsheathed heterosexuality.

And then there were the others. Mincing painted medicine men smeared with ash, red earth, and black beetle juice; who concocted narcotics or cooked up spirits that poisoned people back to life; witchy bitchy creatures, with lady-boy gaits, leaning on long umbrellas and wearing feathers in their bowler hats. She was scared of these men when she was a little girl, and she was scared of them now. They tittered and simpered; they were hated and feared and tolerated and venerated and visited by everyone. Every village had one, and in the towns and cities there were little enclaves of them. People went to them for fortune-telling and the exorcism of evil spirits, as well as for potions and elixirs for HIV/AIDs and other sexual diseases. They specialised in sexual diseases. She saw them very differently now, but still they gave her the willies.

The confident, proud, openly gay men of this country were one of the groups which had helped her to admire this strange unlovable country. And because of them her eyes were opened wide to the sins and sicknesses of her country. Yes, it was the gay men of this country who made real this country's great claims for itself. She and other fellows laughed at the certainty this country had about its moral rank in the world. But in Julian and others like him it did at least project an elegant and assured—and a right and just—attitude to sexuality. Her country, her whole continent, failed miserably in this regard, she felt.

So her disillusion with the House of Journalists was not down to Julian. She was very angry with him for the way he had treated Mr. Stan, of course. But generally she was on his side. It did not seem to her that he was suffering outrageous slights; or that the House of Journalists was facing a threat to its very survival. But she was not as close to the politics of the place as he was. She was just passing through. The House was not her proudest achievement, her greatest passion, a place and ideal she would do anything to protect.

"Jules, man, you do what you have to do. I respect that, brother, I really do. Leave me out of it, leave Mr. Stan alone, but do what you have to do. I'm leaving soon anyway."

She had said this to Julian one night in the hearing of several of us, as well as a circle of staff and volunteers. His guffaw connoted gratitude for her candour and her advice. But we all noted that in the days after, Julian started to take steps, to pull strings, to accelerate Agnes's now oft-stated intention to move out. Not that she needed his help.

Within a week, she had found herself a modest job as an assistant in a photographic agency. The agency knew nothing of her connection to the prestigious House of Journalists or of her past. She applied in all modesty for a modest job—and got it on her merits. She also found herself a modest apartment.

A job, a flat, a start, an end: a break from this place. It was simply time, she told Julian, as they shook hands in his office. (She refused to have a farewell party.) She took with her two bags—one more than she had arrived with, but not much to show for her time at the House of Journalists. She said her goodbyes. There were some tears and cuddles with Mr. Stan, but she did not drag out even that farewell. Then she was gone.

We gather—Julian has his sources—that she is doing well and wishes us well. There are no dramas to report. The extraordinary has become ordinary. Agnes is a young woman making her way in the city. She will—let us break the conventions and confirm what only the future knows—do well.

They may have known nothing of her when she arrived, but they will soon realise what she can be. She will be given tasks and she will perform them well. She will rise fast. She will combine her work in this city with foreign assignments. She will start to move in prestigious circles, and to develop a reputation.

She will soften into this city and its civilisation, wear her hair longer, and swap her street clothes for luxury brands. She will live less modestly, but give back. She will champion human rights causes and progressive politics. She will revisit her home continent and eventually her homeland. She will be reunited with her surviving brothers and sisters. She will visit the graves of her grandfather and sister—and her mother. She will never speak of these deaths. Not to friends, not in interviews. She will win prizes and get invited to things. She will be a success story. She will be happy enough.

Of course, she will sometimes dream of bodies hung from trees or floating bloated down slow brown rivers. Who of us doesn't? She will sometimes dream of a head hacked off a beautiful body and stuck on a stake. The past, real and imagined, stalks us all.

Otherworldly shrieks will pierce the workaday dreams of lovers who will find themselves—most unnervingly—bolt awake, crushing comfort into the thrashing creature in the bed beside them. They will need all their electrified strength to hold her tight, so violent is her distress. She will shudder and whimper in their arms and they will not know if they will ever be able to lay her down to rest. She will be glazed head to toe with a film of fear. And she will piss herself. They will not be revolted. They will stroke her hair and whisper sweet things. They will improvise admirably. They will be shit-scared. It is a lot to ask of these men. They are casual lovers who do not last long. It is a marvel that most are still around in the morning. She will find their bodies crashed out beside her. She will not like to wake them. What conversation is possible over a cup of tea after a night like that?

Most will attempt some when they eventually emerge. But she will see the uneasiness in their eyes. She will let them go. Forming relationships, it is the hardest thing. It is like throwing a rope from one side of an abyss to the other—more often than not the rope will be left dangling. She will come to realise that Alexei was weird, but Alexei was great. He could deal with this—he got off on it. But Alexei is history. She will rarely talk about the House of Journalists—which is closed now anyway. She will rarely think about us—we are all dispersed in our various ways. What of it? This place and all of us in it are in the past and she looks to the future. Is that not the natural order of things?

| TO PUT HIMSELF BACK IN THE HOUSE IS TO FALL THROUGH A FALSE FLOOR

So much for Agnes. What of Mustapha? We are drawing together the loose ends of our story, and Mustapha is a most important thread. Yet before we get to Mustapha we must clarify the position of Adom.

It may be recalled that Adom and Mustapha had hearings before the tribunal scheduled on the same day. And it will be further recalled that Adom was eager to go before the tribunes and lay himself bare. He would expose both his courage and his cowardice to these just and merciful men and women. He would confess that he was both hero and villain, as indeed every man is, if he cares to look into his soul and to tell the truth about himself. Yes, a good man, but also a sinner. He would heap his goodness and his sins on the scales of justice. Let those who would judge give their judgement. Let those who would grant mercy grant mercy. We all in the end answer to God.

As it was, and as we suspected, Adom was denied his precious hearing before the tribunal. There were interventions. From the very highest echelons, it was rumoured. Though not the most high! God Himself has stayed silent for the moment. Here in his earthly kingdom, discussions took place, however. It was deemed politic that Adom's case should not be exposed to an open hearing. It was not in state interests. There were diplomatic considerations. Adom railed against them mightily but in the end submitted. He was granted special temporary status by ministerial order without a hearing. For the moment he remains at the House of Journalists on an extraordinary fellowship.

Julian has fallen in with this arrangement with the greatest reluctance. There is talk that he was not party to all the background information about Adom's case when Adom was admitted to the House of Journalists. There were things he was not told for security reasons, supposedly. We can imagine what Julian would have made of that. There is, after all, both the safety and integrity of the House to think about. The House has always prided itself on cooperating fully with the authorities, but in return it expects to be treated with some respect. He will not have the House of Journalists used. If word gets out, the reputation of the House will be damaged: its enemies are always looking for instances like these to turn against it.

The government appreciated the difficult situation it had put Julian in. *Not me, the House!* Indeed, the House, the minister corrected herself. She had phoned to explain in person the full facts, on privy terms. She acknowledged that it would have been better if Julian had been trusted with them from the start, but he perhaps now realised the acute sensitivities.

It has even been suggested by some devious souls that the visit of the prime minister is connected to the official handling—or mishandling—of Adom's case. That, most of us think, is an unworthy thought. It does not make sense either. Now that Julian knows the fuller story— whatever that is—it is surely most awkward for both him and for Adom that Adom is present on the most important day in the history of the House of Journalists. That is not to suggest that Adom would deliberately cause any embarrassment. Indeed he has endeavoured to keep a low profile in recent days. But that is not easy for such a big man.

Sometimes he has to be prompted or reminded. (For example, when it is realised that he intends to don national dress for this evening's reception, he will be persuaded immediately of the wisdom of wearing something which does not draw so much attention to his impressive person.) Even so, Julian is surely wishing that the arrangements to move Adom on had been concluded before the big day.

There have been complications, apparently. Bureaucratic incompetency, he would like to bet. The inefficiency and inertia of the home department in these types of cases is staggering. But Julian is trying to let nothing distract him today. The Adom situation is certainly an irritant. But there is no point worrying about it now.

Anyway, we were, if you recall, supposed to be telling Mustapha's story.

Julian remembers Mustapha. Yes, Mustapha. He never forgets a fellow, though he remembers some better than others. And he certainly does not put those who are returned out of his mind, if that is what you are thinking. That is most unfair. He has a proud record of supporting all-party calls for the monitoring of the safety of returnees. But if he is asked whether he opposes all returns, the answer is no. And it is the policy of the House not to query the decisions of the tribunal—there is no appeal—as to do so would be to drag the House into the determination-of-claims process, which is beyond its articles of foundation. It would also be a highly political act. The House policy is that fellows are supported in every way to make their claim for status before the tribunes—no other claimants get such a level of support—so if the tribunes make a refusal their decision should be accepted.

Of course, it is most painful for everyone when this happens—though it rarely does, we all should note. And it may be that, on occasion, the decision to refuse is the wrong one. However, as Julian points out, it would be a reckless presumption of the House if it were to say that *every* fellow refused was refused wrongly. Can we, the fellowship, look among our number—not just now but at all times in the past—and say with complete confidence that every one of our stories would stand up to the closest scrutiny? Are there not inconsistencies and omissions, points of embellishment and exaggeration, which talk against the strictest credibility? Do we even know the exact sequence of events, or the order of motivations, which brought us to this place? And we are first-person, not omniscient, narrators, after all. We have a point of view. The truth of our stories is *our* truth, not *the* truth.

Now, these are muddy philosophical waters, and the tribunes, practical people making difficult decisions, do not fish in them. They make the best judgement they can based on the stories they hear and the evidence presented to them. What more can we ask of them? Their judgement consigns us to very different fates. Return for some is a death sentence; while a grant of status offers new life. No doubt, as Julian has said, they, the tribunes, get decisions wrong on some occasions. But as Adom would say, they will have to answer to God for that.

None of this—or very little of it anyway—brings us any closer to understanding why Mustapha was refused, however.

(By the way, it will have been noted that Mustapha is no longer speaking for himself. He too has been silenced, it seems. The conventions of the House of Journalists dictate that outside narrow confines— the rules are perhaps arbitrary and certainly difficult to parse—a fellow loses his own voice. His (or her) point of view will be represented, more or less faithfully, from another perspective—but the subtleties and nuances, the passion and character, of you and I do not always come across as clearly. Singular colour and tone and depth are lost. The fellowship itself will always, in the last resort, speak for its members. It could be said that we are *the* voice of the House of Journalists. But then who exactly are *we*? Our membership changes; fellows come and go. This is the main point of our story.)

Anyway: Mustapha. A closer understanding of why his case for status was refused by the tribunal is to be found in that aspect of his personality—he told us about it often enough—which rebelled against any restriction on liberty. For Mustapha a man is only truly free if he can act according to his own conscience even when to do so is against his apparent interests. Some will see this as a perverse code of honour, and yet the House of Journalists only exists because many of us feel bound by it. Bound to a code of absolute liberty? There are obvious contradictions here. Mustapha would be the first to admit that he is a mass of contradictions. It is the human condition, is it not? But on one matter he has been entirely consistent. *He was not tortured.* We recall him saying it frequently when he was among us. You will too. The House authorities begged to differ. He was told on many occasions that experts could be put up to testify to that effect. He would not have been refused had he allowed the House to take on his case. But he did not allow it. He travelled to his hearing that morning alone: without Adom and without any representative from the House of Journalists. Of course, he was still better off than his fellow claimants at the session. His case file was clearly marked as that of a fellow of the House of Journalists. This was an advantage which he could not dispose of.

What strange business is this, the tribunes thought, that a fellow of the House of Journalists arrives here without the fullest safeguards of that favoured institution? The tribunes are not of a temperament to admire for its own sake independence of spirit or an unconventional approach to their proceedings. But it intrigued them that a fellow should choose to come before them relieved of most of his advantages. It might, depending on their mood, have swayed them towards him. They too sometimes strain against the orthodoxies of the system. They, the tribunes, while officers of the state and servants of the people, maintain an open mind to every case that comes before them.

However, in the end they judged that it was not right to indulge the peculiar disregard for self-interest that Mustapha displayed. They gave him every opportunity to save himself and he gave every indication that he was not disposed to do so. He furnished no evidence or argument that the persecution he faced was of an order of seriousness to justify a full grant of asylum in this country. That left the question of his safety on return.

And it was not clear that even a return home would put him in any great danger. He had been released from prison for "good behaviour"—for which he was to be commended, they felt—having served most of his term. There was no warrant for his arrest, and by his own admission it was futile to protest against the regime of his own country. Again, a pragmatric consideration. He only wanted a quiet life, which was, in their view, very sensible. Moreover, he could, they put it to him, return in complete safety to the country in which he was domiciled prior to his departure to this country. (The claimant, the official record states, nodded his head at this point, as if conceding the evident justice of it.) Yes, the claimant was, they noted, a most reasonable man, and as such must realise that the international asylum system is not designed for the purposes of "beginning again," "enjoying a fresh start," or "having a complete break from the past," understandable though these aspirations may be in someone who has gone through such hardship and upheaval. He had their sympathy and respect, but there were no grounds for a grant of status and no grounds either for a stay on removal. Removal, it should be stressed, to the third country—the country of transit—even though, to reiterate, in their opinion return to the country of origin was itself technically safe. Perhaps the critics of the tribunal system would be good enough to note this fact. There were none in the court of course; the only people there were the tribunes, the officials, and Mustapha. The point stands, however. And pertains in particular to anyone considering a judicial review, which in the absence of appeal is the only legal route open to those challenging their decisions, but which would be in this case, in their considered opinion, vexatious. Though the last thing on Mustapha's mind—the official record can have nothing to say on this, but it was so—was a legal challenge. It was over, it had been settled: he knew his fate. For the first time since he had set foot in this country the inescapable sense of unease lifted.

This will seem perverse to some, no doubt, but perhaps we should try to imagine what was going through Mustapha's mind. We cannot, of course, claim to see into the private universe of his thoughts. The metaphysics of this vast and complex space is closed to outsiders. But he revealed to us, don't forget, his mixed emotions about exile in this country. Many sympathetic and friendly people—we think, in particular, of Esther—saw in Mustapha a sad and lonely man, pitifully reduced by terrible experience, who nonetheless was looking forward. He spent much time alone and was not easy in the fellowship; but he was always polite, courteous, and at pains to fit in as well as he could; and he took some pleasure in the language lessons, among other diversions. Yes, everyone thought he demonstrated determined optimism in endeavouring to acquire this new language, and generally was making the best of life here. All of which reassured those—not just Esther, but the rest of the staff and volunteers too—who so desperately wanted to help him, as they help all of us.

Rebuilding a new life in a new home—that is what it is called; that is what we are all working towards. Most of us, for want of an alternative, go along with it—rhetorically at least. But ultimately, Mustapha could not. We have already heard how stifled he had been in that "little country"—*"consisting of inert memories and hopes that can never be realised"*—which fellow émigrés had pieced out of scraps in the neighbouring capital. The tribunes were right to call it a "third country." It was more than one step removed from home. But if that was the case, then what was *this* country? Certainly not a new home. It was the obliteration of home—an end to looking back and yearning, to mourning and yet hanging out flags. In the ultimation of absolute exile he would be free of the false comfort of diasporic community. There was a heroic logic in this end. And yet now he had booked himself a one-way ticket back to the half-life of the third country. Why? Reasons simple and sad: his spirit and his heart were broken. He looked in the mirror and saw a weary, pathetic figure. No fight, no heroism left. Dismal compromised existence was all he was fit for, he had decided. Snivel-spirited, he was crawling back under a stone to live cramped—and then die.

Not anytime soon, we hasten to add on his behalf. No such grand gesture or release. He will return on a scheduled flight to the neighbouring capital; no need for escort or restraint. He will take the municipal bus from the airport, his duffel bag on his knees, through the interminable sprawl of the city, to that dense, warrened district which the exiled community suffers to call home. He will find a room. He will go to one of the cafés to read the newspaper of the community—and to drink its ersatz coffee. The news from home will be reported with increasing resignation and hopelessness; the coffee will taste ever more bitter. The regime has strengthened its grip, legitimised itself through economic growth, and improved diplomatic relations with its neighbours and the key powers. The exiles playing the old tunes seem ever more scratchy and irrelevant. He will have to find a job. This is his life, his future. He will meet a woman: a country woman (in both respects) strongly reminiscent of his paternal grandfather's cook. Yes, it is the smell of her somehow: bread dough and stone floor. Not unpleasant. There is little in the way of mutual attraction (how could there be; just look at us!) but intercourse of a sort takes place. *Don't mock me, my darling. And do not mock her. We do not enjoy your youth and beauty, Yasmin. We do it on a lumpy mattress under blankets to keep warm.*

Yes, the relationship will be a humiliation to Mustapha—but also a consolation. Without it his loneliness would be intolerable. Loneliness eats into the bone of the exiles living in this bleak city on its steppe. (As it eats into the bone of exiles everywhere.) That is why there are all these clubs and committees and celebrations, failing so pitifully to capture the elegant traditions and liberal civilities of his homeland. He and his lady friend at least have companionship: the sort that involves silent reading by lamplight (him) while knitting needles click (her). Milk boils in a pan on the ring, and the rumble from the traffic on the overpass rattles the window frames. It never stops. The bed with the lumpy mattress is too small, the heartsickness so immense. He will lie staring at the ceiling. She snores beside him: faint echoes of you, AA! The thought is surprising. As a rule, he never thinks back to this place. Or of us, the fellows. The House of Journalists? It is a notion too fantastical to merit serious reminiscence. Was he really ever part of such an enterprise? His few months as a fellow feel uneasily dreamed up. It was one of those brief interludes which have no solidity. To put himself back in the House is to fall through a false floor. He thinks no more of it. He will live here—in this city, in this apartment; with her—his companion and carer—for nearly twenty years.

BUT NOW WE MUST LOOK FORWARD

When Mustapha failed to return from the tribunal hearing that evening there was shock among the fellowship. The smokers among us gathered to discuss the news, even though Mustapha had never been one among our group.

Mustapha, how can that be? Mustapha, but he suffered so greatly! Mustapha, didn't he spend all those years in prison, doing hard labour? Mustapha, if torture means anything, he was tortured.

In truth, these were ritual lamentations. None of us had been close to Mustapha, and within a day or two he was forgotten. This is the harsh truth of our situation. Who was that standing at our shoulder smoking on the fire escape just now? Just another fellow of the House of Journalists, like us, passing through. He will be forgotten too. We are called on to celebrate this fellowship, to take heart from it and see hope in it. This fellowship is the frame within which our lonely destiny is painted in heraldic colours and given grand purpose. But what a bleak blessing it is. What a meagre consolation for family, country, home. We are on our own here, and must make our own way. We cannot spare much sympathy for others.

Mustapha made it to the House of Journalists—a miracle in itself. Thousands don't. But he found no peace here. We are sure he didn't want to appear aloof or ungrateful. He tried to celebrate small connections but the wider connection eluded him. Here was never there— the fabled and haunted past in which he dwelt incessantly. We all know how the past pulls us back. But the refugee must move on in his mind if he is to make any kind of life in his place of exile. And the trouble with Mustapha was that he would not play along with the system here, even when it was trying to help him. He sealed his own fate.

Mr. Stan took the news of Mustapha's refusal very hard. Agnes conveyed it to him in his room, to which he was confined entirely in the early days after his return from the hospital. The good eye filled with tears and the good stump trembled in Agnes's grip.

Agnes was shaken by this reaction. Mr. Stan had not paid Mustapha much attention during his time at the House of Journalists. He was attending to other, higher matters, of course. But a good fellow lost in this way always excites sentiment in Mr. Stan, and in his new condition he trembles on the brink of an excess of feeling more perilously than before.

The House must surely have failed Mustapha, Mr. Stan decided, without troubling to find if the charge would stick. Certainly he, Mr. Stan, had failed him. He was concentrating all his energy—weak and failing—on the petty power politics of this place and in so doing neglected to make any personal connection with the agonies of this fellow. Did Agnes say his name was Mustapha? Yes, of course, Mustapha!

Mustapha, your story will not be forgotten, Mr. Stan vows to himself. And yet, locked in silence, there is nothing he can do to sing it out.

Do not worry, old man, Julian reassures his mute ally. This name, Mustapha, is recorded in the book of the House of Journalists. Along with his story. One among many, and all the more powerful for that.

But now we must look forward. We must look to other fellows whom we can help. We must look to the future, starting with this very important day ahead.

| ALMOST THE LAST WORD

So we have accounted for Mustapha, for Adom, for Agnes, for Esther. But there is one person we haven't dispatched yet—you. Yes, you, AA: the first name in the book of the House of Journalists—by dint of a well-worn device. You may have contributed little or nothing to the grand sweep of our story, but it began with you and now it ends with you. Almost the last word.

So what has become of you? Where are you lurking? What might you do to spoil Julian's big day?

There really is no need to string this out.

You have left the House of Journalists. Yes, that's right—you've gone. Skedaddled, vamooshed. Vanished into thin air. High-tailed. Upped and left sticks.

We choose our words carefully because we mentioned, we think, that no one just *disappears* from the House of Journalists. The place has its own procedures, which it follows to the letter. And as we all know, the government of this country prides itself on maintaining the integrity of its immigration system. It is, we are told constantly, a "listening" government and its citizens have made their voice loud and clear on this issue. So all immigrants are counted in and counted out, recorded and tracked. We are all issued identity cards containing our biometric data. We are told—and why would we dispute it?—that identity fraud and visa violation have been rendered almost impossible. Our progress through the system is constantly monitored against our visa status, as are our whereabouts. Electronic tags, daily or weekly reporting requirements, secure hostelling, and detention are all options, if required, which generally they are. And—make no mistake—the House of Journalists, for all its dispensations and privileges, is locked into this system. And yet it seems, despite it all, AA, you've done what can't be done: you've *disappeared*.

Room 15 was discovered that morning a few weeks ago just as it was when you arrived not three months previously. Bed made, cupboards bare, surfaces wiped down, floor washed: all you had left behind was that unnerving, institutional deep-clean that we never completely succeed in humanizing with our fears, dreams, frailties, and memories. Indeed so complete was the expurgation of personality and presence from Room 15 that it was as if you had never been in there. Never slept, never snored, never cried out in the night. Yes, latterly, there were nightmares. The place was starting to get to you. And yet after going into Room 15—and we all did so in appalled fascination—it was difficult to picture you or summon you to mind at all.

You must have left during the early hours. Yet the volunteer stationed on your corridor did not see or hear you go. He was quizzed in harsh unsparing morning, but could shed no light. Nor could the security cameras conjure up one last image. They recorded only an empty monochromic corridor, untroubled by human comings and goings, with the duty volunteer alert at his post throughout. Almost as strange was the silence on the tape. What had quieted our nightmares? Ours, it seemed, for one night only, was the sleep of the blessed dead. Such peace!

Julian, promptly informed and immediately alarmed, oversaw a tape review himself. No sign of you. Nothing on the corridor tape, the lobby tape, the front entrance tape, the fire exit tape. And not just on that night but on the day before and the day before that. Indeed, when the whole tape bank covering your stay was scanned, not one image of you was found.

And when the records of the House were searched there was no record of you either. AA—Writer, the first name in the book: gone.

But no one just *disappears* from the House of Journalists. *No one!*

By the second day we were being organised into search parties. Led by trusted volunteers, we wandered around the neighbouring streets "looking for any sign" of you or "picking up any information"—Julian was rather vague in his instructions. After a while, the jokers among us started calling out your name as if you were a lost cat. Discipline broke down. The cigarettes came out at street corners and a few fellows sloped into cafés. The descent into farce was obvious even to Julian—who, typically, led from the front. The parties were called back. The episode was not to be mentioned.

For two days we talked of nothing else.

On day three, your departure—the word "disappearance" is officially banned—was finally reported to the authorities. It was an unwanted first for the House of Journalists: a fellow whose status was undetermined was officially AWOL—an "abscondee," an illegal, a fugitive from immigration justice.

We all expected the immigration authorities to descend on the House: to turn over Room 15, to impound the video bank, to flood the neighbouring streets with mobile pick-up squads, to interrogate the duty volunteer, to interrogate us, to interrogate *Julian.* (We have all seen the TV programme *Border Force.*) Julian certainly expected such a response. Instead, after two days of hearing nothing back, Sabrina took a phone call from a low-grade official to tell her that the Immigration Department had no record of an AA, so could the House of Journalists please forward its own paperwork.

Julian immediately instructed Solomon to call a more senior official. How could the Immigration Department have no record of a person they dispatched to the House of Journalists only a matter of weeks before? Solomon asked. Perhaps because no such person *was* dispatched, the senior official ventured in reply.

In a conversation with an undersecretary Solomon suggested at Julian's behest that the Immigration Department may care to admit that it was more likely that it, the department, had mislaid its record of

AA than that the House of Journalists had invented his existence. Perhaps so, the undersecretary conceded, but it was mystifying, was it not,
that the House also had no record of AA.

Speaking to the deputy permanent secretary at the Immigration
Department (the permanent secretary was not available), Julian—who
had taken personal command—suggested that although it was clear
that some people in the ministry thought he was mad and obsessive, they surely did not think him so delusional as to conjure a fellow
out of his imagination. There was no question of anyone at the ministry thinking that he was mad or obsessive or delusional, the dep perm
sec assured him. And they did not doubt that AA existed in some
sense, but—

She was interrupted there and then, with Julian demanding to be
put straight through to the minister herself.

"What on earth is meant by the expression that one of our fellows
existed in '*some sense*,' Barbara?"

"Julian, I apologise if the DPS caused any offence. What she meant
was that, while we do not for a minute dispute the actual existence of
this AA, the complete absence of any records means there is an issue as
to his, as it were, *official* existence. I know it sounds like linguistic leg-
erdemain." (Julian was not really in the mood for Barbara, a former
journalist, displaying her "way with words," and his icy silence conveyed that.) "But you, I think, will understand and appreciate the subtle distinction." (And flattery was not going to work either. Barbara
sensed that but ploughed on in the same emollient tone nonetheless.)
"It is a most unusual case, of course. My officials tell me that they have
never heard of one quite like it. But similar things do happen—less and
less frequently, I am pleased to say." (She never quite stopped being the
politician talking in public.) "Sometimes case notes are lost, certain
clients slip under the radar, new identities are assumed, and all the rest
of it. You deal with the same issues, I know, and deal with them successfully, in the main." (Again Julian gave nothing back. Barbara's tone
hardened this time.) "The fact is, if we have no record of a person it is
difficult to pursue them. Who exactly are we looking for? What breach
have they committed? What sanction would be open to us if we did in

fact find them? We would be chasing shadows. As was the case when you organised a little hunting party of your own, I understand!" (A cheap shot—Barbara regretted it straightaway. Nothing from Julian, but she softened again.) "I understand this AA was something of a troublesome presence." (This wasn't helping. Julian did not care to be reminded that the ministry seemed to have its spies inside the House of Journalists.) "By which I mean, his departure perhaps will not be greatly regretted. And while I think it is right to say that, while troublesome, he was not a danger either to the House or more widely. If we were to carry out a risk assessment, would the threat level of AA justify the deployment of emergency enforcement capacity, with all that means in terms of departmental resources, at a time of fiscal constraint? Forgive me! I am slipping into departmental jargon." (Barbara liked to suggest that she had a great respect for the language, particularly when she was talking to a "fellow" writer.) "You understand where I am coming from, I think? To pursue at all costs an abscondee deemed a low risk is probably not a wise use of resources. And that may well be the case in this case, in which case: case closed." (Laughter: Barbara felt, apparently, that she had deployed sparkling wordplay.)

What was Julian's response to all this? Well, as you can imagine—and of course we immediately assumed you had been plotting for it to turn out this way—he was incandescent. It was a farcical turn of events; it exposed the House of Journalists to ridicule; and made a mockery of the fellowship. All of us heard him shouting down the phone at the top of his voice. The House of Journalists rang with his anger.

"What sort of department are you running, Barbara? Because it sounds to me like the department for laughable Kafkaesque incompetence. The department for half-baked Orwellian double-speak."

He calmed down a bit after that. Apologised. Spoke in more measured tones. But he was not done. "And you may be prepared to write this off as a mystery; to put AA down as a shadowy character who perhaps never existed in the first place; but not me, Barbara—not me! No, I live in the real world, a harsh and unremitting place, in which the fellows are flesh and blood, and the marks of their torture and the evidence of their suffering are substantial. It is a world where the House of

Journalists must exist. For the work it does and for what it represents. No, Barbara, I won't let go. This AA is out there somewhere; he has to be. So I will be on my guard, as I am constantly. Never letting up for a moment. The House of Journalists is mine, Barbara, do you hear that? *Mine.* No one is going to take it from me or destroy it."

"And I'm sure no one wants to," Philip said comfortingly, when Julian returned home that evening and off-loaded with a strength of feeling that was deeply shocking. "You are right about AA, of that I am certain. But it's over. This is his parting shot. Good riddance. Let it go, let *him* go. Who will remember him when the book comes to be written? In a few short weeks the prime minister is coming to give the official stamp of approval to the House. Concentrate on that. You have been vindicated, Julian. Vindicated."

Julian so wants it to be so. And he is giving every appearance today, as he has on every day since you left, that he has been persuaded by Philip. Look at the gentle command he displays as he inspects the line-up of fellows chosen to greet the prime minister. Look at the easy charm he deploys towards funders, stakeholders, and other VIPs. Look at the graceful attention he pays to even the most junior staff, volunteers, and mentors. But look too at the flicker of panic in his eyes and the film of sweat on his upper lip as he is told that the prime ministerial car is pulling up. He moves towards the imposing front door, mouthing the words he will soon say out loud and which should be words of triumph. "Prime Minister, welcome to the House of Journalists."

BUT JUST ONE MOMENT—A POSTSCRIPT

Saw AA this afternoon. You heard. Yes, AA. The very same. Was always with Julian on this one. One was not going to put up with this disappearing into thin air nonsense. Not going to allow you to get away with that. And let's not forget the fellows of the House of Journalists. Haven't they had enough of disappearances? Their names may be written in this book that everyone goes on about; their stories recorded therein. But what about all the others lost in the wars, the uprisings, the political struggles? All those who are languishing in jails and torture centres? All those who fell behind on the long journeys to safety? All those who are locked away in detention centres and then deported? If we want ghosts to haunt our imagination, we have accursed souls aplenty. So there was never going to be any going up in a puff of smoke for you, AA. Not for Jules, and not for Crumb either. One shook your hand, shared a word and a cigarette, and now—to reassure everyone at the very end of this story—one can report a definite sighting. That's right. No doubt about it. But first—slight detour, nothing more—one must mention why one was up in town.

To see one's publisher; to discuss the book; which in its own way adds another little spicy twist, does it not? Meeting took place in their West End offices with one's agent and one's editor also present. Nothing unusual about that of course, but another attendee was a *lawyer*, one Rogers Cook. Now, the presence of a lawyer always unnerves. But just one moment: *Rogers*?

Yes, not Roger singular, but Rogers plural, which was explained, to everyone else's apparent satisfaction, by Rogers being an American. Okay, Rogers it is; but Rogers *Cook*?

One didn't pursue it, but while business matters proceeded one was inevitably diverted by one's own speculation as to whether his parents either had no notion that their son's Christian name was alternatively (and to one's own mind, pleasingly) a verb (perhaps it is peculiar to English English?) or were unrepentant Confederates who through this bestowal entitled their son in the expectation that when he reached young maturity he would live up to his name by sexually assaulting the uncomplaining black woman they employed in their kitchen. If the latter alternative was the case, and Rogers in the United States was as double-entendre-able as in these isles, then it followed that the surname Cook hardly tickled the surface of comic possibilities. Others that suggested themselves instantly were Nunn, Tallboys, and Winterbottom.

So absorbed was one in thinking of more, that the discussion of one's new novella was hardly registering at all, though it was good to surface and to hear that one's publisher and one's editor liked the concept, the outline, and the draft chapter. (Then there was Sergeant, Ladyman, and Pope.) And they also all liked: the core idea, the episodic structure, and the multiple voices.

"Oh, you liked the multiple voices?" one asked. One had been expecting this reaction. (Snowman, of course, but one had other things on one's mind now.) "Why does that not surprise?"

"The multiple voices, yes, but also the episodic structure and the core idea, the concept." The voice talking up was that of Conrad, one's publisher, who for four decades published all the stuff that everyone loved and which was heaped with praise, but who for the past decade has had to publish all the critically excoriated and publically reviled work in one's own voice, one's rediscovered voice, one's *true* voice.

"But the multiple voices certainly worked for you?" one persisted. One of the problems with the true voice is that it doesn't know when to let things drop. (Hoare, Trollope, Pornstar, the Virgin Mary.) It goes on and on—and thinks it is funny to go on and on a bit longer. It isn't funny. It is boring. Conrad has perfected a facial expression that makes this point—and he deployed it to particularly good effect on this occasion, making it clear at the same time (something about the face again) that he had something serious to say.

"The thing is . . ."

He paused. He tensed. One slouched; one smirked. The seriously serious—as this now clearly was—brings out the silly and immature in one, as many an ex would attest. "This is deadly serious, Ted, and all you can do is dick about . . ."

"The thing is . . ."

Conrad was one thing, but the lawyer—Rogers Judge—had also tensed. A tense lawyer—Rogers Dury—unnerves even the most defiant slouching smirker. One sat up straight. One urged him on a bit.

"What exactly?"

"The title . . ."

Ah, yes, the title. Now we were getting to the nub of the matter. This was what it all came down to. Even so, one fulfilled one's obligation to get Conrad to spell it out by playing dumb.

"Well, it's about the House of Journalists, so one thought, 'You know what, let's call it *The House of Journalists.* It's not as if Snowman has copyright.'"

"Ah . . . Well, that's just it."

The lawyer—*Rogers the whole fucking idea*—chipped in at this point. "Or at least that's what his lawyers are claiming, threatening. The law is not entirely clear on the point, but Mr. Snowman's lawyers have an injunction out on its use in any literary context. It is slightly curious, Mr. Crumb, because the papers were served well before you indicated your intention to publish something under this title. It's as if Mr. Snowman had wind."

Up to this point, restraint; at this point, the furies.

Of course he had fucking wind, m'learned, one thought—though one didn't actually say anything out loud at this stage. Muggins farted in his face with that visit the other month. Oh, yes, this is what comes from doing some actual *field research*—what was one fucking thinking? Make it all up, you stupid bastard, that's always been the Crumb motto. Work of the imagination. Never needed to set foot inside the place to know what one wanted to say about it. One's *House of Journalists* is all one's own. It's not real; it doesn't exist; it's just a title for a book; and once you have a title, as we all know, the rest just flows.

"So," the lawyer continued, oblivious to the vile tempest of one's thoughts, "the judicious course would in my opinion be to—"

"Issue a counter-writ," one suddenly bellowed. No question of keeping the furies in this time. No hiding behind multiple voices. One was speaking up again in one's true voice. "Yes, draw it up immediately, Rogers, my friend. Rogers, my wife. Rogers, my five-year-old daughter. Against Messrs. Bastard, Wanker, and Cunt, lawyers for Snowman, under Article whatever of the UN declaration to let me do what I fucking well like, alleging that the client of your client, Mr. Edward Crumb, is being gagged, breached in his humans, denied in his basics, disentitled of his entitled title by this outrageous fatwa. Yes, the volume of piss extracted by Snowman on this occasion cannot be allowed to stand. Crumb and colleagues are not going to be redacted, injuncted, and royally rogered. Issue a counter-fuck!"

So vivid was this outburst that even veterans of similar (agent, editor, publisher) were stunned by it, while the one newcomer (lawyer) was most stunningly stunned. Even the silence was stunned—it was one of those "stunned silences." Publisher, editor, and agent quickly shook it off, but the lawyer was still slack-jawed and starry-eyed until Conrad brought him round with a hypnotist's finger click. Literally.

"Well . . . yes . . . quite . . . maybe . . . I don't know." The poor man emerged still groggy.

One's agent put a hand on his shoulder to comfort him; one's editor refreshed his glass of water and decided opening a window might be an idea.

Conrad turned on me. He still has work to do on his *Must you always behave like this?* face, but even if it had been in better shape it would have fallen on deaf ears, as it were, because one wasn't of course joking, one was deadly serious, one meant every word of it, yes, even on reflection and after consideration—all of which one made clear through one's own facial expression. And subsequently—and at some length, and in no uncertain terms—deploying the power of speech.

Upshot? Stalemate. No meeting of minds could be reached, so the meeting of persons broke up. For the time being the publication of one's *House of Journalists* under any title is on hold. That's what we agreed. But, in truth, between muggins and the gatepost, it's over. Binned. Shredded. Pressed delete. The rest of them can discuss it if they like, but as far as the author is concerned it's a dead letter. Which is a pity perhaps, but hey! It's not as if the work itself—as far as it went (which was not far)—was really any good. The idea was good; the idea was a blast. But it didn't really extend beyond writing something called *The House of Journalists* and then watching the Snowman combust. And, on reflection, that doesn't really do the bigger themes and issues at play here justice, does it? It's not really worthy of those brave fellows, all they've gone through and stand for and put up with. So one is done with it. Let someone else have a go, if they dare.

All of which was going through one's mind as one walked down the High Road here, just a mile or so from the House of Journalists, and only a few streets away from where one was born and raised, where it all began for me. Yes, it may not have been mentioned before, but wherever the action has taken us—and we've dropped in on many parts of the globe—all roads seem to lead back to this single borough. Strange, that. Small world. So anyway, one was walking down the High Road when who should one see on the other side of the street but coming in one's direction?

Well, yes—one gave that away at the start—it was you, AA.

"AA! Here!"

Greatly excited, one was. Hard to convey that now perhaps?

"AA! It's Crumb. Over here."

One had considered of course the possibility that this so-called disappearing might be a way of saying you had been rubbed out, eliminated. But no, that was too outrageous even for the most extravagantly outraged among us. Of course, one was prepared to believe that they were capable of pretty much anything, the fucking murderous bastards, but not on these shores, surely? This is why they negotiate those memoranda of understanding, why they render extraordinarily, why they offshore, surely? So, bumping into you like this, though it might appear to some to be almost *too* neat an ending, was a huge relief. Here was a soft landing; a nice rounding off; rather than a nasty bumping off. (One finds one has gone rather soft in one's old age.)

Yet, as it turned out, one was going to have to work rather harder than that to resolve the whole thing.

Because the response to one's call of greeting was what? Nothing.

Not a flicker. The rest of them on the other side of the street: *they* turned as one to see who was shouting for AA. But they weren't you. *You* were! And yet you just walked on. Not any faster, not as if you were trying to get away, not as if you were pretending not to hear, not as if you wanted to deny it, to escape it, to put it behind you, to forget. No, it was as if it wasn't—you weren't—you.

"AA?"

One was out in the road by now. First, body-swerving a tootling scooter (now picking itself up off the pavement); then bonnet-rolling a white van (its contents now hanging backwards out of the front windows and cunting one with such neck-cord throbbing venom that, oops, it has shunted into the back of a little lady number at the traffics); and finally finding oneself frozen in hands-up supplication before a black cab, reared on its hind legs.

A matter of seconds had passed while all this pantomime passed off. But seconds mattered. True, the rest of the street had stood transfixed throughout, only moving off, and then reluctantly, when one physically waved them on, like a traffic copper dispersing rubber-neckers. *Nothing to see here, move on, move on.* But you, AA—you had kept on walking. You had noticed none of this near-death dicing, you had walked on regardless, heedless, even though it was *because* of you, *for* you.

Phew, AA! One was trembling, one was shagged, shattered, beat— one was hands-on-knees for a moment.

And of course one had also entertained the idea you were your twin, your double, your absolute spit. Like you, but *not* you. Entertained it and rejected it. Because this denial of you was after all *very* you. Not least in its passivity. Because you had not denied it, your youness, you had just not acknowledged it. Your AAness, that is. And that was important. You were you—can we agree on that at least?—but that did not make you here/now/there/then AA. You had stopped being AA when you had "just disappeared" from the House of Journalists, you might say. You were someone else now. Or rather you were you—let's establish that once and for all—but under another name. Your own name, whatever it is, or another assumed for new circumstances and purposes, whatever they are.

One was back in some semblance of active pursuit now, but in the pavement push, only the back of your head was visible. Cause for pause? Not really, because one had had that good view of you from across the street. That first sighting. And it was unmistakably you; though indubitably altered. Not the same fellow with whom one had shared a surreptitious cig in the House of Journalists.

And as one gave chase, lamely, lung-burningly, with decreasing hope of ever catching up, one reflected on that: the single incident. Why was it freighted with so much significance in every version of *The House of Journalists* that is doing the rounds? Because between you and me, AA, sharing a cig in these parts would normally be *nothing* to write home about. Two writers sharing a cig and exchanging a few words would not a plot twist make. You would be working damn hard out here, on these streets, to make a damn thing out of that. And yet, for all that, the whole damn business still seemed to hang on it.

It's a mind-bending little doll's house, that House of Journalists. Two stops on the tube from this very spot, but a parallel universe, it seems. Oh, yes, it's a tricksy box that seduces and mesmerises, and warps and distorts, and plays games with perspectives and any sense of proportion. It throws itself open to share and show a whole world of pain and suffering, and heroism and humanity, and then it folds in on itself, tight, stifling, and suffocating. You are no sooner in the place than you want out. The wise fellow hangs in there just long enough to extract what he wants from the place and then . . .

So all power to you, my friend, for it was clear from where one was standing, hands on knees admittedly, that you, brave man, felt you could take it on. It had defeated one of us, but you were going after the prize. And it was in that instant that one suddenly realised that you were perfectly at home here. Not settled in a new home, so to speak; not finding your feet in a new country, a new city. It was more rooted than that. The feeling one had, with absolute conviction in that instant, was that you were *from* here. Like me. You and I; me and you; the two of us both.

And though one couldn't see you now, it didn't take much imagination to picture where you were going. Back to your crummy flat above a shop, back to your cruddy desk, the same desk you had abandoned in despair not half an hour before. Sounds pretty sad and lonely, perhaps? Desolate. But, come on, think of the fellows. Think of what they have gone through. Use that as a spur to drive you on. And perhaps, as it often does, the walk to the shops for an evening's supply—a decentish bottle of red, a packet of twenty, something you won't eat to eat—has done the trick yet again. It has all fallen into place because you stopped staring at it, thinking about it, *working* on it. Now you just have to get back to your desk, glass in one hand, cigarette in the other, and it will, as they say, write itself.

Printed in the USA
CPSIA information can be obtained
at www.ICGtesting.com
LVHW091138150724
785511LV00005B/392